ANY x SERIES

1

ANY x LOREN

THROUGH ANY FIRE

A SECOND CHANCE ROMANCE

KATHERINE CARTER

To 29-year-old Katie, who thought she'd only ever write one book.
You did it.

First Edition

ISBN: 979-8-9902904-3-3

Editing by Claire Ashgrove
Cover Design and Interior Formatting by Rachel McEwan

Content and Trigger Warnings can be found on page 394

TABLE OF CONTENTS

DEAR READER,

Welcome to Roswell! While I wouldn't necessarily classify this as a dark romance, it contains certain themes you may find dark or disturbing. Trigger and content warnings can be found at the back of the book and on my website. Please prioritize your mental health and check them if you need to. If you wish to go in blind, I hope you have a great time with Cal and Loren.

Enjoy!

Yours faithfully,

Katherine

P.S. I would love if you could leave an honest rating and/or review when you finish! As an indie author, it would mean the world to me.

PROLOGUE

In the dreamscape, he is overwhelmed with her scent. No matter how he tries, he can't escape the bittersweet cloud of sweet almonds laced with a hint of the ripest springtime cherries. It settles over his senses like a warm blanket, and he falls easily into the comforting embrace of familiarity.

In the distance, a woman crosses a busy street. Her chestnut hair yields to the gentle breeze, and he reaches a hand out to touch it.

But he's too far away.

One blink, and she's gone, replaced by the familiar ghost of heartache.

Next to him lies another, but her scent is too syrupy. Crystallized sugar saturated in manufactured vanilla that suffocates each sense, but he leans into it. Anything to chase the ghosts away.

For a moment, he forgets.

In the next, he wakes, and the blonde lying across his chest stirs. His head drops against the pillow, and he stares up at the ceiling. As the dawn floods into the room, not for the first—nor the millionth—time does he wish things had turned out differently.

But that's a useless wish, one that does more harm than good. Nothing has changed. His father is still alive, and there's nothing he can do. So, he slips a hand down to grasp his heavy cock and closes his eyes to pretend the hand that joins his is hers. He groans.

Time to wake up.

CHAPTER ONE

Sometimes, I wonder how my life would have played out if I'd ignored the small boy with intelligent eyes and a curious sort of kindness. I wonder if my father would have been alive to see me get married to a nice man and have two babies—both girls, I think. I wonder if my mother would have put down the bottle, and if my brother wouldn't have felt it necessary to prove himself to a family who couldn't care less about him.

It keeps me up at night sometimes, analyzing the dominoes that fell perfectly against each other to lead me here, and I think about how my life would've been completely altered had I not met *him*.

But here I am, about to change the course of my life once more.

Perhaps it was inevitable.

My palms are slick with sweat, and my heart races, thudding so hard I hear it in my ears. I ignore their pleas for clemency. I ignore the blatant cry to stop, turn around, and go back home. My world has been tilted on an axis, and if no one's going to right it, I'll do it myself.

No matter how much it might cost me.

My fingers shake as I smooth my silk dress. It's dark blue with a cowl neck and barely grazes the curve of my ass, but it was all I had in the closet. With one deep inhale, I step out of the darkness and into depravity. A pounding bass and hazy fog saturates the sticky air as I enter Abstrakt, and prickles of awareness tingle down my spine. A knot swells in the back of my throat. How am I going to breathe in here?

Bodies fill the space from the wall-length bar to what looks like a sunken dance floor. Domed, inset, half-rooms frame the space with crimson couches and mirrored ceilings at each semiprivate table. Sheer black curtains offer the illusion of privacy for each, though only a handful have them drawn. It seems people here like to watch. With more skin on display than I've seen in a while, it's no wonder this place has built a reputation for debauchery in such a short time.

The dark walls display brass sconces and gilded photos of hedonistic activities, fully immersing patrons in a night they won't forget. Abstrakt is as promised: a darkened void where one can lose themselves in pleasure and sin.

Abstrakt only opened its doors a few months ago, but according to anyone who's anyone, it's the place to be. And given the rumors surrounding who I'm looking for, he's definitely someone who'd enjoy this sort of establishment. Word has also spread that an even more exclusive lounge lies beyond the intimidating security, if only you know where to look. A lounge he's probably in, based on the sheer number of people packed in this club. A lounge I need to gain access to.

Loud music, a mixture of pop and electronic, thrums over the sticky air, and each pulse slides against my skin as I cross the room. The heady

4

musk of sweat and lust fills what little space remains, but with each breath, I find another note. Something…sweet.

I've never been one for the underground scene, but circumstances have changed. And to start, all I need is to buy some time. I find the center of the group of writhing bodies and join in. An easy smile slides onto my face, and my arms rise as I melt into the music. I don't recognize what's playing, but the rhythm is hypnotic, and my stiff limbs loosen with each beat.

There's a bar on the right wall, and at one end, a bartender shakes a silver bottle with a light flourish before he strains the clear liquid into a martini glass. His ears are likely already tuned to his next customer. Clusters of men openly watch women dance, sipping from their drinks, lust dripping from their gazes. The bar, like the rest of Abstrakt, is crowded.

If it weren't life or death, I wouldn't be caught dead in a place like this. In fact, the sooner I can leave, the better.

The mezzanine above is almost empty, and I don't see how to get upstairs. It's almost like a viewing catwalk, a gallery for the elite to watch those below. Two men lean against the wooden railing, chatting and laughing at whatever their conversation holds. Neither is who I'm looking for.

Hands slide around my waist and squeeze, and I sink into his hold. *Well, he found me quickly.*

If I hadn't been expecting it, I would've elbowed the asshole. Instead, my hands find his, intertwining our fingers against my belly as we dance together. Then, something heavy locks onto my wrist. A smile slips past my control, and I twirl around, putting a few inches between our bodies. His sturdy grip wraps around me once again, pulling me even closer. Sharp green eyes sparkle with familiarity.

"You know what you're doing?" he murmurs, voice barely audible over the music. There's a slight furrow between his brow. I know he's concerned for me. To him—and the other Bianchis—I'm still the little girl they once knew.

I wrap my arms around his neck. To the crowd, we look like anyone else dancing. I don't acknowledge his doubt. "Thank you, Hudson."

His eyes flick between mine. He nods. "In the back. Two guards."

My gaze slices over his shoulder toward the few inlets in the back with their curtains drawn. One has two security guards on standby. At first glance, one might think they were simply there to watch the room. Upon further inspection, their focus seems to remain on those directly around them, as if ensuring no one approaches.

Hudson draws a deep breath as he slides his hand into mine and turns it over between us. Thanks to Hudson's sleight of hand, where previously bare, my wrist is now adorned with a heavy black cuff about an inch wide. A gold filigree with an A in the center shines against the flashing lights.

"Thank you," I repeat. One step closer.

His lips press into a thin line. "Are you sure you want to do this alone?" He releases my arm and tucks a strand of loose hair behind my ear, his eyes narrowed with a mix of intrigue and concern.

God, I wish I could accept his help. But I've used up all of my favors with him, and I don't want to owe him anything else. "I'll let you know when I'm out."

Hudson pauses. Then he drops my hand like it burned him and dips his chin, all emotion cleared from his face. "Be careful, Lo. I don't want to see you on one of those missing posters."

With that, he melts back into the sea of moving bodies without a backward glance. When I blink, he's gone, the crowd having swallowed his enormous frame, which usually has him sticking out like a sore thumb.

I'm on my own.

The weight of the band pulls my attention, and I sneak another look. It's heavy, weighing down my wrist more than any bracelet I've ever worn. Against the lights, you can almost make out a thread of silver stitched around the filigree. A seam runs from the top through the symbol and down to the bottom, and I press on the gold *A*. It clicks open, but I quickly fasten it once more and glance around to see if anyone noticed our exchange. My paranoia is getting to me. Thankfully, everyone's too involved in their own pleasures to be worried about my accessories. And now it's time to make sure it works.

Crossing the room, I slide against more skin than clothing. Some openly display their lust with sensual kisses, their bodies pressed together, with no mistaking what they're up to. I hold my breath and count to ten as I fight the spike of anxiety that shoots tingles down my spine.

God, I hate crowds.

As the thought forms, I push through the last of it and climb a few steps to exit the sunken dance floor. Two hefty bouncers scan my form, and an amiable smile slips onto my face. My feet move without instruction, closing the distance between us.

"First time?" the shorter of the two asks, voice rumbling over the pumping music. He guards the gauzy curtain with beefy arms clasped behind his back, standing straight as a rod. His eyes zero in on me.

The one on the right remains silent, a scowl etched onto his face. Coupled with a scar that slices through his left eyebrow, he screams *intimidating*.

This better work.

I nod, raising my wrist without another word. The silent one's attention doesn't leave mine as the shorter one taps a device against the black band. We only have to wait a moment until he nods once, then he turns to open the curtain for me.

"Use the Park Avenue entrance next time. Enjoy your evening, Miss."

Park Avenue entrance?

I smile coyly, slipping into the role of a lifetime. "I will."

The curtain falls behind me without fanfare, and I follow the dim hallway. It has the same deep green, almost black, walls, with gilded sconces lining the hall. My heels click on the marble floor, and the farther I travel, the less I can hear the pounding music. Instead, a lower, more sensual thrum rises in volume until I reach the end. A doorway opens to a new lounge, one three times as large with at least half as many people. Velvet couches and ornately carved wooden tables scattered throughout the space create intimate gathering spots, most with only a few people.

Conversations are hushed, and several security guards line the room. Dimmed crystal lamps provide low lighting, and a glass fireplace crackles off to the side. On each end of a lounge, there's a bar, and servers clad in sequined fringe deliver drinks. It's the perfect spot for the high-profile patrons. Just from my initial glance, I spot what looks to be the police chief entertaining a woman who's clearly not his wife. Lovely.

But I gather the reason people are paying top dollar for a membership is the entertainment—high-pitched moans ring out, and the slap of skin draws my attention to the stage in the center of the room. On a circular dais is a group of four people—two men and two women—twisted together like a pretzel. One man thrusts into a woman from behind, who works her mouth on the other man, while the second woman thrusts into the man from behind. Even from the short distance where I stand, I can tell her strap-on is girthy and an incredible length. The man groans, echoing around the room and drawing more than one eye toward the stage. Already, a small crowd gathers to watch, and a woman whispers into another patron's ear. He nods, and she drags him by his belt to a door off to the left. The door opens, and I catch a glimpse of a lengthy hallway lined with doors. Each appears to have a strip light of either red or green tracing the frame, and just as the door shuts, I watch as she picks a green door. As soon as she opens it, the light turns red.

Moans harmonize with each other, and a flush creeps over my chest and neck. A low heat gathers in my belly, but goosebumps break out over my exposed flesh as my sweat cools against the chilly air. The silk dress I picked out earlier is tasteful but offers little to the imagination or in the way of warmth.

"Care to warm up by the fire?" a charming voice says from behind me.

I twist around, and my eyes feast on a gorgeous sight. A young sight—and not the sight I'm looking for—but gorgeous and one step closer to me going home.

A few different plays run through my mind. I could either approach the man I'm looking for directly, or I could draw him to me. The latter feels petty, but I just can't help myself.

The stranger in front of me stands tall, a flirty sparkle behind his eyes. His dark hair is buzzed close to his head, and his brown eyes crinkle as he scans my body. By his youthful look, he must be in his early twenties. And fortunately for me, the perfect patsy.

"I don't know," I drawl, turning back toward the room. "I haven't decided if I'm staying."

"Don't leave yet; you just got here." He moves to stand in front of me, and I take the chance to look him over. His clothes fit perfectly—I'd expect nothing less from someone in this lounge—but he's unfastened the top button of his dress shirt and rolled the sleeves to his forearms. A swirl of a black tattoo peeks out from behind the crisp white material on his neck. He smirks, as if all too aware I'm sizing him up.

"What are you going to do?" I close the distance and walk my fingers up his chest, laying my palm over his shoulder. "Throw me over your shoulder and drag me back to your cave?" My attention flicks to his lips before returning to his brown eyes.

He chuckles. We're inches apart, and I can practically hear the quickening of his heartbeat. His eyes dip to my mouth, and his smirk morphs into a smile. "If that's what you'd like."

He seems sweet, and I almost wish I didn't have to use him like this. *Almost.*

"Caleb." He steps away, but only far enough to extend a lithe hand.

I glance down, conflicted. *All part of the show.* I shake my head and accept. "Loren," I respond, a flirty curl to my lips.

Caleb shakes my hand lightly, and I lean into my role—and my bait.

"How about a drink instead?" His eyes twinkle as he extends an elbow in invitation.

I slide my arm through his with a smile and allow him to lead us toward the closest bar. There's no wait for the upper echelon, it appears.

"Single malt scotch and a..." Caleb trails off as he looks over at me. "You look like a merlot kind of lady, am I right?"

A permanent, sultry smile freezes my face, and I don't dare let it slip. I don't mind red wine—I can drink almost anything with a straight face now—but it's not my preference. I nod.

"I knew it." Caleb's words are proud, as if he was some grand profiler.

The bartender pours our drinks swiftly, and Caleb accepts them without a word. He passes mine over, then leads me toward an empty crimson settee right by the glass fireplace with a hand on the small of my back. The marble on the vent matches the flooring, and the heat is welcome.

Caleb unbuttons his jacket. He sits mostly in the center with his legs sprawled out, one arm thrown carelessly over the back of the couch. He takes a sip from his whiskey and hisses through his teeth.

"Are you sure you aren't missing curfew?" I tease, settling next to him. "Let me see your permission slip." The crushed velvet cushion is soft against my bare thighs, and the fire crackles over the low music. I cross one leg over the other and drape my body toward my unwitting opponent.

Caleb chuckles low, but it doesn't cause even a flutter. "It's difficult to maintain any sense of composure when faced with the full weight of your undivided attention."

I smile coyly and flutter my lashes over the brim of my glass. The silence stretches. I take a sip of my wine, letting it simmer even more. The merlot is lush, with notes of cinnamon and berry, going down easily and warming what the fire can't reach.

"Darling, you wouldn't survive the weight of my undivided attention," I say.

His eyes widen in apparent challenge. He slides closer, reaching for me. His fingers just barely trace the bare skin of my shoulder. "I'm up for a challenge."

My response is low, almost a whisper. "Am I a challenge now?"

Caleb chuckles. "Of course not," he drawls, one finger trailing from the slope of my neck to the curve of my jaw. "You're the prize."

Caleb is objectively handsome, that's without question. Warm complexion, clean-shaven, angular jaw, straight nose, brown eyes framed with full dark lashes…It distracts me for a moment. But only that—a moment. His eyes never leave mine as he leans close enough to share breath.

"But the question is"—his tongue flicks out to wet his lips—"how can I win you?"

With each breath, he leans closer until our lips are almost touching. If I don't stop him, he's going to kiss me. And I don't want him to kiss me…right?

I pull back with a sultry smile. "Perhaps you'll find out."

His eyes shine with obvious excitement.

"*Later.*"

Caleb laughs, relaxing back into the couch, nodding in concession and taking a healthy swig of his scotch. This time, he conceals any reaction.

"I usually get to know a man before I learn what he tastes like."

"Ryan, twenty-three, business, and yes, I'm single. And your name is Loren. There. Now we know each other." Humor dances in his voice.

I settle back, putting distance between our bodies. "Ryan? I thought you said your name was Caleb."

"Ryan's my middle name."

I arch a brow. "And the rest?"

He chuckles and finishes the last of his drink in one swallow. "I just turned twenty-three. I graduated last May with a degree in business. And I think the last one's self-explanatory."

My laughter is raucous, drawing the attention of those around us, as intended. "Actually, I'd like to hear about it in further detail." I gesture toward his face and put on a teasing tone. "How is all *this* single?"

Caleb smiles brightly. "It doesn't have to be."

I still, a smile threatening to break through. He sure is determined. "I hate to break it to you, Caleb, but I think I'm too old for you."

"No offense, sweetheart, but I think I get to decide what's too old for me."

I tilt my head, nodding once in concession. "Fair enough. But there's one thing you'll learn as you get older."

"Oh yeah? What's that?" His tone is light, and I can tell he's not offended by my redirection.

I swirl my wineglass around. "You should get to know someone before you order for them."

Caleb looks to my near-full glass of wine. "Every woman drinks red." He points to the red lipstick stain on the rim. "But you don't?" Then he tucks a strand of hair behind my ear.

I smile, but it's weak.

A crystal tumbler with amber liquid appears in front of me. "She drinks whiskey," a smooth voice says from above.

A voice that's haunted me for years. A voice that swarms my every sense, invades logical reasoning, and heats my blood to a boil.

Callahan Keane.

The greatest heartbreak of my life.

CHAPTER TWO

My heart stops. All noise muffles as I stare at the proffered drink. Caleb speaks, but I don't hear what he says. I'm frozen, suddenly sixteen again, feeling the burning stare of a boy who wouldn't look away from me.

My gaze travels over the scars on his knuckles, the custom silver cufflinks, the perfectly tailored charcoal suit, the clean shave of his jaw, and locks onto his captivating brown eyes. Some things are new—like the scars—but at least one thing hasn't changed. I teeter on the edge, about to fall headfirst back into his pull, when sound rushes back in, and Caleb clears his throat.

"Do you two, uh, know each other?" His earlier confidence seems to have shriveled in the presence of *him*. Something I'm all too familiar with.

A momentary flash of blonde hair and hurried shuffling slices open an old wound with no warning. The silence stretches. Caleb looks between us, a furrow forming on his brow. Callahan doesn't answer, doesn't move from where we're locked. His gaze burrows into mine, and I feel the years melting off like a forgotten popsicle on a wooden dock.

14

"Bunny." It's all he says, his voice soft as he urges me to take the glass from him once more.

My nose scrunches. How *dare* he use that name? My fingers curl around my wineglass. I almost wish it breaks so I can use a shard to stab him in the hand for daring to offer me anything again.

"I'm not your bunny." My tone is scathing. But not nearly as harsh as it could be. "And I don't drink whiskey anymore." I take a healthy gulp of my wine to prove my point.

Callahan raises a brow and removes his offering. He takes a long drink, never breaking eye contact, downing the entire glass and smacking his lips, shoving the tumbler into Caleb's chest.

"Get another. And this time"—his stony gaze slices to Caleb—"keep your hands to yourself."

Caleb frowns but stands anyway. He walks toward the bar, muttering something under his breath. I watch him until I physically can't, and Callahan effortlessly settles into his spot.

His power is tangible, an air of cockiness that only comes from knowing you could change the political landscape with a snap of your fingers. Callahan might only be a year older than me, but he's the newest leader of the Keane family, the largest distributor of premium cocaine in Roswell. According to the news outlets, his father suffered a heart attack in the middle of the night eight months ago, making Callahan the most powerful man in Roswell overnight.

The Keane family and Bianchi family have been in a tug of war for territory for as long as we've been alive, for reasons I've never really understood. The Bianchi family sells weed and occasionally coke, but mostly the green flower. There really shouldn't be a crossover of clientele, but back when our fathers and uncles ran Roswell, there were huge personal attacks that led to a great divide. Any interactions with the enemy were strictly forbidden and punishable by exile. And even though I'm a Catrone, my father was the right hand to Dominic Bianchi until my father's untimely death, which meant Cal and I were enemies from the moment we were born. That didn't stop us, though. The thrill only made it more exciting. For a while, at least.

Instead of responding, I take another drink from my wineglass and look over to the crackling fire. Even though I came here for him tonight, seeing him again has caught me off guard. Cal chuckles, a deep rumbling that reverberates over my skin. Whatever attraction I thought had passed, clearly hasn't.

"You know, the silent treatment is sexy. Means I'm under your skin."

My head whips around, and my gaze lands on his smirking face. "You wish."

He winks. "Of course I do. I'm not afraid to admit it."

I clench my jaw, telling myself I'm refusing to dignify his response with a rebuttal. But truthfully, I don't know what to say. I'd practiced my speech in the mirror for hours. Even so, the words evade me. With each breath that passes, I feel the weight of his gaze taking in every inch of my body. Every nerve comes alive as the memory of his touch burns as hot as it did eleven years ago. We were kids then, bumbling fools who knew nothing about pleasure, but eventually, we figured it out. Many times, in fact. He looks at me now as if he remembers, too.

His eyes devour me, flicking over my face as if he's afraid I might disappear like a ghost. As time would have it, Callahan is even more devastating than he was at seventeen. Wide lips still wet from the whiskey, straight nose, high cheekbones, and a jaw that could cut glass… His brown hair remains parted on the same side as I remember, but it's longer than when we were kids, the wave so effortlessly chic. He smirks, and the dimple I used to dream about appears. I have to force my body not to gravitate toward his. Despite never having fully recovered from the sting of his betrayal, I can't seem to escape his pull. My mouth parts, but I can't find the words. I'm a ship without a life raft, stranded in the middle of his ocean.

Frozen, I can only watch as Cal lifts a hand to tuck an errant strand of hair behind my ear. I suck in a quick breath, and his finger stills, but only for a moment. He drags it tenderly down my cheek, so lightly I'm not sure it even happened.

"Why are you here, Bunny?"

His words are simple, his gentle tone so familiar, but it slices me to the core. A leftover remembrance of when he called me that in our youth.

"I'm here…" I trail off, stalling before I dive headfirst into insanity. "Because I need your help."

Cal's face doesn't change, he just cocks his head to the side. "What do you—"

"Here," Caleb interjects, holding out a fresh tumbler of whiskey.

Cal's jaw ticks, and he refuses to look away from me. After a few seconds, I relent.

"Thank you, Caleb." I trade my wineglass for the crystal tumbler in his hand. "If you could please give us some privacy."

Caleb shoots Cal another glance. He visibly withers and nods. "Sure. I think I see someone who looks in need of a drink, anyway." With that, he discards the wineglass on a nearby table and heads toward a busty blonde.

I turn back to Cal, and tingles rush down my spine. *He never looked away.* The weight of his gaze heats me from the inside out, just as it did all those years ago.

Shoving the drink into his hand, I almost flinch when our fingers brush. He takes the glass, and my hand lingers, until I remember myself and drop it into my lap.

"What's happened?" he questions. "Why are you coming to me?"

Fighting words that aim to cut, to make him *bleed*, I grind my teeth. I need his help, and insulting him won't get me any answers. I have to swallow my pride.

"Mason is missing," I finally manage. "He…" I gulp, gaze dropping to my lap. "He wanted to be made, so they gave him a task."

Cal's rugged finger presses below my chin, tilting my face to meet his gaze. His deep brown eyes search mine. Looking for what, I don't know.

"What kind of task?" he murmurs, his gaze dropping to my mouth for a moment before returning to my eyes.

"They wanted…" Flashes of Mason's kiddish charm and round cheeks hardening into dangerous stubbornness and sharp edges barrage me. I can't find the words, can't say them aloud. I twist my chin from Cal's hold and stare at the crackling fire instead.

"Wanted what, Bunny?"

The nickname tugs at my defenses. This could be a catastrophic mistake, but it's my only option. I meet his gaze once more, ripping open my armor and falling on my sword.

"They sent him on a data collection mission in Keane territory. Wanted him to come back with updated stats on your suppliers. They've seen you've recently lost some territory and thought they could capitalize on your newfound weakness." The words rush out of me and linger, thickening in the air between us.

Cal doesn't speak; he simply watches me. My hands tingle in the silence.

"Is that all?" He arches a brow as if to say my biggest fear is nothing to worry about.

"Is that all?" I repeat, brows shooting up to my hairline. "Is that fucking all? Did you not hear a word I said?" I swear I can feel my blood pressure skyrocket. "Elias sent my baby brother into enemy territory— into *your territory*. We haven't heard from him in weeks, and all you can say is, *'Is that all?'*"

Cal—wisely—stays quiet, and uncharacteristically, without a smirk. He waits, and the lack of reaction confuses me. Did he already know?

My anger sizzles, and I open my mouth to speak, but he cuts me off, slamming his whiskey in one gulp and sniffing the burn away. His sizable thumb wipes a drop he missed from the corner of his mouth, and he leans forward, resting his forearms on his legs. His face is the closest it's been, and his gaze openly searches my face.

"After all these years," he says, voice low, a sharp bite of irritation bleeding through, "you still believe I'm only your enemy?"

My mouth parts, ready to argue, but he *tsks*, cutting me off with a sound so admonishing it stings.

"Oh, Loren, you wound me." He leans forward until I'm forced to either share his breath or retreat.

I refuse to concede.

His burning gaze drops to my lips again. It lingers for a moment, then locks with mine once more. Turbulent storms war behind his brown eyes, until darkness eclipses the brown. Suddenly, I'm not sure this was a good idea. Cal's nostrils flare, and I wonder if he can sense my trepidation.

"As if I could be so lucky," he snaps. The words slice, burrowing deep into an old wound that still remembers.

"What the fuck does that mean?" I grind out between clenched teeth. I've spent the last eleven years *loathing* Callahan Keane—for good fucking reason—and he has the audacity to be angry with *me*? Has he forgotten how absolutely callous he was? Or how he told me he loved me, then turned around and discarded me like trash? Does he think I've forgotten the look on his face when I opened the door and saw that blonde crawling out of his bed? Or the words he threw at my back, wielding cruelty like a whip as I ran? A red haze flashes over me, but I lock it down, lifting my chin in defiance.

"As if you ever could be."

He chuckles low, a scathing sound I haven't heard from him before. I narrow my eyes, and he composes himself, but only enough to speak.

"Oh, you don't know." His words are laced with bitter humor.

My brow furrows, confusion eclipsing my anger. "Know what?" I ask with hesitation.

Excitement sparks in his eyes. He settles against the couch, arms thrown over the back. The patron saint of carelessness. "That I need a wife."

His words stun me, but it's his smile that's the most unnerving. He looks me up and down from where he lounges, watching as the gears turn in my head. Why should I care that he still needs a wife? Every gossip in town tells of the endless rotation of women he keeps company with. If he's still single, it's likely for good reason. And not my problem, either.

But no matter the reason, somewhere deep, *deep* in the recess of my mind, a young girl cries out.

I ignore her.

Instead, I lean back with calculated disinterest. "And why do you feel the need to tell me this?"

Cal scrubs a hand over his jaw and smiles to himself. He exhales deeply, throwing his arm, once again, back over the edge. "Because you'll be my wife."

I grind my jaw shut, trapping the scream that threatens to escape behind my teeth.

"And if you want your brother to live," he says as he gestures to a nearby server for a refill, "all you'll have to say is *I do.*"

CHAPTER THREE

I t's all I can do to not laugh in his face. My fingers fly to my lips, covering the outlandish smile that breaks out. Be his wife? Marry *him?* The thought is so comical it almost eclipses into familiar territory: contempt.

I tamp down my knee-jerk reaction and shake off the humor. Cal leans back and tilts his head, eyes flicking between mine. The silence builds, neither of us breaking eye contact, while the low thrum of music seems to swell into a deafening crescendo—or that might just be my heartbeat echoing in my ears. A knot thickens in my throat, and I gulp.

Cal breaks first, eyes falling to my neck to watch me swallow. I grind my teeth together to stop a triumphant smile from breaking free, turning instead to the crackling fire to watch as the log snaps in two. An apt metaphor.

How does he still have such an effect on me? It's been eleven years since I saw him. Why does he look at me like it hasn't even been a day?

"And what part about marrying me is so comical?" he asks, but the musing tone tells me he's toying with me.

I consider lying. Telling him off. Dragging Caleb back here and sliding my tongue in his mouth. But worst of all, I consider saying yes.

Thankfully, the server returns, saving me from answering as she hands a fresh tumbler to Cal. He accepts it, but his fingers linger on her wrist, halting her in her tracks. He looks away from me, and an old ache throbs. "Come back in ten." His eyes drag over her exposed body, and there's no mistaking the meaning behind his words.

My face heats, blood rushing to my cheeks as the server smiles and leans down to whisper in his ear. I'm not sure what she says, and I don't care to use my imagination. She stands and walks away with a sway to her hips.

I scoff. "It's nice to see the rumors are true."

Truly, let's just call the past five minutes a temporary blip in judgment. How could I ever think Callahan would ever give up his philandering ways? He wasn't the marrying sort. He told me that himself eleven years ago.

I only came here tonight because I'd hoped to speak with him without his constant security detail. They're still here—I recognize one in the corner, though much older than when I saw him last—but Abstrakt guarantees a certain level of privacy. It was my best chance to get him alone long enough to ask if he knew where Mason was. I certainly wasn't expecting him to extort me into marriage, and then somehow still feel jealous when he openly propositioned another woman in front of me.

The sly smile that curls his lips stings more harshly than a sucker punch to the gut.

"Which rumors have you heard, Bunny?" He raises his glass, and my eyes follow the knot in his neck that slides up and down as he swallows. The ice clinks in his drink as he swirls it around. Then he extends his glass in open offer. "Now, now. Don't be shy. It's just the two of us here." He winks one of those brown eyes that's hooded with lust. "We both know you still drink whiskey. Crave it, in fact."

Cal lightly turns the tumbler, swirling the liquid to tempt me. I lean closer, my gaze never straying from his. I'm so close that his knuckles brush my silk dress. It sends a shiver down my spine, but I refuse to show how he affects me.

"Even if I were dying of thirst, I wouldn't accept a drink from you." My body fumes, heating me from my scalp to my toes, and I lie to myself that it's from my anger. "Let alone your bullshit proposal."

Cal grins, his dimple creasing his cheek. "It was hardly a proposal." He pauses for a beat, as if in thought. "Though, I suppose it was. A business proposal, at least."

With another sip of his drink, his tongue darts out to wet his bottom lip, and he sighs. "I don't see what the problem is. I'll help you with your brother. You'll get to quit whatever day job you have. And after two years, if you want a divorce, I'll draw up the papers myself."

My shoulders twitch. *Quit whatever day job I have?* Has he not kept tabs on me like I have on him? Something about that stings, and I fight the urge to reach for the old ache in my chest.

"Why won't you just help me out of the goodness of your heart?" I ask, despite knowing he's going to mock me. Anything to steer me out of that train of thought. "Or is it true you've ruined the last of it?"

Cal leans forward, and a curl from his perfectly tousled waves falls loose. "Didn't you just say we were enemies?"

"Not in those exact words."

"Semantics," Cal says with a dismissive wave. "Why would I help *you*, when all you offer is a less than grateful attitude"—he gestures toward me with his drink—"and a bargain peep show."

My cheeks heat, and I fight the urge to tug on my dress. I'm wearing more than almost any woman in here. And I think I've been fairly tame compared to the hellish torrent I could have unleashed on him.

It's like he's antagonizing me on purpose.

Fine. If he wants a fight, then it's time to lace up the gloves.

"What do I have to be grateful for?" I push his hand away, and the tumbler crashes into his chest, spilling down his crisp white shirt.

Cal freezes, either stunned by my finger jabbing into his wet chest or the vitriol I'm about to spew.

"The only thing I'm grateful for is that I was fortunate enough to be spared your face for the last eleven years. Each day without you was *categorically* better than the last. Even the day my father died was a walk in the park considered to that last morning. Though unfortunately, it appears my luck is up. And you're the only one who can help me." I shrug, mouth pinched together in a mocking frown. "Is that what you want to hear? That the only reason I'm here is because *I need you*, and how I'd rather swallow broken glass than utter those words, but here I am saying them anyway?"

Cal doesn't move, doesn't breathe. The only sign my words have landed is the slight flare to his nostrils. He tilts his head to take a sip of his whiskey, exposing his corded neck.

"Are you done?" he asks, setting the empty glass on the side table and clearing his throat. "Is it my turn now?"

My eyes narrow, but I remain silent.

Cal smirks, leaning forward to speak. "I'll help you," he begins, finger twirling around a lock of my hair, "but I'll need something in return. I wasn't kidding when I said I needed a wife." He drops my hair and stands, holding out a hand for me.

I pause for a calculated moment, then allow him to pull me up. He takes the chance to look me up and down, and my face flushes against his appraisal.

"If you agree to the terms, I'll use every resource at my disposal to help find Mason."

"What do you mean, *find* Mason?" I ask. My heart thumps painfully against its cage. "*You don't know where he is?*"

Cal swallows thickly, his eyes never leaving mine. "No."

I ready to argue, but Cal cuts me off.

"But if you say they sent him into Keane territory and no one's heard from him since, something must've happened. So here's my offer: You agree to marry me within the month and move into the Keane residence, remaining in a marital contract for twenty-four months. In exchange, I locate and return your brother to you, safe and sound. Agreed?"

Two years? My chest tightens, and I gasp in a breath. He's serious. He's actually serious. He'll find Mason, and all I have to do is sacrifice a few years as his…wife.

The thought makes me dizzy, and I sway. Cal steadies me with a hand to my elbow, eyebrows drawing together as he inspects me.

"Mr. Keane?" a voice says from next to us.

The server is back, but she has no drink to offer. The green-eyed monster I thought I was better than rushes to the surface, and my gaze snaps to Cal.

"No women." The two words are piercing, and I see the moment he understands, a minute twitch in the jaw, but Cal covers it easily.

"No men," he counters. "I won't allow my wife to embarrass me in such a manner."

I scoff. "If I were *your wife*, you wouldn't have a damn say over what— or *who*—I do." I hear the hypocrisy, the double standard, but I can't help the fact that he's under my skin, and I need to have the last word.

Cal steps into my space, forcing me to look up at him. The fire crackles behind him, casting a golden glow around his frame. His usually chocolate-brown waves are ablaze with an auburn fire, and his brown eyes shine with a curious emotion.

"The only cock my wife will worship is *mine*." His breath smells faintly of whiskey, and his sandalwood cologne wafts over me. It's a heady combination that sends me back years.

Cal trails a finger along my jaw, speaking softly so no one else can hear. "I hadn't thought to add that into the contract yet, but if you'd like to amend the terms, I'm more than willing to consider it."

"Don't push it." I flick his hand away from my face, and Cal chuckles.

A throat clears next to us, and we look over to the server. A berry blush flushes her rich, brown complexion. She looks everywhere but at us.

"Kyra, dear," Cal says, finally acknowledging her presence. "Meet me at our door."

My mouth drops open. His audacity is astonishing. "What happened to *no women?*"

Cal smirks, a mischievous lilt to the corner of his mouth. "We're not married yet, Bunny." His gaze locks onto mine one last time before he leaves me standing by the roaring fire. "Meet me at sunset on the twenty-fifth at Wisteria Pointe. Wear something white."

I'm frozen, unable to move even as he walks away. What just happened?

"Oh and, Loren?" He turns back around to face me. "Don't be late. I'd hate to chase down a runaway bride. But for you, I suppose I can make an exception."

He spins on his heel with a wink and saunters off, leaving me reeling in the wake of his proposition. Am I actually going to marry this man? *This* man? Callahan Keane, the man who taught me to never trust another again?

My gaze slices to where Cal's led into the hallway of private rooms. *Kyra* opens the door for him, and together, they exit the lounge.

Oh, I am so going to make him regret this.

Since I don't know where the Park Avenue exit is, I turn and head toward the first club, crossing through the dim hallway. The two security guards say nothing when I storm past, cutting through the dance floor that seems to be even more packed and pushing through the stairwell. In the corner, right before the door, I see the dead plant where Hudson instructed to leave the wristband. Pausing, I click the black band open. *How did this night take such a left turn?* I freeze, a knot thickening my throat. If I've used all my goodwill up with the Bianchi family, and I'm well and truly on my own, then what's the harm in keeping it?

Nothing. With a curl to my lips, I shove it into my clutch instead, press open the metal bar, and exit into the night.

The light drizzle from earlier has turned into a heavy downpour, and while it only takes about ten seconds to make my way around the corner and to my car, I still get soaked to my bones. The door slams behind me, and I dig my phone out of my bag, then toss the clutch onto the passenger seat. My hair drips onto the black fabric, but I pay it no mind as I dial Hudson's cell.

It rings twice before he answers.

"You get what you needed?"

"Yes, I did," I begin, still dizzy from the direction my night took. "Thank you, again."

A long exhale comes from the other end. "I hope you know what you're doing, Lo. Did you drop the band where I told you to?"

Mason's face flashes in my mind, and my hold tightens painfully on my cell. If I ever want to find him, then this is what I have to do. I better get used to it now.

"Goodbye, Hudson." I hang up the call. The sound of the rain pouring over the metal roof of my Subaru fills the quiet space and gives me something to focus on. Hudson's contact flashes on my screen, but I decline his call. Instead, I make an online appointment with the nearest bridal shop for first thing in the morning. Upon clicking the submit button, something tightens in my chest, but I ignore it, choosing to shift my car into drive. I step on the gas.

Here comes the bride, all soaked in...lies.

CHAPTER FOUR

I let out a groan that practically reverberates against the walls and slam my head back on the edge of the couch, squeezing my eyes shut. Twinkling laughter sparks next to me, and I feel around for my decorative pillow to launch at Alice's face. It lands with a whoosh of air and an even harder laugh from my best friend. She cackles next to me.

"This isn't funny."

"Coulda fooled me." Alice wipes a tear from her large blue eyes that sparkle with humor. She's twisted her mane of blonde hair into a topknot, leaving a few pieces to frame her fresh face. She's barely older than Mason, and even though I'm four years older, her maturity constantly makes me forget that she's only twenty-three. We met when Mase and I moved into this complex three years ago, and we've been friends ever since.

"I just told you I'm getting married to the man responsible for breaking my heart into a million pieces without so much as an apology. I hate him with every fiber of my being, and you're *laughing*."

She shrugs. "They always say there's a fine line between love and hate." As if that's the answer to everything. As if I could ever love him again. *As if I could ever love again, at all.*

It's a terrifying thought, one I don't want to dissect. Instead, I deflect. "Says the woman who hasn't been on a date in over six months. What happened to that Henry guy?"

Alice's cheeks flame. Her eyes avert to her lap, and she adjusts the band of her grandmother's watch. I've never seen her without it. She's quiet for several seconds, her hands playing with the hem of her bright blue sweater. It's vibrant, but Alice has always been a cheerful woman. Her clothing choices might not be for everyone, but once I got to know her, I realized the eccentric look was an outward expression of her energetic personality. She always sees the good in people, almost to a concerning fault. Her cropped sweater falls to her slim waist, and she wears pink and yellow rose-print palazzo pants with her legs curled under her.

"Student teaching really took a lot out of me last year, and then the serving job in the summer was exhausting. Then the fall semester was harder than I expected." Exhaustion shadows her voice, and I reach a hand over in comfort, stilling the fingers toying with a loose thread on her hem. She accepts the gesture quickly, lacing our fingers together and squeezing tightly.

"I'm sorry. It was just supposed to be a joke," I say.

Alice nods, and I know she's forgiven me. She's like that. Quick to forgive, easy to love. It baffles me how someone with such a rough start to life came out the other side with more empathy than I have in my pinky.

Raised by her grandparents because her mother didn't want her and her dad was just a one-night stand, Alice had an unusual start to life. Her father didn't even know she existed, and her mother never cared enough to remember his name. When Alice was fourteen, her grandparents died, and she went into the system, bouncing around from home to home.

On her eighteenth birthday, a lawyer showed up at her foster family's home to hand her a check. Her grandparents had left her a trust, something she hadn't even known about until the lawyer told her. Her foster family took one look at the number of zeros and kicked her out that same day, saying she could pay her own way from then on. But she refused to touch the money, using only what she needed for necessities and school. And somehow, despite all that, she graduated early with her teaching degree and was about to start her second semester as a first-grade teacher. Pride swells in my chest whenever I think of how far she's come.

When we first met, she had just started college, and over the course of the next three years, we became inseparable. At first, it started more as a big sister-little sister relationship, and she'd ask me adulting advice and dating advice—which, admittedly, I probably shouldn't have told her all men were trash. Then, as the years passed, she blossomed into a beautiful young woman, and now we regularly hang out. Usually half the week, she comes over for dinner, or just to watch a show and catch up.

Tonight is one of those nights. She showed up with a mocktail margarita mix and homemade guacamole while I cooked chicken fajitas. The whole condo still smells like simmering spices and garlic, but my belly is too stuffed to start the cleanup. The end credits of *John Tucker Must Die* roll in the background, and I reach for the remote to flick off the TV. Alice doesn't drink, but she sips from her mocktail, smacking her lips from the tart margarita. Mine is empty on the round coffee table and due for a refill with *actual* tequila, but again—too full to move.

The room goes dark except for the few lamps scattered around the condo. It's not the most aesthetic home, but I'm proud of it. I bought it with the first real paycheck from my novel and spent the next year filling it with furniture and decorations I'd thrifted and upcycled. None of it really matches, but that's what gives it its charm—or so I tell myself.

A television sits atop an antique standing cabinet, someone having replaced the cabinets with glass before I acquired it. I store my collection of DVDs and backup candles inside, along with a few books and other miscellaneous items that don't really have a home. My couch is a brown leather sectional with mismatched decorative pillows and a circular white rug underneath. With white walls covered in random pieces of art and dark hardwood floors, the room gives off an eclectic, cozy vibe that I adore. The rest of my house follows suit, all pieces I've picked up along the way because they spoke to me.

The only thing missing—Mason.

My heart sinks, and I can't help the emotion from twisting my expression. Alice notices immediately—she always does—and she throws herself over the couch to squish me with her love. I can't even blink before her surprisingly fierce grip coils around me like a snake.

"He'll come home. He always does."

I nod into her shoulder, but she doesn't let go. That night, I break in her arms, and she just holds me tightly until the sun rises.

⚭

My feet pound against the sidewalk as I push myself further. Sweat pools against my nape, curling the hairs and dripping down my back. It only spurns me further. My revenge era, female rage playlist blasts in my ears, and the lyrics to "Which Witch" by Florence + the Machine feels more and more relatable with each stride. The sun is bright, warming me just enough as I make my way to Strikers, but the coastal breeze is picking up speed. Typically, Roswell is overcast and wet, but days like today offer the perfect balance for the northeast coast in January. I don't always run to the gym—most days I know I won't want to make the trip back—but today, I need the distraction.

The massive warehouse comes into view just as a stitch cramps my side. My sneakers slap against the concrete, and I barely slow to let myself into the building. Jenna waves from her spot at the desk, but I duck past her with an air kiss, then point to my headphones. *She'll understand.* On my way toward the left side of the gym, I borrow a pair of gloves from the bin and slip them on.

I'm not scheduled to train today, but I needed to punch something, so I choose a quiet corner and warm up with a few combos. I make it my mission to beat up the worn sandbag hanging from the ceiling.

When sweat stings my eyes and my muscles burn from overuse, I finally pause, sucking in a breath that doesn't quite fill my lungs. My vision tunnels, and black spots dot my periphery, making my head dizzy and light.

"Fuck." I rub a gloved hand against my temple and pop my headphones over my neck. The music still blares, reverberating against my collarbone, but I don't have the energy to grab my phone and pause it yet.

"You good, kid?"

Jude's voice startles me, and I nearly jump out of my skin.

"Shit, warn a girl, would ya?"

Jude's brow furrows, and he looks around the gym expectantly. "This is my gym. And I did warn you. I said, *You good, kid?*" An incredulous look passes over his face, and I can't help a snort of laughter.

"Of course that makes sense to you."

"Why wouldn't it?"

I wave him off, the rip of the Velcro audible even against my music. I toss them to the floor and fish my phone out of my pocket to pause the music. There's an unread text from Hudson that I haven't been able to bring myself to open. I know he wants the wristband back, but I have a feeling it will come in handy.

"Why are you here today? You're not scheduled until Thursday."

I've been coming to Strikers two to three times a month for the last eight years, and Jude has trained me almost the entire time. Sometimes, I'll come in and pound on the bags or spar with someone else, but only if I'm really going through something.

And clearly, I'm going through it.

"I needed to work out some aggression."

Jude raises a singular brow, but otherwise doesn't pry. That's what I love about him. He takes you at your word but doesn't get upset if you break it. The only person I've seen him show a modicum of emotion toward is his wife, Jenna. I met her a few years back when he'd already been dating her for over six months, apparently. Then, within the month, they were married. He hadn't even told me. I found out because suddenly, he was wearing a gold band on his finger. When I badgered him for details, his dark complexion had warmed, and the tips of his cheekbones and ears burned crimson. It was actually sort of sweet, so I didn't mention it again for fear he'd never tell me anything else. I honestly never expected him to be the type to settle down, but I like who he's become after Jenna.

He actually asks how I'm doing now instead of just grunting whenever I try for conversation.

Still, his bulky stature would intimidate anyone, grunting aside. He's got to be taller than six feet, and each of his arms is thicker than my head. Jude keeps his head shaved, but a well-groomed dark beard covers the expanse of his chiseled jaw. Several breaks have left his wide nose crooked, and scars mark his torso and knuckles. When asked how he got so many, all he said was *people*. He left it at that, but it was enough for me to draw my own conclusions.

He crosses his tree trunk arms over his chest. "Want to talk about it?"

A smile threatens to break, so I pinch my lips together. I know that was like swallowing glass having to say that out loud. But the offer is sweet, and I appreciate it more than he can know. I shake my head.

Jude pauses, then says with reluctance, "Want to get drunk?"

This time, I don't contain the smile that splits my face in two. "Fuck yes."

CHAPTER FIVE

O n the eve of my wedding, I sit cross-legged on my bed, a handful of pictures scattered on the duvet. My entire life—until I left the Bianchi residence—lies around me. Pictures from my parent's wedding, my birth, our old dog Coco, Mason's birth, the lake house where I learned to swim…and where I fell in love for the first time.

With the weight of my impending nuptials, I feel as if I'm floating outside my body. Tonight, I'd finally succumbed to digging the old, dusty shoebox out of its permanent hiding spot in the back of my closet. Each time I almost forgot about it, some unwanted memory cropped up, reminding me of its presence like a beacon in the night. It isn't anything special, just an old sneakers box, but the contents inside are priceless. One in particular catches my eye. The one I'd avoided looking directly at for the last fifteen minutes.

It's like looking through a portal to another world where life was simpler. It sends me tumbling through time. Down at the dock, I'd sat at the edge with my feet dangling in the tepid water alongside *him*, near a cracked, anchored dinghy. As we spoke, our fingers crept closer until our pinkies touched. Then he finally gathered his courage and grabbed my hand, and we laughed at the awkward tug. That was the first of many trips to the lake house. This picture is from the last.

We spent the entire summer sneaking up north when we could, and when school started up again in the fall…well, that was the beginning of the end. I think we both knew it, but neither of us were brave enough to admit it. To say it out loud.

My hand shakes as I pick up the photograph, a candid shot of a younger Cal as the sun set behind him. His face is how it's frozen in my memories, slightly rounder than it is now, and his shoulders are relaxed. Cal stares out at the water with a serene smile, pointing at something in the distance, but I don't remember what. All I could focus on was *him*. A sharp ache in my chest burns. The photo was from the last time we made it to the lake house. I drop it back onto my bed.

It lands over the crumpled envelope I've done my best to avoid. The worn envelope is wrinkled from years of clammy hands gripping either side, trying to build the courage to open it. He sent it to the Bianchi estate about seven years ago, when I still lived there and my family was whole. It's addressed to Ren Catrone, so I knew it was from Cal—he was the only one who could get away with calling me Ren—but I couldn't bring myself to open it. I told myself it didn't matter what he had to say, didn't matter what secrets the letter could contain. But that didn't stop me from almost opening it about a hundred times. After a while, it became a fixation, so I shoved it into the shoebox to force myself to forget about it.

Even so, temptation drew me to the shoebox. And now, on the eve of my wedding to the sender of the letter that has taunted me for so long, I almost break. It tugs at me, whispering sweet promises that are surely lies. *It doesn't matter what it says,* I tell myself. If Cal really wanted to apologize, he would've found me and said so to my face.

Over the last few weeks, I've cycled through each possible emotion a human can process. First, it was shock, barely registering the soft music played in the bridal boutique. When I was younger, I imagined my wedding to Cal. I thought about the millions of dresses I'd try on, worried about the height of my heels, how I'd do my hair…Every single detail had been planned out until all I was missing was the groom himself.

It was foolish, and I knew it then, too. But it didn't stop me from spending hours fantasizing about the possibility.

I bought the first wedding dress I tried on. It didn't matter what it looked like, if I liked it. It's some sort of silk slip and hangs in a white garment bag in my closet. I can't bring myself to look at it. Teenage Loren would be so mad.

Next it was avoidance, and I threw myself into my work, barely even stopping to eat. If I didn't leave my room, I couldn't notice that Mason still hadn't come home. Alice had to hand deliver each dinner for three nights and practically forced each meal down my throat.

When I hit the anger stage, Jude, Jenna, and I closed down Poor Folks, drinking until almost three in the morning. Upon waking the next afternoon, I remembered why I stopped mixing my liquors and spent half the day puking my guts out until there was nothing left. Jude was, as predicted, back in the gym, teaching a class by ten that morning. I will never know how he does it.

Since then, I've wandered through my days as if heading toward my death. And in a certain manner, I sort of am. I'm ending life as I know it.

Now, I sit on my bed on the cusp of my teenage dream realized, and I think I've finally entered acceptance. Staring at the sum of my life's major events, I can't help but feel a certain ache loosen in my chest. The photos are few, but I place them back in the shoebox.

There's a knock on my door, and Alice peeks her face in. "Hey," she murmurs. She pushes into my room and crosses to me. Her angelic face is flushed, and sweat beads along her temple. Her insanely long blonde hair is in a fierce ponytail, with only a few frazzled pieces sticking out, and her face is rosy. Combined with her athletic wear and damp hairline, I'd wager she just came from the gym. "Ready for tomorrow?"

I summon what I hope is a reassuring smile.

"Hi," I respond as I shut the lid on my shoebox. "I sorta have to be…right?"

Alice openly searches my face, probably looking for any sign I want to run, disappear into the wind. I'd done it once before; I could do it again. Her wise-beyond-her-years eyes narrow as she waits for me to be honest with myself—and her. But the memory of holding an infant Mason flashes in my mind. Our father died in service of the Family almost a decade ago. Our mother is probably swimming at the bottom of a bottle of gin somewhere…I can't run. Not this time.

Moreover, I don't want to.

Alice perches on the edge of my bed and arches a brow. "I don't know, do you?" Her voice is gentle, concern pooling behind her blue eyes. Her sincerity distracts me for a moment. "Are you sure about this?"

My gaze drops to my duvet as I play with a loose thread on my leggings. Her gentle hand covers mine, stilling my anxious fingers. I look up to see concern in the pinch of Alice's brows.

"For Mason, I have to be."

"Lo, we—"

"No, Alice. Any favor I had with the Bianchis is gone. And I can't get any more information out of Leon. It's like Mason's a ghost."

"I know." Her shoulders drop.

"I'll be okay. If there's anything I can be sure of"—my throat tightens over a sudden knot—"it's that Cal can't hurt me physically."

Alice's lips press into a flat line. She shakes her head and stands to leave, then crosses the room and pauses at my door. Gripping the wood, she looks back at me, apprehension furrowed in her brow. "I still think it's a bad idea."

A crestfallen sigh escapes me as I look at the single worn photo I left out. The one that shows a cheesing six-year-old Loren cradling a newborn Mason. "I never said it wasn't."

The next afternoon, I rush through my makeup and tie my chestnut hair in a messy low chignon, only pulling two pieces from the middle part to frame my face. My hazel eyes are slightly bloodshot from the tears I succumbed to late last night—or was it early this morning?—but I've tried to hide the residual emotion with a brown smokey eye and pencil liner. I blink matching brown mascara onto my lashes and swipe mauve lipstick over my lips.

My mind empties as I move on autopilot. Do my makeup. Fix my hair. Get dressed.

I'd already packed my car up this morning, opting to leave mostly everything here, save for my favorite clothes, laptop and notebooks, makeup, and a few other bits and pieces I can't live without. By leaving most of my belongings here, it appeases the trembling part of me that believes I'll return one day. Or rather, in seven-hundred and thirty days, should we find Mason.

My silk robe slides off easily, and I step into a white lace panty. I tuck the matching bra away and ignore the mounting frustration building inside me. Cal will never see it, but something selfish inside me insisted I have at least one thing I would've had if this were a real wedding. A somber weight settles over my shoulders as I slide into my off-white silk dress. It's tapered to my waist and falls just past my knees with a cowl neck and very, very low back. The thin straps are practically decoration; it's not like my small chest needs much support. If not for the color, it could barely pass for a wedding dress.

A quick knock precedes a muffled "You decent?" from Alice, as I look over my shoulder toward the vanity. I do *not* remember the back being this low. Not that I remember much of the fitting, anyway. *Oh well.*

"Yeah, come in," I respond as I move to perch on the edge of my bed and slip into my black heels. With a sharp inhale, I slap a smile on my face as Alice enters.

She looks me up and down and returns my grin. "You look beautiful, Lo. You sure I can't come?"

I shake my head, and her smile wobbles. If I hadn't been looking at her, I would've missed the crack to her facade, but it would be a cold day in hell that I'd bring Alice into Cal's world. She is everything light, and I'm heading straight into the darkness.

I take one last look in the vanity mirror. My face is older, sharper than what I thought it would look like on my wedding day. Sure, one day I dreamed of marrying Callahan Keane. Swirled *Mrs. Callahan Keane* in the margins of my notebooks. Of finally being able to step out of the shadows and into the light with him. But then I woke up. And now I was about to marry him, but for none of the reasons I used to think I would. I used to think we'd marry for love.

How foolish of me.

Mason materializes like a ghost in front of me. His face contorts in silent agony, and even though I know he made this decision, it stemmed from a naive and desperate need to prove himself. What kind of sister would I be if I didn't do everything in my power to save him?

I shake my head, clearing all thoughts of my brother. "I'm ready," I whisper to my reflection.

As ready as I'll ever be.

The sun is only a half-hour away from setting, but I'm frozen in my car. I parked outside Wisteria Pointe ten minutes ago, and since then, I've been trying to build up the courage to open the door. For someone who hates small spaces, this car has always been a comfort. A place I could go to scream, cry, sleep—*anything*—and then return inside as if nothing happened. What happens in the Subaru stays in the Subaru.

"You can do this. It's just another contract," I whisper to myself. My fingers tremble as I reach for the door handle. It's now or never.

With a deep inhale and a sure tug, I open the car door and step onto the street.

Wisteria Pointe is the premiere wedding venue in Roswell, usually booked months, or even years, in advance. I have no clue how Cal could swing this.

The dying light of a winter day bathes the entire building in coral fire. The crisp air chills me instantly, but I suppress the shiver that tingles down my spine. String lights cross overhead, illuminating the path toward the main entrance. There are broad oak trees surrounding the venue, making the space feel even farther removed from Roswell than it already is. Green shrubbery is trimmed to perfection, and lush ivy spirals around the building's cream columns. In the center of the courtyard, a fountain bubbles. Its gentle trickle is at distinct odds with the pressure coiling in my chest.

The beauty of the brick building doesn't even register as I march toward it. I count to ten, inhale deeply, and wrap my fingers around the handle. The pounding in my chest only accelerates when I pull open the heavy cedar doors. With a shake and a mental kick in the ass, I straighten my spine and enter the venue, my chin raised tall and haughty.

Pastel orange light floods into the cavernous room that's filled with white chairs, and my long shadow stretches down an aisle dusted with white rose petals. As if in perfect sync, the entire room turns in their seats to stare. The string quartet playing in the corner falters for just a moment, then resumes its ethereal tune. Hushed whispers break out as I stand stock still, frozen by the sight of my husband-to-be.

Callahan Keane stands on the other side of the room, hands clasped in front of him as he speaks with the officiant. He wears a midnight tux, tailored to fit his broad shoulders and trim waist. His tousled waves are perfectly messy, and memories flash in my mind of my teenage fingers sliding through those same curls.

Finally, it seems he must notice the change in the room, and he turns toward me. If I were closer, maybe I could see his reaction. From here, with the distance stretched between us, his face remains unreadable.

Someone takes my clutch and hands me a bouquet, which I numbly accept, barely noting the lilac and pink peonies. The quartet changes their song and begins playing the wedding march. To me, it sounds more like a death march.

With calculated steps, I walk down the aisle, eyes locked onto Cal's. If anything, it keeps me from scanning the rows of chairs—and from the crushing realization that every seat is full, yet no one here is for me.

I raise my chin, refusing to name the feeling it evokes. As I reach the end of the aisle, Cal's face momentarily flickers between the boy I fell in love with and the man standing in front of the priest. They're so similar, and the familiarity calls to me. It chokes the air from my lungs. Who knew we'd be here, together, after all these years? I plaster something that might pass as a smile on my face, stepping up onto the raised platform. There are three bridesmaids I've never met before waiting in blush chiffon, and I hand my flowers to the closest one.

Cal's best friend, Lucas Alvarez, stands as his best man, while his younger brothers, Matthias and Hale, are his other groomsmen. They're all dressed in matching tuxedos, but they couldn't look any more different. Luc's carefree attitude shines as his eyes refuse to stay still. Gray ink peeks out from his collar and sleeves. When we were teens, he got his first tattoo over his bicep. Clearly, he's gone back for more. Unlike in school, he keeps his hair buzzed close to his head. And despite his relaxed smile, the glimpse of tattoos coupled with his angular jaw and sharp cheekbones, he radiates danger.

Lucas winks when he catches me staring. He's always been a ladies' man, even in high school.

Matthias's scowl is just as I remember and a clear indication of what

45

I'm sure are his true feelings toward this arrangement. He has tied his long brown hair back at the nape of his neck. He's only gotten larger—both in height and muscle mass—since I last saw him. Save for the fact that getting under his skin is one of my favorite pastimes, I would be shriveling under the weight of his glare.

Hale is as any third son would be—flirting with the bridesmaids at my back. It surprises me just how grown up he looks. He looks so similar to Cal as a teenager, with floppy waves and a slightly rounded face, not quite having grown into his features yet. It's eerie, and my heart clutches in my chest.

I would've thought since Matthias and Hale were here that Murphy would be, too, but the youngest Keane is noticeably absent from the sham of a wedding ceremony.

It's not like she's missing much.

"I thought I was going to have to chase you down," Cal says with a hand pressed against his tuxedo. "Way to run down the clock, Bunny."

To my left, the officiant speaks, but his words become background noise. The hairs on the back of my neck tingle, and I clear my throat.

"In these heels? Please."

Cal's eyes drag over me, from the careless curls in my hair, to the polished maroon manicure on my fingernails, over the curve of my waist, all the way to the shine on my freshly shaved legs. He rubs his jaw, covering his mouth so I can't see his reaction, but there's a rigid set to his shoulders.

"You're right. Though I'd love to see you try."

My smile slides into a snarl. "You could never catch me."

Cal smirks. "I think I just did."

"Funny how you think extorting me into marrying you means you caught me."

The officiant clears his throat, and I press my lips together, raising a defiant brow at Cal. Continuing, the officiant's words blur together during his speech. It's traditional and utterly plain. *Where did Cal find him?* And how did he convince him to marry two strangers? The covenant of marriage and all its promises has never felt more like a farce.

"If that's what it takes," Cal whispers, and I'm not sure if I was meant to hear it.

All at once, it's time to exchange rings, and I wonder what mine will look like. Cal twists to retrieve the ring from Lucas, and my fingers tremble. He gingerly lifts my left hand, and he meets my gaze as he recites his vows.

"I, Callahan Keane, take you, Loren Catrone, to be my wife from this day forward. I vow to protect you and those you love until my death. With this ring, I seal my promise."

Cal's words are flat, almost robotic as he vows his...protection. These aren't the vows of a man in love, but then again, mine won't be, either.

He slides a ring onto my finger, and my eyes widen. The oval diamond stretches from my knuckle to the middle joint, nearly dragging my hand to the floor with its weight. It has a simple gold band that fits me perfectly, and as the last of the dying light shines against the diamond, my throat makes the oddest squeak.

"Loren," Cal murmurs, shaking me from my stupor. "It's your turn, Bunny."

My turn. Because we're getting married. Right.

I exhale and turn to my apparent maid of honor to retrieve his ring.

It's heavy and gold and perfectly plain. I face Cal once more, and the vows fall from my lips without a second thought.

"I, Loren Catrone, take you, Callahan Keane, to be my husband from this day forward. I promise to be faithfully yours, and…" I trail off, not sure what to promise him in this moment. My stomach clenches tightly. "And I promise to hold you to your word."

It's a mix between a promise and a threat, and I grab his hand to slide the ring on, but something stops me. I dreamed of this day for so long, but something sour taints the entire act.

"Any day now, Bunny."

I fight the scoff that threatens to ruin the mood and place the ring on his finger.

Sound muzzles out as the officiant declares the seal of our marriage, and before I know it, Cal's lips press against mine. I'm stunned frozen as his heady cologne washes over me, sending me tumbling back through time. He's never changed his scent, and I can't help but wonder if he did that for me. *I doubt it.*

A camera flashes, someone immortalizing our first moment as husband and wife.

Cal's mouth breaks from mine, and he meets my gaze. Where previously blank, a blistering inferno surges behind his brown eyes.

"*Wife*," he practically growls.

"For now," I remind him with narrowed eyes, and his jaw clenches.

Cheers and whistles ring out as Cal and I turn to face the crowd. He shakes our joined hands, leading us back down the aisle. Along the way, he points at guests and makes short, quippy remarks to a few. Cal's radiating charm captivates the room. While everyone watches *him*, I allow myself to do the same. His dimple is out in full force, a blinding smile aimed to bewitch anyone blessed enough to witness it. *Ugh.* I roll my eyes and tug him toward the doors, but we're stopped by an older gentleman in the second to last row.

"Congratulations, young man." The man winks and nods his head at the doors. "Call me after you're settled."

Cal nods. "Thank you for coming, Edwards. I will."

Matthias steps in front of us. "Cal." It's all he says, but there's a fierce glint to his eyes.

Cal nods in apparent understanding, and leads me outside. We exit Wisteria Pointe together, whoops and hollers following closely after. The cedar doors shut behind us, silencing the cheering crowd with surprising efficiency. But I don't have a moment to even think as Cal practically drags me toward a blacked-out SUV parked out front. My car is nowhere to be seen.

"What, we're not staying for cake?"

Cal opens the back door and holds it open, indicating for me to get in. My clutch is on the seat behind the driver, and with a quick peek in the back, I see the bags I had packed. The ones that were in *my* car. Cal arches a brow and tilts his head as he takes me in from where he stands.

"Where is my car?" I can't quite control the hiss to my words.

"You no longer have use for it. It's been returned to your apartment. A driver has been assigned to you. You'll meet him tomorrow."

Heat rushes to my face, burning the tips of my ears. So now I had to rely on him or a driver to go where I wanted for the next two years? Ridiculous.

"I thought I was your *wife*, not your prisoner."

"We both know it's a marriage in name only. You married me for my power. Simple as that. That show"—he waves a careless hand toward Wisteria Pointe—"was just that. A *show*." His smile drops, and he looks off to his left, where Matthias waits. "So thank you, *wife*, but I have other, more pressing, matters to attend. Nathaniel will take you home. We'll speak tomorrow about your brother. Now, in you go." He gestures to get in the car, and I grumble as I slide into the back seat.

I have no more fight in me tonight.

"Sweet dreams, *wife*."

He shuts the door with finality, leaving me with only my thoughts for company on my wedding night.

I should be happy I don't have to put on a mask in front of a few hundred of Cal's closest friends and enemies. I should be happy there's no awkward lingering or silent car ride.

I should be…but I'm not.

Nathaniel pulls away, driving into the dusky night, and I lean my temple against the cool glass.

What have I gotten myself into?

CHAPTER SIX

I f I thought the Bianchi house was grand, it was nothing compared to the Keane mansion. Nathaniel drives us through the gate, and I roll down the window. A gentle breeze streams through the car. The place itself must span half a football field, with too many windows to bother counting. Floodlights illuminate its cream exterior, and men walk the grounds, scanning their surroundings. I wonder what the rest of their security looks like.

We slow in front of a garage door, and Nathaniel clicks a button. The garage opens quietly, and I shield my eyes from the bright light inside. When the car stops, I hop out without preamble. My steps echo as I look around. Several cars ranging from blacked-out SUVs to a sleek sports car are parked. A lone motorcycle waits in the corner. The cherry red Corvette pulls my eye, and I circle it.

"She's a beaut, isn't she?" Nathaniel asks. His voice is scratchy, and I wasn't expecting such a gravelly sound to come from such a lanky man. His salt and pepper hair is short, but he only has a few lines around the crinkle of his eyes.

"She sure is." I look back to the car and think about stealing the keys and running through the gate.

But that would be stupid. Instead, I turn on my heel and face Nathaniel. A young woman enters the garage, and I startle. She can't be older than twenty. The newcomer doesn't seem to feel the weight of my stare; instead, she just gathers my bags and whisks them into the house.

"Not to worry. Tinley will take your bags upstairs." Nathaniel turns and leads the way through the door. "Come, follow me."

We enter an industrial kitchen with at least two of each stainless steel appliance you can think of. In the center sits a long prep table, where a plump woman hunches over, writing in a notebook.

"Darla," Nathaniel says, startling the poor woman. Darla's shoulders jump as if she wasn't expecting to hear anyone. "This is Loren Keane, Mr. Keane's bride."

I fight the urge to roll my eyes, but Darla drops her pen and straightens, dusting her hands on her stained apron and crossing over to us. She examines me from head to toe. While Darla can't be taller than five feet, the stare she's leveled on me sends a shiver down my back. She has coarse white hair tied in a neat chignon and pale skin with smile lines and crinkles around her green eyes, and she wears a gray uniform with a white apron tied around her waist.

Darla props her hands on her hips as she continues to appraise me. Somewhere in the room, a clock ticks with each uncomfortable second that passes, until she finally nods and extends a hand.

"Nice to meet you, Mrs. Keane. I'm Darla Sullivan, the Keane's chef and household manager."

I take her hand, shaking it firmly as I introduce myself. "It's nice to meet you. Please, call me Loren."

Darla smiles, but there's a guarded sheen to her matronly gaze.

"And it's Catrone," I assert, with a pointed look to Nathaniel, who doesn't reply.

Darla's eyes dart between us. She hums and steps back. "Would you like me to show you to your rooms?"

Rooms? Plural?

I nod once and follow behind as she exits the kitchen.

"Nathaniel," I call back. "After I meet with my *husband* tomorrow, I have a social appointment. Will you be available, or should I drive myself?"

"Your security will be available to take you. You will meet Cohen tomorrow after you speak with Mr. Keane."

My chin dips in acknowledgment, and I follow Darla. Lifetimes seemed to have passed since the last time I walked these halls, so not much is familiar. I had to sneak between the shadows, sticking to a very specific route to avoid any unwanted attention. When I think back to those times, my mind overflows with memories of *him*—not his home. I lose track of the turns we take, but the grand opulence spans throughout the entire manor. Hardwood floors, heavy plush curtains, and dimmed chandeliers in nearly every room we pass.

Finally, Darla and I stop in front of a plain door. She opens it without ceremony and ducks into the room. I follow closely behind.

Inside is a medium-sized living room with a couch in the middle. It faces an electric fireplace on the far wall, and a stocked bar cart waits in the corner. Matching curtains hang on windows on either side of the fireplace.

"Through here is your bedroom." She indicates to a door on the left side of the room. "There's also an en suite and walk in. Tinley will stop by at ten, daily, to collect any laundry and make the bed. If you have any specific requests, you may leave them on the coffee table." She stretches a hand toward the glass coffee table in front of the couch, where a fresh vase of flowers and a new notepad sit.

A voice in the back of my head tells me not to get used to this sort of luxury, and my shoulders stiffen.

"Thank you," I reply with a quiet voice. "I think I'll turn in now. It's been a day."

Darla looks me over again, and the lines around her eyes seem to soften. She nods and slips out of the room, leaving behind a faint aroma of vanilla. The door latches softly behind her, and like that, I'm alone.

I step numbly into my new bedroom, and as I look around, it occurs to me that Darla was being literal. Nothing about this space says a man lives here. There's a king-sized canopy bed with fluffy lilac sheets and pillows that appear freshly laundered. More flowers and scenic portraits adorn the walls. On the right side, there's a sturdy walnut dresser and vanity under a vast, arched window where the full moon shines in. A lamp next to the bed is on, casting a small radius of light. Everything combined, this is clearly a guest room. While the revelation is partly comforting, there's a part of me confused by the pit growing in my stomach.

At that exact moment, a growl unleashes from my stomach. Okay, maybe I'm just hungry.

I could either go looking for food—and likely get lost—or I could just go to sleep and deal with it in the morning.

I choose sleep.

As I curl onto my side, I check my phone. There's a text from Alice. *How'd it go?*

I type out a quick response and silence my phone, shoving it under my pillow.

It went.

⌘

I'm up before the sun rises, having spent hours tossing and turning. Two nights of shitty sleep in a row makes for a grumpy Loren.

When I finally can't take it any longer, I turn on the waterfall shower and wash off the makeup from last night, using more luxurious products than I could ever justify buying. It's not until I'm rinsing the suds from my hair that I catch the faint cherry aroma. My nose scrunches up and I look at the bottle. It's the brand I've been using since I was a teenager. I didn't think to bring my own, so how did this end up in here?

My confusion washes away with the last of the soap as I rinse off. While unexpected, it's not exactly surprising behavior from Callahan Keane.

I go through my usual routine, using what I can find in the medicine cabinet and below the sink. After a half hour, I finally wake up. My chestnut hair is glossy, falling in light waves to my chest, and the steam from the shower seems to have helped my puffy eyes return to somewhat normal, though they remain bloodshot. Within minutes, I finish up in the bathroom and then check the time on my phone: almost six-thirty.

The sun peeks through my windows, and I take it as a sign to get moving. As good a time as any to track down some coffee. I snoop through the dresser, finding a drawer filled with lacy panties and matching bras, and heat rushes to my cheeks. My fingers tremble on the edge of the drawer. *He put me in a room where another woman previously stayed?* And he didn't even have the decency to clear out her used panties? I trap a scream in my throat and slam the drawer shut.

Thankfully, the next drawer is safe, and I find a silk loungewear set that feels like butter. I contemplate putting my underwear from yesterday back on, but the thought grosses me out too much. Instead, I pull on the loungewear with nothing underneath. It fits perfectly.

By the time I step into the hallway, the sun has risen, casting the manor in golden light. My steps are purposefully quiet, and I try to remember the way to the kitchen. There were at least three turns to get here last night…right?

After another fifteen minutes—and countless wrong turns—I finally make it to the kitchen. Pans clang and bacon sizzles, and I'm led by my nose to the center of the chaos. Darla whirls around the kitchen, barking orders to a younger chef and checking on whatever it is she's checking on. I stand for a minute, watching as she seems to be in complete peace while in the eye of the storm.

When she spins around to check on a pan of sausage links, she finally spots me. "Mrs. Keane, please take a seat at the dining table. I'll bring you breakfast. Coffee?" She's already onto another burner, stirring eggs and seasoning them with pepper.

"Oh, I was hoping to eat outside, actually. Get some fresh air."

Darla freezes, turning to me. "We eat as a family, no? Have a seat. I'll bring you a plate. Any allergies?"

I guess I won't be eating outside today. *Who all will be at breakfast?*

"No cheese," I say, watching as horror dawns on her face. I raise my hands in reassurance. "It's not an allergy. I just don't care for it." My nose scrunches. "Can only stand it on pizza."

Darla's eyebrows shoot to her forehead, but then she quickly composes herself and nods. "Okay, Mrs. Keane. No cheese."

"Thank you, Darla. And it's Loren, remember?"

She waves me off, and I let it go. "Coffee?"

Darla tilts her head to the side, indicating a brewing pot of coffee. I open a few cabinets around it before I find one with mugs and fill one, leaving room for some cream.

"So you're a snooper, huh, Rabbit?"

Rabbit. Matthias Keane's twist on Cal's teenage nickname for me. He knew just how much I hated *Bunny* back then and decided to annoy me even further by calling me *Rabbit.* He was the only Keane who knew about Cal and me. *I guess not everything has changed.*

I look up to see Matthias glaring down at me. Matthias has always towered over me—not that it's difficult when you're five-six—but I stare up my nose at him, anyway. Sweat drips down the side of his face from his wavy brown hair. He's wearing gym shorts with a towel tucked into the waistband, and nothing else. His toned chest and abs sparkle with perspiration, and my face heats, but I refuse to let him intimidate me. "Searching for a mug in a kitchen is hardly snooping, *Mattie.* Your room, however..." I trail off, delight in throwing the old nickname back at him perking me up more than the coffee warming my hands. When he started calling me *Rabbit,* I started calling him Mattie. Was it petty? Of course. Was I going to stop? Absolutely not. Taking the chilled carafe of creamer from his hands, I turn away from the reddening man in front of me with a roguish twist to my mouth.

"Guess we'll just have to keep an eye on you." Matthias reaches over me to grab a mug and fills it to the brim.

I meet his stare once again and arch a brow. "I don't know what you're talking about. I'm just a simple wife." I flash my ring with a sip from my mug, the freshly brewed coffee mollifying my inner shrew.

Matthias's upper lip curls. "You are a mockery of a wife. And everyone here knows it." At that, he stalks off, but the tension in the kitchen has thickened immeasurably. His insult lands as intended, and my self-assurance wilts under his scorn.

Darla looks between the empty doorway and me, then speaks to her chef. "Lex, show Mrs. Keane to the dining room."

Lex nods and lowers the heat of his dish to a simmer. He wipes his hands on his apron and crosses over to me. His dark complexion is slick with sweat, and he brushes a brawny arm over his face to wipe it dry. Compassionate jade eyes land on mine, and Lex smiles brightly.

"This way," he says, taking off.

His long legs make for covering much ground, and I struggle to keep up. Thankfully, we only have to exit the kitchen and take the first door on the right to find the dining room. Inside, there's a long wooden table with at least twenty seats around it. Candles and fresh flowers serve as centerpieces throughout the table, and a few people have already taken their seat. Conversations hush as we enter, and I whisper a hurried "thank you" to Lex as he abandons me to the sharks.

I step into the grand room, with floor-to-ceiling windows letting in natural light. Two chandeliers hang above the table, and a burgundy, patterned rug sits below the table and chairs. It's nothing short of grand, which I expect here at the Keane residence.

Either I arrived early, or some seats remain empty at each meal. There are two groups of three, each already seated. One group sits at the left end of the table, and the other near the middle. They all watch in silence as I walk around to the head of the right end of the table.

The chair slides out easily, and a hushed gasp echoes when I sit. Why though? There's another man sitting at the other end of the table.

"It doesn't say reserved," I joke with a tight smile, choosing to sip on my coffee.

As if shaken from their stupor, they resume their conversations, this time even quieter than before. There's only a few darted glances to where I sit.

The minutes pass, and I watch the birds on a broad oak tree. They fly around each other and chirp, and I can hear them through the glass, filling the morning with a peaceful ambiance. I zone out, letting the hushed conversations flow right past me.

Then Darla enters, pushing a cart of plated food, and sets them in front of those present. They thank her, and she smiles warmly back at them. With a few more plates on her cart, she looks up to where I'm sitting. Her eyes go wide, but she shakes off her surprise and delivers the plates. To my left, she places a berry parfait, loaded scrambled eggs, crispy bacon, and a few sausage links. In front of me, she places the same, but without cheese on the eggs.

"Thank you," I say, unrolling the silverware and placing the napkin on my lap.

Darla smiles and nods, placing a few other plates with small but distinct variations at the surrounding seats. It seems seating is assigned, then. She tops off my coffee and leaves the pot on a hot plate, then retreats from the room.

I take a large bite of eggs and try not to make a fool of myself. It's delicious—as if I ever thought it wouldn't be—and I make it a point to take one bite of everything before I dig in. I need to look into hiring a chef—possibly even poach Darla herself—when my two-years is up.

Within minutes, more people trickle in and sit down to eat, each one eyeing me as they do. No one says anything to me, but the hushed whispers are louder than they think.

"He's going to lose it," one says.

"Oh, this is going to be good." another comments.

I let the words slide over me. If every seat was assigned, taking someone else's was inevitable. Based on their reactions, I'd wager I was in Cal's. Well, I'd love to see him try to kick me out. I might be his *wife*, but it will be a cold day in hell that I'd let Callahan Keane issue me any sort of order.

As if my thoughts conjured him, the man himself steps into the room. He's furiously typing, his nose practically buried in his phone, but damn, he looks good. Freshly shaved and wearing a pressed blue suit and crisp white shirt, no tie. He makes it all the way to his spot at the table before he looks up, and we lock eyes. His gaze narrows, but he says nothing. I take an unhurried bite of my parfait, never breaking eye contact as I drag the spoon between my lips.

Cal arches a brow and looks around the table to find his breakfast. When he spots it to my left, he sits without a word. He simply picks up his silverware and begins to eat. A hush falls over the room, highlighting the clattering of the silver fork against the ceramic plate. If Cal refuses to acknowledge it, then neither will I. I pick up a crisp piece of bacon and crunch on the end, savoring the maple glaze and the satisfaction of the quiet. Inevitably, people resume their conversation.

After finishing the piece of bacon off, I wipe my hands and fold them on the table. "So about Mason," I begin.

Cal shakes his head. "Not here." He doesn't look around, but the table has mostly filled out, with only a few open spots around us. "Come to my office at"—he checks his watch—"eleven-thirty. We'll discuss your brother then."

"No, I want to talk about him *now*. Every minute, every hour, is another chance for him to be hurt. You already made me wait two weeks. Cal, please." I place my hand on his, stilling his fork against his plate.

Cal freezes, staring a hole into my hand. Then he looks up and searches my face. He's silent, even as Matthias and Luc enter, crossing the room to our side of the table. Open disdain twists Matthias's face.

"What the fuck is she doing?" he spits out, a vein throbbing in his neck, looking like it's about to burst.

Cal slips his hand from my hold and sips his coffee. He leans back and wipes his mouth with his napkin. "And?" His tone is bored, as if it were no bother to him.

Matthias seethes where he stands. "*And?* You've sucker punched me—*twice*, I might add—because I dared to sit in your seat."

A light chuckle escapes Cal, amusement brightening his brown eyes. "That's because you're you"—he waves a dismissive hand toward his younger brother—"and clearly, you didn't learn your lesson the first time."

Luc is silent as he drops a newspaper by Cal and sits on my right, seemingly unperturbed by the new seating arrangement. He digs into his plate. When he speaks, his words are muffled, but I hear them well enough. "You don't have a pussy, either. He's not gonna sucker punch his wife, idiot."

61

It's so minute I almost wonder if I imagined it, but Cal's jaw twitches just before he chuckles. Matthias's face grows redder by the second, but he takes his seat on Cal's left, and it pleases something sick inside me.

"You can try to sucker punch me, Mattie," I reply sweetly with a saccharine smile. "I'm sure that will work out swimmingly for you."

Matthias grips his butter knife until his knuckles are white. "I will if you call me that again." He points the tip of the knife at me.

My smile grows even bigger as I flash my teeth at him. "Matt—"

Matthias lunges forward, but Cal raises a bored hand, halting him in his place. "Not at the dinner table, kids."

"Technically, it's the breakfast table right now," Luc mumbles between bites as he continues to plow through his food. It's been many years since I've seen Lucas, and since he wore a tux during the wedding, I didn't know he's covered in tattoos. Intricate flowers, snakes, and feathers wrap around both arms, and a broken skull is tattooed in the center of his throat. The gray-scale scheme of his tattoos blends the designs together well atop his light brown skin. When he catches me staring, he winks one of those olive-green eyes at me.

"Right," Cal concedes. "Not at the *breakfast* table, kids." He rolls his eyes and shakes out the newspaper, flipping the page in clear dismissal.

"Callahan." His name is sharp on my tongue, and his fingers crinkle the paper where his grip tightens.

He looks up to catch my stern gaze, his eyes flicking between mine until he eventually sighs. He turns his attention to Lucas, who's busy looking between us with a smile like a cat who got the cream, then his gaze swings to Matthias.

"Push my seven-thirty to eleven," Cal says.

Matthias's brow furrows as his eyes dart between Cal and me. *"I'm your seven-thirty."*

Cal just arches a brow in silent answer. I press my lips together to hide my amusement as Matthias upends his chair and storms out of the dining room. Cal watches with thinly veiled humor as the door slams shut behind Matthias's speedy departure, then he turns his attention to me.

A question I'd forgotten to ask earlier bubbles to the surface. "Where's Murphy?"

Lucas stills for a curious moment, then shoves another bite into his mouth, glancing to Cal.

"She's at NYU. She couldn't get leave for the wedding like Hale did. He returned to Columbia straight after the ceremony."

Interesting. Cal and Matthias weren't allowed to go to college. Instead, they took online classes and explored more…hands on learning opportunities.

Cal folds his newspaper and stands. "You have an hour. Let's not waste it." He moves to the door, not waiting for me to follow as he opens it.

I scramble up, abandoning what's left of my coffee and breakfast as I catch the door before it falls shut, following Callahan without a second thought.

Something I swore I'd never do again.

CHAPTER SEVEN

My quick strides fight to keep up with Cal's through the twists and turns of the Keane residence. He doesn't spare a glance to ensure I'm following. He knows this is too important for me to not. It frustrates me he's right.

A few turns later, we enter a library that I don't have time to appreciate because he opens a heavy wooden door and holds it open for me, a look of utter impatience plastered on his face.

Callahan's office is masculine, with a leather sitting couch at one end of the room. On the other, a modern, L-shaped wooden desk sits perfectly organized. Just like the rest of the house, there's not a personal touch to be found. This could be anyone's office.

At the bottom of a bookshelf in the corner, there's a row of records. I gently flip through them, noting the titles and variety. The door clicks shut.

"So, Matthias was right," Cal says as he settles into his desk chair. "You're still a snoop."

I shrug. "What can I say? It's a passion of mine." I cross to his desk and sit in a leather armchair. It's plusher than I expect, and I sink further than I'd planned for.

The air stills as we lock eyes, and it grips me how old he looks. Not old in the sense of gray hair and wrinkled skin, but I see years swirling behind his brown eyes, a sense of tiredness that doesn't come from anything other than a long life. He studies me just the same, and we sit in charged silence for only a minute until he finally speaks.

"Right," he drawls, scrubbing a hand over his jaw. "So, Mason is missing. And you think he's somewhere in Keane territory?"

I clench my jaw and nod.

"And why do you think that?"

He doesn't sound like he believes me, which is aggravating. If I had a nickel for every time a man didn't take me at my word, I'd be fucking rich.

I let loose a sigh and share more than I care to. But if it will help me find Mason, I'll sing like a canary.

"Because Leon said so." I'd practically had to beg on my knees, but the Bianchi son had finally relented. That was all he told me, though. When I asked about specifics, he was tight-lipped.

Cal's brows furrow, and he opens his mouth to speak, but I continue. "He told me about seven weeks ago, Mason came to Elias and him, begging for a chance to be made. Apparently, Mason was tired of not being given any proper work." I suppose the boss of the Bianchi family was amused enough to give him a chance to prove himself, and he had the perfect job.

"What was the job?" Cal asks.

"To gather information on your recent supplier losses and find out where more potential weaknesses lie."

Cal clenches his jaw, presumably in understanding. It was an attempt to claim more territory from the Keane family. I fold my hands in my lap, curling them into fists. Mason is nearly twenty-two—hardly a child—but I still feel responsible for his well-being.

When we moved out of the Bianchi house six years ago, our mother went on her longest bender, running away to god knows where. We haven't seen her since. She could be dead in a ditch, for all I know. It used to irritate me, used to *enrage* me, how she gave up on us, but recently, I've been too busy to spare her a solitary thought. But even before she left, she was lost at the bottom of a bottle on any given day, so for the last decade, I've been Mason's caretaker. He wasn't happy about it, but I made him finish high school. All he wanted was to return to the Bianchis and offer his life in the name of serving the Family. He'd been a foot soldier for the last three years, and while occasionally he hadn't come home for a day or two, it's never been as long as it has been now. Elias won't tell me anything, citing I'm not a part of the Family anymore. I used the last ounce of clout I had when I begged Leon to tell me something—*anything*. And that's when he told me about the mission they sent Mason on and how they haven't heard from him in over a week. But after that, they wouldn't be able to disclose private matters to an outsider. That was weeks ago, now.

"Apparently, Elias was thrilled to let another Catrone join the ranks. Leon then told me it was Elias's idea to send Mason over to Keane territory to do some recon. But it was only supposed to take a week or two."

Cal leans forward to brace against his desk. His shoulders tense, and a thick cord in his neck pulses. "And he thought a twenty-something could find our warehouses without help?"

I shrug. "I don't have all the answers—*yet*—just what I've been able to piece together secondhand." Maybe it went further than just recon, and Mason was supposed to poach distributors. Or—a shiver rolls down my spine—eliminate operations altogether. The thought of my brother killing someone in cold blood chills me to the bone.

"When I spoke with him, Leon said he'd missed his last three check-ins."

Cal's eyes widen ever so slightly. We both know it's never good when someone misses even one check-in.

"I didn't know who else to go to. Leon and Elias won't tell me anything else."

"I see," Cal says thoughtfully.

"If you say he's not in Roswell…Well, I don't know where he could be, then." I slump back into the chair, swallowing around a thick lump in my throat.

"Bunny," Cal whispers. His voice is tender, and my old nickname falling from his lips feels so familiar it hurts. There were nights we'd spend under his covers, hiding from the world and his father, and he'd whisper to me just like he did now. "We'll find him."

My eyes fall to the floor, and I can't help but pray he's right.

"I'll start with Matthias, Luc, and Caleb. They've been looking into the supplier disturbances. Before I sent him off to security detail, Caleb was assisting Matthias and Luc with the…interference we've been experiencing."

Matthias. Great.

"Don't give me that look."

I relax my brows, unaware they'd furrowed and revealed my disdain for Matthias. I deflect. "Caleb?"

Cal's jaw ticks. "Caleb Ferguson. You two met the other week."

Something dark flashes in Cal's brown eyes. Why, he almost seems…jealous.

"Ah, Caleb. I remember him," I say, seizing the opportunity to switch the topic, giving myself time to board up the cracks in my armor. "I liked him. He's very charming."

Cal's nostrils flare as his jaw grinds together.

And just to push him a little further, I pout. "Does he also live on property? I'd like to go say hi."

Cal practically growls as he spits out, "He's busy. From now until forever."

I can't help but laugh. "Is someone jealous?" My words land like a blow, sending Cal back in his seat.

He glowers and digs his phone out of his pocket, tapping on the screen once again. Holding it up to his ear, he never breaks eye contact as he waits for his call to be answered.

"My office. Now."

"Is that Caleb? Tell him I say hi!" An unexpected giggle bubbles out of my chest, and Cal ends the call, dropping his phone on his desk a little too aggressively.

"Callahan, you didn't even tell him I said hi. How else is Caleb going to know I was thinking about him?"

Cal stands and walks around his desk to tower over me. His finger pulls my chin upward until we share our breaths. "Stop saying his name," he commands with a sharp tone. His dark gaze flicks between my mouth and my eyes, and his tongue darts out to wet his lips. "Or there will be consequences."

My eyes narrow. "Like what? Are you going to forbid me from speaking to him?"

Anger sparks inside, and I wonder if he can feel the boiling heat of my stare. Who does he think he is? It's a damn good thing I didn't include obedience in our vows.

At the reminder that this man is my *husband*, a newfound heat coils in my abdomen. A heat I stuff down further, ignoring the building sensation as blonde hair flashes to the forefront of my memory again.

"I was thinking something more along the lines of killing him, but I suppose we could start with a light exile first."

I whip my face out of his hold. "That's not funny."

Cal perches against his desk and crosses his legs, bracing his arms on either side of him. His knuckles turn white from their grip on the desk. "Then it's a good thing I wasn't kidding."

Two quick knocks sound at the door, but Cal doesn't break our stare. He simply raises a brow and lets the air thicken between us. He must see I won't budge.

Finally, he relents.

"Come in." His voice echoes in the room, and a new face enters.

The newcomer looks between us, clearly waiting for an introduction. He looks to be about six feet tall and stacked, with curly hair cut almost in a mullet and a thick mustache. His tan skin is golden, as if he's spent more time outside than not, and if not for the combat gear he wears, I would've thought he was just missing his boots and hat and bull to ride.

"Ma'am." He nods to me, then turns to Callahan. "Yes?"

"Loren, this is Everett, our head of security. He's responsible for our security patrols and all things to keep us and our product safe."

Everett extends a firm hand, and I shake it.

"Nice to meet you," I say.

Everett nods and turns back to Cal.

"Have we picked anyone up by the name of Mason Catrone in the past few weeks?" Cal asks.

The combat cowboy pauses, eyes darting to me. "I can't recall off the top of my head. I'll check and get back to you."

Cal nods. "See that you do." He tips his head to the door, and Everett takes his cue to leave. But before he reaches the door, Cal speaks again. "And, Ev?"

Everett pauses, turning back to Cal.

"Make it a priority. And keep it between us for now."

His eyebrows hitch upward a degree, but then he nods and leaves the room. The door clicks shut behind him, and it feels like an omen.

"I'll call you back when I have more information. For now, enjoy the benefits of being Mrs. Keane." Cal returns to his desk and opens his laptop. Within moments, he's furiously typing, the dismissal clear.

God, his inflated ego is going to be the first thing I'll rejoice in no longer having to be around when our contract is up.

I grimace. "Enjoy the benefits of being Mrs. Keane? Seriously?"

Cal ignores me as he continues to type out what can only be a novel. I almost feel bad for whoever is on the receiving end of his scorn.

The silence stretches, and he doesn't look up from his computer. With a huff, I lean over his desk and push the laptop closed with more force than necessary. His fingers have to slip out of the way or risk being slammed by the force of my anger. Cal glowers but meets my wrath head on.

"You will make this a priority," I reiterate. "And you will keep me informed. Otherwise, I will make your life a living hell. You will rue the day you chose *me* to fulfill whatever archaic marriage requirement you needed to conform to."

Callahan looks between my eyes and must see how serious I am. He opens his mouth to speak, but I raise a hand.

"You *owe* me." My words are hushed, and my voice shamefully cracks.

Cal's nostrils flare, and his gaze drops back to his computer. He lifts the screen, pushing my hand off the back.

"I made you a promise," he says simply. "I'm a man of my word."

"You haven't always been."

It's satisfying to see the blow land, to see him flinch as his shoulders tense. It may have been eleven years since the man in front of me took my heart and shattered it into a million pieces, but at least I knew I was going to survive. That I would eventually be stronger for it. If I lose Mason…God help Cal if I find out he didn't follow through on his word to save him.

I turn and leave, pausing by the door for one last thing. "I have a life, you know. I won't stop living it."

Cal's fingers still on his keyboard, and he looks over to me. "I wouldn't dream of it. As long as it doesn't conflict with any social events I will require Mrs. Keane's presence for, you're free to do as you wish. Within reason, of course. Just make sure you take Graves with you on any outings."

My brows shoot to my temple. "Graves?"

"That would be me, ma'am," a voice says from behind me.

I jump, whirling around to find a man who must be at least six and a half feet tall, with black tattoos crawling up his arms and neck. His tanned olive complexion is warm and thick lashes frame amber eyes. Shoulder-length onyx waves are half tied up in a knot atop his head, and he sports a perfectly trimmed matching beard. The man—*Graves?*—is dressed in all black with a tight, black tee tucked into tactical pants, which are then tucked into combat boots.

What is with the uniform? Everyone dresses like they are in Mission Impossible.

"Loren, this is Cohen Graves, your assigned protection whenever you're off property. He'll also be your driver. Take him with you. *Do not* give him the slip."

Yeah, he looks exactly what you'd expect a personal bodyguard to look like.

I stick out a hand in greeting. "Hi, Cohen. It's nice to meet you. I'm Loren."

Cohen takes my hand and shakes it firmly. "You, too, Mrs. Keane."

I hum in appreciation. "Please, call me Loren." I look pointedly to Callahan. "And it's Catrone."

Cal arches a brow. "Actually," he drags out, smug amusement slashed onto his frustratingly perfect face, "it's Keane. We filed the paperwork on Monday."

Filed the paperwork on Monday? "We just got married last night. How is that possible?" My words come out more shrill than I'd like to admit.

"Mrs. Keane—*Loren*," Cohen amends, "almost anything is possible when you're Callahan Keane."

I scoff. "That wasn't part of the agreement." Callahan said nothing about changing my name. I was quite fond of Catrone and quite averse to Keane.

"Guess you should've read the fine print." Cal flashes his teeth in a victorious smile. "Oh well. Next time."

My eyes narrow. "What else was in the fine print?" The Callahan I knew was devious, yes, but never intentionally malicious. Well, until that cursed morning, that is.

"That would spoil all the fun, Bunny. You'll just have to wait and see."

Cal and I lock into a staring match, neither budging for several moments. Cohen clears his throat.

"Nathaniel mentioned a social appointment, ma'am?"

I grit my teeth and turn from Cal. "Yes, that's right. I just need to find something more"—I glance down at my loungewear and bare feet—"appropriate for going outside. Do you know where my bags are? Nathaniel said Tinley would take my bags to my rooms, but they weren't there when I got in last night."

Even though my question was for Cohen, Cal answers. "Tinley was unaware of our arrangements and brought them to my room instead. I didn't want to disturb you last night, so I waited until breakfast to have her move them to your room. They're there now."

My pulse quickens at the thought of him left unattended with my bags. "Oh," I stammer. I drop my gaze to Cohen's chest, cheeks burning. "Cohen, would you please help me find my way back? This place is a labyrinth."

Cohen chuckles, a deep rumbling that's almost melodic. "Of course."

We turn to leave, but Cal calls out once more. "And, Loren?" He waits until I turn around. "The first of those social events is next week. Find something nice to wear." With that, he pulls out his wallet, takes out a card, and extends it to me.

I arch a brow, unsure if the insinuation should insult me. Does he really think I'm excited to be here, to play "wife" to the boss? That I'm in awe of the glamorous lifestyle the women closest to the nexus of the family receive?

Absolutely not.

But if I have to suffer through two years of social events and appearances as his arm candy, it's certainly not going to be on my dime. I step into his space once again and take his card. Our fingers brush, and an electric zap shoots up my arm. I yank my hand back.

With a prompt spin, I leave without another word. Cohen catches up easily before taking over and leading me through the maze that is the Keane residence. With each turn, my stomach sours.

"So, how'd you get the short end of the stick to be my babysitter?"

Cohen chuckles. "It's actually a great honor knowing the boss trusts me enough to keep you safe. Am I gonna miss the action I saw as Cal's guard and resident enforcer? Of course. But every now and again, you gotta shake things up."

Oh, so he's like, off his rocker.

Cohen laughs again, this time a full belly laugh that has me looking over in confusion. "What? Didn't think this face could grind some teeth in with the sole of my shoe, like stubbing out a cigarette?" He smiles widely, and it only further proves he has a few screws loose.

"No, it's not that I think you don't look capable..." We turn another corner, and he leads me to my door. "I just didn't expect you to smile while describing what I'm sure is an incredibly brutal act of aggression."

Cohen shrugs sheepishly. "What can I say? It's the duality of man."

I hum in agreement, and we enter my reception area. A deep sigh rattles from me. *This place is a maze.*

"It took me weeks to figure it out. You'll get there," Cohen says.

I realize then I said that out loud. His words are meant to be reassuring, and I give him a tight smile.

"I know." That was what I was afraid of.

One day, I'll know this place like the back of my hand. And then another, I'll have no reason to, and I'll forget. One day, our contract will end, and with that, so will our marriage.

Why is there a part of me that hopes that day never comes?

CHAPTER EIGHT

Just like Callahan said, my bags were sitting behind the couch in my sitting room. After being surrounded by all the wealth of the Keane residence for the last twelve hours, it makes the pitiful three bags of clothes seem inferior. I grimace. Cohen plops down on the couch and pulls out his phone.

"I'll just be a few minutes," I say as I grab the handles of the three bags and waddle over to the bedroom.

Cohen waves me off from where he lounges. "Take your time. I've got nothing else to do with my day." He never looks up from his phone.

Right. *Babysitter.*

I bump the door open with my hip, and shut it behind me with my foot. My bags land in front of the wooden chest at the end of my bed with a faint *thud.*

Unzipping the worn blue gym bag, I pull out its contents. At the bottom of the bag remains my trainers, along with some towels, tape, and icy hot patches, which I leave in the canvas bag. I stuff the rest of the gym clothes into a dresser drawer, one *not* filled with another woman's underwear. Then I pick a random top and a pair of leggings to throw on, along with a pair of socks and my sneakers.

At the thought of the used panties of whichever woman lived in this room before me, my face floods with heat. In an act I can only describe as irrational, I yank open the drawer and scoop out all the underwear, then march over to the bathroom and toss them in the small trashcan. It overflows immediately, spilling her underwear onto the floor. Fuck. I bend down and shove the underwear to fit the trashcan, until all that's left is a mountain of another woman's silk.

I stomp out of the bathroom and return to my task at hand. Working on autopilot, I hurriedly French braid my hair to keep it out of my face. Jude taught me very early on just how easily an opponent can use it against you.

In my pocket, a ding chimes. Without thinking, I slip out my phone and check the screen. Six missed calls and at least ten text messages from Leon, getting progressively more aggressive with each text: *Loren…*Followed by: *Call me, Lo. This is serious.* All the way to: *What have you done?*

Why would Leon care so much about my life? Hudson made it clear that I used up the last of my goodwill with the Bianchi family when he helped me get the wristband for Abstrakt. My shoulders tighten as I grind my jaw, frustrated with the audacity some men have. It's impossible to live up to their contradictory expectations, and when I finally take things into my own hands, somehow it's the worst thing I could do.

His words swirl in the back of my mind, but I refuse to let him sink his misplaced anger into me. Shaking off the texts, I clear the messages and mute his contact so I won't be notified the next time he tries to reach me.

When I'm done, I sling my gym bag over my shoulder and exit my room. Cohen looks up from his phone, and his eyes narrow.

"I thought you said this was a social appointment."

I press my lips into a thin line to hide my amusement. Jude would fucking die if he knew I was using him as an excuse to get out of my newfound gilded cage. But alas, my frayed nerves mean I'll need to punch something besides Cal's face if I have to sit on my hands while he searches for Mason.

"Yes, it is a social appointment. At the gym."

"You know we have a full gym in the basement, right?"

I didn't, but that is handy information. I shrug. "Your gym doesn't have what I need."

Cohen huffs a laugh. "You haven't even seen it, so how would you know?"

When we pull up to Strikers, I get the distinct pleasure of seeing Cohen's face light up.

"You kickbox?" His words are disbelieving, but his tone tells me he's impressed.

"For about eight years now. Jude is my instructor, and I'm here a few times a month."

Cohen nods, eyes sparkling with interest as we walk into the gym. It's in a warehouse, with four rings in the center of the space. There are dummies, bags, weights, and smaller spaces lining the walls where people can train independently. The distinct and familiar smell of rubber, powder, and sweat wraps around me.

"Hi, Loren!" Jenna waves from the front desk. She's tied the top half of her shoulder-length blonde hair into two buns atop her head, and her round cheeks are flushed. She probably just finished her workout—a perk to working at the front desk at a gym. And being married to its owner. Jenna and Jude have such an insane story that when she first told me how they met, I was in utter disbelief. It happened all under my nose, too. Granted, Jude and I hadn't really shared anything personal by that point, so why would he tell me about his love life? Now, we make Jude our designated driver whenever Jenna, Alice, and I have a girls' night out.

"Hey, lady. He in a sour mood still?" Jude wasn't thrilled when I told him what I was doing. Between shots of tequila and a few Irish car bombs, I finally spilled what had me in such a funk. Well, Jenna had done most of the probing, but Jude listened to each slurred word, his face reddening either from the liquor or the information. Something tells me it was the latter. But then he surprised me when he shared just how much he knew about this world, and he spent the better part of an entire session last week trying to talk me out of it. Apparently, he's got connections he could've asked for help, but they were on the other side of the country. I informed him I didn't have that sort of time to wait, and he stormed out of our last session. This is my first session back, and we haven't spoken since.

Jenna's face scrunches, which that tells me all I need to know. Then she glances to my left, where Cohen stands silently. He fits right in with his tactical gear, and his eyes scan the gym.

"Jenna, this is Cohen Graves. My personal bodyguard for the time being."

Jenna's brows shoot to her hairline, but she quickly recovers and extends a hand to Cohen, who shakes it once.

"Bodyguard, huh?" Then she turns her blue gaze to me. "Thought you could take care of yourself just fine. Or what have you been doing for the past decade?"

I huff a laugh and shrug. "Yeah, well, it's not really my choice. At least he's pretty to look at."

Jenna eyes Cohen up and down and grins. "That's very true," she says with a wink. "Any chance you'd be interested in teaching self-defense classes here? Even with the recent...abductions"—Jenna visibly winces—"trying to get women to sign up for classes is next to impossible. Having some eye candy as an instructor might help fill out our classes, but our trainers are stretched thin as it is."

Cohen's face reddens, and a blush creeps over the ridge of his nose and tips of his ears. He opens his mouth to speak, but an even grumpier man cuts him off.

"You realize I'm standing right here, woman?" Jude says as he appears from the doorway of the office.

"Oh, I'm aware." Jenna turns back to her computer, a smug smirk painted on her face.

I don't hide my snicker.

Jude turns to me to glower. "You're late." He stalks off into the cavernous warehouse.

I roll my eyes. "No, I'm not," I call after him, then turn to Cohen. "I'll be done in an hour."

With that, I leave Cohen behind and trail after Jude. When I catch up to him at the ring, I reach into my bag to grab the tape for my wrists. As I pull the roll out, I freeze. I'd completely forgotten about the rock on my left hand.

As if Jude hears my thoughts, his gaze zeroes in on my ring finger, and he scoffs. I slip the ring off and toss it unceremoniously into my bag.

"You know, the normal reaction is to send a gift or even just say congratulations," I say with slight irritation bleeding through my words. I know Jude wanted to help, but I'm a grown fucking woman. And Callahan was my best bet to find Mason, so if marrying him is what it took, then that's what I was going to do. Why did I have to keep justifying my actions?

I finish taping my hands and shove them into my gloves, then slide under the rope and enter the ring.

"A normal reaction to your friend marrying one of the most dangerous men in Roswell is to tell that friend they're being a fucking idiot." Jude stuffs his hands into his pads and throws them up for my warmup. He levels me with a stony stare. "And you're being a fucking idiot."

My first punch takes him off guard, and he absorbs the impact with a muffled grunt.

"And you're being an asshat." I throw another punch, this time with less force. I'm not trying to pull a muscle just because I'm getting pissed at one of my longest friends.

We fall into a familiar routine, and before long, we're sparring. I refuse to speak, instead channeling my frustration with Jude, with Callahan, with Mason, with *everyone* into my workout. Sweat trickles down my spine and over my temple, stinging my eye as it drips. I hiss and swipe an arm over my forehead. Jude pauses, his chest heaving and sweat darkening his gray muscle tee. My breath is labored, the physical exertion having lessened my animosity. Though only a fraction.

Jude readies himself to go again, bouncing on the balls of his feet as he approaches me. Then he just has to open his fucking mouth. "I'd rather be the asshat, as you've so lovingly described, and face your wrath, than have you die because nobody told you that you were making a fucking mistake."

I'm suspended, the fervor of his words stunning me just long enough to fully evade his right hook. It lands on my ribs. A *whoosh* escapes me and I double over, cradling an arm around my torso, but the ache piercing my chest is a vestige of his words, not his blow.

"Deep breaths. You'll be fine." Jude places a gloved hand on my back and leans down. He rubs his hand in what he probably thinks is a soothing motion, and I suck in a breath, straightening. But I can't seem to meet his stare.

"Says you," I gasp. The digital clock on the far wall shows it's only been forty-five minutes, but I can't be around him anymore. "I gotta go." I duck my gaze and lift the rope but freeze, finding a stone-cold Cohen staring Jude down. Anger swirls behind his dark eyes, and his jaw ticks. I can practically hear the murderous vitriol he wants to spit at my friend.

I shake my head and hop out of the ring, ripping off my gloves and tossing them into my bag. I wipe my face and neck with a towel and sling my bag over my shoulder.

"I'm fine," I grumble in a hushed voice to Cohen, who finally looks away from Jude. "I'm gonna go rinse off. Be back in five."

Cohen nods curtly, then returns his glare to Jude, who's already left the ring and is stalking back to his office.

The women's bathroom is smaller than the men's since there aren't as many women training here, and I head straight for it. There are two shower stalls and three toilet stalls, and I turn on the last shower. With nimble fingers, I untie my braids and throw my hair into a bun, keeping it out of the water. Four minutes later, I'm dressed in a comfy pair of cuffed gray sweats and a cropped black hoodie. I put on a fresh pair of socks and stuff my feet into a pair of black slides, then shove my sweaty clothes into a separated compartment of my bag. The bathroom barely had time to fill with steam by the time I leave.

The muffled hits of gloves landing on bags filters back in. Cohen leans casually against the entrance to the bathroom and kicks off the wall to trail after me as we leave. I wave to Jenna but refuse to look toward Jude's office, instead, heading out into the chilly January day. Misty rain falls from a dark cloudy sky, and I smile to myself. I love the cold and the wet. It was one reason I never left the northeast coast.

Cohen and I jog over to the car and jump inside, where Cohen cranks the heat. My hands tingle as they thaw in front of the blower, and it reminds me to put my ring back on. Its weight is something I'll need to get used to.

"Big ring," Cohen says from the driver's seat.

It is a big ring, and the oval diamond is breathtaking. I like the ring— love it, even—but what it symbolizes ruins any sense of beauty it could ever represent.

I nod. "Yes, it is." There's a sadness to my words that I don't think someone I've known for all of five minutes will pick up on, so I let it go.

"So," he says after an awkward moment of silence, "do you have a favorite shop to get your gowns from?"

Right, I need a dress. For my first public outing as *Mrs. Keane.* I didn't pack any formal dresses—because why would I?—but it's not like I really had any. I made good money from my books, but it wasn't fuck-you money like the Keane's are used to. Most of my income goes to taxes and then bills. I was now on the third book in my latest series, and my editor needed the next set of chapters by the end of next week, and the final chapters for the ghostwriting contract by the following Monday. Which is a problem because I haven't written a word since Mason went missing.

"No. I wouldn't even know where to begin," I say honestly. Because seriously, who has a favorite boutique? I do most of my shopping online, and since I work from home, most of my clothes are athleisure.

"Alright, I think I know a place." Cohen shifts into drive and takes off. The misty greenery passes in a blur as we get onto the highway, and I lean my temple against the cool glass. The ride is quiet. Peaceful.

After about fifteen minutes, we take an exit and drive for another few miles on the main road, until we enter a parking lot. It looks like an outdoor shopping center but for luxury labels. Just in the first few stores, I see Prada, Chanel, and Cartier.

My eyes widen, and I turn to Cohen. "Seriously?"

His brows pinch together as he parks.

"You brought me here when I'm dressed like this?" I gesture to my sweats, slides, and hair that's still damp from my workout.

He shrugs. "Your money's just as good as theirs. Better, in fact."

He has a point. I open my door and grab my wallet from my gym bag, following Cohen as he leads me through the land of luxury, straight toward a midsize boutique called Amor. Soft, melodic music plays in the background, complimenting the white marble floors and natural light. There are a few displays of clothes, and two associates chattering about the mannequin they're styling. Cohen clears his throat, and they slowly turn. They're both objectively beautiful, with glossy hair and perfectly tailored dresses.

The snootier-looking of the two eyes me up and down. Her lip curls disdainfully. "May we help you?" Derision drips from her painted lips, and she crosses her manicured hands over her chest.

Her haughty attitude and the weight of the rock on my hand spurn me, and confidence floods my body. My shoulders straighten, and I lift my chin, refusing to let her make me feel less than. "I'm looking for a dress. Something formal, but will make my husband jealous of anyone who sees me in it." I walk over to one gown on display and run my hands over the material. "Something just borderline of scandalous."

The woman's eyes flash wide at the sight of my ring, and her smile turns practically feral. "Of course, ma'am," she rushes out. "Here, follow me to the dressing room."

Cohen—thankfully—opts to sit in an overstuffed chair and wait. I follow the saleswoman and enter a grand dressing area with a raised circular platform in the center of the room. Mirrors cover the entire left wall, while the right side contains extra-wide changing rooms. A plush cream couch and matching chairs rest along the far wall, and the saleswoman guides me to one.

"Here, have a seat, and I'll bring out some options. Would you like anything to drink while you wait? Water, coffee, champagne?"

I shake my head. The saleswoman's smile falters at my lack of excitement for her sudden gold star treatment, but she disappears quietly and returns with several options.

We spend the next half-hour trying on various dresses and styles. They're all beautiful, but something about them isn't calling to me. Finally, Cora—the snooty-turned-simpering saleswoman—brings out an emerald beauty. I slip it on, and it hugs me like a glove. The woman in the mirror looks out of place with her messy hair, but I can't help but feel beautiful. It's a strapless, floor-length emerald dress with a slit all the way to my hip. The neckline is almost sweetheart, but either side above my breasts comes to a point instead of the usual rounded edge. Each step I take reveals my entire left leg. I tug the strap of my thong over my hip to hide it. I won't be able to wear any underwear with this.

It's perfect.

Cora enters the dressing room and pauses, her mouth parting in obvious approval. "That's it," she says. "Now for shoes." She gently places a few boxes on a nearby chair.

Thirty minutes later, Cohen and I are back in the car and heading back to the residence. I bought enough to fill the trunk, including several other dresses and a few pairs of shoes. The entire ordeal was like a second workout entirely. I yawn and cover my mouth.

"Shopping must be *so* exhausting," Cohen mocks in a lilting tone.

I just shrug, because he isn't wrong. "Sorry, am I boring you? It was your idea to go shopping. I would've been fine ordering something online."

There's a distinct curl to his lips, but he doesn't respond. He just flicks on his turn signal and merges onto the highway.

I grab my phone and call Alice. When she answers, I don't even give her a chance to breathe before I'm asking, "Want to watch a movie on Facetime tonight? I miss you."

"As if you even have to ask." She laughs. *"Burlesque?"*

I smile and ignore the hulk of a man who does his best not to listen in. But by the wry twist of his mouth, it's obvious he can't help it.

CHAPTER NINE

I haven't seen Callahan in over a week. I've asked Cohen about the efforts to find my brother, and all he had to say was that they were still following leads. Each time I've tried to get a hold of Cal, I've been told he was busy, and it's honestly tiring to hear the same update—that there's no update. I've been doing an hour of yoga each morning just to corral my blood pressure. It's not helping.

Alice checks in every other day or so, and I welcome the familiarity. After our Facetime movie date the other night, I realized how much I miss her. But guilt swirls in my belly; I don't want to bring her into this world any more than I already have. She's young and needs to focus on school.

So, I spend most of my days trying to distract myself by finalizing my chapters for my editor. A large part of me holds immense satisfaction, knowing I've exposed some of the darkest aspects of the Bianchi estate without them ever knowing. Writing under the pen name Bea Page, I've gained decent popularity with my *Lovers of Sin* series, a series of romances based on a crime family that deals in drugs and scandal. My readers are practically feral over the tension I've built between the gray areas, exploring what it truly means to be moral and where the line blurs.

They'd never expect just how real the darkest aspects of my books are. Details I've pulled directly from years of listening to my father or from Cal himself. No one ever expects truth sprinkled into the pages of their favorite dark romance, but when I needed to support Mason and myself, I found myself drawn to the impossibility of it all, and I had my first novel finished within two months.

When I'm finally satisfied with the ending of book three, I pen a quick message to my editor that the files are ready, and then set off to get ready for my first event as Mrs. Keane. I fight the urge to roll my eyes, and instead, hop in the shower. The 'social event' Cal told me about last week has finally arrived, and a part of me actually looks forward to it. Or at least to get out of the house.

After two hours, I'm mostly ready, just touching up a few details as the playlist switches to "Knock You Down" by Keri Hilson. The song blasts through my suite as I finish my hair. I've twisted it into a low chignon—seems to be my go-to style these days—and pulled a few face-framing pieces out. My eyes are a smoky bronze, and I apply a gloss to my lips, rolling them together to evenly coat the nude color.

I straighten with a slight wince and take one last look in the mirror. Turns out I still bruise fairly easily, and my ribs are purple from Jude's hit. But I've had worse, and thankfully, my dress covers it. The emerald gown fits perfectly and is easily the nicest I've ever worn. I wish I'd thought about jewelry, though. As it stands, I'm wearing only my rings, and the only earrings I brought are gold studs that hide behind my hair. *Oh well.*

After rolling my almond oil onto my wrists and dabbing the excess onto my neck, I turn off the bathroom lights and grab my clutch. It strains to close around my phone, ID and cards, and the tube of gloss inside, but I don't have time to find another. When I exit my room, I'm surprised to find a sharply dressed man lounging on my couch. I freeze in the doorway, and when he doesn't look over right away—too engrossed in his phone—I take the chance to fully appreciate him. He's wearing a black tux with a white dress shirt and a black bow tie. His hair is perfectly tousled and his face freshly shaved. When his jaw ticks, unbidden thoughts of dragging my tongue over the curve of his neck flash through my mind.

I mentally scold myself. Yes, while Callahan remains one of the most attractive men I've ever met, he's also one of the most conniving. When I walked in on that woman crawling out of his bed all those years ago, I sealed my heart off to him forever. Even knowing it would be impossible to feel that way for anyone else, I walked away. I've had feelings—even loved—since then, but it's never been the same magic we somehow made. Being so close to him after so long is like being suffocated with nostalgic memories from the past, mixed with a somber understanding that sometimes life doesn't work out the way you want it to.

"Come to collect me? How gentlemanly of you." My words are saccharine and steeped in sarcasm.

Callahan looks up from his phone and freezes. His heated gaze drags over my body from the tip of my head to the point of my heels, and I can't help but feel a certain warmth swirl inside me. He tucks his phone into his breast pocket and stands, buttoning his tuxedo.

Cal smiles and steps into my space. His clean shampoo and sandalwood cologne washes over me, and I fight the pull my body demands.

"I am, if nothing else, a gentleman." Dark eyes flicker to my lips and linger.

"Kyra from Abstrakt would beg to differ, I'm sure."

At the mention of the server from the lounge, Cal chuckles darkly. "You can't tell me you're still jealous of her. That was over a month ago."

My eyes roll of their own accord. "Of course, ancient history." Honestly, it just goes to show how much he hasn't changed. If only for the fact his business is successful—though with the warehouse fires, maybe not for much longer—I wouldn't have as much faith in his ability to help me find Mason. But if there was one thing I could always count on, it was his bloodthirsty need to be right.

His gaze drags over my body, licking me from head to toe. Heat flushes my chest and warms my cheeks.

"My, that's a beautiful dress."

A flutter stirs inside me, but I tamp it down. "Thank you. It was very expensive." My eyes narrow, but Cal just chuckles, the deep noise rumbling from his chest.

"Oh, I'm aware. I received a notice from my bank."

I smirk. "So expensive, and yet not nearly enough fabric." I bend my left knee, drawing his hooded gaze over my smooth leg.

He doesn't bother hiding the gleam behind his eyes. My lips curl into a smirk, but I turn toward the mirror, giving Callahan a view of my backside. I pretend to finish my touch ups, fussing with my hair and swiping a maroon nail under my lip gloss. My lips smack together, and a muffled groan sounds from behind me. In the mirror, Cal's lustful gaze is glued to my ass. I stifle the grin that threatens, twisting on my heel and watching with distinct pleasure as he averts his gaze.

90

"I have something for you."

This piques my interest, and I arch a brow.

"Turn around."

I'm curious, so I do as he says. Cal reaches into his pocket and pulls out a velvet box. It snaps open, revealing a beautiful Van Cleef necklace. The petal blossom pendant is dainty, resting on a thin gold chain. Cal's hands are steady as he latches it around my neck. My fingers numbly press against the necklace. It's almost affectionate, the way his fingers linger on the curve of my neck.

"So." He clears his throat, aptly changing the topic and putting much needed space between us. "Are you ready for your first public appearance as Mrs. Keane?"

"As if I have another choice."

Cal surprises me, speaking softly, almost as if he cares. "You always have a choice."

"That's not how life works." Anyone who thinks otherwise is delusionally optimistic. And I am nothing if not a realist.

Cal cocks his head and studies me. I can practically see the gears spinning. He nods and steps backward, offering his arm. I accept, sliding my own through his and holding on to his bicep. He guides us out of my suite and toward the garage.

"Perhaps," he finally says. "In any regard, all you need to do tonight is show off how in love we are. Mingle with the other wives, enjoy a few glasses of whiskey. Have fun." He says those final two words with a pointed look.

"Have fun." I scoff and shake my head. "Have you made any progress with my brother?"

Callahan opens the door to the garage for me, and Nathaniel hops out of the driver's seat of a black SUV to let us in the back seat. I climb in, and Cal shuts the door, then walks around to the other side. He gets in, opens a compartment, and pulls out two crystal tumblers and a bottle of aged whiskey. Before I can refuse the drink, it's poured and in my hand. Cal clinks his glass against mine, then swallows the entire drink in one go. I sip mine gently, determined to nurse it.

"Not yet," Cal answers my question. "Luc is still tracking down our people. It seems fear is spreading with the recent fires."

I take another sip of my drink to calm my speeding heart. But either from the moving car, or my trembling fingers, I spill a dribble down the side of my mouth. In a flash, a thumb drags across my chin. Cal brings his finger back to his lips, sucking the whiskey from the pad of his thumb, never breaking our eye contact.

"We're just getting started, Bunny. I'm sure Mason's just fine. But I'll have Luc give a progress update in the morning."

I'm still stunned. All I can do is nod, and we continue the rest of the drive in silence.

Ten minutes pass in relative awkwardness, where I pretend I'm not acutely aware of every breath Callahan takes. When we finally arrive at another too-large-for-life mansion, I feel the first flutters of doubt. For so many years, I've held such anger and resentment toward Callahan, despite my best efforts of telling myself I'm long since healed, and now I have to put on the show of a lifetime, pretending to be madly in love with him.

Pretending?

"What did you tell everyone?" I ask, breaking the tense silence as Nathaniel rounds the car to open our door. "About how we met and why we left right after the ceremony?"

Cal straightens his bow tie and answers. "To the public, we were childhood friends and secretly dating for the past year. I asked you to marry me in September, a week after your birthday. You broke down in tears and readily accepted." Cal smirks, clearly pleased with the story he's spun. "We took a short honeymoon and now are back to life, as per usual."

"But how did you get everyone at the venue so last minute? That's what I don't get."

For the first time all night, I see a shimmer of something I can't identify behind his brown eyes. He looks away from me for a moment, and in the darkness, I can just make out him swallowing thickly.

"The venue had been booked for weeks. I just needed a bride." His words are hushed, as if it pains him to say them aloud.

At his confession, a rock settles in the pit of my stomach. Of course. How could I forget? I don't know this man in front of me. He told me in Abstrakt that he needed a wife. I was available and in desperate need of his help. As much as it tugs at an old ache, he has been nothing but honest since then. It's me who's inflated his flirty nature and natural charm to the chance that maybe somewhere, deep down, he might still have feelings for me.

Once again, I'm reminded that he's honest—most times to a fault.

I nod. "Right. Who doesn't shop for their bride like an airplane SkyMall catalog?"

Cal doesn't respond, but his jaw ticks as we exit the car. Like before, he offers his arm to escort me into the residence. An attendant at the entrance opens the door, and we step into a wall of warmth.

Cal twists to whisper in my ear. "Remember, we're madly in love."

I don't respond, but I tighten my hold on his arm in understanding.

We enter the party that's already in full swing, and I still don't know what we're doing here. If I cared more, I'd ask. As it stands, I don't think I want to know any more than I have to about Callahan and his dealings.

Cal leads us around the room, introducing me by my new name, then leaves me with a group of women and slips into an office with at least two other men. The women chatter about other social events, and I do my best to stay engaged, but I just can't help my wandering eyes and ears.

At a slight break in the conversation, one woman in particular turns her attention to me. Perfectly poised in a wingback chair, she sips a glass of red wine. The crackling fire warms her deep complexion, and a gracious smile plays on her lips. She appears to be in her early fifties, and she's twisted her midnight hair into an elegant up-do. "Mrs. Keane, it's lovely to meet you. I don't believe we've met yet," she says, placing her wine on a glass side table and extending a slender hand adorned with a diamond tennis bracelet. "I'm Helena Edwards. Welcome to my home." It takes a second, but it sounds like she has the ghost of an English accent swirling around her words.

I step forward and accept her greeting. "Loren Keane," I introduce, shaking her hand firmly.

The corner of her mouth curls an infinitesimal degree. Her surname rings a bell, and I try to place it, but nothing comes to me. The obvious wealth is magnificent, and I can't help but wonder how they acquired it. On the far wall, an enormous painting of a navy crest with a ship and a sweeping wave stretches nearly from the floor to the ceiling. A vivid memory surfaces of Cal thanking a man named Edwards at our wedding. "Forgive me, but Edwards, as in the Edwards shipping conglomerate?"

A twinkle sparks in Helena's brown eyes, and she dips her chin.

"That's right." She picks up her glass and leans into her chair. "But such old news. Tell us about your husband. How was your honeymoon?"

At the mention of Callahan, my palms turn clammy. This is it, the big show. I smile brightly and wave her off, as if I'm shy and embarrassed to be the center of attention. I hope it's convincing. "We've known each other since we were kids. It took growing up to realize we had it right the first time." I leave it at that. I should've spoken with him more about what our cover story was, and I plan to rectify that first thing on the car ride back.

Helena nods as if she understands. When she doesn't respond, I know she's wanting me to continue. Instead, I wave off the attention and attempt to spin the conversation elsewhere.

"But you know how the honeymoon stage goes. This home, though, is beautiful. Did you design it yourself?"

A bemused brow lifts, but Helena allows the change, chatting for the next twenty minutes about their recent renovations and interior design. It's a trivial conversation that I tune mostly out. Though being in a place like this, where there are such clear divides between the gender roles… well, it's fascinating. I wish it wasn't a faux pas to whip out my phone and take notes for inspiration in my next novel.

As the clock strikes nine, I rise and go hunting for a drink. "Excuse me," I whisper, as I snake through the women and leave the sitting room.

The mansion is even bigger than the Keane residence, but thankfully, the party is contained to one wing. I follow the sounds of chattering voices and elegant, low music to what can only be described as a ballroom. Its vaulted ceilings are painted a soft cream and stone columns line the walls. Ivy crawls up each one and onto the ceiling, into intricate designs of flowers and sparrows. A string quartet plays gentle music in the back corner, a cover of a song that's familiar but I can't place the name of. On the left side of the room, there's an extensive bar. Helena has covered the remaining walls with a considerable amount of art—so much so, it feels like a private museum.

The dimmed chandeliers cast a faint, warm glow over the guests. They gather around scattered cocktail tables and in front of the art, talking among themselves. Boisterous laughter and raucous conversations liven the party.

I make a beeline for the bar.

There's only one person waiting for their drink, so I stand on the other side of the bar and patiently await my turn. The seconds tick, and with them, I thrum my fingers on the glass counter. A yawn threatens to escape, but I trap it with a press of my lips. Before long, the bartender takes my order and places a crystal tumbler of whiskey in front of me. I thank him and then wander the room. I'd rather not get sucked into another conversation I'm not ready for.

I sip on my whiskey, enjoying the warm burn it leaves in its wake. The heat spreads to my fingertips, and the coil in my chest loosens. Cal still hasn't returned, but I imagine he's striking some deal with Isaiah Edwards, Helena's husband and the founder of the Edwards shipping conglomerate.

"Who would leave such a beautiful woman alone in a den full of vipers?" a voice slithers from behind me. There's a bold undercurrent of an accent that I can't quite place.

Chills erupt down my back, and I'm instantly on guard. Carefully, I turn and try to hide my apprehension.

The man in front of me is attractive, with a trimmed beard covering the expanse of his jaw and styled black hair. But while his face might be pretty to look at, something evil seeps behind his eyes. His midnight-blue tuxedo is well tailored, complete with a black bow tie. My nose scrunches. He smells of gin, and something sharp, but sweet.

"How do you know I'm not a viper myself?" I raise a brow and take a sip from my whiskey. He's got me backed up against a wall, with only a cocktail table between us.

The man huffs a laugh, and the sound sours my stomach. "As if someone so beautiful could ever be deadly."

He slides closer, but I throw up a pointed finger, stabbing him in his chest as he sways toward me. I push him back, and he stumbles only slightly before straightening himself.

"Oh, Ms. Catrone, that wasn't very nice," he says, eyes narrowing. He raises his glass and points at me. "Actually, it's Mrs. Keane, now, isn't it? Where is your husband, Mrs. Keane?" He pretends to look around, arching a brow and tilting his head.

My mouth parts, ready to ask him how he knows my name, but he cuts me off.

"Ah"—he *tsks* and waves me off—"that's not very important, is it? I'm sure he's putting out much bigger fires. So difficult to get any face-to-face time with him lately, wouldn't you agree?"

He takes another step closer, but I hold my ground. The sardonic attitude, which he clearly loves, only leaves a bitter char in the back of my throat. His voice is slick, and the hair on the back of my neck rises.

"Why, Mrs. Keane, I'm positively sure that will change here soon." An oily smile slides onto his face, and a spark of something I can't quite decipher flashes behind his eyes. A pit of dread sinks deep in my belly.

"Though it's a shame he can't be in two places at once."

CHAPTER TEN

I shove the deep discomfort of this stranger knowing my name aside and bury it beneath my rising anger. I lift my chin, but I refuse to take my eyes off him or answer, watching every minute movement as he smirks. He looks triumphant, but I don't understand why. Because he knows who I am? While that unsettles me to my core, it's not entirely impossible to know who married one of the most influential men in Roswell just last week.

He looks me up and down and sniffs obnoxiously, then tosses back the last of his drink. "Goddamn, the pictures don't do you justice. Just looking at you makes me want a cigarette." After carelessly dropping the glass on the table, he reaches into his breast pocket and pulls out a pack. A waft of smoke carries on the air as he pulls out a fresh cigarette. He places it between his lips, then talks out of the side of his mouth.

"Care to join me outside? I'll make it worth your while." His brows waggle as he brings a lighter to his mouth and lights his cigarette. Smoke billows toward me as he smiles menacingly around the rolled paper.

"No," I say with finality. "Excuse me." I grab my clutch and skirt around him, but his hand whips out to catch my arm.

If he doesn't let go of me in about half a second, I'm liable to break his fucking nose.

"Let. Go."

If words could melt, he'd be a puddle on the floor. The stranger just pulls the cigarette from his mouth and blows the smoke off to the side. He opens his mouth to speak, but a server rushes in.

"Sir, I'm afraid you can't smoke in here. Please, put that out at once!" Their voice shakes with the order, but the man just laughs.

"Of course. What was I thinking?" His sardonic tone is made only more irritating by the look he gives me. He takes another extended drag, then drops the lit cigarette into my glass, which is still half full of whiskey. It sizzles, burning out. He blows the last of the smoke in my face, but I refuse to show weakness and wave it away. His cheeky attitude only serves to further irritate me, and my grip tightens around my glass. I'm surprised it doesn't shatter in my palm when the server finally interjects once more.

"Here, ma'am. Let me take that for you," they say, grabbing the glass and rushing away from the tense storm brewing.

I arch a brow and tilt my head. "Good evening, Mister…" I pause, waiting for him to fill in the blank. The smoke still clings to the air as he smiles, a slithering coil to his lips that sours my stomach.

He ignores my obvious attempt to learn his name. "And to you, Mrs. Keane." He winks and strolls away, hands stuffed into his pockets. He swaggers through the room with little rush, even looking back as he exits the room to toss a wink back at me.

When he's finally out of sight, I breathe a sigh of relief. My shoulders slump, and a fog clouds my brain. What the hell was that? The oily residue left over from his slimy gaze sinks to the bottom of my gut and settles like stone. Something about that interaction goes further than just becoming unnerved. He looked at me like I was a prize, one he'd yet to win.

The unease compounds, morphing into a distinct sense of foreboding, and I resolve to find Callahan. But before I even take a step, the man himself bursts into the ballroom.

To anyone else, he might seem collected, but I can see the panic rippling off him in waves. His eyes frantically search the space, and I can't help but hope he's looking for me. I take a step out of the shadow of a column, and his gaze instantly catches mine.

With brisk strides, he crosses the ballroom and crushes me to his chest. His arms band around me, giving me no choice but to accept his embrace. Under his jacket, his heart pounds mercilessly. This is the first I've seen him this unkempt.

He inhales deeply and freezes.

"Why do you smell of smoke?" he asks as he pulls back. Shadows shroud his face, and his hands slide to my upper arms, holding me as if I would float away should he let go.

My nose scrunches. "I was just about to come find you. I just had the strangest interaction with this creep." A shiver rolls down my spine.

Cal's eyes shutter. "What happened? Did he hurt you? Who was he?" His questions rush out, one after the other, and seem to warm my chest more than the lingering traces of whiskey.

"I'm fine, but he spoke to me like he knew me. Like he was expecting me here."

Callahan wraps a hand around my elbow and practically drags me toward the exit. We rush through the Edwards's residence without so much as a goodbye.

"Callahan, slow down."

He doesn't.

"Cal, what's happened?" My voice comes out higher than I'd like.

Cal finally slows as we reach the exit. His jaw ticks, and his shoulders tense, but he slows.

"There's been another fire. We lost some good men tonight."

My steps falter.

"There was a note left. A note addressed—" Cal freezes, a look of horror flashing over his face before he collects himself. We're paused on the steps in front of the Edwards's residence, and the bitter cold rushes in, chilling me to my bones. Callahan's grip tightens on my elbow, but I pay it no mind.

"Addressed to who, Cal?"

Callahan shakes his head and drags me toward the SUV. Nathaniel smokes as he leans against the grill, but when he sees us approaching, he quickly stubs out his cigarette on the bottom of his shoe. He rushes to the driver's seat to start the car. The rumbling of the SUV coming to life is deafening, and I flinch.

Then I'm sailing, thrown backward. My head slams against the pavers. Sound muffles as a fire encompasses the SUV, smoke already reaching high into the sky. The scalding heat from the flames blisters, and I struggle to scramble backward. Callahan's face appears in front of mine. His eyes are wide, his pupils blown until there's barely a sliver of his usual deep brown. He mouths something, but the ringing is too shrill

101

for me to hear. Dark flashes of men carrying massive guns pass next to us, and Callahan points to the east, then turns back to me.

The fucking car just blew up.

I try to look around him, but his hands clamp gently on either side of my face. He keeps mouthing something, but I don't understand. *Is he asking me if I'm okay?*

I run a mental check over my body. I'm sore, and the palms of my hands sting. My head throbs lightly, and I instinctively raise a hand to my temple, only to find it slightly sticky. My trembling fingers come back wet. Slick, warm blood coats my index and middle fingers, and I look over to Cal. He curses.

Gravel crunches next to me, and my head snaps over as Cohen drops beside me. He flashes a bright light between my eyes. I flinch, raising a scraped hand to shield my eyes.

"Are you okay?" His words are muffled and come out garbled. Then he says something to Callahan that sounds like *concussion* and *head wound.*

I nod, and the buzzing from earlier quiets. Callahan's shoulders rise and fall with heavy breaths, and his gaze darts around, bouncing from me to the car currently in flames, to the dark forest surrounding the Edwards's residence.

"We need to move," he seems to shout, though the words are still muted.

Cohen stands and offers me a hand, helping me rise to my feet. He scans my form and lingers on my temple. A warm trickle of blood slides over my cheekbone, and I quickly move to wipe it.

"I'm fine," I whisper, shocked because the damage could've been so much worse. But then I remember—"*Nathaniel.* Where is Nathaniel?"

The fire blazes over the melted shell of the SUV. The roof and top half of the vehicle is gone, and in that moment, I realize there's no chance Nathaniel survived. While Callahan stays silent, my bottom lip trembles, and I quickly cover my face to hide the emotion. I didn't know Nathaniel very well, but he was kind to me.

Callahan approaches me with caution, his arms raised gently in front of him as if I were going to bolt. "We need to leave." He looks to Cohen. "Now."

"Could this be—"

A sharp bark from Cal interrupts Cohen. "Not here."

Cohen dips his chin in understanding.

Just then, a bright light floods the driveway as a nearby garage opens silently. Callahan replaces Cohen's hand and guides me away from the car that's still burning. In the garage, Isaiah Edwards steps calmly toward us.

"Run into a spot of trouble, yeah? Here"—he tosses a key fob to Cohen, who catches it with ease—"take the Audi. I'll send over the reports, as discussed."

Cohen clicks the fob, and the headlights of a midnight SUV flash. Callahan opens his mouth to speak, but a sudden spell of wooziness overtakes me, and I sway. Cal tightens his grip, looking over at me with such concern that a long-forgotten emotion swells in my chest.

"Let's go." My voice trembles and sounds disconnected. I take a step forward, and my knee buckles. I go down, dropping like rocks to a riverbed, but Callahan catches me before I hit the ground. He swings me into his arms and carries me to the back seat, then settles me against the cream leather. Black dots fill the edges of my vision, and I rub a tired hand over my temple.

Callahan's worried gaze meets my own as he seems to catalog every detail of my face. I'm sure it's filthy and scratched, just as my dress is in tatters. Somewhere along the way, I lost a heel and scraped the bottom of my foot. Kicking my other heel off, I reach for my seatbelt, but Cal beats me to it. His face is inches from mine as he stretches the belt over my body, and I hear every quickened breath. Under the smoke and burning rubber, his sandalwood scent breaks through. It calms me. The moment the seatbelt clicks into place, I exhale deeply.

Callahan takes one more look at me and shuts the door. He throws a muffled expletive and climbs into the other side. Cohen hops into the driver's seat, and we take off into the night.

As we pass the fire, a tear slips out of the corner of my eye. A crowd has gathered on the front steps of the Edwards's residence, with similar looks of horror painted on each face. My fingers tremble as they reach toward the cool glass, leaving smudges from their touch.

Three seconds.

That's all it would've taken for us to have perished in that explosion. The realization is unnerving.

My hands fall to the middle seat as we drive away. The flames from the fire blaze through the night, only seeming to grow with distance. I squeeze my eyes shut, sinking into the leather in exhaustion. The lightest touch presses against my pinky, and I want to fight the comfort it offers, but I can't. I'm not strong enough. Not tonight.

Instead, I lean into it. On the middle seat between us, our hands touch only by the skin on our pinkies, but I tip my head back, letting the feeling of safety wash over me.

Lulled by the near-silent car, I fall asleep.

CHAPTER ELEVEN

What I can only assume is about ten minutes later, a gentle hand touches my shoulder. Pain throbs through me sharply, and I shoot up in my seat on a wince. My hands fly to my temple. Cal's hand lingers on my shoulder, but then he pulls back.

"I'm fine," I placate, despite the dizziness making a quick return.

"No, you're not. You probably have a concussion." Cal hops out of the back seat and skirts around the rear of the car to open my door. He helps me get out, and my feet wobble on the epoxy surface. "Let's get Doc to have a look at you and get you cleaned up."

I chuckle, trying to ease his obvious tension. "Well, I won't say no to that." Despite knowing I was going to wake up with a few more bruises than I already had, and a low-grade concussion, I was fine. Unlike Nathaniel.

Cal gently guides me through the kitchen, but instead of turning right like I'm used to, we go left. Down a short hallway, there's a door, which Callahan opens without knocking.

It's a sterile, beige room with an exam table, sink, and cabinets lining the farthest wall. Upon our entrance, a thin woman works swiftly to open a medical kit. She doesn't bother to introduce herself as she ushers us inside. I'm skeptical of her credentials—she doesn't wear a white coat or scrubs, but instead a plain T-shirt and dark pants—but it's not entirely surprising that Cal has a doctor on site. She moves hastily to tie back her dark hair into a low bun. It's streaked with gray and the faint lines around her brown eyes leads me to believe she's in her late fifties. She has golden olive skin and round glasses perched on her nose. There's a distinct lack of surprise on her face, which suggests she's used to Callahan needing urgent medical care. The thought churns my stomach.

The doctor directs me to sit and proceeds to check me over. Her fingers gently prod at my injuries, and she takes extra care to look at my scalp. Thankfully, the bleeding has stopped, and an antiseptic wipe clears away any dried blood.

Then, for the second time, a bright light is shone between my eyes, and I squint. Before I know it, she's put the light away and has moved on to checking out my palms.

"Any dizziness, confusion, headache?" she asks as she inspects the cuts on my hands.

I nod. "Just dizziness and headache."

She dips her chin in acknowledgment, cleaning the scrapes with an alcohol pad, and I fight a wince. As she works, she glances over to Cal. "And you?"

Callahan stiffens. "I'm fine."

I scoff, and he looks over to me.

"I am," he insists, but he sounds like a petulant child.

I arch a brow. "We were in the same explosion, Callahan. Just because you have six inches and almost seventy-five pounds on me doesn't mean your head is any less fallible than mine."

The doctor sighs, as if this isn't the first time she's dealt with his particular brand of stubbornness, and she performs the same check over on him as she did on me. She pulls out her small pen light again and flicks it between his eyes.

Then she turns to her medical bag and ruffles through it for a moment. She pulls out a small container and shakes it, pills rattling around in the bottle. "These are your basic Tylenol. *Anyone*"—she shoots a pointed look to Cal—"experiencing symptoms of dizziness or headache should take two every six hours." Then she puts the bottle in my hands and pats me on the shoulder. "You don't have a concussion, but if your dizziness gets worse, come back and see me."

At that, she ushers us out and closes the door behind us. A clear dismissal. I glance over my shoulder and back to Cal, whose presence overwhelms me. His hair is disheveled, and a filthy combination of dirt and ash covers his face. His bloodshot eyes likely match my own. In short, he's a mess. But it still calls to me, and I find myself gravitating toward him. I pray he can't see the thrumming of my pulse.

Cal clears his throat and glances down the hallway.

"Let's get you cleaned up. Then we can meet with Everett and Matthias. We have much to discuss."

My tongue thickens in my mouth, so I just nod. Callahan places a soft hand on the small of my back and guides me to my room. The heat of his touch is scorching, and I don't even think he's realized he's touching me. The entire walk is silent, save for the sound of Callahan's shoes clicking on the floor. With each step, my mind races to fill in the blanks of what just happened, and before I know it, Cal is depositing me at my door.

His lips press into a thin line. Moments pass in a tense silence. Then, he finally speaks. "Take as long as you need. Then come to my office."

I open my mouth to speak, but can't seem to find the words. If I say what's actually on my mind, I'm liable to make the night worse—so instead, I just nod. Disappointment momentarily flashes on Callahan's face right before he dips his chin and turns away. His steps echo the thudding of my heart until he reaches the door on the other side of the hallway, about ten feet down. He pauses with his hand wrapped around the doorknob. I'm suspended, heart in my throat for what feels like an eternity. I try again to speak, but Cal shakes his head and leaves me standing in the hallway. Alone. The door latches softly behind him.

Oh. Callahan's room is only a few feet away from mine. My mouth parts. *Oh.*

With that newfound information, I head inside my room and make a beeline for the shower. I try to avoid my reflection in the mirror, but the call is too difficult to ignore.

The woman in the mirror looks like hell. Her hairline is stained with blood, her eyes red with dark purple bags underneath. Dirt covers her face, and her dress is ruined.

It pains me—both physically and emotionally—to peel off my dress, and I toss the singed garment to the floor. I turn the shower on and wait impatiently for it to warm before finally saying fuck it and hopping in. The icy water slices over my skin, stinging where broken. I rush through washing my body, slowing only to wash my hair delicately.

Thankfully, none of my cuts are deep, but I still move with as much care as I can manage.

Ten minutes later, I'm dressed in loose loungewear and unraveling the cord to my blow-dryer. When my hair is half dry, I leave the bathroom, grab my phone, and head to Callahan's office. I only make one wrong turn—progress—and when I approach the office, muffled voices argue behind the closed door. My feet falter, but I press forward, leaning my ear against the wood.

"How did this happen?" Cal says. His voice is strained, and I can only imagine the look on his face.

"We're still investigating. Edwards hasn't sent over the security footage yet." I can't tell whose voice that belongs to, but I want to be in this conversation.

Without knocking, I twist the doorknob and enter. Thick tension heats the room as the men angrily turn toward me. Callahan visibly checks me over, and I note his hair is also damp. Unlike my need for comfort, Cal has put on black combat clothes. A tight tee stretches across his broad chest, and his tactical pants are tucked into combat boots. The angry pinch between his brows softens when he looks me over, eyes darting from my drying hair down to my bare feet.

"She shouldn't be here right now," Matthias grumbles with an arm thrown out toward me.

Cal doesn't look away from me. Instead, he addresses me. "How are you feeling?" His voice is gentle. Tender.

A pang in my chest stings, but I tell myself he's just checking on my well-being. He'd ask the same of anyone. "I'm fine."

I step farther into the room and shut the door behind me. Matthias stands next to the bar cart, a glass of some amber liquid in his hand, while Everett sits on the leather couch. Cohen leans against a bookshelf while Cal perches against his desk. I move to sit in one of the leather chairs in front of Cal's desk, but Callahan stops me from passing him. His hand catches my wrist and doesn't let go. I lift my gaze to catch his, and he softens more.

He dips his chin and lets me go.

"She stays," Cal instructs as I sit in one of the guest chairs. "What do you mean Edwards hasn't sent over the footage yet? It's been an hour."

"I haven't heard anything else. Your guess is as good as mine."

"Let's remedy that."

Cal pulls his phone out of a pocket and types something, then places the call on speaker. The phone rings twice before a deep voice answers.

"Keane," Isaiah Edwards answers.

"Edwards." Cal's voice is strained, and his jaw ticks. "Care to share why you haven't sent over your security footage yet?"

Isaiah lets out a sigh, and something in me tells me we aren't getting that footage.

"It's been wiped. Has to be a professional job. We have some of the best tech money can contract, and it's as if a ghost blew up your vehicle."

Callahan's grip on his phone tightens until his knuckles turn white. I swallow over a thick lump in my throat and shift in my seat.

Isaiah continues, "Would've appreciated if whoever you pissed off blew up your car in front of your house instead of mine." His tone is playful, but there's a thread of annoyance in his words.

"It's your house, Edwards. It's not too far a stretch to believe that was meant for you."

Isaiah remains pensive, as if considering Cal's words. "I've made it a point to ensure my enemies wouldn't dare try me in my own home. Could you say the same about yours?"

Callahan's eyes narrow as his gaze darts to Everett. "Perhaps someone isn't very keen on our partnership taking root."

"Perhaps. But as it stands, we've reviewed what footage we do have and found nothing out of the ordinary."

Nothing out of the ordinary? So someone could sneak onto the Edwards's property, plant a bomb in Cal's car, detonate it at exactly the right moment, and get away scot-free? There has to be some sort of evidence.

The skin around my wrist tingles as if it remembers the stale touch of the man from the party. Cal looks over to me and must notice my distaste. He lifts the phone once more. "Send it over anyway. Get me the hour before."

Isaiah sighs. "Fine," he relents. An audible *click* signals the end of the call.

Cal tosses his phone onto his desk. "We'll find him."

"He said the strangest thing. He asked me where you were, and then waved it off and said you've got bigger fires to be putting out than escorting me. I thought he was being satirical, but now…"

Callahan scoffs, and his grip on the edge of his desk tightens. "What else did he say?"

I think back to the conversation. "Most of it was a lot of nothing, just a guy trying to unnerve me. He had an accent, something European. He said something about looking at me and needing a cigarette before he reached into his pocket and pulled out a pack and lit up. A server came rushing over and told him to put it out, so he dropped it in my drink. I about threw it in his face, but the server took it from me."

Everett crosses his arms, and a deep scowl creases his face. "Did he know you?"

I nod. "He called me Ms. Catrone before he corrected himself. It felt like he was trying to intimidate me. But our wedding was in the papers with profiles on both of us. At the time, it wasn't as unusual as it is now because anyone could've known who I was."

"It could be connected to the fire and the note."

Matthias's words are like a shock to my system. "*The note.* What did the note say? You got cut off by that fucking bomb."

Callahan looks away from me as he stands and pours himself a drink from the bar cart. He slings back the whiskey, then pours another and takes it back to his desk.

"It was…" He trails off, voice suddenly catching. He tosses back another healthy swallow and hisses as he wipes the corner of his mouth with his thumb.

I stand and lean over his desk. "It was *what*, Cal?"

Tense silence builds as he refuses to look at me. Instead, he stares at his almost empty glass, rolling it around his hands, watching as the last drops of the amber liquid pool at the bottom of the tumbler. Finally, he looks over to me. "There was a note found on the gate in front of the warehouse that was burned down."

Through whatever cosmic force, I know whatever he's about to say will change everything.

"What did it say?" The words wobble out of me.

Cal's nostrils flare. "It said, '*Til Death Do You Part, Mrs. Keane. Until then, your brother will do.*'"

The words hang between us, thickening into a deadly storm of electric anxiety and muggy tension. I don't know what to say, and I collapse back into the chair, curling my fingers into fists and dropping them into my lap. The weight of the implication presses on me.

"Mason," I whimper. His face materializes like a ghost, battered and bruised. It's like a sucker punch to the gut, stinging harder than Jude could ever manage. I knew I'd wasted too much time.

I look back to Callahan and find his usual defenses missing. He openly searches my face, and I see a flicker of doubt that's quickly replaced by resolve.

"We have to find him." My words seem to change something in Cal.

The air thickens until it lodges in the base of my throat.

"What happened tonight?" I ask Cal.

His jaw ticks, and he looks to Matthias.

Matthias stiffens, his knuckles turning white where they grip the arm of the couch. "At approximately eight-fifty, the Culver Street warehouse was set on fire. Redding and his team were on site, and there were eight casualties. Any product left was compromised."

The clock on the wall ticks loudly until it's almost all I can hear. I draw in a shaky breath. *Eight dead.*

"And Redding?" Cal asks.

A prolonged pause follows. Matthias shakes his head. "He didn't make it."

Callahan curses and slams a fist on his desk. It echoes throughout the room. A tense quiet follows. Everett enters again and crosses the room to sit on the couch.

This time, it's Cohen who chimes in. "Who called it in?"

"Barley. He was on his way in for inventory when he noticed the flames. He called Redding, and when he didn't pick up, he called Everett."

"Who are among the dead?"

Everett lists the other seven casualties, and while I don't recognize any of the names, my heart breaks for them. When he finishes, there's a somber silence. But only for a moment.

The next instant, Cal's office door slams open and crashes into the wall as Lucas shoves into the room. Ash coats his buzzed head, and a scowl mars his face. He barely spares me a glance and snaps, "The footage was wiped."

The room is icy as his words simmer in the air between us.

"Which cameras?" Matthias asks.

Luc scrubs a hand over his face, smearing ash and dirt. "All of them. Inside and out. They were all wiped clean of the last twenty-four hours."

Just like at the Edwards's residence. Shit.

A *ding* chimes from Cal's laptop. He opens it, eyes narrowing at the screen. "Looks like Edwards came through."

His words ring out like a clang of a bell, and we rush to gather around his desk. We spend the next fifteen minutes tracking the stranger to a blue Tahoe, and Everett jots down the license plate. He steps outside to call someone, presumably to have it tracked.

"Why'd they target us in front of Edwards's home?" Cal mumbles.

"Before the note at the fire, I would've suspected a coincidence." Luc's voice is drenched in fatigue, and he scrubs a tattooed hand over his buzzed hair.

"Nothing is a coincidence." My voice cracks from disuse, and I grab Cal's glass of whiskey and finish it.

Cal looks up from the screen to meet my gaze. Something flashes in his brown eyes, and I feel a tug on my chest.

"No," he says, throat bobbing. "No, there's not."

"Someone who doesn't want us using Edwards to ship product overseas?" Matthias's question keeps us quiet in thought. So that's what we were doing there…

"Perhaps. However, we've been quiet about the partnership. Only a select few know we've been meeting."

We continue to investigate.

For the next hour, we pore over the conversation from every angle, analyzing every possible meaning. No one recognizes him, but the footage shows a tattoo peeking out of his sleeve. Everett enhances the still as best he can, but it's still grainy.

"Is that a *D*?" I point at what looks to be the point of a dagger. It slices through the top of a curved, capital *D*.

Everyone gathered around the computer leans closer. We work through the footage, shot by shot, trying to get a better look, but his sleeve never recedes any further. Cohen furiously types out a text to someone while I tuck that intel in the forefront of my mind.

The only thing we could gather was that he was likely involved in both the car bombing and the fire at the warehouse, and that because of the timing of both, there was likely more than one person involved.

With that realization, my stomach turns to stone, and prickles break out over my skin. That multiple people want me dead is jarring, something I've never encountered before.

Growing up in the Bianchi house, I was no stranger to death. Granted, except for my father, the Family typically hid the more gruesome details from me, but that doesn't discount the several dead bodies I've seen over the years—or learned of various methods to dispose of them.

And when my dad died, I was—of course—sad, but I wasn't that upset. Somewhere along the way, I realized my father was the one responsible for his death. He may have died in service to the Family by taking a bullet that was meant for Elias's father, Dominic, but it was his own fault for choosing to involve himself with a criminal organization. Death is part of life. It's natural. But when faced with my mortality, it's shaken me to my core.

I look to Callahan. He's deep in conversation with Matthias and Everett and doesn't seem to notice my staring. His eyes are stained with purple shadows, and his five o'clock stubble only highlights his exhaustion, but he's still the most beautiful man I've ever seen. It was true eleven years ago, and it's true to this day. Only now, I have the distinct feeling that whatever future I saw flashes of might not come true at all.

When a purple haze settles over the horizon, Callahan dismisses Everett to double security surrounding the remaining four warehouses in Roswell. If the technology was failing them—or being tampered with—more eyes on the ground could help catch the perpetrator. Cal also instructs Everett to assign leaders to each security detail at the warehouse, who will ensure shift changes are smooth and cameras are working properly. The crews are stretched thin as it is, but no one speaks their nerves aloud.

Without anyone noticing, I slip from the room. I trudge back to my suite and fall into bed with a heavy heart.

As a war picks up outside this manor, a similar one wages inside of me.

CHAPTER TWELVE

The next morning, I wake with a tension headache. By the time I get out of the shower, the Tylenol Doc gave me kicks in, easing the low throbbing of my skull. I'm not usually one to wash my hair so frequently, but it was necessary. The fresh hair and clean scent of my soap settles something in me, though I swear I can still smell the singed car in the back of my nose.

The necklace Cal gave me is still around my neck, and for a moment, I consider taking it off, then dismiss it. I love peonies, and the blossom shape is beautiful. I hate how well he knows me.

Shaking off the annoyance, I dress in a pair of navy capri leggings and a geometric-patterned, hot-pink sports bra. It leaves a sliver of my midriff showing. The girls are bound tight, but a little cleavage still shows at the top. I plan to get some cardio in today after almost a week and a half of avoiding Strikers and its particularly grumpy owner.

As I make my way to the kitchen for a quick breakfast, I scroll through my phone, clearing notifications and checking on my messages, but there's nothing of importance. Two seconds later, I smack into a hard chest.

"Ow." I rub my nose and glance up at Cohen's concerned gaze.

His brows furrow. "You seriously going to work out after being in an explosion not even twenty-four hours ago? I don't think Doc or Cal would think that's very smart."

The mention of Cal having a say over how I live my life stirs a wound not quite healed.

"I'm just going to find a treadmill and get some movement in. Don't worry, Dad, I'll be fine."

The face Cohen pulls at my choice of words is comical. He's frozen as if he just sucked on a warhead when I push past him. When I make it to the kitchen, he finally catches up with me.

Dressed in his usual black combat gear, dark circles ring his bloodshot eyes, a testament to a similar late night. Mindlessly, I drift toward the coffee and pour myself a mug. Cohen grabs the pot from me and pours his own while I get the creamer from the fridge. A healthy splash into mine, none for Cohen. Leading up to the explosion, we'd fallen into some sort of routine. Most mornings we would meet for coffee, then he'd eventually follow me around until he realized I had no plans to leave, and he'd wander off to do his own thing. I'd taken to bringing my laptop to either a library, patio, or even a random balcony I found that's off another empty guest room.

My editor seemed to be happy with the chapters I sent last week, but as an author, there's always another project waiting. Today, I had to finish the autobiography I'm ghostwriting for a high-profile tech entrepreneur. He hired me about six months ago, and the final draft is due tomorrow morning.

Andy Thorne is an impressive man, to say the very least. I interviewed him for almost sixteen hours, and his personal assistant gave me her direct cell number for any further questions. I only had to finish the final chapter, then put the finishing touches on the afterword. The project was a love letter to his late wife, which I found entirely too sweet. They'd found each other later than most and had two girls together in the late nineties. Despite loving her fiercely, Andy spent much of his marriage buried in work. It put a strain on their marriage until neither of them were happy, he claims.

But everything changed when his wife ran their car into a tree in a remote area with the girls in the back seat. She'd taken the girls, and they were on their way to the lake for a few weeks to get some space from Andy. After they crashed, the car caught fire. Her seatbelt was stuck, and her youngest was knocked out. Her oldest was in shock and couldn't move or speak. It was only thanks to the help of a couple passing through at the same time that they were rescued before the car succumbed to the flames. Andy claims it was the wake up call he needed.

Tragically, only a few years later, his wife died in another horrific car accident. After rushing to the hospital, he learned she was dead on arrival. He said the crushing guilt for prioritizing his work over his family was debilitating, but he had to press on for the sake of their children. From then on, he scaled back his work to raise them. He still maintained his position as CEO of Thorne Enterprises, but he delegated any duties he could in order to spend as much time as possible with his daughters.

Now, he was determined to share their story. To implore others to not make the same mistakes he did. His plan was to market the memoir as all the best secrets of his best business practices, when in reality, it was a plea to other men to not take their life at home for granted. When he shared his wife's tragic passing, I couldn't help but feel immense sorrow for a woman I'd never met.

I move around Cohen and grab a parfait from the fridge as he trails behind me. I head toward the backyard, and Cohen only laughs once when I make it there without a single missed turn.

"See? I told you you'd get the hang of it." He smiles, and I wonder—not for the first time—how he's single.

Fuck it. I'll just ask. "Why are you single?"

Cohen nearly spits out his coffee but manages to compose himself. He swallows over the cough and covers his mouth with a large hand. "Excuse me?"

"Oh, come on, we both know you're an attractive guy, and sometimes you can be funny. What, are you a serial cheater or something?"

A twinkle shines in his dark eyes, and the corner of his lip lifts. "I never said I was."

My jaw drops. "What? You've never said anything." He has never once mentioned a girlfriend or partner.

Cohen smirks. "You never asked." With that, he takes another sip of coffee and shakes out a newspaper he picked up from somewhere.

I stare at him, mouth gaped open like a fish. "Well, are you?" I finally manage.

He looks over the paper and shrugs. "Yes."

I crumple and toss my napkin at him. It breezes over his arm and falls to the ground. Laughter bubbles out of his chest, and after the shock wears off, I join in.

"Dick," I cough under my breath.

Cohen just winks and returns to his newspaper.

"So, how did you get into the family?"

Lucas has been Cal's friend since middle school, and I'm honestly surprised he never found out about us back then. Or if he did, he never said anything. Cohen and Everett were the unfamiliar faces of the group, and if I'm going to be here for the next two years, I might as well get to know them. Well, Cohen at least. I haven't seen much of Everett so far.

The breeze picks up, a chill wrapping around my body. But after spending so long inside, I welcome the brisk air. Cohen sighs, folds the newspaper, and tosses it onto the table. It lands with a crinkle, and he laces his fingers together, settling deeper into the wrought-iron chair as he gives me an appraising look. After a moment, he finally speaks.

"I was a fighter."

I raise a brow. "Was?"

Cohen smiles, but it doesn't reach his dark eyes. Invisible memories play in the chilled air between us, but I'm not privy to their story. His hands twist in his lap, and he cracks each joint.

"Was." He doesn't elaborate further, picking up the newspaper, effectively dismissing me.

We end up sitting on the patio for another fifteen minutes before the clouds start to roll in. It was already brisk, but I don't want to get caught in the rain.

I gather the trash and empty mug and drop them back off in the kitchen. Then I turn to head to the gym and realize…

"Where is the gym?"

Cohen lets loose a deep sigh and shakes his head. "Some trainer you are," he jests, leading the way.

"Hey, I never claimed to be a trainer. I just happen to train."

He opens a door for me and waves me off as I pass through. "Tomato, potato."

I flip him the middle finger and take in the massive gym. Machines of all kinds take up a third of the space, while treadmills and a stair master sit in the back. Free weights line the mirrored wall, and punching bags hang in the center. Heavy electronic music blares from a sound system, hiding the usual sounds a gym creates.

A few guys pause to watch us enter, but I pay them no mind. A man on one treadmill pulls my attention, and I find myself frozen, stuck to the floor and fighting to keep my tongue in my mouth. Callahan runs at a breaking pace, sweat dripping over his bare torso. A towel hangs from the arm of the machine, but I'm about to burn it and offer myself in its stead. Muscles I don't remember him having at seventeen ripple with each stride, and I take several moments to just watch him before a voice whispers next to my ear.

"I can pass a note to him, if you'd like. He's here every day during second period."

"Shut up." I smack Cohen's chest and turn toward a clearing with mats and bands. Dropping to the floor, I stretch my dormant muscles.

Standing up, I shake out my quads and reach an arm over to the side. My ribs had finally stopped hurting from Jude's unchecked punch last week, but I think the fall from yesterday only compounded the ache. My body is sore, and not the kind you get after a hard day of labor or a good workout.

With one long exhale, I straighten, ready to get some steps in.

"What the fuck is that?"

I snap to my left to find a fuming Callahan. Sweat drips from his hair, his temple, his abs—everywhere. His chest rises and falls with heavy breaths, and his hands curl into fists. His face is red, though I can't decipher if it's from his workout or his outrage.

I scan the gym, trying to see what's made him so furious, but don't find anything out of the ordinary.

"Good morning to you, too," I say with a shake of my head.

Cal scoffs, stepping into my space. I can smell his sweat and remnants of his sandalwood cologne, and my mouth waters. His shorts are slung low on his hips, his chest glistening from his exertion.

"That's not from the explosion last night. Tell me what the fuck happened."

A frown tugs at my mouth, and I try to figure out what he means. "What are you talking about?"

"*This*," he snaps as he rips up the hem of my sports bra until my breast is almost exposed.

The heat from his palm radiates over my skin, stirring a flutter in my core. The yellowed bruise spanning from the bottom of my ribs to the top of my hip is on full display. Another day or two, and it wouldn't even show, but of course, with my luck, Cal would see it. Callahan's hand shakes with anger as his gaze snaps back to mine. "What is *this*?"

My eyes roll of their own accord, and I bat his hand away. "It's a bruise." Steam practically shoots from Cal's ears, and I amend, "Or at least, one that's almost healed. As in, I'm fine."

Callahan's hands prop on his hips, and my eyes are drawn to the sexy v-cut of his abs. A dark trail of hair disappears into his shorts, and my eyes flick to the towel stuffed into the waistband, covering his cock. His jaw clenches, and I see the gears turning.

"What happened?" he repeats, fuse shortening to a dangerously low wick.

I ignore him, opting to use the treadmill he just vacated. Callahan follows on my heels and stands in front of the machine as I press and hold the speed to get it up to a jog.

"Sparring gone wrong." My words are simple, and I do my best to ignore the man puffing out his chest in front of me. It brings me immense joy to dig under his skin.

"You spar? With who?" He looks around to Cohen and spots him lifting weights on a bench. "*Graves?*"

I can't help it—a laugh bubbles free before I can stop it. Cal's face snaps back to me, and his eyes immediately draw to my breasts. I press my lips into a thin line to fight the smile that wants to break out.

"No. My coach. I was distracted, and he clocked me. It's fine."

"That bruise is almost healed. It probably hurt like a bitch when it happened." Cal's voice remains steeped in anger but has taken a curious turn into concern.

"It did. But as you can see—I'm fine."

"I don't want you sparring with him anymore."

My indignant scoff only brings him back around to anger. "You can't tell me if I can spar or not." I decide to ignore him for the rest of my jog.

But instead, Cal pulls the emergency stop cord. He holds it in his hands, and I groan, popping my feet on either side of the treadmill as it comes to a slow stop.

I give him a look that says *seriously*, but he ignores it.

"I didn't say you couldn't spar. Just not with him."

Crossing my arms in front of my chest, I arch a brow. "Full offense, but you can't tell me who I can and can't see."

Callahan crosses to the back of the treadmill and slides up behind me. In the mirrored wall across from us, I watch as he puts his hands just outside of my own and lowers his face to whisper in my ear. "I am your *husband*, and if I say another man isn't allowed to put his hands on you, then I will cleave any hand that does." Shivers roll down my spine, and I meet his gaze in the mirror.

"Besides, if you want to spar, you have me." He grins, but it's almost more like he's baring his teeth. *You have me*, he says. Something in my stomach sours.

When I speak, my words are quiet, and I try to cover the hurt behind glacial indifference. "Don't say things you don't mean." With that, I push out of his cage and leave the gym, resolving to take a walk around the perimeter instead. I could use the fresh air.

Cohen notes my departure, and I can see him groan as he tosses his weights back on the rack and lopes after me.

"I'm staying on property, don't worry. Just going for a walk. You can finish your workout."

He looks me over and must see that I need some space and time alone. Nodding, he backtracks to the weights. The blaring music cuts off when the door slams behind me.

For the next hour, I re-familiarize myself with the landscape of the Keane residence. I've seen most of it from a distance, but it was good to know the gate toward the farthest east wall still exists. Only now, it has a security camera directed toward anyone who'd use it. Warmth spreads in my chest, and I test the handle. It doesn't budge—I hadn't really expected it to—so I look around the brick wall for the clue. After a moment, I see it. One brick is slightly darker than the rest, and I give it a tug. It scrapes around, just barely loose. Pulling harder, I almost fall on my ass when it finally comes out. A smile breaks out, and I shove my hand into the hole.

A key rests exactly as it did eleven years ago, but when I inspect it, it's different. Silver instead of brass. *I wonder when it changed.*

It slots perfectly into the wrought-iron gate, and the handle turns effortlessly. The gate creaks open, and I slip out. It's only minutes until I'm surely caught, so I look for the matching brick on the other side of the wall. Scanning the nearby wall, I locate it.

Cal had devised the system when we were in school. A loose brick on either side so I could lock the gate behind me whether I was coming or going. I'd have to wade through the bushes and use this forgotten gate to sneak in the middle of the night, but at least I got to see Cal. The camera is new, though.

Not wanting to push my luck, I return to the garden and lock the gate behind me, placing the key back in its hiding spot. I return to my room with an emotion I don't want to name swirling in my chest.

All these years, and he left the door open for me. At any point, I could've returned.

I'm not sure what to do with that information.

CHAPTER THIRTEEN

As I finally open my laptop on the balcony of a random guest room, I settle in for a lengthy writing session. I have three drinks with me: my hydro filled with ice water, a can of diet coke, and an iced coffee. I light a honeycrisp apple candle and crack each knuckle on my fingers twice.

A little over eight months ago, Andy's lawyer reached out to the publishing house I'm contracted with, and after a few rounds of interviewing, he selected me as his ghostwriter. It's an opportunity I can't waste, so the final manuscript has to be perfect.

Thankfully, the words I'd been struggling to find are suddenly unlocked, and I finish the final chapter of Andy's book within an hour or so. I hit save, and move to the afterword. This was a more difficult project because Andy's voice is so different from my own. I'm used to writing fiction and romance, and while Andy's love for his late wife could truly rival a modern-day love story, finding the right time to blend his adages with business had been more difficult than I'd originally thought.

As I sit on the breezy balcony, re-reading the highlights of the last few chapters, I realize how I want to write the afterword. My notebook sits open on the table next to me, and I flip through it, looking for the letter that Andy's wife wrote him just a week before her sudden passing. He said it wasn't uncommon for them to write love notes to each other— it was something their counselor had suggested—but this one stood out to him. When she died, he clung to it like a lifeline. It was an adage about love and life, but I can't remember her exact words.

After frantically searching, I realize I don't have the copy. That's strange. I turn inside and head to my room to check my purse. But it's not there. Tipping my face to the ceiling, I try not to scream. I know it's just a copy that Andy gave me, but I shouldn't have been so careless with it. Thinking back to six months ago when he gave it to me, I remember—I left it in my desk at home.

I grab my phone and dial Alice.

"Hey, babe." Her voice is cheery.

My heart squeezes. I miss her. "Hey, hun. I left a letter on my desk in my office and need a copy. Can you take a pic of it and text it to me?"

"Sure, but I'm at the school right now. Can you wait an hour?"

School? It's Sunday. Why was she at school on a Sunday? I try not to groan, but I know I'm inconveniencing her. I could go myself, but it would take forty minutes round trip. Delayed gratification was never my strong suit.

A laugh chimes through the phone. "Sorry, I forgot who I was speaking to. I guess I can wrap up early. I'm getting pretty hungry, anyway."

"*Thanksyou'rethebestIloveyou.*" My words run together, and Alice chuckles, hanging up the phone without further preamble.

Now off to kill a half hour.

I opt to take a quick shower, washing my hair and blow-drying it straight. When I've finished with my skincare, I glance at my phone and frown.

It's been almost an hour.

I dial Alice again. It rings for a minute before I get her voicemail.

"Hi, you've reached Alice. Leave a message at the beep, but remember, if you don't have anything nice to say, don't say it at all."

"Hey, hun. Did you make it home yet? Call me."

Another ten minutes go by, and I can't stop my knee from bouncing. Alice always calls me back within minutes, or at least texts me she'll call me later. I check my phone again. Nothing.

I dial her again. It rings and rings, droning in my ear as something nefarious swirls in my chest. Again, I get her voicemail.

"Hi, you've reached Alice—" I hang up.

Slipping into my slides, I grab my keys and head toward the garage. Something is wrong. I can feel it in my gut.

The walls blur past as I hurry downstairs, only stopping when a hand grips my elbow. A breath whooshes out of my chest, and I try to yank my arm out of the grip, but it doesn't budge.

"Where are you in a rush to?" Cal's voice is laced with misguided anger, but his deep brown eyes dart between mine as if searching for a lie.

"I need to go home. Something's wrong."

His brows furrow together. "Home? You are home."

An exacerbated sigh escapes me. "No, I need to go *home*. Alice was supposed to send me something, but she didn't, and now it's been an hour, and she's not answering her phone." Panic swells in my chest as I say it out loud. What if—

Hands cup my cheeks and tilt my face upward. His touch derails my panic, but doesn't dismiss it. Brown eyes flick between mine. He nods. "Alright. Let's go."

I don't even question it, just turn and continue my path to the garage. Cal is close on my heels, silent as he slides into the driver's seat. When the engine turns over, I focus on the rumbling beneath my seat instead of the worst possible outcome.

What are the chances something bad actually happened?

Considering the threats on my life lately?

Shit.

No, she's probably fine. She probably got sidetracked at school, as she often does, and is now stuck in traffic.

Traffic at five p.m. on a Sunday?

My fingers curl into the armrest, leaving behind crescent moons from the tips of my almond manicure. I turn my face to the passing trees and buildings. They blur together as we drive the twenty minutes to my complex, and I let my mind wander anywhere except toward Alice.

A few minutes later, Callahan pulls up to my condo. Before the car is fully parked, I hop out and rush to the front door. Cal is right behind me, a sharp warning thrown at my back. I ignore it. When we reach the porch, he falls silent. My stomach sinks, bile rising in my throat. The doorframe is cracked. It looks like it was kicked in.

"Stay here," Cal instructs, sliding his pistol out from his side holster. He enters my condo with precision and sweeps the first room, disappearing from sight.

My heart thumps against my ribs as my imagination runs wild. Was Alice here when the break in happened? My nerves frazzle, and I wait as long as I can—about ninety seconds—before I follow inside. With a gentle push on my door, I listen for any signs of someone besides Cal. The house is silent, so I creep inside. My blood runs cold, a chilling dread seizing me as I take in the scene unfolding before me.

Fluff is scattered around my shredded couch, and the cushions are tossed all over. Glass crunches underfoot, and I look down. A broken picture frame lays abandoned. I reach a trembling hand to pick it up. The wooden frame is empty, but it used to have a picture of Alice and me.

As I carry the frame farther into my condo, a knot lodges in my throat. Cabinets in the kitchen barely hang on by their hinges, dishes shattered on the floor, clothes strewn all over…It's a mess, and the intrusion tugs on old wounds, tearing them open and forcing me to bear witness to them all over again.

With each broken item, reality begins to set in. And Alice still hasn't called me back.

Cal comes into the living space and holsters his weapon. Immediately upon seeing me, his mood changes, and he marches right up to me. "I thought I told you to stay *outside*."

My panic makes it impossible to mince my words. "Clearly they aren't here anymore."

"You didn't know that when you came inside, though, did you?" He crosses his arms in front of his chest, and his jaw grinds.

I wave him off and turn toward my room. "Is it like this everywhere?"

Cal doesn't answer, so I glance at him, but he won't meet my gaze.

"I'll take that as a yes." I trudge forward, pushing into the hall and heading toward my room. It's as if I'm stuck in a nightmare, where the hallway gets longer and longer the farther I travel. Prickles break out over my skin.

Pushing the broken door to my room open, I survey the damage, numb. If the living room was bad, this looks like a tornado crashed through it. The corner of my bed frame is broken, and my lopsided bed lies on the floor, the mattress partially slid off. My clothes are ripped and thrown all over, my shoes broken in half. Holes are punched in the wall, and the arched window above my dresser is cracked, letting in a chilly draft.

Even worse, the shoebox of memories I'd left on top of my dresser is nowhere to be seen. The only pictures of my once complete family are gone. Cal's letter is *gone*. The letter I spent years obsessing over. I told myself I didn't care, it didn't matter. *But it does. It did.* And now I'll never know what it said. It tugs at a deep ache in my soul.

I'm stuck, frozen in my spot. Each hole in the wall, each strip of ripped fabric, stings as the violation settles into my bones.

Callahan silently approaches, hands stuffed in his pockets. For once, it seems he doesn't know what to say. Doesn't have a quippy remark. The silence stretches for several seconds before I find the strength to move.

I turn, heading toward my office. A gracious numb swathes my senses, and I feel like I'm floating outside my body. My desk is torn apart, and papers are scattered everywhere. The letter Andy entrusted me with is gone, but that's the least of my worries right now. Broken pieces of my life crunch under each step toward the desk, and my hands tremble. Written in scribbled handwriting on a blank piece of paper lies a message.

Her blood is on your hands. It should've been you, Bunny.

CHAPTER FOURTEEN

Scattered drops of blood pool in the middle of the page, as if the person writing had been bleeding. Bile burns the back of my throat. Denial cloys me like a suffocating blanket, and I pull out my cell to dial Alice. The phone rings in my ear, and in the distance, the lilting tune of "Hey, Soul Sister" by Train begins to play. I follow the ringtone, dread weighing down each step.

It leads me back to my room. *"Hi, you've reached Alice—"* I hang up, dialing her again.

The ringtone starts back up, but it sounds muffled, almost as if it's buried under something. I rifle through my shredded duvet, and I find it just as the ringtone ends.

Horror widens my eyes as I reach a trembling hand toward her cell. Dried blood cakes the corner. I straighten, but my eyes lock onto a pair of underwear also covered in blood. They're not mine, either.

Bile floods my mouth, and I can't help the vomit that follows. Cal finds me on all fours and coughing, eyes burning with tears. He strokes a hand down my spine, and my heart thud in my ears.

After a minute, I suck in a sharp breath and stand, looking away from the broken bed and bloody underwear.

Cal breaks the tense silence. "We'll find her. And we can have a crew here in an hour. They'll clean this place up in a few days. Don't worry." His hand tentatively presses against my shoulder, and I explode, channeling the crushing grief into rage. Blistering, misplaced fury.

"Don't worry?" I scoff, my heart racing. "My best friend has been raped and abducted. Do you think I give a flying *fuck* about my house?" My words fly like knives, and I watch with bittersweet pleasure as they land.

Cal remains silent, taking my vitriol on the chin. But a moment later, the misplaced anger shifts into a curious blend of guilt and shame that swirls in my chest. My cheeks flood with heat and embarrassment, and I drop my gaze, unable to voice my conflicted emotions.

As I'm staring at my feet, Cal's phone rings from his pocket. He fishes it out and doesn't even glance at the caller ID before answering. Muffled voices filter through, but I can't make out any words.

All I can see is the myriad of emotions that flicker over Cal's face. Rage, frustration, annoyance…glee. A spark of manic elation storms behind his brown eyes.

"Where did you find him?"

Cal is quiet as he listens, a pinch forming between his brow. "And he was carrying her over her shoulder? Did you get her to the hospital?" Muffled voices respond, and Cal nods along with whatever they're saying. Hope blooms in my chest, praying it's news about Alice.

"He had the same tattoo?" Cal's gaze slices to me. "We'll be there in ten," he says, voice gruff and sending an icy chill down my spine. Then he hangs up and stalks out of my room. "We have to go."

"Was it Alice? Did they find her?" I scramble over my broken belongings and chase after him. The ruined condo blurs in my periphery as I try not to look at it. I wonder if I should worry about my door, but immediately dismiss the thought. There isn't anything of value in here. Not anymore.

Cal pauses at the driver's door, looking over the hood at me. "Does Alice have black hair?"

Crushing despair chokes the breath from my lungs, and I shake my head. We load into the car, and the rubber tires squeal as we exit my complex.

If I couldn't see just how concentrated he was, I'd probably be terrified for my life. As it stands, Cal's eyes never leave the road, and his knuckles grip the steering wheel so tightly they turn white.

"Where are we going?"

Cal ignores me, or perhaps he doesn't hear me. His jaw ticks, and his grip adjusts on the wheel as he presses the accelerator further.

"*Cal*," I try again.

Finally, he looks over to me. His eyes soften the briefest fraction.

"Everett and Graves found one of the kidnappers. He had a woman knocked out over his shoulders, who he was carrying in broad daylight. He had the same tattoo on his wrist."

His words explode like a bomb, settling in my stomach like rocks.

We speak at the same time. "Ho—"

"They've taken him back to the house to interrogate."

That quiets me. They're going to…interrogate him?

"And by interrogate, you mean…" I trail off, waiting for him to say it out loud.

Cal doesn't answer, just presses his foot further on the gas.

Torture. They're going to torture him.

Good.

Eleven minutes later, we arrive back to the Keane residence. Cal's barely turned the car off before he rushes into the house. I follow, barely catching the door as it slams in my face.

"Cal, wait!"

He doesn't. He tracks on, twisting through the Keane residence with me on his heels. When we reach an area I've never been to before, he finally stops. I almost slam straight into his back.

"Loren, leave. Go to your room. You're not permitted to see this."

"Not *permitted?* Who are you—"

In the next breath, he whirls around, hands gripping my upper arms as he stares into my soul. Something akin to panic flashes behind his eyes, and it stills me.

"Ren," he whispers, a broken plea for me to listen, "please. Not now. I can't deal with you, too."

That hits me like a truck.

"*Deal* with me? Am I something to be dealt with, Callahan?"

He doesn't respond. Instead, he glances down to the floor.

I see.

"Fine. I'll get out of your hair. God forbid I offer to help."

Callahan hardens, his shoulders turning rigid. "As if this is something I'd ever want your help with," he spits. "Now *go.*" He doesn't wait for me to respond. He slips inside without another word.

I catch a glimpse of the space, and there's not much to it. A cramped concrete room that's brightly lit and empty. Other than the man strapped to a metal chair in the dead center of the grim room.

The door slams with finality, and I fight not to flinch. My eyes drift down the hallway, noting three other industrial metal doors, and a chill shivers down my spine. They're each numbered, and the one Cal disappeared behind is labeled as *one*. Frozen, I stand, trying to make myself leave when I finally realize: I don't want to leave. Who the hell is he to think I'm not useful? Sure, I haven't tortured anyone before, but I'm not morally opposed to it, especially if it's a life or death situation. And with Mason missing and Alice abducted, likely by someone who this captive could lead us to? Yeah, I'd hand over the crowbar.

My mind is made up. I'm not leaving. Not yet, at least.

When the screams start, my fingers curl into fists. When the crying starts, I hold the memory of Alice's bloody underwear in the front of my mind. When the prisoner finally cracks, I press my ear so tightly against the door it could leave an imprint.

His words are muffled, but I can hear him well enough.

"What's your tattoo mean?" Cal asks.

There's no response. A muffled blow lands.

Cal asks again, "What's the tattoo?"

The man groans, and another hit lands. Finally, he answers. "The Disciples."

Disciples? That's creepy as fuck.

"Why are you here?" someone asks calmly. I think it's Everett.

Another blow lands, and a muffled grunt follows.

"Don't make me ask again."

The threat lined in his words sends shivers down my spine. I press my ear tighter to the door and hope I can hear his answer over the pounding of my heart.

"There's a…a new partnership in town." That's all he says. Another blow lands.

This time, it's Cohen who speaks. "What partnership?"

"All I know is I'm supposed to pick up"—he spits—"girls and take 'em to a drop off spot. That's all. I don't talk to anyone else."

Silence falls.

Drop them off? My heart sinks, and I know in my gut they're not being let go. No, they're being sentenced to a far worse fate. The knowledge chills my blood, and my palms grow slick against the door, but I squeeze my eyes shut in hopes I can hear better.

"What about the fires?"

"Fires? I don't know anything about any fires."

Another blow lands, and the man cries out. "I swear, all I'm s'posed to do is get the girls. I don't know anything about any fires!"

It's quiet for a few moments. They must be deliberating. Then I think it's Cal who speaks. It's difficult to tell through the door.

"Where are you getting them? The girls?"

The man doesn't answer. Blow after blow rains down until his cries fill the room. Then he grunts, and grunts again.

"*Where?*" Cal growls. Either their torture works, or the man has no more fight.

He sighs, a wet, shaky sigh that sounds like a broken man. "Abstrakt. And some other clubs to make sure we fly under the radar."

Abstrakt? A shiver rolls down my spine as Hudson's warning that night I went into the exclusive lounge flashes to the front of my mind. What had he said? Something about not wanting to see my face on the missing posters. Does he know something about this?

"And where do you take them? The women?"

There's no answer, just heavy breaths and a strike. The Disciple hisses and swears but still refuses to answer. Another blow, another cry, another scream, before he finally relents.

"Fuck, it's different every time," he cries. "Sometimes it's a motel, or a warehouse, but I get a text to my burner with the address, and I have to deliver them by midnight. After that, I do it again the next night at a different club."

The room goes quiet, and I press my ear harder against the door, trying to pick up on anything that I can.

"You're not gonna find anything on it. We delete everything right after we receive it."

I can only presume they frisked him for his phone.

Then, Everett speaks. *"Who do you report to?"*

His voice sounds distant, as if he's farther in the room, possibly behind the Disciple. It's a terrifying tactic to interrogate from behind where they can't see you, can't predict what you're about to do.

"I asked, who do you report to?" Everett repeats, but his words are steeped in rage and impatience. Another blow lands, and the Disciple curses.

When he speaks, his voice is tattered, almost in weary acceptance that he won't be leaving this room alive. "The Apostles," he finally groans. "They tag the targets and signal them to us. We sprinkle a little something in their drinks and deliver them as asked. The Apostles send an address to our cells. For each woman, we get five-hundred bucks, and with enough overall, we can become an Apostle. We are their loyal Disciples, but I don't know anything more. We aren't told anything else."

My stomach sours with the weight of that information. So many women being taken, never to be seen again. I fight the urge to gag.

"How many of there are you?" Callahan asks, just as my hands begin to tremble.

"I don't know exactly. They spread us out, and we're not s'posed to reveal our identity to anyone."

There's a tense silence. When the man screams, it twists into a gargle.

"Fuck, Cal, why did you kill him? We could've—"

Cal cuts him off. "He didn't know anything else. He'd be a waste of resources and time to keep him alive."

I take several shaking steps backward. Then I turn and run, but have to stop short, almost smacking right into one of the maids, Tinley. Her eyes widen into saucers as apologies fly from her lips. She carries a tray of food. It's curious, but I don't have time to question it—or her.

"Tinley, hi," I start, breathless and frantically looking back toward the torture room. "I'm headed to bed. Please tell Mr. Keane I don't want to be disturbed."

Tinley's brows pinch together only the slightest touch, but she dips her chin in concession. I skirt around her, flying back to my room as I try to put together the pieces of my plan.

Cal doesn't think I'm very useful? I lived my entire childhood in the Bianchi estate. My father was the right hand to one of the most dangerous men in the past few decades. Although he was undoubtedly disappointed I wasn't a boy, he still brought his work home and sat me on his lap to teach me the business.

When he died, I vowed to forget all the lessons he forced upon me, only to be visited in my world of fiction. But perhaps…perhaps, it's time I remember.

CHAPTER FIFTEEN

B efore the clock strikes ten in the evening, I've dressed in the tightest dress I could find in my closest. It's dark red with tiny straps and falls just over my ass. I've smoked out my eyes with black shadow and a deep maroon lipstick paints my lips into a sultry smile. After adjusting the necklace Cal gave me, I add a new pair of small hoops and put on a pair of slides. I have no desire to sneak around this house in heels. I'm fairly certain I'd be caught immediately.

Against the dimmed lights, my ring sparkles, drawing my attention to the enormous diamond. *Well, that won't do.* Ignoring the confusing swirl of guilt that stabs me when I slide the ring off, I place it on the bathroom counter. Instantly, my hand feels lighter, and a frown tugs at my mouth.

Keep going.

I grab a pair of heels, throw on an oversized hoodie, and pray I don't run into anyone on my way out. Thankfully, the house is quiet as its residents wind down for the evening. I creep through the shadows of the Keane residence to the back gate, unlock it with my spare key, and slip away. Once I'm about twenty minutes away from the house, I finally dare to call a car.

Then it takes another fifteen to get to Abstrakt. When the car slows in front of the dark alleyway, I suck in a sharp breath.

"You sure this is it?" the driver asks, trepidation clear in his tone.

I look around, and all I see is stained concrete, a few broken bottles, and soiled newspapers. But what sticks out the most is the couple dressed way too nicely sauntering toward a rusted metal door: the aforementioned Park Avenue entrance to Abstrakt.

"Yep." I slip off my hoodie and slides, stepping into my heels and pretending to forget the rest as I exit the car. The door slams shut. Without skipping a beat, the driver takes off. I follow the couple closely and see for myself how the upper echelon enters Abstrakt. Clicking the wristband on, I can only pray it hasn't been deactivated.

Down the stairway, the walls change from concrete to partially painted, and Abstrakt's decor bleeds through. A gold sconce here, a gilded frame there. The dark green paint appears in choppy sections, as if the painters never finished the hallway, but in strategic blocks. It's strange to not blend the decor seamlessly, almost as if they want you to acknowledge you're entering the new space.

The couple in front of me holds on to each other tightly, chattering between themselves as we descend. When we reach the bottom of the stairs, one taps their bracelet on a diamond panel on the wall and waits for it to turn green. It chimes, and then the woman opens the door and shuts it behind her. Her partner follows suit. Again, I pray that the bracelet still works.

My heart beats wildly as I approach the panel, and when I hold the wristband against the metal plate, an anxious buzz frazzles under my skin. A second later, it chimes, and the light turns green. I enter Abstrakt with a relieved sigh.

It's as I remember, debauchery running wild as drink flows steadily. This time, a group of three performs on the platform, with a man thrusting sharply into his female partner. Another woman lays on her back below them, licking the woman on top while she reciprocates. Their moans ring out, and the slap of his body against hers is rhythmic and mesmerizing.

Turning from the erotic scene, I resolve to get what I need. Cal has his tactics, and I have mine. And while women are going missing from Abstrakt, it's likely from the main floor, so I don't believe I have to worry about that here. *I think.*

As I step farther into the room, hope crackles in my chest. Many are here tonight, and I'm sure I'll find something of use.

I head to the bar. Only a few wait before me, and my fingers tap along the epoxy as I tune my ears to nearby conversations. Within minutes, I quickly realize Abstrakt is a goldmine for information, where one man's gossip is another man's blackmail. I was so focused on finding Callahan last time that I didn't even realize just how safe its patrons feel to speak freely. My fingers itch to take down anything of interest, but so far, there isn't anything about the Disciples or the missing women.

I order my whiskey and float around the room. It's busy, so I do what any pretty woman would do, and slide into conversations with a simple laugh at a man's joke before twisting the conversation into where I need it to go. When I don't find anything, I move on.

Until—

"Oi, you just be glad you've been given this chance. Not many get the opportunity to impress the Prophet himself. Don't fuck it up."

My ears prick up, and I drift closer to the conversation, pretending to join the one next to theirs. I perch on the arm of a sofa with my back toward the group and plaster a welcoming smile to my face, nodding along to the conversation in front of me.

"I know. I'm not gonna fuck it up, mate. I want this as much as you. It's been too long we've been overlooked." A *ting* chimes, as if they clinked their glasses together.

"But not anymore."

"Not anymore."

My lips curl into a triumphant smile. It's time I kick it up a notch. Twisting in my seat, I catch a glimpse of the dagger tattoo on one of their wrists. Disciples. But these two didn't exactly seem like they were out snatching women. Perhaps Apostles, then?

"Have you wrangled your lot?" one asks.

I take a sip of my whiskey. Perhaps I spoke too soon.

"Got a few last minute additions, but should be ready for Friday."

Friday? That's only five days from now.

"I'm three short. Trying to get a few more tonight, but we'll see. Otherwise, I'll have to go hunting myself and drive them directly to the port. I'd much rather give a few of the girls a test drive instead."

"I hear ya." His voice is slimy, and it unnerves me how it seems to coat my senses. "I tried one sluts out last night and"—he lets out a long breath—"I'd bet money she was a virgin."

My blood boils, and I fight to keep my rage from spilling onto my face. These guys deserve to be in Cal's concrete room and never leave. At least not breathing.

Alice and Mason's faces materialize in front of me like ghosts, and I stuff my nerves down until the tightness in my throat eases. Throwing the last of my drink back, I plaster on an amiable smile and droopy eyelids, slouching over further in my seat. My arm dangles out, and I toy with the empty glass in my hand. Then I stand and stumble, cursing under my breath as I catch myself.

One man I stood beside tries to catch me, but I spin away, toward the Disciples. I stumble a few steps forward and watch my targets line up in my periphery. One stands, immediately putting an arm around my waist. I have to suppress the knee-jerk reaction to throw him off.

"Well, *hello there*, miss," he drawls, a playful squeeze to my waist. His smile stretches across his face but doesn't reach his eyes. Oily black hair slicked back, combined with a too-large suit and a gold hoop through one of his ears. His bloodshot eyes droop and scan my body while he licks his lips. "I'm Roy. Care for a drink?"

It's a chore, but I remember my game and nod vigorously, covering a coy laugh behind my hand. "Why, yes, Sir Roy. How'd you know I needed one?" For some reason, I've picked up a bit of a southern accent, but I roll with it.

Roy's eyes spark, and he starts to lead me to the bar. Instead, I whirl out of his arms and let myself fall onto the lap of the other Disciple. Laughter peels from my lips, and I playfully swat at the man's chest.

"Oh, I'm sorry"—I hiccup—"I seem to have lost my footing."

The Disciple's hand slides across my waist and holds me to him.

"David, let her up so we can get a drink." Roy's words bite, and he extends an impatient arm to help me up.

I playfully push it away. "I'm pretty comfy here. But will you get me

146

a glass of champagne? We're celebrating tonight, boys."

"How's that?" David's eyes light with unnerving glee as he shifts me on top of him. *Gross. Maybe I didn't think this through.* "What are you celebrating tonight?"

I let loose a flirty sigh. "Don't you mean, what are *we* celebrating tonight?"

Roy chuckles and raises a brow. His greasy face shines against the dim light, and his voice rumbles out of his thin chest. "And what are we celebrating tonight?"

I mockingly groan, as if they should already know. Roy steps closer, and when a hard length pushes against my hip, I roll out of David's grip to sit next to him on the couch instead.

"Well, I just got gifted a membership here, and you guys…" I trail off, but they don't seem to catch on. "Aw, something good must've happened for you guys, too. Come on, don't be shy!"

Roy smiles brightly as he looks to David and then back to me. "Well, now that you mention it, we're about to be partners in a *very* lucrative business."

I gasp and clap my hands wildly, as if truly unable to contain my excitement for them. "You guys must be really smart then, huh?"

The compliment only further inflates their confidence and loosens their lips. *God, and it was so juvenile, too.* David shrugs, and I lean forward, listening intently. He smirks, settling against the couch and taking the last gulp of his drink. Then he smacks his lips, and an insidious gleam shines through his bloodshot eyes.

"You could say that, little lady."

Little lady? Gag.

He smiles, but it seems more like he's baring his teeth than emoting any sort of happy emotion. "We've recently partnered with a shipping company, and now we get to take our wares worldwide."

"Worldwide," Roy reiterates with a matching smile. They look to each other, and then turn their pointed attention back to me. "Now, how about that drink?"

Chills erupt down my spine while my heart thuds. You couldn't pay me to drink anything these men might give me.

"Let me just use the little girl's room first," I say with a tight smile. When I stand, I feel David's evil stare slither down my backside. "Be right back."

I turn and have to freeze or otherwise run into a familiar stature. Leon's dark gaze narrows as he looks me over. He looks a little worse for wear, dark scruff covering his jaw and purple shadows underneath his eyes. He wears a black shirt, sleeves rolled to his elbows and tucked into dark charcoal slacks. His tan skin looks paler than usual, but it could be because winter's blocking out the sun. He's young, only a half a year younger than Mason, but tonight, he looks years older than twenty-one.

His eyes soften, and when he speaks, it's almost as if he's seeing a ghost. "Loren."

My name sounds wrong falling from his lips, and I offer a weak smile. "Hey, Leon. Have you heard from Mason?"

My words seem to shake him, and he visibly shutters. "What the fuck are you doing in a place like this?" Anger rattles out of his chest, and his face flushes. He pointedly ignores my question.

Instantly, I'm on guard. My eyes narrow, nostrils flaring. "And why wouldn't I be allowed in a place like this?" I bring my wrist in front of me to flash my wristband. "Seems you're wrong."

Leon's jaw clenches, and a fierce grip freezes my hand in front of him. He brings it closer to inspect, and he inhales sharply. Rocks settle in my belly like stones in a riverbed. I try to wrench my hand out of his hold, but he tightens his grip.

In my periphery, Roy and David stand and move to leave. Roy raises his hands in defeat and says, "Sorry, man. Didn't know she was yours." Then, they're gone.

"I'm not." My words slice out, and Leon flinches. What the fuck is his problem?

"You could've been."

I freeze, and all sound outside our bubble deafens. Leon watches my reaction with thinly veiled humor sparkling in his dark eyes.

"If I knew you were going to run off and marry the first guy who promised to help you find your brother, I would've told you I could help."

My eyes widen. He'd practically slammed the door in my face when I went to him for help all those weeks ago.

"But now"—he steps closer into my space and lowers his voice— "you are the enemy. And your husband's latest partnership only solidifies that."

My eyes flicker between his, and I can tell he believes every word he says.

"Hudson—"

Leon cuts me off. "Hudson isn't privy to the sort of information I have access to." His words are sharp, and the heat of his anger is blistering. "I thought you wanted to find Mason."

My eyes narrow. "Of course I want to find Mason."

Leon smirks, and his hold on my wrist slides up to rest on the nape of my neck. With a light squeeze, he leans closer. "Let me help you." His words are sickly sweet and coated in double meaning.

I open my mouth to respond, but I'm cut off by a gruff voice standing next to us.

"Get your hands off my wife."

CHAPTER SIXTEEN

L eon's gaze cuts to Callahan and narrows, but after a moment, he does as Cal asks. In the next breath, Cal has wrapped an arm around my waist, and he tugs me to his chest. The heat of his palm pressing against my hip is possessive and intoxicating and stirs a need I thought I was long rid of.

"Callahan Keane," Leon grinds out. "Your *wife*"—his gaze darts over to me and lingers—"seems to have found herself a membership. It was simply a lucky coincidence I found myself with her here tonight. Who knows what could've happened if she was left to her own devices? As I'm sure you must be aware, controlling Loren Catrone isn't an easy feat." He pulls a cigar from his jacket and bites it between his teeth around a smile.

"You must not know Mrs. Keane as I do, Mr. Bianchi. She's particularly...*agreeable*"—he brushes a feather-light touch over the crown of my head—"if given the right motivation."

I grind my jaw shut and jerk my head from his petting. He simply returns his hand to my waist and tugs me closer.

"Now if you'll excuse us."

Leon's nostrils flare, and then he clears the sour look from his face. He grabs the cigar and waves it in dismissal. "Always a pleasure, Keane."

Cal doesn't look back as he tugs me away. "Wish I could say the same, Spare."

I steal a glance backward, and Leon's face reddens with Cal's insult. He's always been particularly bitter about the fact he was born second, but apparently, he grew out of it a few years ago, settling into his role as right hand to his older brother. Though young, the Bianchi household trains their men from the time they learn how to walk.

Cal's grip tightens as he pulls me to the exit. His icy demeanor practically burns, and I struggle to keep up with his quickened pace in my heels.

When we exit the lounge, we're alone in the stairwell and begin the ascent to street level. Our steps echo as the silence simmers, but in the next breath, Cal presses me against the wall. The concrete is cold against my back, but not as glacier as Callahan's gaze. He pins me to the wall with a hand on either side of my face, leaning close until we share the same breath. His shadowed eyes flick between mine, darting over the rest of my face before he finally speaks.

"*What* the fuck were you thinking?" he growls.

My wrath rises to match his, and I straighten against the wall. Cal shifts closer until our lips are mere breaths away. His sandalwood cologne washes over me and I suck in a breath. Cal jolts like I electrocuted him, recoiling away. The movement shocks me back into my fury.

"What the fuck was I thinking? That I might get some fucking information you clearly weren't able to. I thought I might find where they took Alice. And guess what? I did."

Cal inhales sharply, and he looks away. "How did you know?"

I roll my eyes. "Know what, Cal? Be a little more clear, would you?"

He rips away from me and scrubs his jaw with a bandaged hand. Dots of blood seep over his knuckles, and I reach a trembling hand out to touch it, but then remember myself. I pull my hand back and curl it into a fist.

It does the opposite, and his eyes zero in on my left hand. I curl it into a fist, but not before he grabs it. His eyes narrow with obvious fury.

"Where the fuck is your ring, Loren?"

A chill shivers down my spine. I straighten, refusing to cower beneath his intoxicating rage. "At home. It wasn't conducive to my plan to advertise that I'm married."

Callahan stills. Abstrakt's music pounds through the door and a single light flickers in the stairwell. It's ominous, but not nearly as dangerous as the man in front of me. Cal crowds my space, slipping a hand to grasp my chin.

"Don't ever take off my ring again. You are *mine*. Whether you like it or not."

A churning heat thrums low in my belly. His possessive demeanor is confusingly attractive. But I can't let him know that. As if he has no idea of my internal war, he continues with his barrage of questions. "How did you know to come to Abstrakt?"

The question draws to light information I'd rather stay hidden. He knows I listened.

I raise my chin a fraction and stare down my nose at the man huffing in front of me. Tense shoulders rise and fall with each choppy breath, and shadows eclipse his face.

"*How did you know?*" he shouts. His rage echoes in the empty stairwell and shakes my defenses.

I narrow my eyes and cross my arms over my chest. "I never vowed to be obedient."

Callahan curses under his breath. An unyielding finger presses beneath my chin, forcing me to look up at him. Storms brew behind his brown eyes.

"Must I shackle you to my arm so you don't run off unprotected again?" The threat washes over me, but I see nothing but cold promises in his stare.

I don't respond, refusing to give his tantrum further fuel. His gaze dips to my lips and returns to mine once again. He releases a deep sigh. "If that's what it takes."

With that, he drops a hand to my arm and tugs me up the stairs. We exit into the quiet night. Across the street, Cohen leans against a black SUV. I do my best to ignore Callahan as he opens the door and practically shoves me in.

Then Cal reaches over my body, trying to buckle my seatbelt for me, but I swat his hand away. He arches a brow but shuts the door and rounds the back to enter on the other side. With a practiced ease, Cohen slides into the driver's seat, adjusts the mirrors, and then smoothly starts the engine, a low hum vibrating through the car.

Cal types furiously on his phone. I tune him out, choosing to lean my forehead against the cool glass. The city lights blur as we speed back to the residence, not a sound in the car other than the thrum of the engine.

When we finally reach the garage, he hops out and opens my door. But not for any obvious, chivalrous reason. No, instead he places a firm hand on my lower back and guides me to my room.

"I'm quite capable of finding my way to my room, but thank you for the chaperone," I say with a roll of my eyes.

Cal just grunts and continues to push me down the hallway. But when I go to open my door, he tugs me further. Toward his room.

"Cal, what are you doing?"

He doesn't answer. Instead, he opens the door and gently prods me inside. With a quiet *click*, I'm shut in his room with him. I spare a glance and note it's set up similarly to mine, though much larger. Instead of a couch and sitting area, there's a desk and office chairs in front of the fireplace. Like mine, there's a bar cart in the corner—though unlike mine, it's clearly in need of a restock.

A door on the right is open and looks to lead to his bedroom, but I turn on my heel and glare at the man in question. He ignores me, flipping the lock on his door and prowling toward me. I straighten, raising my chin and a singular brow, but he just huffs a laugh and passes me, heading straight for the bar cart.

He pours himself a generous glass of whiskey and rounds the desk, perching on the edge as he stares at me from over his tumbler.

"Cal, why am I in here?"

He smacks his lips and swirls the amber liquid in his glass. A gentle breeze from a cracked window chills me, and my nipples harden under my dress. His eyes draw straight to them, and he takes another sip.

Finally, he speaks. "You said you found where they took Alice."

With cautious hesitation, I nod once. My gaze never leaves his.

Cal places his glass on the desk and rolls his sleeves to his elbows. Muscles ripple with each twist. I find my gaze drawn to the tendons on his wrist.

Cal notices where my eyes have fallen and smirks, crossing his arms and raising a brow. "Then where is she?"

My lips curl into a coy smile. Tilting my head, I leisurely take three steps toward the brooding man. "Now you're suddenly interested in my intel?"

Callahan remains silent. I pick up his glass and take a small sip, relishing the warmth as it travels down to my belly. Heat gathers low and unavoidable as I breathe in his sandalwood cologne and masculine shampoo. Cal's nostrils flare as I lean closer.

"I thought I wasn't capable?" I ask, circling his desk and putting some much-needed space between us.

Callahan's shoulders stiffen as I drag a nail over his wooden desk, clattering over a fountain pen, humming over his desk pad, crawling up his arm, and finally coming to a rest over his shoulder. He doesn't turn, doesn't move other than the tick in his jaw. His back is warm against my chest, and I press my breasts against his shoulder blades.

"I never said that."

"What else could you have meant?" I prod further. "It was always about how capable I was. Even then, even now."

Cal's head turns toward me, but I slide a hand into his waves and clench, halting his movement and tilting his head up. Bending down, I whisper against the shell of his ear, "You never believed I could handle it. And that's the part I find most insulting."

I straighten abruptly and toss his head away, crossing in front of him once more as I sip from his glass.

"I never thought you weren't capable," he says with a low voice that rumbles from his broad chest. His hair is mused from my contempt, like he just rolled out of bed. *Or rolled into bed. With someone.* The ghost of his wavy locks lingers between my fingers.

I clench my hands and snicker. "Of course you've rewritten history so you're the knight in shining armor."

Flashes of bruises and love bites covering the neck of a whiny blonde bombard me. As if it were yesterday, an image frozen in time, depicting the shock hitting Cal's teenage face like a Mack truck. Then came his words, about how I could never survive as the boss's wife, how I could never truly satisfy his needs, how he'd never sink so low as to marry from such a disposable bloodline. Shivers erupt over my exposed skin. The memory of the pounding rain slices me to the bone. I'd fumbled with my car keys before dropping them into a puddle. The car was still warm, but I didn't feel it. Couldn't focus on anything except watching the streetlights change from red to green.

Cal grinds his jaw and stares at the wooden flooring. Seconds tick by. Emotions I thought were long buried bubble to the surface. While most of me wants him to fight, to maintain this semblance of an arrangement, the other part of me is just so tired. Tired of carrying this grudge. Tired of wishing I could meet someone, *anyone*, who could erase his ever-present claim on my soul.

Cal sighs. When he finally breaks the tense silence, his brown eyes are dull. "I may have said it…but I never meant it. Not a single word."

His words hang in the air between us, and I feel each like a lash. But pretty words wrapped in honey mean nothing when it doesn't change the fact that I caught him in bed with another girl. She was a grade above us in school, and for the rest of the school year, I was forced to see her perfect face and golden hair until she graduated and eventually left. It was death by a thousand cuts—or in this case, a thousand blonde hairs.

My gaze hardens, and the flush of my anger rises over my chest, my neck, all the way to the tips of my ears. Through clenched teeth, I try to speak. "Well, I'll never know if that's the truth, but it doesn't change the fact you slept with Brielle Waylan."

Cal's shoulders drop, and his face contorts with what looks like pain. Good. He opens his mouth to speak, but I throw up a hand.

"I don't want to hear it. The day I walked in on you was the best day of my life. It was a cruel reminder that I don't belong in your world." I step closer, and my hands tremble. "But that never meant I wasn't capable. Just that I shouldn't bother with wasting my love on someone like you."

Callahan grinds his jaw and stands, stepping into my space. I tip my face up, feeling each heavy breath he exhales. A second later, he steps away and stalks to his bedroom. The revived anger coursing through my blood heats as I'm once again dismissed by the man who consumes my every waking thought. I turn on my heel to leave.

Before I can make it to the door, Cal cuts me off and grips the frame, his voice lashing out at me like it did all those years ago. "Where do you think you're going?"

I freeze, my hand on the doorknob. "Anywhere away from you."

I unlock the handle, but when I twist the knob, a bandaged hand slams the door shut. The other brushes against my hip. Through the dress, I can feel the heat of his touch, but it only serves to fan my flames. I do my best to ignore the growing need between my legs.

"I'm going to bed," I say in defeat.

A growl so low I might've thought I'd imagined it rumbles over the shell of my ear, and his strong body presses me into the door. I know he's so close that if I turn my face, our lips would almost touch.

"Then this is probably a bad time to tell you that you've been moved."

My eyes widen, and I whirl around, but Cal gives me no leave. I'm pressed against the door, and Cal drags his bandaged hand to tuck a strand of hair behind my ear, smiling like the cat that got the cream.

"If you're going to sneak out at all hours of the night, then you need to be monitored."

I open my mouth to argue, but he just continues.

"And if you're going to be reckless with your life"—his gaze drops to my lips, then flicks back up to meet mine—"then I'll just have to be your personal guard. To make sure you come home to me in one piece, darling. You understand, of course."

Blood rushes to my cheeks, warming my face. Of course, the asshat would take any excuse to twist me into an obedient little wife. But if that's how he wants to play it…

I smile, and Cal has the decency to be unnerved. He frowns.

"Careful, Callahan. You might just make me think you care."

I duck out of his hold and stroll across the room into his bedroom. It's one of the largest bedrooms I've ever seen. Cal's soft steps follow behind me, and I hide any reaction from my face.

Toward the back of the room, there's a king-sized canopy bed with red velvet curtains tied open. *How entirely pompous.* A couch sits in front of a mounted television that could easily pass for a home theater installment, along with low tables on either end of the couch. To the left, there are French doors leading out to an expansive balcony, one with a much better view than the one I've been working at. Petulant jealousy tugs at me, but I ignore it, choosing to take a guess at one of the two other doors and hope it's his closet.

I open the door, and my mouth parts. It's almost as big as the guest room I've been staying in. Curiously, I note my clothes have already been hung on the right-hand side. I turn on my heel and raise a brow to the man leaning against the doorframe with his hands stuffed in his pockets. He keeps a blank face, but the slightest curl to his lips gives him away.

"So that's who you were texting in the car."

He shrugs. Stepping into the closet, he opens a drawer and pulls out a pair of charcoal sweats. Without a care for his decency, he begins undressing. My cheeks heat, and I spin around. I desperately want to watch, but I can't let him know. Instead, I rifle through the drawer under my hanging clothes. Once again, the top drawer is filled with women's underwear. I can't help a rush of anger, and I slam the drawer shut so hard it rattles.

I move to the next drawer, where I'd found the loungewear in my old room, and sure enough, there are a few sets. I grab the first I see and move to leave the closet, but stop short. Cal is standing with a bemused smirk, his arms crossed, sweats slung dangerously low on his hips. His torso is deliciously bare, but I refuse to give in to my base desires.

"Taking out your rage on my poor dresser, Bunny? That's not very nice."

My cheeks heat, and I know he's enjoying my frustration. "I don't think it's very nice to shove a drawer full of your flavor of the night's panties in my face, but we can't all get what we want, now can we?" With that, I push past him and stride toward the other door a few feet away.

"You don't like the panties I bought you, Bunny?"

Those were—*are*—mine? It stops me in my tracks, and my cheeks flood with heat. I can't believe it. From the gleam in Cal's eyes, he's having the time of his life watching my brain malfunction. With a growl, I stomp away and head into the other door.

Thankfully, it's a bathroom, as expected, and I quickly lock the door behind me. It actually pisses me off even further to see how perfect his bathroom is. A massive claw-foot tub sits in the center of the marble floor, and a separate alcove off to the right holds what is likely a toilet. A dual-headed, waterfall, glass shower takes up a third of the space, with extra jets lining the wall. In the gilded mirror hanging above the Jack-and-Jill sink, I take stock of myself. It feels like it's been ages since I snuck out, but with a quick glance at my phone, it's barely even midnight.

A bone-deep fatigue settles over my shoulders. Deciding I don't want to see Cal again just yet, I turn on the shower and wait for the room to fill with steam. As I step beneath the water, I do my best to banish the sting of betrayal. It's always two steps forward, three steps back with Callahan.

Sure, all these years have passed, and now he says he didn't mean the words he so harshly wielded, but I'll never know the truth. Because no matter what he says now, the only thing I can trust him with is my brother.

The realization is like a punch in the gut, and all I want to do is sleep for ten years. But as life would have it, that's just not an option. Alice is now missing, too, Mason is god knows where…

I pump shampoo into my hand, and this time, it doesn't faze me that Cal has my brand in here, too. I rinse and condition my hair and wash the feel of Roy and David's hands from my body. If I closed my eyes, I could still feel the press of David's erection. A shudder rolls through me.

It was time to get serious.

And it could actually work in my favor that Callahan wants to stick by my side until the person gunning for our lives is caught and my people are found. He won't have the option to toss me off to the side and ignore my badgering, no matter how much he wants to.

Resolution solidifies in my gut, and I step out of the shower with a shifted mindset. By the time I exit the bathroom, Cal is sitting on the bed with his computer on his lap. As if he has no other speed than furious, he types so quickly I can't imagine he's not misspelling every other word. A pair of glasses with a thick black frame perches on the bridge of his nose, giving him a sort of Clark Kent look. Unsurprisingly, I find it rather sexy.

Fuck.

When I approach the bed, I instinctively head to my usual side—opposite of Cal. It stops me in my tracks. Once upon a time, at the lake house during our very first sleepover, we realized we both preferred the right side. We spent almost an hour arguing over who would get to keep 'their' side until we eventually passed out with me rolled on top of him, leaving it as a moot point. The next night, Cal went straight for the left side. When I asked him why he was giving up so easily, all he had to say was how the night before was the best night of sleep he ever had, and if losing his side meant he got to sleep next to me, then so be it.

And tonight—right now—he's on the left side.

Warmth swirls in my belly, but I pay it no mind. Instead, I pull back the covers and slide into the softest bed I've ever lain on. On the bedside table lays my ring. I slip it on and do my best to ignore the man typing away. I plug my phone in on the bedside table, then wrap the comforter around my shoulders. Without speaking, Cal switches off the lights and lowers the brightness of his laptop. As I drift off, all I can notice is how quietly he seems to type.

CHAPTER SEVENTEEN

The next morning, I wake to a hard body pressed against me. The bed is warm, and I snuggle deeper into the soft blankets, only to feel an equally hard length nestled against my ass. My eyes fly open, and my breathing quickens.

Sunlight streams into the room through the French doors, and I squint, the harsh morning light too bright. An arm around my waist squeezes, and a face nuzzles my neck and inhales deeply, a soft moan sending a zap straight between my legs.

Blaming the momentary lapse in judgment on the fact that I'm practically still asleep, I allow myself this reprieve and wish, for a moment, that this could be my life. In a heartbeat, a future I thought long dead flashes in my mind. I see smiles worn easily, banter thrown without second thought, first—and last—kisses. I see it all.

One night, we cuddled—not unlike we are now—beneath the duvet of his bed, trying to keep quiet so his father wouldn't catch me in their house. But he just kept tickling my ribs, teasing my body. His eyes were brighter than the stars in the sky, twinkling as he rolled me below him. He pulled the duvet over our shoulders, and he looked down at me with such unadulterated joy.

I love you, I'd whispered against his lips.

The memory dissipates as Cal's wandering hand freezes, and his body stiffens. A deep sadness burrows into me, and I close my eyes, pretending to still be asleep. Cal's breathing hitches as he slowly extracts his body from mine. He curses under his breath when he rolls away. But I lie still, pretending not to have felt his body pressed against mine, pretending not to have tasted a slice of my deepest desire.

I must do a good job. The bed dips, and his soft footsteps pad away until a door opens and shuts quietly. The shower turns on, and I exhale deeply, throwing my arms out of the comforter.

For a few minutes, I let myself lie there with an empty hollow in my chest. But the time for wallowing is over. Scrubbing my face, I decide to sneak out while I still can and tiptoe to the closet to change. By the time I'm in fresh clothes—another pair of capri leggings and a cropped tank—the shower turns off.

Swearing, I realize my phone's still plugged in. I sneak back to the bed and grab it, but jump in the air when the bathroom door is yanked open.

Cal emerges with steam curling around his wet body, chocolate brown hair almost appearing black as it drips onto his shoulders, a white towel tied low—dangerously low—on his hips. His jaw is freshly shaved, and my eyes drop to the knot in his throat. It bobs as he swallows, and I gulp. Cal freezes, mid-scrub of a hand towel against his hair as he takes me in. I must look like a deer in the headlights, and all excuses fizzle from my brain as a drop of water slips over his pecs and ripples over

164

his abdomen. My gaze zeroes in on the dark trail of hair that disappears under the towel, and it embarrasses me to no end when Cal's shoulders shake with laughter. I gulp and tuck my phone into my waistband, turning to leave without giving him any further satisfaction.

"Loren," he calls after me.

I pause with my hand on the door. I look back, only to watch him saunter toward the closet, hand holding the knot of his towel in place.

"Thought you could sneak out on me?" He laughs as he opens the closet door, dropping the towel to the floor with a wink over his shoulder. "Give me ten, and I'll join you."

Heat flushes my face at the sight of his bare ass flexing as he moves to grab a suit. My cheeks flame, but I can't pull my eyes off of him. After entirely too long, I turn from the show he clearly wants to put on. But not before I find out that he's wearing skintight, black boxer briefs under his impeccably tailored navy suit. Then he heads back into the bathroom.

Five minutes later, he exits the bathroom with styled hair and a gleaming smile. He looks perfectly refreshed and ready to start the day. It bothers me how unbothered he appears.

Smothering the annoyance, I plaster on a fake smile and refrain from shoulder checking him to get into the bathroom myself. After I brush my hair into a pony and scrub the grime from my teeth, I breeze past him without looking at him. Cal chuckles and opens the door for us to leave, extending an arm for me to lead. God, his laughter is just as I remember. But this time, instead of it slicing open an old wound, my chest warms, and I have to stifle a smile.

Instead, I flip him the bird, and then make for the kitchen. His steps ring out behind me, the heel-toe clicks of his loafers against the floor sharp. We walk in silence, and by the time we reach the kitchen, it's obvious—at least to me—that I just don't know what to say to him.

I move to pour myself a coffee at the same time he does, and our fingers brush, but I smack his hand away. With one hand, I pick up the pot and grab a mug with the other. A petty part of me delights when I pour my mug to the brim, leaving all but a drop for Callahan. He smiles and reaches over me, cloying my senses with his familiar cologne, grabbing a fresh mug just as Darla hands us a new pot. I take a stubborn sip of my coffee to make room for some creamer, and my eyes twitch at the bitter taste.

Cal doesn't speak, just pours a mug until there's an inch of space and trades it for the one I'm struggling to drink. Then he places the creamer on the counter and watches me, sick satisfaction gleaming in his brown eyes, as I give in and doctor the drink to my liking.

"Thank you," I mumble under my breath, even though it pains me.

Callahan simply smiles and raises his own mug in cheers, turning on his heel.

"Thanks for the extra coffee, Darla," he says to the busy woman, who just waves him off.

He leaves the kitchen, and like a puppy, I follow. We step into the dining room, and the conversations lower to a hush. Cal rounds the table and sits at the head, while I take a seat about three spots down from him.

He sighs in apparent annoyance, but remains silent. Instead, we both drink our coffee as we wait for Darla to bring in breakfast. I recognize more people around the residence, and it seems only a select handful—or two—are invited to breakfast each morning. After the first few days, I noticed everyone mostly sits in the same spot, and curiously, an extra chair was added to either side of the table. Not that I ever felt bad for taking someone's spot, and as much fun as it was to poke Matthias, I found the convenience quite practical. If I'm to be here for the next two years, I might as well have my own spot at the table—both literally and figuratively.

Speak of the devil—in the next breath, Matthias, Lucas, and Everett enter, heads low as they speak in hushed tones with each other. They barely look up to find I'm seated farther than usual, and they take their seats around Callahan. Darla follows, pushing in a cart full of plated food and gets to work setting out each meal.

When she gets to me, my stomach noticeably grumbles. Lucas, who sits next to me, freezes and looks over with wide eyes.

"Do you"—his eyes dart around, stage whispering—"have a monster inside of you that you forgot to warn us about?" He gulps and stabs a fork into fluffy eggs and offers me the bite. "Here, little monster. Here you go. Please don't hurt us."

In the corner of my vision, Callahan takes notice of us, and I decide to have some fun with it. Leaning forward, I slide my mouth around the fork and swallow the eggs. A sharp cheddar melts in my mouth and my face contorts. I groan, taking a hefty gulp of my coffee to clear the aftertaste.

Luc's brows pinch with confusion over my obvious disgust, just as Callahan barks out a laugh. Luc looks to him for clarification while I take a drink from my water.

"She doesn't like cheese," Cal says around a laugh, digging into his food.

I roll my eyes and pick up my fork, diving into the bacon, hash browns, omelet, and strawberries in front of me. Within minutes, I've successfully fed the monster inside of me, as Lucas so affectionately called it.

Cal tosses his napkin onto his empty plate. Then he stands, buttons his jacket, and rounds the table to help me out of my seat. I grumble but allow him to slide the chair from under me, and we head out of the dining room and toward his office.

"Five minutes. My office," he throws over his shoulder, placing a hand on my lower back and guiding me down the hallway.

When we get to his office, he shuts the door behind us softly and sits at his desk. I fall onto his leather couch, placing some much-needed distance between us.

"So, would you like to tell me what happened last night before they get here?"

I don't pretend to not know what he's talking about. I thought about it last night, and if this operation really is as big as I think it could be, I definitely couldn't do anything on my own.

I groan and bury my face in my hands. Last night...

Finding the Disciples. Overhearing where they're dropping the women off. *Leon.* The words tumble out of me, but I share it all, everything I heard. While I'm in the middle of my recap, the door opens, and in strides the three musketeers.

"What is she talking about?" Matthias asks, upper lip curling over the fact I'd already claimed the leather couch.

"She was just explaining how she snuck out last night to go on a fact-finding mission at Abstrakt. You know, the club where women have been abducted from, never to be seen again?" Pure, unadulterated rage shakes out of Cal and thickens in the air between us, and I finally get a glimpse of how he actually felt about my so-called mission.

Luc's disbelieving face whips toward me, and his eyes widen. "You did *what?*"

168

I shrug. "I was in the lounge; I wasn't in any danger."

All but Cal's eyes widen at the admission. They must know exactly what happens in that lounge.

"And besides, I found out where they take the women. Two Disciples—or Apostles, I suppose—couldn't help but brag about their new lucrative business, and I overheard them talking about dropping the last of their victims at the port."

The room goes silent, my words imploding like a silent bomb. The seconds tick by as the heat noticeably rises, my palms growing slick as sweat prickles the nape of my neck.

"The port?" Cal grinds out. "Are you sure they said the port?"

I nod once, and Cal swears.

"Think it's Edwards?" Matthias asks.

I'd wondered if Callahan's new business partner had any ties to the ships that might have additional, undeclared wares on board.

Cal's jaw ticks, and his gaze slices from me to Everett. "Get the shipping manifests for the past six months, as well as the projected schedule for the next two. We can't afford any miscalculations or jump to any conclusions. If it's Edwards, I want to be damn sure before I accuse him."

Everett nods and strides toward the door.

"Wait," I call toward his back.

He pauses with his hand on the door as all eyes turn to me. Alice's sweet face materializes in my mind and my heart skips a beat, but I shake off the emotion. Alice needs me to be focused.

"They said something else. They said…" I pause as my throat cracks. "They said they needed a few last-minute additions, but then they should be ready for Friday."

It was now Monday. Which means we only have four days to save my friend from being shipped to god knows where. The tension coils in the room until it snaps.

Callahan swears and nods to Everett, who leaves without another word. Matthias and Luc look at each other, opening their laptops at the same time. I stand and cross to Cal's side. He barely spares me a glance until I clear my throat. Dragging his eyes from his screen to mine, he waits for me to speak with obvious impatience.

"Any word on Mason?"

His pupils dilate, and he inhales sharply, glancing over my shoulder to Matthias. I turn, bracing for the worst, the longer they don't speak.

After several seconds, Matthias's mouth flops open like a fish as he tries to find the words. "No," he grinds out, looking to Cal. "We haven't found him yet."

A deep hold on my chest loosens, and I release a long breath. "Well, why didn't you just say that?"

Again, Matthias looks at Cal before speaking. "We've ramped up our security presence at all four remaining warehouses, as well as increased our eyes on the street. Though there haven't been any attempts on another warehouse yet, there's been no mention of seeing anyone matching Mason's description at all. We've also contracted a firm to... scan the public cameras and run facial recognition, but to no avail. It's like he's vanished from Roswell." Matthias drops his gaze and has the decency to look ashamed. He swallows, returning to his laptop, his updates now complete.

I turn to Callahan. "He hasn't been spotted anywhere?" My voice hitches up an octave, and fear bubbles in my chest. It's been five weeks, and he's nowhere to be found? That can't mean…

"Loren," Cal whispers, voice low and full of trepidation, "it doesn't mean he's dead."

The word itself strikes me like a bullet and knocks the wind from my chest. I suck in a breath but can't seem to find oxygen. Black spots crinkle the edges of my vision. Then I'm pressed into a chair, and a soothing hand rubs along my spine. Calming words fall from Cal's lips, words of comfort and encouragement, but I barely hear them.

Mason can't be dead. He might be a certified idiot, and hellbent on proving himself to a man that couldn't give two shits about him, but he's my only connection to my family. My mom is god knows where, my dad is dead…All I have is Mason.

Callahan continues to stroke my back, brushing my hair away from my face and offering me water. I take a sip, and then down the rest of the glass. Then I practice my breathing, controlling it and letting my fears sink into the recess of my mind, a problem to deal with another time. It helps, and the tremble in my fingers begins to ease.

A shrill ring jolts the last of me from my panic attack, buzzing following in my waistband. I exhale a shaky breath and check the caller ID. I swear, heat flashing through my body and prickling against my palm. Answering the call, I shoot up from the chair and start for the door.

"Kate, hi." Given the past twelve hours, it's not surprising that I forgot about my deadline *and* that I was supposed to meet with Andy Thorne, his lawyer, and my agent—Kate—this morning, but it doesn't ease my guilt.

Cal wraps a steady arm around my waist, halting me as I try to pass by. *I have to go,* I mouth.

His hold tightens, and he arches a brow, mouthing back, *Why?*

"Loren, where are you? You were supposed to be here ten minutes ago. Is everything alright?"

I squeeze my eyes shut and try my best not to focus on the fact that Cal's palm is warm against my exposed skin, but shivers break out anyway.

"I'm sorry, Kate. I lost track of my morning. I'll be there in twenty. Can you stall for me, please?"

Cal's gaze narrows with my words, and he doesn't take his eyes—or his hands—off me.

Kate sighs. "Yes, but get here ASAP. You know how big a deal this is."

Shame washes over me for a brief second. I'll just explain what happened—or a modified version, at least.

"Of course, I'm leaving now." I hang up and stuff my phone back into my waistband, then look up to Cal. "I have to go. I have a business meeting that I completely spaced on. It's downtown, and I'll be back in two hours, but I have to leave now."

Cal snorts, tossing his head back, humor dancing behind his brown eyes. "Oh, Bunny. If you think you're going to whatever that meeting is, you're sorely mistaken. You're seconds after coming out of a panic attack and in no state to handle whatever business that's for. Now sit down." He tries to push me back.

I plant my feet and press a hand against his chest. "Cal, this is important. I have to go."

I search his eyes for any chance of mercy but see none. So I pull out the big guns and smooth my palm against his chest instead of pushing him away. His gaze openly searches my face, his jaw rigid. Resolution settles in his eyes.

"Fine. But I meant what I said last night; where you go, I go."

A laugh bubbles out of me before I realize he's serious. His posture doesn't change, doesn't suggest any sense of humor, and I sober.

"Fine, whatever. But I have to change, and we have to leave like five minutes ago."

Cal nods and releases me, and I rush back toward his room. As I reach the end of the hallway, I hear him bark orders to Matthias and Lucas to continue their search.

Five minutes later, I'm dressed in my high-waisted, flared cream slacks with a powder-blue satin blouse tucked in, and my camel tote slung over my arm. There was obviously no time to put any makeup on, so I straightened my ponytail and swiped a mauve lipstick and my mascara to apply in the car.

Callahan is already waiting, leaning against the SUV with a foot propped behind him. As usual, he's typing on his phone, but when he hears me enter the garage, he looks up from his screen. Rushing past him, I have no time to appreciate the slight part to his mouth or the wandering trail of his eyes as they follow me to the back seat. Without waiting, I open my door and slide inside, then rifle through my purse for a compact. Cal rounds the car and gets in the back with me, and Cohen climbs into the driver's seat.

"Well, good morning to you, too, Your Highness," Cohen jokes as he starts the engine. "Too busy for us mere peasants?"

I laugh and reach forward to smack him on the arm. "Shut up."

"And where are we headed?" Cal asks as he puts his phone away, leaving all his attention squarely on me. Heat climbs up my chest, my neck, from his undivided attention, so I turn my own to my compact.

"Perial Publishing." I swipe my lipstick on and wait for the best time to apply my mascara, cursing under my breath that I forgot my eyelash curler. *Oh well, this will just have to do.*

"Perial Publishing? Why are we going there?"

Cohen's question tugs at my chest and scrapes at the wound not fully scabbed over. They really didn't keep any tabs on me since...

"I have a meeting," I say simply, hoping they'll leave it at that. Technically, I signed a non-disclosure agreement when I was contracted to ghostwrite Andy Thorne's biography, plus, I quite like the fact that they've clearly underestimated me.

Fourteen minutes later, we pull in front of the three-story building where the publishing house offices are on the second and third floors. Cohen slows to a stop in front of the loading zone, and I hop out before anyone can say anything. Callahan swiftly catches up, placing a gentle hand on my lower back like a doting husband would.

As we approach the glass double doors, Cal steps away to hold one open for me, and when I pass by, he whispers, "If there's a door you're walking through when I'm with you, I'll hold it. Don't charge forward on your own. Understand?"

I give him a sarcastic smile, rolling my eyes as I pass by. Then he returns to my side, following as I lead to the offices upstairs. I wave to a few people I've met from prior visits and enjoy, with smug satisfaction, as Cal becomes further confused by my being here.

After climbing the stairs and rounding a corner, we come upon a visibly flustered Kate. Her golden skin is warm, her cheeks flushed, her jade eyes frantic. She's twisted her dark hair into a low bun, but a few frazzled pieces have escaped, suggesting her nerves have gotten the better of her. She notices me immediately and rushes over.

"He's getting ready to leave; we need to head in there *now*." Kate does a double take at Callahan, and a question forms in the pinch of her sculpted brows.

Cal extends a hand to introduce himself. "Callahan Keane, Loren's husband."

Kate's brows shoot to her hairline as she looks between us, stunned speechless. Finally, she composes herself and says, "Looks like we have much to discuss."

I nod, mouthing, *Later*, and turn toward the boardroom. "Wait here." I gesture toward a reception area where a leather couch and glass coffee table sit.

Cal just smiles and stuffs his hands in his pockets. "I think I'll sit in. It would be good for me to learn more about *my wife's* business dealings." A flicker of stubborn determination flashes in his eyes, and I relent, needing to get into that meeting.

Kate strides forward to open the door, but Cal beats her to it and holds it open for the both of us.

I take a deep breath and plaster on an apologetic smile as I walk in, an apology already waiting on my tongue. "Mr. Thorne, thank you so much for your patience. I apologize for my tardiness, but I bring good news that I think you'll be excited to hear."

Andy Thorne and his lawyer stand, both wearing light smiles. Andy rounds the conference table to shake my hand. He's an attractive man in his early fifties with perfectly styled salt and pepper hair, and he wears a navy pinstripe suit. He waves off my apology.

"Bea, please. Call me Andy. It's good to see you. And it's not a problem; I was looking for an excuse to cancel my next meeting, anyway. You saved me the trouble of wasting an hour."

I smile, and the tension that gripped me earlier melts away. Cal's body presses against my back, so close there's no mistaking he's staking a claim. It's a struggle, but I keep my irritation off my face and step to the side to introduce the two men.

"Mr. Thorne—" He raises a brow, and I start again with a smile. "Andy," I correct. "Please allow me to introduce my husband—"

"Callahan Keane," Andy says, his eyes widening. The room heats, tension palpable and thick.

I glance between the two men, who seem to be in a standoff, sizing each other up silently and frighteningly. Next to me, Cal's stands rigid and ready to detonate.

CHAPTER EIGHTEEN

"**T**horne." Cal finally extends a hand, his jaw ticking as he waits for Andy to accept.

But he never does. The older man stills, fury brewing in his blue eyes, and his hands curl into fists at his sides. Then his gaze slices to me, obvious concern softening the pinch between his brow. "Your name isn't Bea Page, is it?"

I shake my head. Cal stands at my side, a possessive arm curling around my waist.

Andy inhales sharply, his eyes widening infinitesimally. "You're Loren Catrone." It's not a question. But hearing my maiden name doesn't offer any comfort, like it once did.

"It's Keane, now," Cal amends. His hand squeezes my hip, a visible claiming.

Andy's fury bubbles to the surface once more, redirecting back to Cal. "*How could you?*" Decades of hurt shadow the three words that tumble from Andy. Confusion prickles my nape. "You're supposed to protect the women in your life."

Cal says nothing, his hold tightening on my hip. I can't see his face, but his ire blisters through my satin blouse.

I frown. "Andy, how do you—"

"How can you keep her safe, when the only one she needs protection from is *you?*"

A gasp parts my lips. "Mr. Thorne—" I try again, but he cuts me off with a hard look.

"I don't expect you to understand." With that, he strides from the conference room. Steam practically rolls off his suit jacket, following behind in a cloud of wrath. When he reaches the double doors, he pauses, looking over his shoulder. "I'd advise to be more careful with who you align yourself with, Loren, but you've already gone and married the fucker." Andy's wrath slides over to Callahan, who takes a step forward in front of me. "But it's *his* family who ordered the attack. *His* family that threw the explosive into the car that killed her infant son. She ran into the pharmacy for two minutes. Two fucking minutes." His voice cracks. "She was forced to watch from the shadows as her child burned in front of her, with nothing she could do except flee for her life."

He pauses, throwing over his shoulder, "Good luck, Loren. You're going to need it."

Callahan steps forward, blocking me from Andy's view entirely. "Is that a threat, Thorne? I don't take threats lightly, no matter who they come from. You come for her, and you'll have the entire Keane enterprise raining hell on you and your business."

Cal's promise hangs in the air.

Andy visibly deflates. "It's not a threat; it's a warning. Danger follows you wherever you go, Keane. Protect her. You won't get a second chance." The older man leaves, the doors shutting behind him.

Kate's color has drained from her tanned skin, leaving her unusually pale. She stammers, mouth opening and shutting. "I'm going to go... check on him." She turns and leaves herself.

My hands tremble, but not from Andy's words. No, it couldn't be that. Not when Callahan Keane stands in front of me, wielding the entire expanse of his power and reach to protect my life against an empty warning. His promised protection settles over me, and a sense of peace coils around me for the first time since we were teenagers.

Cal turns, but I can't let him see the emotion in my face, so I cross to the window that overlooks Bengal Street, searching for anything to take my mind off the catastrophe. I spot Cohen, who sits on a bench next to the entrance of the publishing house, talking on his cell. Cars drive by on the street, people going about their normal lives, undisturbed by the events that have shaken me to my core.

It baffles me how people can live their lives with no clue to the dangers they pass by daily.

Cal comes to stand beside me but doesn't speak. His presence fills my every sense, and I struggle to hold on to my convictions of keeping him at arm's length.

"I guess we should leave," I resign.

Cal's warmth heats me from behind. "Graves is on it."

Cohen stands and heads to our SUV. This part of downtown is no stranger to the elite, and luxury cars line the curb, many of them blacked-out SUVs.

Below us, Andy Thorne storms out of the building. His strides eat up the distance of the sidewalk until he reaches his car. His driver jumps to get in the front seat. I can practically hear the slam of his car door, and I wrap my arms around myself as I wait for him to leave.

But he never will.

Flames engulf the SUV, and a heartbeat later, the *boom* of the explosion rattles the windows. Before I can even think, I'm slammed to the floor with Cal's body covering mine. After a breath of pure silence, car alarms blare, and screams fill the quiet.

"Are you alright?" Cal asks, sheer terror written on his face. His eyes dart over my face, my body. Cal visibly shudders when he realizes I'm fine. Confused, but fine. Cal jumps to his feet to look out at the destruction.

Oh, my god. Cohen.

I rush to the window and search frantically for the bodyguard I'd grown close to, but there are too many people surrounding the flaming car. Swarms of people, and none of them doing anything but staring in horror.

Cal checks his phone, and a wave of relief washes over his face. "Come on, we need to get out of here." He wraps a firm hand around my arm and tugs me away from the window.

"Wait"—I resist against his tug, planting my feet with little success— "we need to find Cohen!"

Cal looks over his shoulder and must see the terror written on my face. "He's fine. He's waiting for us in the back alley. We have to go *now*, Bunny."

Confusion clouds me, but I finally relent, picking up my bag from where it fell and grabbing Cal's hand. He leads me down the stairs, and we pass a distraught Kate, who's on the phone with someone as tears run down her face. I open my mouth to call out to her, but Cal leads me away with a jerk of our joined hands.

Down the stairs, we tumble as people blur past us. Instead of turning toward the entrance, Cal leads me toward the back.

"How do you know there's an exit back here?"

He looks over at me, his face impassive. "There's always another exit."

We round a corner, and sure enough—an industrial metal door. In the next breath, Cal pushes me against the wall and pins me with a look that says, *stay here*. He reaches under his suit jacket and grabs his gun from who knows where, before raising it in front of him. A quick push on the metal bar, and Cal silently and efficiently slips out the door to clear the alley. I wait, counting in my head to ten until my nerves finally get the best of me. Creeping forward, I nearly jump out of my skin when Cal's head appears back around the door.

"Fuck, you almost gave me a heart attack." I grasp my chest.

Cal doesn't respond. In fact, he barely acts as if he heard a word I said. Instead, he just opens the door farther and tugs me outside.

In the back alley of the publishing house, a black SUV waits for us. The weight of relief is crushing, and a breath shudders out of me. Callahan opens the back door for me, and I jump in, practically climbing over the center console to squeeze Cohen, who grunts and pats my arm awkwardly.

"Shut up and accept my love. I thought you were a goner." My voice breaks, but I only squeeze him tighter.

"Okay, sucker, that's enough. I'm fine. You can let go now."

"Loren, let the man go. We need to leave."

The echo of the explosion rattles around in my head, and I nod as a terrible sorrow fills my chest. Cohen might have lived, but Andy Thorne couldn't have made it.

I fall back into my seat and squeeze my eyes shut. He was a great man, and I could feel just how much he loved his wife and their daughters. He didn't deserve to die this young, and certainly not in a flaming explosion, just like—

"Oh, my god." My jaw falls to the floor, my heart speeding.

"What, Bunny?" Cal asks.

I twist to face him. "When I first interviewed Andy, he never mentioned anything about an attempt on his wife's life. She died in a car accident a few years ago, but it was just that—an accident. But he just said her infant son died in an explosion—a car bomb."

The dots connect but make little sense. What a cruel twist of fate to die in the exact way your wife almost did all those years ago?

"There were a few black SUVs out there, and this isn't the first time a car has been blown to bits right in front of our eyes."

Cal doesn't seem to appreciate that piece of information, and his shoulders tighten, jaw grinding together. Cohen exits the alley and takes off for the Keane residence.

"Was it meant for us?" My voice shakes, but I get the words out somehow.

"Possibly. But Thorne was a powerful man. It's entirely possible it was a direct attack and nothing to do with us."

While his words might be true, there's a silent understanding thrumming in the car that it feels connected, like there's a puzzle laid in front of us, but we only have half the pieces.

Cal dials on his phone and lifts it to his ear, recapping the events of the last fifteen minutes, probably to Everett or Matthias.

Leaning my temple against the glass, I close my eyes and try not to picture the second car bomb I've witnessed in the past week. Never in my life have I been so close to the danger of this life, and yet, after a few weeks of being married to Callahan Keane, and it's like my entire world is imploding. Is it always like this with him? Or am I just special?

Cohen merges onto the highway, and I stifle the laugh that threatens to escape me. I close my eyes, the cool glass icy against my temple, but a window sounds like it cracks. My brows furrow, and I lift my face, only to be slammed to the back of my seat as Cohen steps on the gas.

"What the fuck?" My voice is shrill, and my knuckles are white where I grip the door handle.

Cohen swerves, and I slide across the bench, not having put my seatbelt on earlier. Another crack in the window, and I realize—we're under fire.

CHAPTER NINETEEN

"**W**here the fuck did they come from?" Cal barks as he twists around, gun still in hand. He looks out the back window.

"Blue Tahoe." Cohen swerves again, passing a compact car. "Shit, they're right on us."

Another three shots hit the rear windshield, and cracks spiderweb out from each bullet.

"I thought these cars were bulletproof!"

Neither Cal nor Cohen respond—which, honestly—fair. They're a little busy at the moment. But in the next moment, another few shots hit the rear glass before the Tahoe accelerates and comes up to my side. I duck below the line of sight. Cal slides across the bench and rolls the window down, enough to return two quick shots. He ducks below the glass when they volley back.

His body covers mine, and I can feel the thumping of his heart on my back. Wind whips through the car as our speed increases. Cal straightens, one hand still pressed against my spine to hold me down.

I inch my body up, peeking over the glass. Another car approaches on our left, boxing us in, and the window rolls down. The glint of a barrel appears.

"Cohen! To your left!"

Cohen's head jerks, and he immediately swerves to hit the newcomers, barely throwing a "Brace yourself" before we make impact with the other car. If this were a movie, they'd lose traction, spin out, and probably flip a few times, effectively eliminating them as threats. But this isn't a fucking movie. There's barely a dent in the side of their car. All they do is get closer to us.

In the driver's seat, Cohen is doing what he can, but he can't seem to ditch them. Fear threatens to drown me, but I shake off the numbness in my fingers and make a split decision.

Ducking up, I push Cohen forward and grab the gun tucked into his waistband.

"*Hey*," he protests, but the car on our left fires another three shots, and his attention is pulled back to driving.

I slide over to the left side, just in time for Callahan to shout, "Sit the fuck down, Loren! Do not engage, do you hear me? You will *not* roll that window down."

More bullets hitting the side of the car cut off his words. He returns fire with three quick shots and their windshield shatters. The blue Tahoe speeds up and splinters off, taking the nearest exit. A new car takes its place. We're starting to really gain speed on the highway, and Cohen's panicked gaze meets mine in the rearview mirror. He must see what Cal can't. He nods, stepping on the gas and gaining a slight lead in front of the two cars.

I sidle up to the left side of the car and peek out the window. The car on our left seems to have two people in it: a driver and a shooter. I check the gun and find it's fully loaded with twelve rounds—I've got twelve chances to get them off our ass.

Tucking one leg under myself, I roll down the window. Another shot hits the glass, and I flinch. It cracks where the bullet hit, and I roll it down another few inches. The car falls back, then skips around a slower car in the left lane and zooms back up to meet us.

Taking my chance, I fire a shot and hit the glass directly above the driver's head. A perfect hole splinters the glass, but the windshield doesn't shatter. The gunman leans out his window and fires back. I barely twist in time to miss the bullet. He fires again, then pulls back inside the car.

"Goddamn it, Loren, stay inside the fucking car!" Cal shouts from his seat across the bench, but another shot brings his attention back to his shooter.

"Worry about your own car, Callahan!"

I turn back to mine and fire another shot, this time just as the passenger leans out the window. It misses by a fraction.

It scares him off, though, and he retreats once more.

I pop back up and fire two quick shots at their front right tire. They hit on target, and the tire deflates. They fall back. Just for good measure, I shoot another three shots into their engine. They stall out completely.

Sweat prickles at my hairline, and my pulse practically jumps out of my skin, but I slide over to Callahan just as he lands a head shot to the driver. The car loses control, and the gunman tries to grab the wheel, but all it does is send them into a tailspin. They flip, rolling twice before sliding onto their side and crashing into the median.

Cohen whoops, pumping a fist in the air as he screams, "Get absolutely fucked!"

His infectious laughter fills the car, and I can't help but join in. Cal glowers, but the slight upturn of his mouth tells me just how relieved he is.

We pull off the next exit, our vehicle littered with dents where the bullets hit, windows splintered and barely hanging on, shattered glass dusting our clothes, the footwells…but after it all, we survived. Cohen takes the back roads to get home, and I fall into my seat, cheeks hurting from smiling so big. My head lolls over to look at Cal, who's already looking my way.

Our eyes meet, and a stutter in my chest takes me by surprise. My breath hitches, and I fall into his trance. Seconds pass, neither of us speaking, neither of us daring to be the first to look away. Then, a sharp inhale, and his gaze snaps to my cheek, and he slides closer, a timid thumb swiping over my cheekbone.

He pulls his thumb back, and I see blood. And a shard of glass.

On instinct, my hand reaches up to cradle my cheek. *So that's why it stings.*

"It's just a scrape," Cal whispers, wiping his thumb on his trousers and sliding closer. He crushes me to his chest with a hand cradling the back of my head as his shoulders shake. "It's just a scrape, it's just a scrape." His whispered words repeat over and over, as if reminding himself I'm alive, if just a little hurt. The warmth of his chest and his sandalwood cologne fill me with a sense of peace and security I wasn't aware I desperately needed.

Cal's heart thuds under my cheek, and I close my eyes, wrapping my arms around his body as I let myself accept his comfort. We stay like that for minutes, somber against the low rumble of the car and the gentle breeze flowing through the cracked windows as we drive past the gates of the Keane residence.

Matthias stands waiting in the garage, arms crossed, as he watches us park. His permanent scowl is missing for once, and when Cal opens the door and climbs out, Matthias visibly deflates.

Cal reaches back into the car for me, not letting me go more than a second without his touch guiding me. He tugs me to his side, and when we pass Matthias, he tosses over his shoulder, "My office in twenty. We're going to see Doc."

Matthias opens his mouth, likely to argue, but Cal doesn't stop to listen.

"If it's just a scratch, Cal. I can clean it and throw a bandage on it. I'll be fine," I say.

He doesn't respond right away, just continues to direct me toward Doc's office. When we arrive, he barely pauses to knock before we stride in.

Doc looks up from her computer, glasses perched low on her nose. She immediately stands.

She chuckles and raises her glasses to rest on the top of her head. "Twice in a week, Callahan? You should take better care of your wife."

It's the wrong thing to say.

Her teasing tone is lost on Cal, who snaps back. "Do your fucking job, Martha, and never comment on mine again. I pay you to heal. So *heal.*" He gently pushes me forward, a direct contradiction from the defensive anger seeped in each word, and leaves the room. The door slams shut behind him.

I grimace in apology. "I'm sorry, Doc. It's been a rough hour."

Doc—Martha, apparently—nods in understanding. "No, it's me who should apologize. I know better than to poke fun at his ability to keep you safe."

A flurry of butterflies erupts in my belly, but I tamp down the silly emotion. Still, my curiosity gets the best of me. "What do you mean by that?"

Doc approaches with an alcohol pad and swipes it over my cheek. It stings, and I flinch, a hiss escaping between my teeth. Her lips press together in silent apology.

"I started working for the family about nine years ago. Young Callahan used to see me daily for various remedies. Cuts, stitches, bruising, things of that nature." She dabs ointment on my cheek, smoothing a bandage over the cut and snapping off her gloves to throw them away. She sits down in her office chair and leans against the back as memories seem to play behind her eyes. "He had so much anger in him it needed an outlet. Turns out, he'd gone and joined an underground fighting ring at Strikers just to deal out the pain he was feeling inside."

An underground fighting ring? At *Strikers?* How come I'm just now hearing about this?

"Anyway, the excuse he gave me for years was that he was just training so he could protect his kingdom one day. That if one day he had to, he'd be prepared against any threat. Against any enemy."

I always knew Cal felt the weight of his role more than others might. It was written into his very DNA. After spending years watching his father—Nolan Keane—attempt to live up to his older brother's legacy of bloodshed, it was bound to affect young Cal. We all knew the story: Daniel Keane—the heir to the Keane family and Nolan's older brother—

was involved with Tony Bianchi's eldest daughter—Mia Bianchi. The Keane patriarch killed Mia, all to control his son. Instead, it drove Daniel mad, and he spent the next two years causing more chaos between the families than ever before, solidifying the rivalry in blood and leading to Arthur Keane's death. Eventually, Daniel took his own life. Nolan then assumed the role as head of the family until he had a heart attack in the middle of the night, just over eight months ago.

Callahan grew up soaked in the blood of Daniel's actions, and I always knew he felt a certain responsibility to uphold the divide between our families. It was a lucrative and competitive business, and he played the cards he felt compelled to play.

"When did he stop?" I finally ask.

"Stop?" Doc's brows pinch, and she shakes her head. "Darling, he's never stopped. He's just learned never to lose."

CHAPTER TWENTY

When I leave Doc's office, Cal's waiting outside the door. He's pacing, running his hands through his hair. When he hears me, his head snaps in my direction. His eyes frantically search my face, noting the bandage. A breath rattles out of his chest. "You okay?"

I nod and pass him, intending to head straight to his office. Cal's long strides easily catch up to my pace, matching my speed once he does.

"Everett, Matthias, Luc, and Graves are waiting in my office. Do you need anything before we start?"

My steps falter for the briefest moment. I shake my head. "No, I'm fine. Let's go."

When we enter his office, the guys are locked in a heated conversation, arguing about something too quickly for me to understand. Cal crosses over and yanks Lucas out of the chair in front of his desk, then indicates I should take his seat. A blush creeps into my cheeks, but I sit.

"Update." Cal's voice has turned harsh, a clear indicator to the mindset he must've shifted into.

All four men talk at once, and Cal holds up a hand. "Everett, go."

"We received an email not two minutes ago, and we've been debating the validity of it."

Cal leans forward and clasps his hands together. He raises a brow in silent order for them to continue.

"Well"—Everett's gaze darts to me and pauses, but Cal waves him on, so he continues—"it seems someone is claiming to know who the Disciples are and wants to meet to discuss the information they've acquired."

Cal hums and scrubs a hand over his jaw. Stubble from the day darkens his face and gives him a rugged look that churns a low heat between my legs.

"Could be a trap," he muses. "Who's the sender?"

This time it's Matthias who speaks. "It's an anonymous address. We sent it off to be traced, but it will take at least a day or two for any sort of answer."

"And when are they looking to meet?"

"At ten o'clock."

That was in eight hours. It would have to be a judgment call, and it was times like these that I was glad I wasn't in Cal's shoes and responsible for making the right choice.

"Was there anything else in the email?" Cal asks.

Everett grimaces. "Not much. Just that they knew who the local leader of the Disciples is and where they can be found. The address they gave is to a restaurant, but it closes at nine-thirty."

"So, they're either friends with the owners or the owners themselves?" My question seems to remind the other men I'm still here, and Matthias's scowl returns.

"What is she doing here, anyway? This isn't something she should be involved in; she's a Bianchi."

Callahan slams a fist onto his desk. When he speaks, his voice rumbles with rage, and his eyes narrow on his brother. "She's a Keane, and you will treat her as such, or so help me, Matthias, I'll strip your rank and send you to babysit a fucking tree. Do you understand me?"

Matthias quiets, but his hateful gaze slices over to me, and the heat of his fury blisters.

"With Andy Thorne being blown to bits this afternoon, it's awfully convenient we're getting an invite to meet with someone we know nothing about."

Cohen's words ring true, and a shiver of fear ripples over me.

"What do you think Andy meant about how your family was the one who tried to kill his wife the first time?" I ask. "That there was a car bomb outside a pharmacy, and an infant that died."

Cal swears. "Fuck. I didn't even realize what he was saying at the time." He looks to Matthias, who appears ashen.

"Could it be?" Matthias whispers.

My brows scrunch together. "Could what be?"

A wordless conversation passes between Cal and Matthias. For several seconds, we wait for somebody to speak. Finally, Cal does.

"Our uncle loved a Bianchi. Mia."

Elias and Leon's aunt. She died a long time ago.

Cal continues. "Our grandfather told him to end it, but Danny refused. Mia was pregnant. And she was the love of his life. Months later, after Mia gave birth, our grandfather ordered the hit. He'd waited long enough for Danny to choose family, so our grandfather chose for him. They threw a molotov into her parked car, outside the pharmacy. Later, they discovered a car seat in the back. Pieces were blown across the street. Reports always said she was in the car, too."

"Or so we thought," Matthias adds. "If she escaped, she never returned."

"Andy's wife's name was Charlene. Not Mia."

This time, it's Lucas who speaks. "People can change their name, Lo."

"Everything else he said lines up with her being Mia," Cal says.

It does. And if Andy's wife was Mia Bianchi...

"Cal, if that's true, I understand why Andy was so upset to see you today. You represent all of his late wife's past life and trauma." Cal nods thoughtfully—and morosely. "But why were you so upset with him?"

Cal visibly deflates. "A few years ago, I tried to hire Thorne Enterprises for our IT security, but he wouldn't accept the contract. When I assumed leadership after my father passed, I tried again. This time, I offered to triple the rate, but he staunchly refused. We were growing at an impossible rate and needed to increase our security; our enemies would love any opportunity to take a shot at us. When Andy rejected us yet again, it wasn't only a blow to my ego, but also a hit to our organization. It left us vulnerable." As he speaks, his tone morphs from bitter resentment to slow understanding. "We hired Garrett and prayed his skill set would be enough. I'd like to say that so far it has, but the recent wipes of our footage has him on my shit list."

If that's all true, it's likely no amount of money would've convinced Andy to accept the contract. Any attempt would've been met with the same outcome: Cal's further embarrassment. But fuck, there's still so much unknown about this.

Cal's gaze snaps up, and I realize I must've said that out loud.

"You're right. There's so much unknown right now"—he scrubs another hand over his tired face—"but ten o'clock gives us eight hours to prepare. Luc, find out everything you can about the restaurant and who owns it. Find out which territory they pay security fees to. If it's an outlier or the Bianchi's, we need to know. Everett, get a team ready to join us. They'll surround the building at least an hour prior to the meet. Matthias, follow up with Garrett about tracing the email, and let us know immediately if anything comes back sooner than expected. Understood?"

Each man nods, filing out of the room. I'm left alone with Callahan, who lets out a deep exhale and closes his eyes. Even though it's barely afternoon, a bone-deep tiredness tugs at my eyelids, and I can't help but wonder if he feels the same. My fingers itch to reach across the desk and take his, to lace them together and squeeze so tightly my knuckles turn white. So instead of ignoring my instinct to stand and leave, I finally give in.

My fingers tremble as they reach over, but the warmth of his hand smothers any final hesitation. I lace my fingers between his and squeeze, and to my surprise, he squeezes back. Cal doesn't open his eyes though, just holds my hand as we sit for a minute in silence, holding onto our sanity and each other with only our grimy hands.

The silence thickens, but it's not uncomfortable. Finally, Cal looks up, and a sadness I haven't seen in him stares back at me with open pain.

"An inch to the right, and I would've lost you today. And if we'd been any closer to the car that night at the Edwards's, I could've lost you then, too."

My heart thuds. Yes, we've escaped death a few times now, and I wonder once again: is this his life, or am I just special?

"I can't exist"—he moves a fist in front of his mouth and clears his throat—"in a world where you don't, Ren."

It's so quick, the slip of his mask. Then he visibly shakes himself back into the hardened Callahan, turning in his chair and breaking all contact with me. "It was a mistake to assign myself as your personal guard. I can't do my job and keep you safe at the same time. Matthias will take over as your primary guard, and Graves will remain as your driver and secondary. Now go. Take a shower and get some rest."

With that, he opens his laptop and begins to type away. I'm frozen where I sit, utter shock washing over his declaration. But once the numbness wears off, I'm left with a deep sadness that wrenches and contorts inside of me. *He can't be around me anymore.*

My mouth flops open like a fish a few times before I'm finally able to get my voice to work. "Fine. When should I be ready to go by?"

This causes Cal to freeze, his fingers pausing on top of his laptop until he finally looks up at me. "Ready?" he scoffs. "For what?"

"To head to the restaurant tonight."

Cal barks a harsh laugh, and I fight not to flinch. "Loren, if you think for one fucking second that I'd ever allow you to enter a situation where I don't know what the outcome will be, and can't guarantee your safety, you've lost your mind. You're staying home, and that's final." He pauses and shrugs. "In fact, thank you for reminding me of your rebellious nature. I'll be sure to place two guards on our door tonight to ensure you don't leave until morning."

A swell of anger mounts inside of me, and it lashes out without a second thought. "That's ridiculous. You don't need to put guards on your door."

"*Our* door," he corrects. "And based on your extracurricular activities the other night, it would stand to reason I do. Now go. Get cleaned up and get some rest."

I scoff incredulously, but he's dead serious.

He's also right.

With a deep grumble, I stomp from the room. It might be petty, but I slam his office door with more force than necessary.

My anger leaves me in a whoosh, and I'm left feeling empty. Empty and filthy. I march straight to "our" room and into the shower, not even waiting for it to warm. I take my time washing my hair and scrubbing the dirt from my body. My bandage gets soaked, so I peel it off and wash my face and behind my ears. Then I shave my legs for the first time in a week, and by the time I exit, my fingers are pruned. With a quick glance, I discover the scrape really isn't that bad, and I forgo putting a new bandage on. It takes fifteen minutes to blow-dry my hair into soft waves. When I glance at the clock on my phone, I see I've only killed forty-five minutes.

Fuck. This is going to be a long night.

I end up spending the afternoon hunched over my laptop and throwing myself into my edits for the first half of my book. It's the only thing that can make me lose hours, and right now, if I don't keep my mind and hands busy, I'm liable to do something I shouldn't. Like find out who Cal placed to guard our door, and then find out from Darla what their favorite snacks are, and then ring her to deliver those favorite snacks and see if it tempts them to leave the hallway. Or head out to the balcony and see just how high up it is. Unfortunately, it's a straight shot down onto brick pavement that would *not* be pleasant to land on.

But, you know, those are only things I would do if I wasn't forcing myself to keep busy. I totally didn't try them and struck out…

Hours fly by, the sun eventually setting, the moon taking its place. The cloudy sky makes for a gorgeous sunset, and I kill about fifteen minutes just watching it from the balcony. Then I light a candle on the coffee table and pour myself a glass of whiskey. A second glass follows quickly after, and I find myself checking my phone more often than ever before. The action infuriates me. When did I revert into a teenage girl waiting for her boyfriend to call her? Cal wasn't my boyfriend.

No. He's my husband.

For once, the title doesn't send shivers down my spine. Instead, a flurry of butterflies takes flight in my belly, and I pinch my lips together to fight the smile that threatens to appear.

Husband.

At eleven o'clock, I scroll through my phone again, clearing notifications. My messages have gotten out of control, with unread texts from Jenna, Jude, Kate, and…Leon? Why was he texting me? I thought I was basically dead to him.

Clicking on his thread, I can't stop the gasp that escapes. Text after text begging me not to go to my meeting with my publisher today.

Lo, stay home. I can't explain, but I'll make it up to you.

Loren, don't go to your meeting. Take it virtually, if you have to.

I thought I told you to stay home! Fuck!

Lo?

Loren are you okay?

LOREN ANSWER ME!

They came, a handful of minutes between each text, and I reach a trembling hand to cover my mouth. He knew? That Thorne was going to be attacked? And that I was going to be meeting with him? How could he have known?

As the questions swirl around my brain, another text comes through.

Guess you made it out okay. But I thought you should know just exactly what kind of husband you married.

I can feel his derision through the text, and my brows furrow in confusion. What does that mean?

Then an image comes through. Then another. And another. They're shot from a short distance, but based on the surrounding decor, it's Abstrakt. But it's not the location that he's talking about. No, it's Callahan being led by the hand into a private room by Kyra. One shot, they're entering a private room. The next, Kyra throws a sultry smile over her shoulder. The final, of the door shutting behind them. Acid burns in my throat, and my stomach clenches in anger.

He's at Abstrakt? With Kyra? The woman he slept with *two weeks* before we got married. I know he didn't owe me anything then, but when you have a plan to be faithful to someone, call me crazy, it shouldn't fucking matter when the date on the marriage certificate is. Steam practically pours from my ears. He's supposed to be meeting this anonymous email sender, and instead, he's at a fucking sex club?

My blood heats to a boil, and I shoot to my feet. I pour another glass of whiskey and toss it back. I drain two more, stewing in anger and a profound sense of disappointment, before the fuzzy blanket of alcohol hits me.

I should've known better. What does everyone always say? *People don't change.* Cal might have gotten older, filled into his generous muscles, and taken on some additional responsibilities, but he's still just a man. I swallow another hefty gulp of whiskey, and it should concern me it doesn't even burn anymore, but it doesn't. Instead, all it does is make me stew harder.

Ten minutes pass, then twenty. The candle I lit hours ago is down to its last inch of wax, and I stare at the flickering wick and lose track of time.

Eventually—finally—the door handle turns, and in walks my husband. His tie is missing, jacket slung over his arm, top button undone, and sleeves rolled to his elbows. The disheveled sex hair is the nail in his coffin. My husband just betrayed me. Again.

CHAPTER TWENTY-ONE

CALLAHAN

T he car ride is smooth, but the short drive to the restaurant does nothing to quell my rising anger. Being summoned isn't something I'm used to, and it sure as shit won't happen again. They might have caught me in a momentary lapse of misfortune, but once we get whoever's torching my warehouses and sort out Loren's missing people, it will be back to business as usual.

My fists itch to slam into a worthy opponent, despite still healing from my last brawl. Three nights ago, when Loren slept soundlessly in her room, I realized I couldn't take it anymore. Her constant presence has ensured my dick hasn't gone soft in two fucking weeks. Everywhere I go, she's there. At breakfast, in the gym, and now I can't even go outside without finding her typing away on her computer on the balcony. She's invaded my every fiber, and it's worse than a death by a thousand cuts. Each time I catch a whiff of her shampoo or perfume, it's like a monster slips into my skin, commanding me like a puppeteer. Her rivalry and fight stings, but more than that, it makes my cock weep.

Now she sleeps in my room, in my bed, inches away, and yet, I can't do anything about it. All she sees when she looks at me is the same asshole who broke her heart. My jaw grinds together at the memory, but then we slow, the car coming to a stop in front of an Italian restaurant.

I've never been here before—I've had no reason to, as it's on the outskirts of Roswell, just outside my territory—and so I'm on edge. Matthias and Luc exit the vehicle and fall into place behind me as we approach the glass double doors. It appears dark inside, with only a dim orange light cast from somewhere in the back. Silhouettes move around inside, while a few seem to sit at a table. Everett and two teams arrived earlier and have surrounded the building as backup, but I hope to god we don't need them. It's taken all I have to find the manpower to cover the remaining warehouses and enhance security around my house. I'd rather not lose any more tonight.

"Ready?" Matthias asks as my hand lands on the cool, metal door handle.

"You know what to do if it goes bad."

Matthias's face hardens—he hates the reminder. If it turns out to be a trap, he's to extract himself and get to Loren immediately, keeping her safe and making sure she stays alive. He's never admitted it, but I know he still blames her for my abrupt descent into madness when I ended things with her. When he realized the old Callahan—the older brother he looked up to—wouldn't be returning, he harbored a deep resentment for Loren. It's clear he hasn't let go of it yet.

I turn back to the door, pushing into the restaurant as heads turn, marking our entrance. Like a little slice of Italy, murals of grapes and wine are painted on rustic almond walls. The restaurant is filled with round tables covered in white linens and unlit candles sitting in the center. At each table except one, the chairs are flipped onto the tops of the tables. At least three armed men stand near the back, hands clasped and standing at the ready.

In the center, one table remains with its candle flickering. The air is tense, silent as we approach. Three men, all at least in their mid-thirties or later, sit with a woman, who seems young. Their whispered conversation comes to a hush as we get closer, all four of them turning to us.

"Well," I begin, stuffing my hands into my pockets, "you've got us here. Now, who do I have to thank for sending us that incredibly vague email?" My gaze scans the men who remain seated, but they give nothing away. They look to be your typical guards, all built like they live in the gym.

The woman purses her lips but doesn't speak. With a careful eye, I size up each of them to see who appears to be the leader. One man has a scar slicing through one of his eyebrows, with a scruffy beard and a bald head. Another has bandages on his knuckles and leans with his arms thrown over the backs of the chairs on either side of him. His lip is split and bruised, but it clearly doesn't bother him. The last has a sharp look to his eyes, as if he's taking in much more than his partners.

As the seconds tick, I find my irritation growing. They have the nerve to summon me here, and now they won't even speak?

I open my mouth to tell them to fuck off when the woman stands. She places the tips of her fingers on the table as she leans forward. The men jump up, rising a half second after she does.

"Callahan Keane," she says, voice smoky and rich.

I take three steps closer to the table, never breaking eye contact with her. The closer I get, the better I can see her. Dark lashes frame her green eyes, and upon closer inspection, they appear bloodshot.

Freckles splatter over the ridge of her nose, and her auburn hair is pulled back into a ponytail. She's dressed in all black, with a turtleneck tucked into jeans.

"It appears you have me at a disadvantage." I look around the room. "You seem to know me fairly well, but you've yet to even introduce yourself. Your manners could use some work."

Her nostrils flare, but her green eyes never leave my face. "Who I am is inconsequential, but you may call me Rose."

I'm silent, waiting for *Rose* to get on with it. I'm already feeling the prickles on the back of my neck that begs for me to get home and put Loren back in my sights.

Rose rolls her eyes and takes a seat, waving a hand for us to do the same. After a hesitant breath, I sit down. The screech of the chair legs on the wooden floor is sharp, but no one pays it any mind.

"Thank you for coming. I have information that you'll likely be very grateful for." With that, she slides a flash drive across the linen tablecloth.

Matthias swipes it, turns it over, and inspects the small chip. "What's on it?"

Rose doesn't look away from me. "It's where you'll find the Disciples and the missing women."

My shoulders stiffen, and my eyes narrow on her. "And how would you have this information?"

Rose waves my question off. "Here's the deal: You will take this information, and you'll use your considerable manpower to stop the shipment from leaving on Friday. In exchange, you'll capture their leader and bring him to me."

I slouch back in my chair, throwing one arm over the back of Luc's.

"And why would we do that?"

The corner of Rose's mouth twitches, and she leans forward. A menacing gleam shines in her eyes, and a ferocity that wasn't there before comes barreling across the table. "Because you need all the brownie points you can get to offset the secrets you're keeping from a certain Mrs. Keane."

The threat slices across and straight through my defenses. Unfortunately, there are no shortages to the lies I've told Loren, both then and now, so it's impossible to know which she's referring to.

"And how do we know the intel you're sharing is accurate? Where—or who—did you say your source is again?"

Rose's jaw ticks.

"Oh, that's right"—I snap and lean forward—"you haven't. So, all this pomp and power means nothing if you can't tell me how you've verified each line of intel. And frankly, I don't know you well enough, *Rose*, to take you at your word."

A deep scowl contorts her face. Then, the man sitting at her right leans over to whisper in her ear. She listens, the irritation melting away with a reluctant grumble. With a single nod, she speaks again. "As a gesture of my goodwill, here's a missing puzzle piece you've been searching for: Peter Agapov."

My brows furrow. *Peter Agapov.* Why does that name sound familiar?

A rumble sounds, and I realize it's a chuckle coming from one of Rose's entourage.

"Peter's recently found himself interested in achieving what his father couldn't: territory in Roswell. His father—Ivan Agapov—tried for decades."

Ivan Agapov—now that's a name I remember. The Russian entrepreneur has been trying to cross into Roswell ever since my father took over operations. Ivan runs a modest shipping company out of Moscow, using the containers to mask his additional imports—mainly drugs—but only delivers product to Quebec. He's wanted to alter his routes to include ports in the States, but my father rejected his proposition. Ivan's product wasn't up to the quality Dear Old Dad wanted, so he sent him packing.

"I see you're putting it together. Now here's where it gets interesting: Peter's spent his life going unnoticed by his father, who believes himself to be infallible. Though almost sixty, he has yet to announce his heir. Peter has it in his head that if he can free up some of the claimed territory, then he can swoop and claim it for himself. His older brother hasn't shown interest in the business, so Peter is trying to get his father's attention."

"So, you're saying Peter's responsible for the warehouse fires and deaths of our soldiers?" I ask.

Rose smiles, but it's more like a baring of her teeth. Something flashes behind her eyes, too quick for me to catch. She drops a photo on the table, and it's of a man who looks to be in his twenties, tall but lean, black hair, beady little eyes. "Peter's responsible for a lot more than that. But yes, he's behind the fires and deaths. He's also behind the women going missing. From what I've discovered, his father is unaware of the doctored shipping manifests and the extra weight they're suddenly reporting."

This guy? He doesn't look like he'd be capable of putting on shoes with Velcro straps, let alone something of this magnitude. But he bears a striking resemblance to the man Loren described at the Edwards's dinner and who we saw in the CCTV footage.

"Who's he working with?"

Rose's brows jump the slightest hair, as if she's surprised by my question. But she covers it quickly and brushes me off. "No partner. Just a lot of manpower. Manpower that I don't have to go up against. And I need him *dead.*"

I pretend to think about it for a moment, letting Rose and her crew believe I'm considering it. Honestly, it seems too easy.

I push from the table. "Thanks for the stories, but it's time for us to go now. We only meet with credible sources, and given you can't prove anything, I have no choice but to cut the evening short. Have a good night."

Matthias and Luc follow closely behind as we march toward the exit, but before we can reach the door, two armed men step in front of it. I look over my shoulder to find Rose still seated.

"We're not finished. Please take your seats."

I sigh. I'm at my fucking wits' end, and my fingers itch to get back to Loren. "Do you really think two men can stop me from leaving? You seem to know my name, but do you know who I am?"

"I know much more than that, Mr. Keane. For example, who you've been keeping in secure room four, in your basement."

Like a punch to the gut, the breath in my chest is stolen. How the fuck does she know who's down there? My gaze slices to Matthias. He looks back, his frustration clear. I can almost hear him say, *I told you it was a bad idea.*

Not for the first time, he's right.

I trap a growl behind my clenched teeth, and a ripple of fury rolls through me. In an alternative universe, I execute everyone in this room, save for Matthias and Lucas, but it appears Rose has much more to offer than convenient information.

I stalk back to the table. The air warms, tension palpable, and the vein Doc always worries over throbs in my neck. I grip the back of the chair with too much force, feeling the wood groan as I take my seat again.

"And how the fuck do you know who's in room four?"

Rose laughs, a twinkling sound that's almost sinister. Then she sobers, her brows pulling into a furrow as she tilts her head. "Why would I reveal all of my secrets?"

The men beside her grin, chuckling between themselves.

"Do you believe me now, Mr. Keane?"

My upper lip curls in distaste. I won't admit it aloud, but I recognize she must have a reputable source. It's frustrating that she won't reveal him, but part of me—a small, *infinitesimal* part—respects it.

"Fine. Assuming you know the identity of our *guest* in room four, and that your intel on Peter is true, then what's in it for you?"

Rose curls her lips into an intimidating smile. "Like I said"—she sips from her wineglass and licks her painted lips—"Peter's life is *mine.*" Her voice is a growl, her knuckles almost white against the glass.

It's odd—the request. Rose doesn't appear to be a bloodthirsty murderer. But I suppose I've seen worse come in much smaller packages. And as long as Peter is dead and his efforts thwarted, I don't particularly care who wields the knife.

"How do I know you'll keep a certain guest's information private?"

Rose just shrugs. "I see no reason to make that my business. For now."

Her threat hangs in the air. *Don't cross me, and I won't cross you.* It'll have to do for now. Rose watches me carefully, and I see the moment her eyes widen with the realization I'm on board. Her smile turns rueful. She stands, extending a lithe arm across the table.

I rise and accept her terms. Unsurprisingly, her handshake is firm.

Once the tentative partnership is sealed, we dive into building a plan.

"Where are the women being held?" Lucas asks, not sharing the information Loren discovered on her ridiculous undercover mission at Abstrakt.

This time, it's the man next to Rose who speaks—Jace, I think I heard someone call him. "They're being held at the East Port, in two different shipping containers. They've amassed more women than originally planned for, but Peter won't refuse his ambitious lackeys."

Of course he wouldn't.

"Which shipping company?" I ask, needing confirmation that Edwards hasn't been plotting against me. It would be just my fucking luck that my first partnership as boss is one where I get double fucking crossed.

"Saint International."

A sweet breath of relief escapes my chest, only to be replaced by the immediate rage that someone thought Roswell—*my city*—was open season.

"Do you have their shipment manifests?"

Rose nods, gesturing to the man on her right. He reaches below him and pulls out a folder, then lays out the registered routes for the next seven days.

"Have you identified which ones likely have the women on them?"

"Not yet," Jace responds. "We have a program running that's looking for discrepancies, but since they've flown under the radar, it's unlikely we'll have an answer soon."

"While it runs," Rose interjects, "we need to devise a plan to stop the containers from leaving the port."

I scrub a hand over my jaw and nod, my gaze flicking over the shipping manifests.

"Do you know where Peter's staying now?" Matthias finally speaks up.

I look between him and Jace, who are busy sizing each other up.

"Yes, but from what we've gathered, not every lackey has turned in their women. So, if we go straight to Peter's motel, we risk spooking everyone and losing all those women. And I refuse to lose another soul to Peter fucking Agapov." Rose's voice rises in anger as she spits out each word. This sounds personal.

"So, we'll find out which shipping containers the women are being held in, rush it with manpower on Thursday night, kill any Disciples, and then hand his head on a platter to you? Do I have that right?"

The silence ticks on as Luc's question lingers. Rose nods.

"What's stopping them from changing the shipment date to Thursday? Or even sooner?"

It's valid, Matthias's question. Compounding anger and a thirst for justice for Loren's best friend sparks in my chest. Yet another innocent harmed because of her connection to me. The familiar feeling burrows deep, and my fists itch to cave someone's face in.

"Peter won't lose this chance, not when he's so close to the final deposit that will secure his father's approval. He's aiming for the biggest payday, and that means giving his men time to deliver the most women they can. They won't leave early."

As she speaks, I nod along, the answer making sense. This is Peter's big break, and he won't risk the best payday he'll ever see.

"Thursday, then." My voice is low, rumbling across the table in a growl. "Until then, we find out which containers they're in. Thursday, we surround them and crush Peter and his fucking Disciples."

The table is quiet, then each person nods.

"And if we can't find the right containers in time?" Jace asks.

My gaze slices to Rose, who looks back at me with the same fierce determination shining behind her green eyes.

"Then we'll chase them across the ocean."

Rose curls her lips into a frightening smile, unblinking as we come to agreement. I take my first impression back; she's more bloodthirsty than most.

I stand, and Matthias and Luc join me. "We'll be in touch, then."

"So we shall," Rose replies.

Our exit is swift. Luc hops into the driver's seat and starts for home. But the thoughts still swirl around, and I realize I need more information.

"Luc." He meets my gaze in the rearview mirror. "We need to stop by Abstrakt."

Lucas nods and sets off for the club. I settle into my seat, loosening my tie and running my hands through my hair with a groan as the city blurs past us.

If someone wants Roswell—*my* city—they're going to have to try a hell of a lot harder.

CHAPTER TWENTY-TWO

LOREN

My heart sinks, but I snap to my feet, swaying only a little. I don't give him a chance to speak before I jab a finger into his chest and push as hard as possible. He doesn't move. A growl splits from my chest, a noise I've never produced before, but I ignore the novelty and throw all my vitriol into my words.

"Shoulda known you couldn't keep it in your pants. You never could." My words slur, but I ignore it, embracing my ire. Fury licks down my spine, flushing my chest with heat.

Cal's eyes widen, and he searches my face. His gaze flicks to the half-full tumbler of whiskey in my hands and then darts back to mine. His brows pinch together as he asks, "Are you drunk?"

I wave him off. "I asked first." Then I remember the glass in my hand, and I finish the remaining gulp. With a sarcastic flourish, I spit out, "Maybe. But only because you showed me your true colors. *Again.*"

I don't bother hiding the pain radiating from my chest. It stings, and I hate how it feels. Fueled by too many glasses of whiskey and vicious jealousy, I push into Callahan's space and drop the glass on the rug. It lands with a *thud*, but I ignore it.

Cal's breath hitches when I wrap my arms around his shoulders and tip my face to his. His heart beats wildly against my chest, and I lean closer, eyes drawing down to his lips, then back to his darkening gaze. All those years ago, I ran from him. But now…now I'm going to show him what he's been missing.

"What are you—" he whispers.

I silence him by pressing my mouth to his. Cal stands frozen, rooted to the ground for two heartbeats, then his arms slip around my waist and tug me closer. I fall into his hold, a soft moan slipping out as I finally kiss the man I've pretended to hate for the past eleven years.

Cal's lips are as soft as I remember, but the reminder of how he acquired his expertise, my cloudy brain sparks in outrage, and I kiss him with more heat. His tongue slips into my mouth as I claw at the hair on the nape of his neck, trying to fuse our mouths together. But it's not enough. A fire has caught, flushing my skin and thrumming between my legs. Cal nips at my lower lip and growls, moving his hands to cup my face as he devours me.

It's not enough, it's not enough.

I slip a hand down his chest, feeling his taut muscles under my palm. Cal breaks for air, his wet lips swollen as he looks at me from under hooded eyelids.

"Fuck, Ren. I wasn't expecting that."

A smirk teases the corner of my mouth, and I grab his waistband. With one hand, I unbuckle his belt and slide it off before he can even look down. The pictures Leon sent flash to the front of my mind, and the green-eyed demon takes over again, rushing forward to kiss him again. Where I once ran from his betrayal, now I lean into the challenge, if only to satisfy my cravings for the night.

That's not why you're mauling him, Loren.

I shoo the thought away, happy to live in my denial, either because the alcohol makes this feel like a dream or because I just don't have it in me to care right now. My tongue tangles with his as a buzz lights over my skin, hands fumbling with the buttons of his trousers.

Suddenly, firm hands land on my shoulders and push me away. "Wait, Ren—just *wait.*"

I scoff, slamming my lips to his and work his zipper down. But in the next breath, his hands clamp around mine, stopping me from going any further. Indignation sparks, and I groan like a petulant child. The several glasses of whiskey almost topple me, and I stumble away from his denial.

"I—I can't. I want you—*god, I want you*—but you're drunk."

Cal looks at me, unrestrained desire shining in his brown eyes, and it's the final straw.

"Fine, I'll do it myself." I turn on my heel and cross to the bed, where I fall into the plush mattress with a giggle. Slipping a hand down my leggings, I find that sensitive spot and strum with quick, tight circles. My eyes close, head falling back on the pillow as a breathy sigh escapes. It's been too long since I had a release. With each stroke, the heady combination of constantly being around my greatest love and an abnormal amount of whiskey takes me higher and higher toward that peak.

Steps sound next to the bed. When I open my eyes, Cal is standing

214

next to me. Shadows eclipse his brooding face. He watches me through hooded eyes, his pupils so dilated they're practically black. His breath comes in heavy puffs. My mouth parts on a heavy moan as I circle faster, then faster again. We're locked in a battle, neither daring to look away. It fuels me, sending me closer to that peak with each circle.

Right as I'm about to launch into the abyss, Cal grabs my wrist. Then, fast as a bolt of lightning, he whips my hand from my pants, eyes zeroed in on my wet fingers. My hips buck, needy and still seeking the release he just stole from me. A whine slips from my lips. Cal goes rigid, his icy stare pinning me to the mattress. My breath stalls as he lifts my fingers toward his face, but at the last second, he freezes once more. His expression clears, and he flicks my hand away. He doesn't look at me when he stalks from the room, muttering to himself.

His residual shame coats me, tainting my almost orgasm in humiliation. With a swipe of my fingers against my leggings, I turn off the bedside light and curl onto my side.

It takes hours to fall asleep, the alcohol burning off with each second that passes, shame settling in its place. By the time the sun begins to cast its golden fire into the room, I finally slip into unconsciousness.

Callahan never returns.

⌀

I could only sleep a few hours when I finally give up. Before I knew it, the sun had risen to its peak in the sky, and it was time to face the damage from last night. But after a few moments of deliberation, I decide to procrastinate and head down to the gym. After almost an hour there, I take pity on those around me and head up to shower.

Flashes of last night barrage me as I scrub my hair. A heat, one not from the blistering water, flushes my chest as I try to escape from my mind. Shame pours over me like a rainstorm, and I step out of the shower to dry off. In the fifteen minutes it takes to dry my hair and dress, I run through at least four counterarguments that might save a scrap of my dignity. But as I shimmy into a pair of jeans and a soft cream sweater, the shame is still there, no matter the argument I try to form.

So instead, I head downstairs, searching for coffee and answers—though not necessarily in that order.

When I get downstairs, the house is abuzz with an energy I haven't felt since I moved in. It's ominous, the way people seem to walk on eggshells around the inner circle—though perhaps because insults are being thrown like knives. The dining room is empty, most everyone spilling into the hallway as Matthias pushes into Cal's space, a fierce finger stabbing Cal in the chest. He whispers his words too low to hear, but the threat is obvious.

Cal straightens, eyes narrowing further with each word.

"Are you done?" Cal asks in a calculated tone. His jaw ticks as he waits for Matthias to respond.

Finally, Matthias spins on his heel and swiftly exits. He pushes past me, shoulder checking me as he steams by. I stumble, though only for a moment, until a hand at my elbow steadies me. Looking up, I find Cal's furious gaze trained on Matthias. I jerk my arm from his grip.

That catches his attention, and he turns his gaze to me. But he doesn't release my arm. His brown eyes soften for a moment, then heat returns with a startling flash. His gaze locks on my lips. It's all the reminder of last night that I need, and a flush erupts over my skin. This time, when I pull my arm from his grip, he lets go.

"I need to talk to you. About last night," he says.

I scoff, rolling my eyes. "If you think I need details, you've taken too many blows to the head." I skirt around him, but he steps to the side, blocking my escape.

I try again, but Cal counters. I blow out a breath and throw my hands onto my hips. Cal arches a brow, stuffing his hands into his pockets.

"*About how the meeting went*, Loren."

His words bring back a rush of why I'm here and why I need him. I concede with a groan. "I need caffeine."

Cal smiles, a dopey curl to his lips that has my stomach fluttering. He dips back into the dining room and returns with a coffee in each hand. The one in his left hand black, the one he offers a light caramel—just how I like it. I arch a brow but accept the coffee, following closely behind as we head toward his office.

When we get to his office, he immediately heads for his desk and slumps into it with an air of defeat that's so unlike him. He exhales deeply, then takes an extra-long drink from his coffee. I'm transfixed by the way his throat bobs with each swallow. Then I note the fresh wounds on his knuckles. There's a bandage around one hand, while the other is only slightly scraped. *What happened last night?* When he finally speaks, I'm jolted from the trance he put me under, immediately feeling the blood rush to my cheeks. *He caught me staring.*

Pieces of the bitter—and hazy—events from last night flash in my mind. They meld with the years-old hurt from eleven years ago until they're practically indistinguishable. Acid burns in my throat, and I chase it away with several sips of my creamy coffee.

Finally, Cal sighs and begins. "Is this who approached you at the Edwards's residence?" He slides a picture across his desk.

I lean forward to inspect it, but it's obvious from the start. I nod, a question forming between the pinch of my brow.

"This is Peter Agapov. His father runs a small shipping company. Peter's trying to get a foothold in Roswell. By force. He's the one behind the warehouse fires and the missing women. They plan to traffick them overseas. Alice is due to be shipped out with the rest."

My heart thuds, and I suck in a breath. Heat washes over me, prickling my skin with each word Callahan speaks. Despite Peter's image already having been burned into my memory, I study the picture. My arm is partially in the frame, and you can see me gripping my glass of whiskey tightly. At that moment, I'd been praying for escape, for Cal to come rushing in to save me from the man who was so entitled to my personal space.

And now he has Alice.

All thoughts of finding Mason take a back seat. Mason chose his path—stupidly, if I might add. He chose to approach Elias and Leon. And just like our father, his choices are his own. Do I want to save him? Of course, I do. I'll never stop looking for him.

But Alice?

Alice is innocent. A complete bystander who got caught up in the wrong crowd—*me*.

Resolution settles over me like a heavy blanket. I shove my anger aside—the *hurt* aside—and turn my focus back to Callahan. "What's the plan?"

CHAPTER TWENTY-THREE

Cal shares the plan to raid the port on Thursday night. My fingers itch to go now, but he explains why we have to wait. I don't like it, but I understand. All my thoughts turn toward Alice, and my heart breaks.

So, after spending an hour poring over the details of Callahan's meeting with Rose, I find myself back in our room with a heavy heart. Everyone around me gets hurt, and I'm starting to wonder if I'm a magnet for heartbreak.

The cursor on my laptop blinks at me, and I stifle a groan behind my fists. I rest my chin on my knee, my leg propped on my chair, and stare at the blank page, searching for words. A quick email from Emma—my editor—told me she loved the conclusion of my last book. It's all building up to a war between rival families, and it's hitting a little too close to home right now. After about twenty minutes of staring at the screen, I let out a groan and slam the laptop shut. It's proving to be way too difficult to focus on what's fiction when everything feels too real.

The sun dips low, painting an ethereal sunset over the clouds. Pastel pinks and oranges melt together, fluffy wisps of clouds drift off farther and farther. I cross to the bar cart and pour myself a drink. Based on the conclusion of my meeting with Cal, there's not much I can do right now, and it's killing me. They have a plan; they have the people. It's all hinging on finding the right shipping container and waiting for Thursday night.

It's the waiting that's getting me. My knuckles are tired from being cracked, my scalp sore from the amount of times I've run a worried hand through my hair. Perhaps a drink will settle my nerves.

One drink later, I realize while it may not help with the anxiety, it does well to distract me. I spend another fifteen minutes perusing a bookshelf, finally picking a copy of Romeo and Juliet. It sends a jolt of excitement through me. *How did I miss this before?* The spine is worn, suggesting I'm not the first to read it. My fingers trail along the cracks, and I picture Callahan curled up in front of a fire with this in his hands. It brings a forlorn smile to my face. I spend the rest of the evening reading the worn paperback, ignoring the heavy drag on my eyelids.

Finally, when the moon shines brightly into the room, I give in. I curl on my side under the covers and tell myself it doesn't bother me I haven't seen Cal all day.

When sleep finally drags me under, I feel the rustling of the mattress. The softest shift telling me that Callahan finally came to bed. It's too late, I've already fallen asleep.

The next two days follow in the same manner.

As I try to write, I find my well of creative inspiration all dried up. What's usually an endless supply of ideas is now a barren pit of dusty ash. So, I've spent the past forty-eight hours roaming the vast halls of the

Keane residence, eating a few meals with Darla, and doing exactly what Matthias accused me of that first morning—snooping.

Unfortunately, I find nothing of consequence. I'm tempted to look through Cal's office, but the man never seems to leave it—other than to sneak into his room late at night when I'm already asleep.

Thursday afternoon rolls around, and my nerves are fried. My knee won't stop bouncing, and my hair resembles a rat's nest from the number of times I've hiked my ponytail up. In times like this, when it feels like the walls are pressing in on me, I usually turn to my car or Strikers. But seeing as how my car is at the condo, and I haven't made up with Jude yet, I'll have to settle for the gym here.

The thought of Jude brings an extra weight of guilt down on me. In the past several weeks, my life has been in jeopardy more times than I can count. It doesn't escape me that all he wanted was for me to be safe, something he's always been vocal about, but I couldn't see it at the time.

It's a lofty realization, one that means I owe him an apology.

But it will have to wait until this is over. I can't bear the thought that trouble might follow me right to Jude's doorstep. He doesn't deserve it, and I could never endanger Jenna and the rest of the gym by rushing over there.

So instead, I spend the next hour on the treadmill, pushing myself faster and faster until sweat drips down my spine. My feet pound against the belt, my pulse thrumming in my neck with each mile. When I can't take it any longer, I head upstairs to shower. The sun is setting—another hour closer to the ambush.

After scrubbing away the last of my grime and a layer of skin, I wrap myself into a thin satin robe tied at the waist. The cut on my cheek is almost healed, and it doesn't look like it's going to scar. My hair drips onto my shoulders, so I towel it until it's dry enough, then I pour myself a healthy glass of whiskey. It seems the amber liquid is my only friend these days. The first sip burns as it slides over my tongue, but I relish the sting. It's something Cal taught me when we were young—to savor the moments that are fleeting, even if they burn you. The thought stills my hand, but only for a moment.

I cross the room and settle onto the couch, then pick up the worn copy of Romeo and Juliet again. I'm about to finish when Cal finally enters the room.

His steps are soft, and I don't look up from my page. He comes to a pause, standing next to my shoulder as I continue to ignore him.

"Ren." His voice is soft, a gentle reminder of who he can be when he wants to be.

I let loose a sigh and take another sip of my whiskey. It warms my throat, settling low in my belly.

"Ren, please."

Finally, I look up. A frown mars his handsome face, souring my stomach. "You can barely look at me. Tell me, what happened?"

I scoff a harsh laugh. "We don't have enough time in the world to even start." With that, I return to my book, but Cal pulls it out of my hands. He doesn't speak, he just waits for me to acknowledge his presence.

With a roll of my eyes, I finally meet his gaze. "You went to Abstrakt."

His brows pinch, and his eyes narrow.

"To see *Kyra*."

Eyes widening, realization sparks behind them. His throat bobs, and he scrubs a hand over his jaw. It's darker than usual, the stubble after

222

a long day shadowing his face. He looks good. *Too good.* And it kills me. Because here I am, still sleeping in his bed, even though I swore he'd never hold a place in my heart again. But somewhere over the last few weeks, he weaseled his way back in. With each stolen touch, each lingering glance, I didn't—*couldn't*—know I was already a goner from the moment I agreed to this insane plan.

I cross to the French doors to watch the moon. A bright, full moon illuminates the bedroom. Cal drops his jacket, and it lands softly on the wood floor. His steps sound behind me. In the next breath, he crowds my space, blocking my view of the moon and cupping my face with his calloused hands. His thumbs swipe over my cheeks, so gentle and so familiar.

His throat bobs. "Ren, I didn't betray you."

I try to tug my face from his hands, but his hold tightens. It's firm, but not painful, and my skin flushes from the dominance. Cal's eyes search mine. My pulse quickens, the heat from the whiskey flushing my face. The quiet stretches as we stand in the darkened room, no other words exchanged besides a silent pleading behind his brown gaze.

"*I didn't.*"

Each time he says it, it's like a blow to the chest.

"Don't fucking lie to me, Callahan. I saw it with my own eyes. *Both* times." Outrage tingles in my fingertips. They tremble at my side as Cal continues to hold my face.

Cal's frown deepens. "Both?" he asks. He shakes his head as if shooing away a thought and continues. "Ren, you're not hearing me. I never betrayed you. Not then, and certainly not now. Why would you think I've cheated now?"

His confession mixes with the light buzz from the alcohol, and I struggle to make sense of his words. He never cheated? A sardonic laugh erupts from my chest.

"So now you're a liar, too?" Another laugh, this one of pure, unadulterated rage. A snarl slides onto my face, and I wrench myself from his grip.

"Loren, I haven't—"

I cut him off with a wave of my hand, heading toward the closet. "Don't even bother."

A firm grip grabs me by my bicep and yanks me back to his chest. He doesn't let go.

"Do I need to get on my knees and beg? Crack open my chest to show you how broken I am?" His voice is sharp, so close to snapping. "Is that what you need from me?" His chest rises and falls with tight breaths, telling me just how thin his patience is running.

His words linger in the dim room. Tension sparks where his grip tightens, and I suck in a silent breath. The heat of his firm body scorches through my satin robe, muddling my senses. I hum noncommittally. "It would be a start."

I'm thankful he's at my back because I don't have the fortitude I used to. I'm already so close to letting go the pain I've carried for so long. It's exhausting, and I'm ready to leave it in the past.

Cal's other palm curls against my hip, squeezing tightly. When his forehead gently presses against the back of my head, my eyes close on instinct. It's as if he can't bear to let go of me long enough to follow through with his offer to get on his knees and beg. Truthfully, I wouldn't mind him on his knees before me, but right now, I don't want him to let go, either. With the realization, I can't help but lean into his hold. My head tips back the slightest degree to rest on his shoulder.

When he speaks, it's a low whisper that rumbles through my bones. It makes it easier to listen with him standing behind me.

"Ren, Bunny, I never betrayed you. I…" He trails off, and my traitorous heart stops beating as I wait for him to finish his sentence. "My father found out about us. He told me to end it—or else—and I knew what his father did to Mia. I had no doubt my father would do the same to you. And so, I made the choice that Danny couldn't. But I knew you'd never believe me if I said I didn't love you anymore. I had to"—he gulps, his embrace tightening—"to hurt you. So badly you'd never even look at me again."

A thick knot swells in my throat. Cal trails a feather-light touch over my hip, the satin robe disheveled. It's barely tied at the waist, and his fingers play with the hem of the fabric.

"But I never slept with her. You know how Luc moved in that summer?"

I nod slowly.

Cal continues. "Well, she'd spent the night with him, and I slipped her into my room five minutes before you were to show up. It was the only thing I could think of. And the biggest regret of my life."

Sometime during his confession, his hold on my bicep turned into an arm binding around my waist, clutching me to him as if he feared I'd run away. I can't speak, can't move, can't think. All of this…was a lie?

"Ren, please. It's plagued me every day for the past four-thousand two-hundred and twenty-four days we were apart, each one more agonizing than the last. There were weeks where I couldn't get out of bed. Months I don't even remember. It got to a point where Matthias didn't recognize me anymore. And when I looked in the mirror, I couldn't either." He sighs, and I brace for whatever he was about to say. "When you showed back up in my life, I knew I couldn't resist you anymore. So, I told you I needed a wife."

I suck in a shaky breath, my heart pounding so fast I can hear its thrum in my ears.

"But I didn't need a wife. I needed *you*."

I squeeze my eyes shut. "But that night, after the meeting, you went to Abstrakt to see Kyra…"

Cal tightens his hold, and I feel the pounding of his heart against my back. I count the heartbeats, all the way to fifteen until he speaks again.

"Yes, I was at Abstrakt that night, and I saw Kyra, but—"

"So, which is it? You didn't betray me then, but you did now? I know I'm not really your wife, Cal, but I thought you respected me enough not to break your promise to me." The words feel wrong in my mouth, but I speak them anyway, no longer wanting to hide behind quips and banter. When I finish, silence takes hold for a long beat.

Then Cal sighs, and my heart cracks, another tear slipping over my cheek. We were so close. *I* was so close.

"Ren…Kyra works for me. She's an inside agent who reports any useful intel she picks up during her shifts. I met with her after the restaurant because I needed to know if she knew anything that could verify what Rose told us. And that night, she did. Parts of it, at least."

I suck in a breath. *He didn't have sex with her?*

"Whenever I'm there, I act like a client, and we head into a room so it's not suspicious. But I've never touched her. Never even looked at her, Bunny. I haven't looked at another woman since you came back into my

226

life. My bed might have been warmed by women over the years, but no one has ever replaced the ironclad grip you have on my soul."

If not for the hold around my waist, I would've collapsed. His confession coils around my heart, squeezing until it bleeds.

"But…" The word trembles out of me, and I twist around in his hold. His arms slide around me, hands grazing the curve of my ass and leaving no choice but for me to stay. As if I could ever leave now that I know.

Cal's brown eyes shine with emotion, and for the first time since I saw him in Abstrakt, I see past his mask. The charm he wields, the devil-may-care attitude he employs. It's all an act. An elaborate show, but a show, nonetheless.

This time, it's my hands lifting to cup his cheeks, to hold on to him tightly. His bottom lip trembles, and my eyes flick down to it for a moment before returning to his tormented gaze.

"Why didn't you tell me sooner?" My words are barely a whisper, a buoy thrown into the crashing waves of his turbulent storm. I can only pray he takes my offering.

His mouth opens and closes—once, twice. Then he shuts his eyes, tipping his face to the ceiling. My gaze is drawn to the bobbing of his throat.

"I tried." He exhales. "I sent you a letter—" He shakes his head and starts again. "My life is dangerous, Ren. So dangerous, you don't even know." He speaks to the ceiling as if he can't bear to face the reality in front of him.

"Cal, I may not have been born a Bianchi, but I was raised in that home, too. My father was the right hand to Dominic Bianchi for twenty years. You know that. You don't think I learned a thing or two from it?"

My imploring finally breaks through to him, and he shifts to look at me once more. His eyes are glassy, and the steam from my earlier anger evaporates before me.

"I'm stronger than you think, Callahan."

The slightest curl to his lips appears, and drawn to his presence, I press closer until we share the same breath. Maybe it's the alcohol, maybe it's the validation that the love I carried for him for so long never really left, because I knew somewhere deep down he would never actually betray me like that. His words feel true. It never made sense why he let Brielle into his bed, but suddenly it does.

"You are, without a doubt, the strongest woman I know. And because of that, I don't know how you could ever forgive me. I may have been a kid when I broke us, but I've lived with that decision every single day since."

"Why didn't you come find me, then? That letter could've been lost in the mail." My cheeks flame. Knowing that I never opened the letter, instead clutched it to my chest every night for six months, is slightly embarrassing.

Cal sighs. "It had to be your choice, Ren. I had to respect your decision that you were done with me. With *us*."

It was admirable, and so like the Callahan I knew. He was constantly warring with his father over the tasks he was assigned. Some days, it was like meeting different people entirely. But he never took my choices away from me. Many of the punishments he told me about still haunt my dreams. I tried to wrangle control over the dark stories, writing the worst of the scenes into my books as some sort of cathartic therapy. Sometimes, it worked. Most times, it made my heart ache.

"When you moved out of the Bianchi residence, I couldn't even trust myself to keep tabs on you. I was afraid if I saw you were dating anyone, I would've been charged with multiple counts of murder."

My nose scrunches. "Multiple?"

"I would've killed whoever you were dating and their entire bloodline. Obviously."

Laughter rumbles from my chest, but it trails off when Cal doesn't join in.

Shit, he's serious.

"So that's why you didn't know about my writing?"

This time Cal does smile. "No, but you better believe I binged the first half of *Lovers of Sin* the first chance I had. By the way, it sounds vaguely familiar." He smirks, squeezing my hip with a knowing twinkle behind his brown gaze.

His observation is on point. The first book was based on one particular assignment his father subjected him to, where he had to seduce a woman fifteen years older than him. It's twisted—*sick*—because Cal was only sixteen when his father sent him off, and the woman was in her late thirties. But in my book, he was in his early twenties, and she was only thirty, and by the end, they fell in love. Everyone ate it up, and it launched my career as an author. My cheeks flame. *Callahan Keane has read my words.* I do the only thing I can: change the subject.

"The letter you sent. I never opened it." The confession tumbles out of me. Ever since the break-in, it's haunted me I'll never know what secrets were folded between its pages.

Cal's dark brown eyes widen. "You never...?" Disbelief rings through his tone.

I shake my head. "I kept it in a shoebox with a handful of pictures my mom took over the years. It was stolen in the break-in." My chest aches with each word, and I reach for the phantom pain.

"That's why you never met me…"

Met him?

"I'm here now." My words are a quiet confession, and I pray he understands the double meaning. My arms slip around his shoulders, and my fingers play with the hair at the base of his neck. With his smile, a tension long pressed around my shoulders dissipates.

Then he frowns. "How did you know I went to Abstrakt to meet with Kyra?"

The confusing barrage of texts from throughout that day returns to the forefront of my mind, and my smile slips away. "Leon texted me. He sent me pictures of you going into a private room with her." I arch a brow, and a spike of jealousy heats through me. "You're incredibly convincing."

Cal glowers and tips his forehead against mine. My eyes slip shut. The contact is so familiar, and yet so foreign. It only lasts for a moment.

When he speaks, it's practically a growl. "Why was Leon texting you?"

I sigh, slightly amused by his obvious jealousy. "He'd been texting me all day, apparently. I actually wanted to talk to you about it because it's really weird. He was blowing up my phone, begging me not to go to my meeting at the publishing house. It was like he knew something was going to happen."

Cal's nostrils flare, and he swears under his breath. "Why didn't you tell me earlier?"

"I muted his notifications. I didn't see the texts until that night. Then it sort of took a back seat to everything else."

Cal swears again, this time louder. I don't speak, unsure of what to say.

He kisses my temple and whispers against my face, "I'm not mad at you, Ren."

I let out a deep exhale.

"I could never be mad at you. If I'm mad at anyone, it's myself."

Cal catches my gaze and tips my chin up with a single finger. Our lips are a breadth apart, and the heat of his body threatens to set me ablaze.

"I'm sorry, Loren. I'm so fucking sorry." His apology rumbles out of his chest, and I desperately want to believe it.

"I owe you an apology, too. I shouldn't have been so hostile toward you in Abstrakt. I just…didn't know how to be in your presence again or how to pretend I didn't care."

Callahan looks at me with something warring behind his eyes. Then a flash of heartache, before finally: resolution. A smile slides over his lips, giving way to a mischievous smirk. His hands slip over the curve of my neck, fingers trailing over the thrum of my pulse and cupping my jaw. He tilts my face to his and whispers against my lips, "I'm going to kiss you now."

Without waiting for me to answer, he slams his lips to mine. I fall into the kiss, sliding my arms around his neck and dragging him closer, if that were even possible. His lips are as soft as I remember, both from years ago and the hazy kiss from the other night. He slides his tongue against the seam of my lips, demanding entrance. My fingers coil around his hair as his slide over my waist, the curve of my ass, picking me up. As he walks me a few steps backward, a moan slips out when my back softly lands against the wall. I tighten my legs around his waist. My robe becomes even more disheveled. One tug on the belt, and it would fall right off.

Cal smiles, eyes hooded with lust as he trails a hand over my neck, squeezing gently. "Fuck, I've waited so long for this." He groans, then slams his lips back to mine.

The kiss deepens and heat gathers between my legs. I feel like a teenager again, grinding my center against the bulge in his pants. The thin satin material of my robe is all that separates my skin from his trousers, and it drives me higher and higher, knowing one swipe could expose me. Cal's hands knead my thighs, pushing the black material upward, and I gasp. With a shift of his hips, he bumps against my center in the most delicious manner. I moan into his mouth.

"You make the sweetest noises." Another kiss, another groan. "Tell me, does it still drive you crazy when I kiss you"—he drags his lips to the soft spot behind my ear—"here?"

My eyes flutter shut, my head falling against the wall. I writhe in his grip as he brushes open-mouth kisses over my neck, my jaw, a whimper escaping my lips with each touch. After my skin is on fire, he finally returns to my mouth. With a roll of his hips, he coaxes another groan from me. It's maddening, and I can't help but find myself drawing near that edge with barely even a touch. After years of dreaming, years of wishing...

Knock knock.

Someone is at the door. "You ready, Cal?" Luc's muffled voice filters through the door, and my head snaps over.

Cal groans, but this time not from pleasure. He places one final kiss on my neck and slides me down his body. My robe is ruffled, barely tied together with my hip exposed to the heated air. Cal's gaze drags over my body, and he reaches for me but stops. His hand curls into a fist, and he bites it.

"Fuck," he swears, turning on his heel and adjusting his pants.

I'm left standing with weak knees, barely able to support my weight. When Cal almost reaches the door, he curses again and turns back. His long strides eat up the distance, and his hands go straight for my face, cradling my jaw as he places one gentle kiss on my lips. "This should only take a few hours. We'll finish this when I get back."

I nod, my face still cradled in his hold.

"Come back to me in one piece. Otherwise, I'll have to kill you myself."

Cal chuckles. Instead of answering, he grips my hands and squeezes them tightly before striding to the closet. When he returns, he's dressed in blacked-out combat gear. He gives me a fiery look while he adjusts his erection in his pants. My breath catches in my throat, cheeks flaming. But then the reminder of what's happening tonight comes rushing back, and my heart lurches. All I'm able to do is sit on my hands, and it's killing me.

Cal spares me one last glance before he leaves, a lingering look that promises more than his last words. He'll return. There's no alternative.

CHAPTER TWENTY-FOUR
CALLAHAN

"According to the ledgers, they're in lots forty-three and forty-four." Rose points to a schematic of the port, her finger tapping on the southern lots. "Each row is stacked three to four containers high. They're in the bottom containers."

"Sounds easy enough," Matthias grumbles.

I smack him on the back of his head. "Nothing about this is easy. Or did you not notice that they're using the Bianchi lots?" Rage bubbles in my chest, and my gaze slices to Rose. "Is Bianchi their partner?"

Rose looks between Matthias and me, hesitating. Then she shakes her head. "No. I couldn't find any connection between Agapov and Elias, so I can only imagine that means they're sailing under the radar with their exports."

I scrub a hand over my jaw and nod, relief loosening the knot in my chest. "It doesn't make it any simpler. If Bianchi catches us, it's terms for war."

Rose's brows furrow. "War?"

I sigh. "Our fathers established rigid rules that we must follow. When they weren't, the streets were painted with blood."

"Why?"

Matthias and I look to each other, neither knowing exactly what to say, or *if* we should say. Finally, after a few tense seconds, I explain. "Our uncle was in love with a Bianchi."

"Cal—"

I raise my hand. "It's not our secret to keep anymore."

Matthias sobers and nods. Rose glances between the two of us, her eyes wide and posture tense.

"Our uncle was in love with a Bianchi," I start again. "Mia. They fell in love as teenagers, and our uncle would've died for her."

"He almost did," Matthias spits out.

Rose's brow furrows, but she doesn't speak.

I scrub a hand over my jaw and continue. "When our grandfather— his father—found out they were secretly in love, he offered our uncle two options: either end things with her and she'd live, or don't, and he'd kill her."

Rose's mouth parts, a hand landing on her lower belly. Jace shuffles closer to her.

"Our uncle refused, and a few months later, our grandfather followed through. One day, her car exploded, killing her instantly. Our uncle lost it, unable to cope with the pain of losing her. But the Bianchis blamed our grandfather, and what started out as mild rivalry turned into outright enemies overnight. Territory lines were drawn and enforced. From there, the rest is history. It's been decades of bloodshed, but the past few years have been peaceful." I leave out the most recent discovery that Mia might have survived and changed her name.

"And if the Bianchis find you here tonight?"

"It's grounds for immediate retaliation," Matthias says.

His declaration is sobering. Quiet falls over the group, no one daring to speak.

I clear my throat. "Then I suppose we shouldn't get caught."

It's completely dark by the time we reach the port. I've pulled the men I could spare, leaving the rest to guard the remaining warehouses and the residence. But most importantly, Loren. Matthias and Luc lead their teams from the north side of the port, and Everett and I lead ours from the south. In total, we have about twenty-two men.

Rose and her men march behind us silently. She insisted on coming along, refusing to wait in the car like I'd asked. She said my responsibility wasn't to ensure she stayed alive—that belonged to the men she traveled with—but to save the women and deliver Peter Agapov to her.

Still, something protective tugs deep inside of me, but I shake it off. I need to stay focused and not think about the fact I can still feel the heat from Loren's cunt grinding on my cock. With that thought, my dick hardens, and I have to shake that off, too, focusing on the present. I won't get killed because I can't stop thinking about getting my dick wet.

It's not about getting my dick wet. It's Loren I can't help but think about sinking into.

I focus back on our task and readjust my grip on my gun. We're clearing the port from both ends, working toward lots forty-three and forty-four. At this time, we can only assume the Disciples entered falsified ledgers and are working with an unknown player. It's tedious, taking the time to clear the port even as tensions rise, but if I want my men alive, we can't just go rushing in.

The air is crisp, a mist forming and threatening to come down harder with each minute that passes. Row after row of metal containers line the port, stacked three, four containers high. After ten minutes of working through the stacks, we reach the Bianchi lots. We wait in silence until Matthias, Luc, and their team come into view. Their faces are set in stone as they round the last of the shipping containers.

Matthias nods once, and we both approach the containers.

"Three, two," I count, hands reaching for the metal rod locking the container, "one." We both yank our respective rods out and pull open the doors. Rusty screeches break the quiet night. Then the yells begin.

A stunned man hops from his seat and reaches for his gun, but I fire off a shot before he can pull his weapon. Everett takes out another, and we enter the shipping container. It's dark and quiet—too quiet. When we reach the end, I frown in confusion. There's only a ladder and a bucket. I glance inside, but it's thankfully clean. Well, it's dirty as fuck, but it isn't filled with human waste.

"They should be here," Everett murmurs, however obvious.

One of his crew flicks on a flashlight and shines it around, illuminating the container.

"If they aren't here, why did they have a guard?"

The question plagues us as we walk back outside, only to find Matthias and Lucas exiting their container with similar masks of confusion.

"No women?" Matthias asks.

I shake my head once, then turn to Rose. Anger thrums through me. "You said they'd be here."

Rose clenches her jaw. "All the data pointed to these containers. Are you sure they aren't here?"

Luc scoffs a chafing laugh. "Unless they're hidden behind a false wall, then yeah, we're pretty—"

I yank Matthias's flashlight from his hands and stalk back inside, all the way to the edge of the container. Luc's words trail off in confusion. Tapping to feel for hollowness wouldn't work with this sort of container, and there's not a false wall to be found. The light shines over the empty container, but there's nothing here.

With a sharp exhale, I tilt my face upward and groan. It's then that I see the cutout above. A ragged square is slightly tilted, like an askew vent in a ceiling, and my gaze narrows, slicing down to the ladder on the ground. My lips curl into a triumphant smirk, and I lean it against the wall. Climbing to the top, I lift the metal like a vent and push it off to the side. I pop my head into the shipping container above, scanning the flashlight through the space, and my stomach settles like stone. A group of terrified women huddle in the corner, with two in the front shielding the rest with their arms.

Their faces and clothes are stained with dirt and probably blood, and a stench permeates the room. Flies buzz around, and I suppress a gag. It's been a while since I've encountered an imprisonment like this, and my nose isn't used to it anymore.

I pull myself into the container and lift my hands, curling my shoulders to show I'm not a threat.

"We're here to help."

They flinch as if I'd struck them. My words are lost on them. They tremble as a group, and with each step closer, some openly cry. "I promise, we won't hurt you."

Everett climbs into the space, and one woman lets out a whimper. Other than a woman who throws a hand over the trembling brunette, no one breaks from their huddle. No one believes my words. And why would they?

As my mind rapid fires how to gain their trust, I almost miss their flinch when another person appears. This time it's Rose.

"Hey, hey." Her tone is soft, and I step aside to let her by. She approaches them gently, and they look at her with hope shining behind their shadowed eyes, but I can tell they're confused. I don't hear what she says next, her voice so quiet as she reassures them. Taking a few steps back, I ease the pressure of my presence.

About a minute later, Rose turns back around. "Okay, they'll come with us."

As if they had a choice, I want to grumble. Instead, I nod and stand at the opening. One by one, we help bring the women down to the ground floor. They immediately form another huddle. By the time the last woman is down, they're shivering more than trembling. "Get them some blankets," I shout, indicating for Rose to follow. Time to get the second group out.

This time, I scope out the container to make sure there isn't a threat, before sending Rose up first. Jace swears, but Rose holds up a hand and climbs the ladder, not paying him any mind. I follow close behind to make sure we can help their descent, and also to ensure Rose doesn't get hurt. I wouldn't blame any of these women for striking first and asking questions later.

After another ten minutes, all the women have been brought down and counted. *Twenty-six.* Fury sparks in my chest that this many women have gone missing and no one's batted an eye or lifted a finger, except to print a few missing posters.

As the women are being handed blankets and water, I scan each face, looking for Alice. Loren sent me a picture of the two of them from some bar a few years ago, and I admit, it was difficult for me to even notice another woman in the picture until Loren snapped her fingers in front of me. Loren wore a red and white checkered top tied under her perfect breasts and the tiniest Daisy Duke shorts imaginable. She had braided her hair on either side of her face and was wearing dusty brown cowboy boots. She said it was from when they went line dancing for Alice's twenty-first birthday. All I could think was how I wanted her to break out those shorts again so I could peel them off her myself.

The thought makes my dick go hard again, and I will it to soften as I scan each woman. God fucking forbid they think I'm hard because of them. I might not be a righteous man, but I'm not pure evil.

When I reach the last group of huddled victims, my heart sinks. Alice isn't here.

"Fuck."

Lucas walks over to me, likely about to confirm the same.

"I've been showing her picture around. No one's seen her."

A curse falls from my lips, and I scuff the bottom of my boot on the concrete. If Alice wasn't here, where could she be?

It takes another fifteen minutes, but Everett, Luc, and the rest of our men get the women loaded into cars and taken to the hospital. They'll brief them on the way there and encourage them to report what happened, but leave any Keane involvement out of it. We don't need to be answering questions right now.

It leaves Matthias, Graves, Rose, and her three men. The misty night picks up, the rain falling in thick drops.

240

"Where the fuck is Peter?" Rose spits, furiously shaking in her boots. The ground seems to tremble even though she only comes up to my chest. Or that might be the thunder that booms, storms swirling in the cloudy sky.

I shake my head. "Alice isn't here either."

"Think Peter still has her?" Matthias asks.

"It's a possibility. But they're supposed to leave at 0600 this morning. That's only a few hours from now."

Rose shakes, and Jace pulls her into a fierce hug. All it does is remind me of the woman waiting for me at home. My cock aches, and I whistle sharply, indicating it's time to leave.

"I hope you didn't think you could come into my lots and there wouldn't be any repercussions." Thunder rumbles, lightning flashing, as Elias Bianchi's voice rings out in the dark of night.

My blood chills as I turn and face the leader of the Bianchi family. My hand rests on the butt of my gun, and a tightness coils around my chest. I haven't spoken to him in person in years, before we were both leaders, and this time…this time, everything has changed.

This time, it's grounds for war.

Fuck.

CHAPTER TWENTY-FIVE

LOREN

Time seems to crawl, like watching a pot of water that will never boil. Nothing can distract me, nothing can pull my attention away from the fact that Callahan is somewhere right now, in the direct line of fire, as he fights to eradicate a poison. My hands tremble, and I clench them into fists. The moon shines brightly into the room, reminding me that every minute that passes, the more likely the fight has turned sour.

With a frustrated groan, I shoot to my feet. If I can't keep my hands busy, I'll keep my feet busy. Roaming the halls of the Keane residence, I take in the home with fresh eyes. I don't know when I learned each hallway, but after a few weeks of living here, I don't get turned around anymore.

It doesn't help.

I spend over an hour just walking the halls like a ghost, my mind still racing toward Callahan. The only change is that I'm now near the depths of the residence, where I've only been once before.

A muffled noise catches me by surprise, and I startle. Then there's another groan, and I'm creeping forward, eyes darting around to make sure I'm alone. The coast is clear, so I press my ear against the first door. There are no sounds behind it. I move to the next, but again, nothing. I try the third door, still nothing. Finally, the last door—the fourth and final door. I creep toward it with my heart pounding in my chest. My face presses against the cool steel of the industrial door, and I strain to hear over my racing heartbeat.

"Ma'am, you shouldn't be down here."

My head snaps up to see Tinley's nervous face. Her auburn hair is half up in a topknot, the bottom in loose curls that fall just above her shoulder. Freckles splatter over the ridge of her nose, and her deep red brows pinch together. Draped over her arm is a blanket. She looks between me and the door, and I straighten, a lie burning the tip of my tongue, but nothing sputters out.

"Right," I murmur, ducking past her and rushing up the stairs. I feel her eyes burning a hole through my back with each stair I climb. In my crazed mind, did I imagine that noise behind the door?

When I reach the top, I turn. Tinley opens the fourth door with a few taps on the keypad. The door slams shut behind her, and I take it as my cue to leave.

I sigh, a deep unsettling paranoia washing over me. *What's taking so long?*

Another hour wasted, and nothing to show for it. I'm upset that my moment with Cal was cut short, but I understand. Still, my heart swells with emotion from his earlier confession. *He still loves me.* I can only pray that he comes back alive and in one piece. *And if he does, I want to reward him.* My pulse quickens, hazy images of pulling him into me sends a wave of need through me.

With a renewed desire to pick up where we left off—and to keep my hands and mind busy—an idea sparks. I straighten my hair and shave my legs. Then, after rifling through our closet, I slip into a dress I might wear to Abstrakt and put the barest hint of makeup on. Another glance at my phone. It's only been forty minutes. I groan, my eyes rolling so far back into my skull it practically burns. Then, I fall onto the bed, pulling my top leg up and posing, fluffing my hair over my shoulders.

I feel like I'm in the movies where the woman tries every position to be casually found in.

Unlike the movies, fatigue washes over me. My eyes flutter shut. *Just a quick nap.*

Minutes or hours later, a chime rings from my phone, and my heart lurches into my throat, and my eyes snap open. I dive for the device, almost losing it in the comforter it in my haste. A text flashes from an unknown number.

Park Ave Motel. Room 324. Twenty minutes. Come alone, and she'll live.

Then, a photo comes through. Terror spikes through me and my hand flies to my mouth. *Oh, my god.* The picture shows Alice tied to a bed. Tears and old makeup run down her cheeks, and her lip is split. A dribble of dried blood pools at the corner of her mouth. Her hair, usually in a messy ponytail, fans around her shoulders, stringy and greasy as if she hasn't washed it in days. Her blue eyes plead with the camera, her face contorted in obvious pain. Dirt and blood stain a once vibrant yellow sweater. But what's worse is that the top left corner of the screen has circles showing it's a live photo. I press down and hold, and after a moment, the picture comes to life. Her cries ring through my screen, her lips wobbling as blood and saliva dribble out, shooting me straight through the chest. At the last second of the live photo, the glint of a bloodied knife enters the frame.

My brain fries, and I realize Alice won't be at the ports. Cal might be off saving abducted women from their fate, but no one is going to be there for her. I throw myself out of bed, pausing only to slide into my black athletic slides. I dash through the residence and pray I don't run into anyone. The words *'come alone'* ring in my head like church bells, and a sense of dread settles like stone in my belly. As I enter the kitchen, I run into Lex. He freezes mid-swirl as he mixes some sort of brown batter together. His brows pinch, and he opens his mouth, but before he can ask why I'm up so late, I'm already in the garage.

"Shit." All the SUVs are taken, leaving the cherry-red Corvette and a sleet-gray Ducati. I rush around the sports car and throw myself into the driver's seat. The keys are in the ignition already, and without a second thought, I twist them. Fear grips me by the throat, stealing all awareness away from the rumble of the powerful engine under me. I click open the garage and jerk backward as I step a little too forcefully on the gas. The Corvette responds to my touch, and it takes me several minutes to get the hang of the drive, lurching forward each time I have to tap the breaks.

Speeding through Roswell, I pray I make it in time.

As the city blurs past, I glance at the clock. *Three minutes.* Nausea burns in the back of my throat, but I press on the gas harder.

Two and a half minutes later, I screech to a stop in front of the motel. It barely even registers that it's the closest motel to Abstrakt.

The night is quiet, but my footfalls thunder against the pavement, slides slapping with each stride. After locating the stairwell, my body drifts around the corner as my arms catch the railing. I pull myself upward, using my momentum to take each stair two at a time. By the time I reach the third floor, I'm gasping for breath, but I have no time to spare.

My vision blurs as I run along the walkway, searching for the room my friend is in.

Three-sixteen.

Three-eighteen.

I round the corner and slow. At the end of the walkway, the light in the concrete ceiling flickers ominously. It's as if all sound ceases. My vision tunnels. I know in my gut that it's the room at the end of the hall. I gulp in three breaths, trying to calm my racing heart as static fills the silence.

What am I going to do when I get inside? A checklist appears in the front of my mind. First, disarm whoever has her. Then, save Alice. I grimace. Some plan that is.

Each step feels like lead as I march toward uncertainty. Fuck, I hadn't even told Cal where I went. What if I die here? What if this is it for me? A tear falls down my cheek, but I don't wipe it away. I reach for my phone, pulling it out only to see the clock. It's been twenty-one minutes.

Without another thought, I text Cal three simple words. Three words he deserves to know if these are my last moments on this earth. And if by some miracle I make it through tonight—well, I'll deal with the repercussions then.

When I reach the door, my hand raises to knock, but then I decide on the element of surprise. I reach for the knob, praying it's unlocked.

Instead, the door whips open, and my hand closes around thin-air as a greasy-faced Peter Agapov grins widely. He looks worse than when I met him at the Edwards's residence. Dark bags shadow his dull eyes, his cheeks hollow and more prominent than before. Stains darken his white undershirt to where I question if it was even white to begin with. He wears black jeans with the fly unzipped, and my stomach drops.

He grins, but it doesn't reach his eyes. Instead, they sparkle with sick, hungry pleasure. "I'm glad you're smart enough to listen." He turns sideways, beckoning me inside.

On the bed, Alice lies limp, her chin dangling onto her chest. Her yellow sweater is crusted with both fresh and dried blood, and her fuchsia skirt is bunched around her waist. Bile rises in my throat, and I rush in, but Peter grips my arm as I try to pass.

A long sniff along the column of my neck, then he licks the shell of my ear, whispering, "I like when you're obedient." This time, his Russian accent is obvious.

I shiver, unable to answer as I jerk out of his hold and rush to Alice's bedside. Her eyes flutter as if she's struggling to open them.

"Alice," I plead, hands cradling her face. "Alice, open your eyes." I swipe a gentle hand over her tangled hair, and my eyes burn. Slicing my gaze to Peter, I hiss, "What did you do to her?"

Peter smirks, pure evil shining through the twist of his lips. "Nothing she didn't ask for." His words are sinister and confirm my horrible suspicions.

I stand, shielding what I can of her body, and cross my arms. But when I see his eyes drop to my cleavage, I drop them, cursing myself for wanting to be sexy for Callahan. In my rush, I'm still wearing a tiny dress that's cut low and barely covers my ass.

"What's it going to take?"

Peter huffs a laugh, rounds the bed, and comes to a stop in front of me. His finger trails over my exposed collarbone and up to my chin, tilting my face to his. Everywhere he touches, an oily burn follows. I grit my teeth, refusing to give in to his mind games.

"What is it going to take? You should know, little bird. Nothing in this life is free."

With a flick of his finger, he slips the strap of my dress over my shoulder. It falls off, but I'm not exposed yet. Fury courses through my veins.

"I'm not for sale."

My words are futile. He caresses my shoulder again.

He smiles. "Anyone can be bought. And I just happen to know your price."

CHAPTER TWENTY-SIX

As if on cue, Alice moans, dragging my attention to her. Peter grips my chin firmly, refusing to let me look toward my friend. His fingers tighten, surely going to bruise, as he dips his face toward mine. Rancid breath washes over me, and I suppress the gag that threatens.

"Or will you let her take your place? A cold pussy has never stopped me before." His implication sickens me, and my skin flushes with fear. "But she'll never know. She'll be dead. So, which is it going to be? You"— his finger trails over the curve of my jaw, twisting my face painfully toward Alice—"or her?" He whispers the words in my ear, sending a shiver down my spine.

Another tear slips over my cheek. I squeeze my eyes shut.

Peter laughs, a rumbling that quickly turns into a cough. He lets go of me, grabbing his chest. It drags me out of my trance, and my sights zero in on him.

I grab his arm, twist it around his back, and kick behind his knee, forcing him to the floor. But he takes me with him, yanking me by my arm and throwing a fist. The blow lands on my side, the pain instantaneous. But I ignore it, launching a blow at his face. He blocks it and counters. With a twist, he's suddenly on top of me, and his hands fly to my neck. He squeezes and laughs.

"Oh, little bird." He licks his lips and grinds his cock into my belly. "You're gonna have to try harder than that."

My body flails, hands pulling at the squeeze on my neck.

"Don't you know I like it when they fight?"

My mind is screaming. *Fight. Hit back. Do something.* But for three heartbeats, it's all I can do to stay above water in my mind and pull at his grip. Peter must think I'm succumbing to his touch—he smiles and tugs his cock out of his jeans. He strokes himself with one hand as the other pins my wrists above my head. Alice groans, and my head lolls over to her. Even from the ground, I can see the tears in her eyes. I mouth, *I'm sorry.*

She blinks, awareness returning to her with each second. Looking from her body to mine, she jerks in her restraints, hands reaching for me even from where they're tied.

Fight, she mouths, just as Peter slides my dress over my hips. *Fight,* she says, face red from strain.

It's like a douse of ice-cold water, and I snap back into my body. With strength I've never known, I slam my head forward, knocking Peter's skull with a force that ricochets through both of us. My head throbs, and a warm trickle slides down my temple. Peter shouts and lets go. Sharp ringing echoes in my ears, but I pay it no mind, using every moment he gives me.

He raises a hand to his forehead, then pulls bloodied fingers away, swearing. I don't wait. With a pounce, I fall into muscle memory. My blows rain down, not stopping until he's groaning on the floor. When I'm satisfied he's down, I rush to Alice and start working on her ties. My fingers fumble with the rope, but even as they burn, I work the knots loose until one arm is free.

"Loren," she moans, head flopping back against the wall. Her lashes are wet with fresh tears, and nausea burns in the back of my throat. I move onto her other arm.

"Loren!" Her voice is alarmed, and I spin around.

Peter stands, a hand on his temple as he stumbles toward the bed.

"Fuckin' bitch." He spits, blood dripping from his nose and mouth. He swipes forward, and I duck out of the way, but he grabs me by the neck, hands squeezing tight. Black spots dot my vision as my hands fly to my neck. He tightens his hold, a maniacal smile splitting his face in two.

I throw another punch, and his hold finally breaks. We go blow for blow, and a disturbing realization occurs to me. Peter might look lanky, but he's holding his own. As we circle each other, he licks his lips, and I notice for the first time that his pupils are blown. Drugs, then. Whatever he took—or has been taking—is clearly giving him a leg up. I've taken down Jude a few times over the years, so incapacitating Peter shouldn't be a problem. But when I spar with Jude, there's always a limit. Alice groans again, and I realize if I want to survive, I can't have any limits.

Peter swings, and I dodge, but the two queen beds make it difficult to move around.

Blood trickles down my temple, likely from the headbutt. I ignore the tickling sensation. My muscles are loose, adrenaline rushing through me and keeping me on my feet despite the blow to the ribs earlier. I throw another punch, but it doesn't do nearly enough damage. Whatever he's taken has clearly affected his pain tolerance. He lashes out, trying to catch me, but his fingers slip as I yank myself away. A growls splits from his chest and he spits on the floor.

"I'll be easier on ya if you stop now. Another second, and I'll rip your holes apart, stuffing anything I can find inside ya."

I let his threat wash over me, focusing on the fight. He lurches for my neck. I have to end it.

He's breaths away when I reach the bedside table. Without another thought, I rip the lamp from it and swing it over my head. A *crack* rings out. Peter's hold immediately loosens as he collapses onto the floor, a river of blood rapidly staining the aged carpet.

I blink, waiting with a breath stuck in my throat for him to get up again. But after a few moments, he doesn't. I skirt around his body, doing my best not to look at the pool of blood spilling onto the floor, and rush to untie Alice's other hand. Tears roll down her face as she gains more awareness.

"Loren." This time when she says my name, it's filled with relief.

My arms slide around her for a quick hug before I pull her to her feet. She sways, and I slide my arm around her waist to lead her toward the door. When we reach the exit, I take one final look at the man bleeding out on the carpet. I'm glad he's dead—or rather, that he will be soon. I let the door swing shut behind us without an ounce of guilt.

It takes a few minutes to get Alice down the two flights of stairs, and by the time we reach the car, there's a fresh layer of sweat over both of us. I help her into the passenger seat of the Corvette and gently lay the seat back as far as it will go. She immediately passes out.

"Alice?"

She doesn't respond. I try again, gently shaking her shoulder. "Alice. Wake up, honey."

Shit, she needs to go to the hospital. My head throbs, and my throat is scratchy, but I can't think about my injuries right now. The soft latching of the car door is like a gunshot in the quiet night, and I fight the flinch, rounding the front of the car to slide into the driver's seat. My hands tremble as they reach for the seatbelt. I suck in a deep breath. *Fuck, that really just happened.* Squeezing the steering wheel, I put the car into drive and get the fuck out of the parking lot.

The hospital is another ten minutes away from the Keane residence. As the drive passes, the fine mist from earlier has turned into a steady pour. Usually, I love the rain, but tonight…tonight, all it does is make my stomach clench as I try to focus on the road. To get Alice to the hospital safely.

I take stock of my injuries. While my neck slightly hurts, I don't think there's any real damage. My body's a little sore from being thrown around, but nothing I won't survive. The memory of Peter's cock grinding into my belly floods my mouth with acid. I look over to Alice's sleeping body. It might not have happened to me, but I was fairly certain it happened to her.

He didn't suffer enough.

Alice groans, and I turn my focus back to the drive, pressing harder on the gas pedal. I'm so focused that I don't notice another car pulling up beside me, the window rolling down, and the glint of a barrel shining against the moonlight.

CHAPTER TWENTY-SEVEN

CALLAHAN

"Keane."

My blood freezes, time somehow slowing with each breath I exhale.

"Bianchi."

Leon Bianchi stands to Elias's left, and a swarm of men step out of the shadows. With only Matthias, Graves, Rose, and her men, we're outgunned, and it's painfully obvious.

"Did you think we wouldn't find you here?" Elias chuckles callously.

My hands itch to pull my firearm, but I hold them still. We don't have the upper hand, so if I can deescalate the situation, that's what I have to do.

Maybe in the past I would've been reckless with my life. Back when I didn't care if I lived or died. But things have changed. Loren's silken body flashes to the front of my mind, and it's like I can still feel the heat of her against my palms. Her breathy moans ring in my ears, and I have to physically banish her from my brain to keep from sporting an erection in front of the Bianchis.

"I was hoping you might understand, given the circumstances." The shipping containers were on Bianchi territory, but Rose said the Bianchi's weren't Agapov's partners. It's a gamble, but I have to make Elias understand.

"And what are the circumstances? You stealing product from one of our shipments?"

Rage boils my blood. I glance to where Rose stands behind Jace. She subtly shakes her head no.

I take a chance. "And what product do you think we just stole?"

My footsteps echo on the concrete as I approach the wall of Bianchi soldiers. Matthias and Graves step with me, showing a unified front, despite not knowing if I'm leading them to their death.

Elias regards me with open disdain. He snaps, and a ledger is placed in his hand. His eyes skim over the manifest, but I interrupt, my voice booming across the port. Rain steadily falls, soaking us and chilling me to the bone.

"Let me help you out: women. Women were being held inside those containers and were due to be shipped out to their demise first thing tomorrow morning. We received a tip that the missing women in Roswell were being held here, and it turns out, it was credible. The women are en route to the hospital now." My eyes narrow, and fury surges through my body. He might not have known what was happening right under his nose, but it's still his fucking responsibility.

Elias's nostrils flare, and he shoves the ledger back to Leon. "What did you just say?" He breaks from the line and strides up to me until our toes are practically knocking.

"You had over two dozen women, filthy and freezing, pissing in a fucking bucket right under your nose. You should be grateful we showed up when we did."

The color drains from Elias's face, shock evident and seemingly genuine. He swallows thickly, eyes dropping to the ground when Leon speaks.

"And you just had to be the one to swoop in and save them? Don't you have your hands full with your burning warehouses and whore of a wife?"

A killing calm slices over me, and I turn the full force of my fury to Elias's younger brother. He's practically a child, can't be older than twenty-one, and yet, here he stands with his chest puffed out like some prick. He has the nerve to act tough when all along he's been texting my wife and feeding her lies. I could make him weep for his mother in less than fifteen seconds. A red haze leeches in my periphery.

"What did you just call my wife?"

Elias goes rigid, clearly hearing the threat laced in my words.

Good.

Leon has the gall to scoff, opening his soon-to-be-wired-shut mouth, but I silence him with a single stare.

"Call her a whore one more time. I dare you." A manic smile curls my mouth, and I drop the mask I don for polite society. It's a chore, but necessary when dealing with all I deal with on a day-to-day basis.

Leon tries to speak again, but this time it's Elias who silences him.

"Enough." The single word has Leon rolling his eyes, muttering something under his breath.

Unfortunately for the Bianchis, I overhear it. Within moments, I raise my firearm. Matthias follows suit, electrifying the chilly air. In a heartbeat, the Bianchi line has their own guns. Within seconds, the night's taken a dangerous turn.

We're severely outnumbered, but I can't let the disrespect slide. Not only is it a slight to me, but it's a slight to Loren, and that can't stand.

Elias is the only one who doesn't raise his piece. Instead, he glances around at the amount of firepower now front and center, humming with curiosity.

"This didn't have to take such a turn, Keane."

"It never would've if he hadn't married that whore," Leon says.

I don't know who gets the first shot off, but I know mine misses Leon by a hair. He ducks at the last second, hiding behind a barrel as the men take cover. Shots ping around the shipping containers, and I dive behind the open door from lot forty-three, Graves right behind me. My arm stings, and I swear, a quarter-inch graze on my left shoulder.

"Why the fuck would you do that? We're out-fucking-numbered," Matthias shouts from beside me. He pops out to fire off a few shots and returns to cover. Where there should've been a return volley, there's only silence and rainfall.

Graves dips his head out for a flash before ducking back behind the door, a shot ringing out toward him. He curses.

Rose, Jace, and her two other guys—I hadn't bothered to remember their names—are crouched behind another container, but they don't flee. Instead, Jace and another return fire. My respect for them rises. They could've left us high and dry, but they're staying.

When I glance past the shipping container door, there's a body lying face-down in the center of the loading zone. The flickering light above doesn't provide much to see by, but I know he's not one of ours.

Leon pops out, and I shoot another bullet his way. Then, suddenly, he's turning and running. In fact, the entire Bianchi force turns tail and leaves just as fast as they came. But they leave the body of their fallen, and I can't imagine they plan to return for him.

257

My steps are quiet as I cross the loading zone, head on a swivel and gun raised in case they decide to double back. When they don't, I crouch to the body, only to swear when the chest rises with a laborious breath.

With a heave, I roll the body over. Shock courses through me as Elias's bloodied face meets mine. His eyelids are heavy, and blood floods his mouth with each cough.

"Let's go!" Matthias shouts from the shipping container.

A torturous feeling swirls in my chest, something I haven't felt toward someone besides my wife in a long time: guilt.

Elias groans, and a weak hand lands on my arm, begging me to help him. I could leave him. My father would leave him.

Fuck.

I mutter something shameful under my breath before calling for Graves to help me.

"We're not seriously taking him with us." His tone is disbelieving.

I don't bother with a response other than to tell him to grab his legs.

Rose drives up with the last SUV, and we load Elias into the back. Jace climbs in after him and Matthias gets in the passenger seat.

"I'll drive."

Rose arches an auburn brow but moves to the middle row without otherwise speaking. Graves's gaze glues to her ass as it climbs over the seat, but Matthias smacks him upside the head. I jump in the driver's seat, needing to feel the pedal under my foot as I press it to the floorboard.

How did that go so fucking wrong?

I don't even question the fact that Rose and Jace stayed in the car with us. Jace watches Elias in the back with a trained eye, while Rose sits across Graves. Her two other men stay behind, working to clean up what they can and removing any evidence of our presence.

When we're almost to the hospital, my phone dings. I pull it out of my back pocket, and ice freezes my chest. There's a text from Everett, but more concerning, one from Loren.

Sent twenty-one minutes ago.

I love you.

What the fuck?

I open the tracking app linked to the microscopic chip on the necklace I gave her—she had a habit of running off, and clearly, it's paying off—and find that she's two streets over, heading in the same direction as we are.

"What the fuck?" I repeat, this time aloud.

"What?" Matthias asks. His nose is buried in his cell.

"Loren's driving down Fifth Avenue, heading toward the hospital."

Matthias's fingers pause from where they're typing on the screen. "And?"

"If she was coming from the house, she'd be driving east, not west. Why was she out this late, knowing everything that's going on?" I keep her confession to myself, the words thawing my chest, but the peace is short-lived.

"Something's wrong."

I pull my gun out, and we drive toward where her dot moves. When I see the red Corvette, vengeance swirls in my chest. I raise the gun, ready to rain hell on whoever has my wife.

CHAPTER TWENTY-EIGHT
LOREN

With a startle, I realize it's Cal behind the gun. A black SUV sidles up next to mine, and he looks in the car, noting Alice knocked out in the passenger seat. He puts his gun away, and through the rain and wind, Cal gestures wildly for me to pull over. The tight coil that's been wrapped around my chest loosens.

Pull over, he mouths again.

I look around for the nearest stop and spot a parking garage at the end of the street. I drive toward it, my foot shaking on the gas pedal as Cal falls in line behind me.

The garage is dark, with flickering fluorescent lights that only show how badly in need of repair it is. There are a few scattered cars, but for it being almost two in the morning, it's fairly empty.

I pull into a spot, throw the car into park, and turn to Alice. She trembles in her sleep, mumbling something under her breath. I press a gentle hand to her shoulder, but she doesn't wake.

"Alice, it's okay. We're safe now. See?"

Alice doesn't move. Something shatters inside me as I watch her shake and tremble. Doing the only thing I can think of, I crank the heater to warm her. The motel room was freezing, and I don't know how long they held her there.

My door is yanked open, and Cal's furious face appears next to mine. His gaze flicks over to Alice, softening for only a moment. When it slices back to me, all his anger rushes to the surface.

"Get out," he hisses. Steam practically billows from his nostrils as I climb out of the sports car. He shuts the door with more force than necessary, the slam echoing around the quiet garage.

I grab his arm to tug him away from the car. "Was that necessary? She's been through hell and doesn't need you scaring her."

A throbbing vein appears in Cal's neck, his face flushing with anger. For the first time since he appeared, I get a good look at him. He's soaked, his black T-shirt is filthy and stained in some spots. *Blood.* His hair is windblown, like he was in a speed chase. On his left shoulder, my eyes zero in on a bloodied tear through his shirt.

"What happened?" I ask as I reach for his arm.

He allows me to pull him closer, his chest heaving with rage as I inspect the wound.

"It's just a graze."

It's just a graze, he says as blood drips all over his arm.

"*Again,* I ask. What happened?"

"I should ask you the same thing." His thumb wipes away the drying blood on my temple, and I wince. There's a low throb, but I ignore it.

We're a macabre picture: bloody and soaked in the middle of an empty parking garage.

261

Cal rolls his shoulder, tugging his arm from my grip. Then he crowds into my space, his heated gaze flicking over my face, then my body. His eyes narrow at the rip in my dress, where Peter almost succeeded in his vile plan.

"I think I should ask you that," he grinds out between clenched teeth.

I stammer, gaze dragging back to the car where Alice lays. "He had her. Peter. He said to come alone."

Cal tips my head back, and his heated gaze drags over me. There must be some bruising already showing on my neck, and my temple throbs. I swallow thickly, and he releases my face. The past few hours have been an out-of-body experience, and my mouth flops open, but no words follow. I look back over to the car. "Alice needs a doctor. Right now."

Cal exhales deeply, his chin dropping to his chest. Then he waves to the SUV. Matthias hops out. His trained eyes scan the garage as his long strides reach us in no time.

"Get Alice and our *guest* to the hospital."

Matthias stills. "You'll be on your own, Cal."

Callahan just waves him off, eyes never leaving mine. "Did you end it?"

I know what he's asking. Did I kill Peter? I nod solemnly, but the guilt never comes. I killed a man tonight, and yet…I'm glad he's dead. My fingers twitch where they held onto the lamp, and Cal doesn't miss a beat. He grabs my hand, lacing our fingers together and squeezing my palm.

"Park Ave Motel. Room 324."

Then he looks to Matthias and nods. "We're fine for now. Get her to St. Thomas. Call Everett on the way and have him clean up the scene at the motel room."

Matthias looks between us, a pinch between his brow. But he turns on his heel without argument and quietly opens the door. He gently slides his arms under Alice's trembling form. Her head lolls backward; she's completely unconscious as he carries her to the back seat of the SUV. A woman I don't recognize hops out to give Matthias room for Alice, and then she slides into the passenger seat. Matthias drapes Alice's unconscious body along the seat, her head laying gently on Cohen's lap. He looks down at her with such sadness that my own heart breaks.

I have so many questions. I don't recognize half the people in the car, but no one looks like they need medical attention. So, who is Cal's *guest*?

Matthias jumps into the driver's seat. The tires squeal as he peels out of the parking lot.

When we're alone, Cal takes another step into my space, forcing me to take a step back. He hunts me, predatory and calculated, until my back presses against the cold concrete wall. Cal lifts a bloodied hand to sweep a lock of wet hair behind my ear. I suck in a breath. I knew he'd hate that I left, that I went on my own to meet Peter, just like I know he's going to unleash his fury on me any moment.

Cal leans forward, and the heat of his body warms my exposed skin. My nipples pebble under my satin dress, scraping against the fabric as his chest grazes mine.

"I'm not even going to ask why you did it," he starts, voice low and rumbling out of his chest, "because I know why. There's little that would stop you from protecting those you care about."

I nod, never breaking his eye contact. His hand lands on the wall next to my face, caging me in and offering no escape from his fury.

"But that doesn't mean you should've gone alone. You should've called me, Ren. Why didn't you call me?" His eyes plead with me for an answer, but I don't have one.

"He gave me twenty minutes to get to the motel. There was no time."

"There is always time. When it's your life on the line, I will *always* make time. I would've let the entire mission fail, lost every single one of my men and every single one of those women, burned every single bridge I had to ensure your safety."

His breaths come out heavy and hot as the air heats between us.

"Cal," I whisper, the words trembling out of me. "I'm okay. It was touch and go there for a second"—his nostrils flare, but I continue anyway—"but I did it. I'm not the girl you used to know. I can take care of myself."

Cal scoffs, but I see the pride warring with concern behind his brown eyes. As much as he must hate to admit it, I'm not the fragile teen he once knew. Then his gaze dips to my lips and over my body. He *tsks* as he takes in my satin dress. It's short, torn at the hem where Peter almost ripped it off. Callahan's jaw clenches, and his hands slide down my body, landing on my thighs.

The memory of Peter's grip burns, but Cal's touch already chases it away. My lower lip trembles, and Cal catches the movement. His brow furrows. The sudden realization of how close I came to giving up, to giving in…

Cal must sense that I'm about to break—in a blink, he whirls me around. My hands fly to the concrete wall to steady myself, and I twist my head over my shoulder. Cal's hands squeeze my thighs, bunching the material.

"And this is the dress you wore? In your *twenty minutes* to get to the motel?"

It works. His jealousy over the dress I picked out for him distracts me from my panic, and the thought sends a spark of electricity down to my core. I arch my back the slightest degree. The adrenaline rush, coupled with the kiss we shared earlier, melts into a heady combination, and the low heat between my legs turns scorching.

Cal chuckles, fully aware of his effect on me. A firm hand draws circles on my inner thighs, chasing away more of Peter's touch. Cal pushes me further against the wall of the parking garage. His body crowds mine, the heat from his attention intoxicating as my head tips against his shoulder.

"Are you trying to kill me?" The words slip out on a pained groan as one massive hand grips my waist, pulling my ass against his firm cock.

It's a delicious tease, feeling the promise behind his combat trousers. I huff a laugh. "If I wanted you dead, I would've smothered you in your sleep already."

His grip tightens on my hip, and he laughs. The sinful sound reverberates throughout the garage while the rain patters outside.

"Loren, you've been tempting me with death since you were sixteen. And I'm tired of pretending like you haven't." With each word, his hands travel between my legs, finding that aching spot and circling with a rhythm that rapidly builds the pleasure curling inside me.

I burn for his touch, arching my backside, silently begging him not to stop.

He doesn't. Instead, his lips find my neck, and he lathers kisses until he reaches my ear. Gentle nibbles on my lobe drive me wild, and his heated breath groaning in my ear as I whimper only serves to spin me higher.

"God, you drive me crazy."

I bite my lip and try to hold back my groan, but it still threatens to slip out.

"We're alone now, Bunny. Let me hear you." Another suckle on the soft skin behind my ear, and I follow his command, a rough moan echoing in the garage. His fingers circle faster, my pulse quickening as I near that edge.

As I ramp up to throw myself over, Cal freezes. The burn between my legs sputters out as my eyes rip open. I try to turn myself around, but he pins me in place, ruffling up my dress so it's shucked around my hips. I hear a clink of a belt buckle and the rip of a zipper moments before the blunt tip of his cock slides over my thong. It's soaked through, and he smears my wetness over his cock, shoving the material aside and slamming into me to the hilt. I groan, the fullness stretching me in a way I hadn't felt in so long—too long.

"God, you're so tight." He groans. "Fuck, I've missed you." His words are said with reverence, as if I am the only deity he worships.

I lose myself to his rhythm, forgetting altogether that we're in a goddamn parking garage, as Cal thrusts into me. A hand slips the strap of my dress down, exposing my left breast to the chilly air. He circles my pointed nipple with an expert touch, tugging on it and flicking the nub until he grasps my entire breast in his hand, using it as a handle as he rides me from behind.

"Cal," I whimper, the ache between my legs spurning me higher and higher.

He hears my plea and slips a hand through the trimmed hair on my pussy to strum my clit. The palms of my hands scrape against the concrete wall with each snap of his hips as he rocks into me, but I can't find it in me to care. It only takes another few thrusts before I'm quivering, ready to explode on his cock.

"Ren." My name is a prayer on his lips, and it's all it takes for me to burst, coming on his cock with a cry as his hips sputter. Two more pumps, and he explodes inside me, falling on top of me as we press against the wall together. His heavy breath washes over my heated face, and I can't help but smile.

A breath later, he pulls himself from me with a hiss. I look around to the car that's several feet away and groan.

"Not ten seconds after I've finished inside of you, and you're upset with me. Seems to be a record."

I turn around and roll my eyes, but Cal isn't focused on my face. His predatory gaze swipes over my flushed skin, the sheen of sweat on my collarbone, my exposed breast and rosy chest, and lastly—the cum dripping between my legs. I gesture toward the trail of his orgasm. "That's why. And we didn't even use a condom." If it weren't for my surgically implanted IUD, I'd be worried about the risk of pregnancy, but knowing his colorful history—my stomach sours—an STD isn't entirely ruled out just yet. "I need a tissue, please. Are there any in the car?"

A gleam shines behind his brown eyes, and he takes another step into my space, head tilted and smiling deviously. "You are my *wife*, Loren. If you think I'm letting you clean my cum from your skin, you'd be wrong." As he speaks, his hand slides up my thigh, rubbing his orgasm into my skin like it was lotion. "And if you think I'm taking this pussy any way but bare, you'll be sorely mistaken."

A flurry erupts low in my belly at the possessive motion, and I gasp. With careful steps, he guides me back to the Corvette. He only stops to lift me onto the hood. It's warm against my thighs, but I welcome the heat.

Cal slams his lips to mine, raising his hand to the apex of my thighs and circling my clit once again. The leftover tremors from my earlier orgasm have me extra sensitive, my body putty under his command. He works me higher and tighter, fusing our mouths together all the while. When I'm about to come for the second time, he pulls away from my face, still circling my clit. I'm panting on top of the Corvette, eyes drooping with lust as Cal licks his lips.

He kisses me again. "Tell me," he whispers against my lips, pushing his cum back inside me with his sinewy fingers. "Tell me who this pussy belongs to."

I gasp, the sensations too much for me to handle. I squeeze my eyes shut as my hips thrust into the palm of his hand.

"Tell me, *wife*." His words are hissed through clenched teeth, and my eyes part to find him wholly focused on my every whimper.

"You. It belongs to you," I groan.

Cal curls his lips into a sensual smile. "And who am I?" His touch never slows, never falters.

When I fly off the edge, the only words I scream are, "My husband."

CHAPTER TWENTY-NINE

The car ride is quiet, giving me time to think about what just happened. *He hasn't brought up my text.* I glance at Cal. His jaw clenches, knuckles white on the steering wheel, but he must sense my eyes on him. A hand slips onto my thigh and squeezes once, twice.

A flutter erupts in my lower belly, and I squirm in my seat. He still doesn't pull his gaze from the road, but his lips curl into a knowing smile.

When we're almost home, I finally break the silence, opting to deflect back to him. "So, are we going to talk about how you were shot?"

Cal lets loose a light sigh, rolling his shoulder. He barely even flinches with the movement, and I take it he's going to be fine.

"A slight misunderstanding."

Misunderstanding. Laughter bubbles in my chest and spills into the car. Cal finally glances over at me, a twinkle of humor sparkling his brown eyes.

"Misunderstandings usually comprise of running late to a dinner reservation, not getting shot."

"I wasn't *shot*. It's just a graze."

My eyes roll with false annoyance. The fact that he's sitting here with me, that I'm alive, that Alice is alive…Well, it just feels like things are finally starting to work out. I can only pray we'll find Mason, too.

Cal's phone rings. He winces as he shifts to pull it from his back pocket.

"Yeah?" His gaze slices to mine. "What?"

My brows furrow. His eyes widen, and a curse falls under his breath. "You sure?" he asks whoever is on the phone.

They answer, a muffled response I can't make out. Then his head drops. He ends the call and turns his attention back to the drive.

Something instinctive inside me recoils, knowing what he's about to say is going to rock me. I brace myself, fingers curling around the seatbelt as I wait with a knot lodged in my throat.

"Agapov…his body wasn't in the room. He's gone."

No. No, that can't be possible. There was so much blood—too much blood.

Cal must read the panic on my face. His hand finds mine, and he laces his fingers through one trembling hand, but it barely curbs the walls from pressing in on me. Once again, the memory of his touch burns like acid on my skin. I rip my hand from Cal's, swiping them over my body, my legs. Time slows to a crawl as the city lights blur together. My breath comes in short, hollow inhales, and it's not until Cal's arms slide under my legs that I realize we're home.

He lifts me out of the seat, cradling my trembling body to his chest as he walks me through the residence. I want to argue, to push him toward Doc to get his wound taken care of, but I can't speak.

All the way to our room, he carries me. When we reach our rooms, someone has already lit the fireplace. He passes straight through to sit me on the couch, heading into the bathroom. The shower turns on, and then Callahan returns to me. I can feel my feet again, so I stand, just as Cal slips his hand into mine. His dark brown eyes flicker over my face. He nods, gently pulling me into the bathroom.

Steam envelopes my body, and I fight to surface from the panic. Cal carefully undresses me, with a quiet "up" as he taps my arms to drag my dress off. It's not until scorching water blisters my skin that I jolt back into the present. Cal has ditched his own clothes and drags us into the shower. His hands graze my body with a gentle foaming soap, washing the dirt, blood, and filth from my skin with careful motions. His touch isn't sexual, he isn't seeking to turn me on. He's taking care of me. It's gentle and instinctive, the way he lifts my arms to scrub my body, his hands barely skimming my breasts, the dip of my waist. He guides me to sit on the bench and kneels, washing my legs and feet where the worst of the filth lies. Somewhere amid the tussle, I lost my slides, and my feet are grimy and black. Cal takes his time to wash each foot, cleaning between my toes as reverently as he can. It's a sight to behold, the most powerful man in Roswell on his knees before me, washing the dirt from my skin.

When he's finished, he lifts my right foot and places the softest kiss to the top of it. My tongue seems to be glued to the roof of my mouth, so instead of thanking him verbally, I pump soap into my hands and return the favor. His eyes flutter shut as I massage the shampoo into his scalp. When it's all clean, I tilt his head back to rinse the suds from his hair, then repeat with his conditioner. The quiet isn't tense; instead, it feels like safety. To be so trusting of the person you're with that no words are necessary. There's an unspoken understanding that it's not sexual. Cal is taking care of me, and I'm doing the same. That's it.

When I'm finished, Cal stands, and the glorious sight of soapy suds slipping over his toned frame stuns me. The blood has washed away from the wound on his arm, and I eye it nervously, but Cal stops the turn of my head with a gentle press on my chin. When I meet his gaze, his brown eyes soften, and butterflies take flight in my belly once more. This time, though, they're full of tender appreciation more than anything.

Cal pumps shampoo into his hands and massages my scalp. The suds percolate in my ears, and my eyes close on instinct, my head falling into his hold. There's a faint cherry scent and I smile. *He used my soap.* A gentle rain clears the shampoo, and I smile softly as he works the conditioner into my hair.

After another rinse, he pulls me to my feet and into his arms. His lips press tenderly to mine, stitching more than just our injuries together. After narrowly escaping horrific fates, somehow we found each other. Again.

Cal tips his forehead against mine. The warm water falls over our shoulders, our bodies, and when he speaks, his tone seeps with disbelief.

"You love me?"

I'd been expecting it. Somewhere between him instinctively knowing I needed his touch back in the parking garage, to carrying me from the car and taking care of me in the shower, I knew it was the right call to send the text. I sent it, thinking I wouldn't make it out of that hotel room. And yet here we are, holding on to each other in our bathroom, breathing life into the other with each exhale.

I look into his eyes, unable to gather the courage to say them aloud.

I know it's silly, but a part of me—the part of me that still mourns for our lost love—needs him to say it first. I need Cal to open that door, to let me in. Once and for all.

He smiles, reading the truth behind my silence. Water slides over his skin, darkening his brown hair and dripping over the tip of his nose. He laughs, a quick, triumphant laugh, before "thank fuck" falls from his lips, and he slams his mouth onto mine, kissing me like I'm the air the keeps him alive. Teeth clack, tongues dance, fingers slide to hold my face to his, and I wrap a leg around his hip.

His wide palm slides down my neck, my collarbone, and settles on my breast. Squeezing once, twice, he groans into my mouth as he flicks my nipple. Callahan swallows each moan as he winds me up with barely a touch.

It's like he remembers, just as I do. Our bodies meld together with the touch of a long-forgotten lover, but with the added passion of escaping near death.

We kiss like that for several breaths. Then he pulls his face from mine, though it looks like it pains him to do so. The shower has chilled, and he turns it off before handing me a fluffy towel from the heating rack. The warm cotton envelopes my body, and I almost moan. I must not be completely successful in my attempt to smother it, because the look Cal shoots me could scorch the earth.

We towel off, and I try to dry my hair as best I can without pulling out the blow-dryer. I don't want to lose any more time with him tonight. While I work on taming my hair, Cal applies ointment and a bandage to his bicep. When we're finished, he drops his towel on the floor and leads me by my hand toward the bed, bypassing the closet entirely. He smirks, pulling back the comforter and falling onto the mattress. He tugs me on top of him. The air is chilly, but he pulls the comforter over us, providing instant warmth.

Our legs tangle together, and I press my face to his chest, feeling the beat of his heart under my cheek. Cal brushes a feather-light touch over my arm, swirling nonsensical patterns into my skin. Goosebumps erupt over my exposed skin. He gathers me close, his breath washing over my face as I burrow into his hold.

When he speaks, his voice is low, and his heartbeat pounds under my cheek. "Ren, everything I've done in this life has been to get back to you. When my father died, I knew it was selfish, and I knew it was dangerous, but I couldn't keep myself from you any longer. You no longer lived at the Bianchi estate, and I sat with whether I could keep you safe for months. Since we've been married, each time your life has been at stake has been like a knife to the chest. But every morning when I see your surly face made brighter by a coffee that's more cream than coffee, or when you have a productive day of writing, or how Darla never once forgets your aversion to cheese…It's like the perfect balm on my soul that whispers I was justified in bringing you closer to danger, just so I can have you again."

Cal sweeps a thumb over my cheek, and I tilt my face to his. He continues, "I've loved you from the moment I knew what the word meant. Any breath we spent apart, I dreamed of one day being back here with you. I knew it was foolish but, Ren, I've never loved anyone like I love you. Never been *consumed* by someone like you've consumed me. And the only thing I learned from all our time apart is that I never could. You're woven into the fabric of my soul. Without you, there is no me."

His words heal something in me, and the ache that used to throb between my ribs doesn't feel as sharp. Sure, there's a dull pain from the remnants of knowing we spent so long apart when we could've been together, but I can't think like that. I can't spend my life wishing it had worked out one way, not when I have Cal here in front of me, giving me everything I've been wishing for. I don't know what to say; my thoughts are a jumbled mess. So instead, I crash into him.

His lips tangle with mine, our bodies fusing together, finally reunited after so long apart. His hand slides down to cup the curve of my ass, pulling me closer. One of his legs slides between mine, notching up into my center. I can't help it, I grind myself on his thigh, moaning into his mouth. He swallows each sound, drawing them out as one hand settles on my hip, dragging my body back and forth over his thigh.

"That's it. Ride my leg, Bunny." His words are a growl against my lips, and I whimper. His free hand sweeps my damp hair behind my ear, pulling my face back with a firm grip as he stares deeply into my eyes. Cal watches intently, hooded gaze flickering over my face, my parted lips, the pulse in my neck. He growls, slamming his mouth to mine. *Devouring me.*

Back and forth I grind on his leg, the slick from my arousal making a mess, but it only seems to spurn Cal on further. The hair on his legs is soft, teasing against my swollen sex, and the heat builds in my core as I lose myself to the rhythm. Cal whispers depraved filth into my ear, and my eyes flutter shut, chasing the release he's sending me hurtling toward. He takes his time, dragging my center over his thigh in an agonizing pace, speeding me up and slowing me down, easing me off that cliffside with each drag of my hips. It should shock me just how well he plays my body even after so long apart, but it doesn't. Even when we were teens, he learned what strings to pull so quickly my head spun.

As the bright moonlight shines into the room, I lose myself in him. My pace falters, and right as I explode, Cal captures my mouth with a searing kiss. I groan into his mouth, but he just kisses me with even more ferocity, holding my weight as I tremble on top of him. My heart thuds, and I pull back, gasping for air and bracing myself using Cal's shoulders.

Cal smiles, eyes twinkling and dimple making an appearance. "Good job, Bunny."

Heat flushes my face and chest, the blood rushing to my cheeks. His praise warms something inside me, and I fight the urge to hide from his affection. Cal notices and sweeps a gentle thumb over my cheek. I nuzzle into his palm and sigh, the throb of his hard cock poking my side. My eyes pop open, my mouth watering.

I slide down Cal's body until my lips are inches from his rigid length. I reach a tentative hand to grip at its base where dark, trimmed hair tickles the length of my pinky. Cal hisses when I make contact, groaning when I squeeze it tighter. Watching from hooded eyes, his nostrils flare when I slip my fingers down my body, rolling them around my soaked entrance and thrusting inside three times. When they're sufficiently soaked, I wrap my fist around his cock once more, slicking the shaft with my arousal and orgasm.

Cal groans, head tipping backward onto the pillow as I work him over. The moment my lips press to the crown of his cock, his eyes fly back open. For several strokes, he just watches, a mix between awe, lust, and disbelief swirling behind his brown eyes. I pick up the pace, using my fist to twist and squeeze the base of his cock that I can't fit in my mouth. Cal's hand sweeps my hair over my shoulder, gathering it in his fist as his hips thrust upward.

My gaze slices to his as I relax my jaw and flatten my tongue, giving him the chance to fuck my throat.

"Fuck," he hisses through clenched teeth. "That's it, Ren. Swallow my cock down." His strokes are slow but sharp as his hips thrust his rigid length into my mouth. Salty precum mixes with my saliva, and I swallow around his length, eliciting a groan from the man below me. The crown of his cock hits the back of my throat, and tears burn in my eyes, but don't spill over just yet.

Heat gathers in my core, never fully having left from my earlier orgasm, but I keep my attention on the way Cal's fingers grip my hair, the way my body presses against his, the way his length fills my mouth. Cal thrusts faster, harder, and the first tear slips over my cheek.

"You look so beautiful like this." His words are oddly reverent and tugs at something in my chest. Cal continues to thrust, and his free hand slides into my hair, gripping the strands and pulling my face even closer to his pubic bone. It triggers my gag reflex, and I choke on his cock, but he doesn't stop.

Cal doesn't ask—he takes—and it has always been my downfall.

His thrusts speed until tears are streaming down my face, the little air I can breathe in through my nose causing black dots to appear in my periphery. The salty mix of precum and saliva pools in my mouth, spilling over my chin with each thrust.

Then Cal explodes in my mouth with a groan, holding the sides of my face over his cock as ropes of cum shoot into the back of my throat. His hips shudder under me, a shaky laugh escaping from his muscular chest. Before I can swallow, his thumb hooks into my mouth, pulling my jaw down so he can admire the pool of cum on my tongue.

He *tsks*, a devilish curl to his lips sending a bolt of electricity to my core. "That's my pretty wife." He shoves his thumb into my mouth, and I suck on it for a beat until he pulls it out, tipping my jaw shut in silent command.

His cum is salty and thick, but it slides down my throat easily. My lips curl into a sweet smile as I climb up his body. Cal's touch is gentle this time, swiping the tears away and placing a tender kiss against my brow. We fall into an old, yet familiar, routine, as Cal cleans me, and I use the bathroom. No words are exchanged, just two souls dancing in the moonlight of revived memories and familiar steps.

We find ourselves back in the bed, slumber tugging at my eyelids as I lay on his chest. Our legs tangle once more, and I breathe a sigh of relief at the comfort. Cal's arms band around me, holding me tightly to his chest as we drift off.

I'm slipping into unconsciousness when I think I hear him speak. The words are muffled, or wrong somehow, but it almost sounds like an apology.

CHAPTER THIRTY

We don't leave the bed for two days. Time seems to slip away as we lie together, relearning each other's bodies and sharing the highlights of our time apart. The first morning after, Tinley shrieked when she entered the room, thinking we'd already left for breakfast. The poor girl is probably scarred for life after seeing Cal drive into me. He didn't even stop, just turned back to me and covered my body with his. From then on, food was delivered to his desk, and we shut out the rest of the world.

Alice was released from the hospital yesterday, but she won't answer any of my calls. I know she needs to heal, but I can't help but feel sick with guilt. I want to show up at her apartment, but Cal has talked me out of it. Instead, he sent Cohen to check on her. It eases some of the crushing guilt, and when Callahan trails his fingers down my spine, I forget everything besides his touch.

But eventually, all good things end, and we had to return to reality.

Hot air blows on my face as I dry my hair into waves, while Cal shaves the three-day scruff off his jaw. Our eyes keep catching on each other's in the mirror, a knowing curl to my lips matching his. By the time we make it downstairs, we've already discovered just how selfish we can be with making others wait. Twice.

Cal's lips are tender but chaste when he pulls out my chair at the breakfast table in the dining room. Fresh roasted coffee wafts in the air, and I doctor the mug to my liking, the creamy blend warming my bones and filling my stores. Or that may be the way Cal keeps staring at me from above his newspaper.

"Earth to lover boy," Lucas teases with a wave of his tattooed hand in front of Cal's face. "You in there still?"

Cal rolls his eyes, shaking out his paper and ignoring Luc flat out. It brings a smile to my face, which Matthias catches immediately. He's still sour toward me, but less so than when I first moved in. I often wonder if we'll ever be friendly like we were as teens, but part of me knows not to get my hopes up. Well, if I have to prove to him I'm all in, so be it.

"Any word on Peter?"

A fork clatters onto Luc's porcelain plate, the clang ringing out in the newly tense silence. I shift uncomfortably in my seat as I wait for an answer, but no one seems to want to say anything.

Cal clears his throat, swallows a bite of food, and takes a sip of water. "Everyone is searching for him."

The table seems empty, but I'd just thought we were late to the meal. My brows furrow. "Have you reached out to Rose?"

Matthias and Lucas look nervously between each other. "We have, but she's unlikely to tell us she's captured him if he's still alive."

Cal's fingers curl into fists on top of the table. My blood runs cold, and I shove my hands under the table, the warmth of my thighs defrosting them. My bottom lip makes for a decent distraction as I gnaw on it, but I can't avoid the question for long. "Any updates on Mason?"

The air turns tense, silent as my question hangs. Cal's throat bobs, and he doesn't answer. Matthias and Lucas are also noticeably quiet.

"Listen, Ren," Cal starts, his tone oddly placating. "No news is good news at this point. If our tech contact can't find him, that's not the worst thing in the world. It means he hasn't found him dead"—Cal winces but continues—"or alive. We're still looking for him. Okay?"

The information isn't surprising, but it doesn't stop the blanket of guilt wrapping around my shoulders. I knew when Mason shared he wanted to follow in our father's footsteps that he was risking his life every day. With each day that passes, I'm finding that glow of hope dimming. There's still one year and eleven months left on our marriage contact—though I think it's probably void by now.

I need to prove that I'm in this. For good.

"And what about the warehouses?"

Luc smirks, but Matthias's brows shoot to his hairline. He folds his arms over his chest. "Why are you so suddenly interested in our business, Loren?"

"Isn't it my business now, too, Mattie?"

He growls, the sound reverberating across the dining room table.

Settling into my chair, I let his obvious annoyance fuel me. "I think it's about time I did. This is my legacy now, too, Mattie. You guys seem to forget that I grew up in the Bianchi house. Have you even considered what I might know about their operations?"

Lucas and Cal look impressed, but Matthias just rolls his eyes.

"What could you possibly know?"

My smile makes him flinch.

Fifteen minutes later, we're in Cal's office downstairs. I'm sitting in front of Cal's desk while Lucas sits beside me. Matthias opts to lean against the bookshelf behind Cal's desk, while Cal sits on his throne. The clock on the wall ticks as the silence stretches. Luc taps his fingers against the desk, and Matthias does his best to look anywhere but at me.

"So, what you're saying is..." Cal trails off, confusion pressing down on his brows.

"Their systems are archaic, and part of the reason they've been so difficult to track is because they only keep written records. There's nothing to hack."

Matthias scrubs a hand over his jaw. Dark circles shadow his brown eyes. *I wonder how much sleep he's been getting.*

Lucas looks astonished. "That must take...hours—no, *days* longer than it should. And what are the checks to ensure accurate reporting?"

"It's a pretty tight-knit circle. Each leader reports their division's operations to their supervisor, and so on, until only the Bianchi brothers have access to the entire operations. Leon assumes most of the responsibility of balancing it and presents the reports to Elias."

Matthias whistles, shaking his head in disbelief. "Handing that much unchecked power to someone who's not the boss is never a good idea."

My nose scrunches. It's *Leon.* All he did as a kid was chase Hudson, Elias, and me around. He's always looked up to his brother.

"Anyway," I continue, "obviously they share the same desire to grow, both in power and territory, but from what I can tell, Elias has had a difficult time implementing any change. The last time I visited the Bianchi estate, Elias had the same ledger sitting on his desk that his father did." Not that I have much room to talk. I still used a planner, too.

Cal frowns. "When was the last time you visited the Bianchis?"

A knot thickens in my throat. "About a week before I went to Abstrakt."

His nostrils flare, and the heat of his stare pins me to my chair. We sit in tense silence for several moments until Luc clears his throat, releasing us from our trance.

"I had to ask about Mason. But they told me they couldn't give an outsider any confidential information. That's when I knew I was on the outs with them. I used the last of my goodwill when I asked Hudson to slip me a wristband for Abstrakt."

While I speak, Cal is silent, but his outrage seems to dissipate from his features. His shoulders relax, and his signature smirk appears once more. "And thank god he did."

My eyes roll of their own accord. They sent Mason into Keane territory and told him to scope out their warehouses for god knows what reason—my brows shoot to my hairline. Cal shifts in his seat, leaning forward with his elbows on his desk.

"Take me to a warehouse."

They all protest at the same time.

"Absolutely not."

"Fuck no."

"No chance."

I try again. "Take me to a warehouse," I pause, holding up a hand to Matthias when he opens his mouth to argue again. "Let me see what it looks like. I've known Mason his entire life, and until seven weeks ago, we lived together. I know how he thinks, how he operates. As much as

I hate it, I understand why he did what he did. My brother's desperate to be accepted. But if you take me to a warehouse, maybe I can put myself in his place and see what he would've done. Maybe I…" I trail off, clearing the desperation from my throat.

Cal's brown eyes flick over my face, searching for something. Then, he nods curtly.

"You can't seriously be considering this," Matthias says. "Agapov is still MIA, and just because he hasn't gone back to another warehouse doesn't mean he won't."

Cal turns to Lucas, who shrugs. "We haven't pulled back security yet. If there's any time to visit, it would be now."

Then Cal turns back to me, but his words are for the brooding man behind him. "I think you're underestimating my wife, Mattie."

A warm flurry erupts in my belly, and blood rushes to my cheeks, but I don't break eye contact with Callahan. There's a mischievous curl to his lips, and I stifle the matching curl to mine.

Cal nods once. "Fine. But we wait until nightfall."

CHAPTER THIRTY-ONE

Tires crunch over gravel as we enter the compound. Someone drags a gate open, and the clang of the metal chain is deafening in the quiet evening. It shuts behind us with a foreboding slam. I fixate on the building as we approach, my heart racing when I imagine Mason sneaking in. I can see it now, Mason sticking to the shadows and slipping in unnoticed. While he's only gotten both taller and broader with age, he's learned how to sneak around unnoticed. Rather, *he thought* he was sneaking around unnoticed. What he wasn't aware of was anytime he left, it was because I allowed him to. Still, he got a thrill out of testing my limits. A ghost of a smile curls the corner of my mouth.

Cal rounds the car. He's taken me to one of the three remaining warehouses. They used to have six, but two were torched before I met Cal in Abstrakt, and one since we married. They've had to merge operations between the remaining buildings.

This one is two stories high and about the size of a common drug store—the irony isn't lost on me. It's also the farthest from the heart of

Roswell. It would take a suspiciously curious individual to even find it. If one were to pass by, you wouldn't think anything nefarious was going on inside. It's a building with a beige shiplap exterior out in the middle of nowhere. There aren't any windows, but in the center, there's two enormous barn doors. As we roll to a stop, the door on the left slides open, and Luc exits.

Dust billows from under me when I hop out of the car, and the moon shines brightly from its peak in the sky. There's a chill to the air, but my beige cashmere sweater is warm. I tucked it into a short brown skirt with sheer brown tights. Chestnut riding boots cover up to my knees. My hair is loose around my shoulders, gently blowing in the wind. After spending almost an hour in the car, I stretch an arm to each side, hiding a yawn behind my hand.

Cal rounds the car, and the heat of his arm wraps around my waist. He wears a pair of black trousers and a tight white tee stretched across his broad chest. A black holster wraps around his thigh. Even though the air is crisp, he doesn't seem to mind the cold.

Luc's steps are leisurely, and when he reaches us, he wears a bright smile. "Hey, boss. Ma'am."

"Luc." Cal dips his chin, nodding toward the warehouse. "How's it handling the increased load?"

"Good, so far. We still need to bring in most of the Thatcher House product, but it should be delivered by the end of the week. The first shipment to Edwards is due tomorrow morning."

With that, we trail inside as Lucas fills Cal in on the daily operations. His voice echoes in the cavernous space, and I catch Cal watching my reaction from the corner of my eye. Inside, there are rows and rows of tables, places for workers to sort and pack cocaine—though no one besides security is here at this time of night. Dim fluorescent lights provide just enough to see by, but it's still dark as we walk the length of the building. Two guards patrol the building inside, and I'd bet there are more outside that I didn't notice. One in particular catches my eye. Caleb Ferguson. He notices me and freezes, eyes widening before darting to Cal, who's busy with Lucas. He doesn't look back at me, and instead, studiously avoids my attention.

Cal passes a careful eye over each station, murmuring to Luc as we walk. Inside his warehouse, his mask hardens, gaze narrowing and unrevealing of any thoughts. It's unnerving watching the transformation, almost as if he turns into a different person.

Lucas and Cal continue their visit while I linger back, taking in the space. There's a pungent, slightly sweet scent to the air. The cocaine, I suppose.

Cal notices and moves to my side to whisper in my ear, "Let me know what you find." Brown eyes meet mine, and he arches a brow.

I nod, hopeful I won't have to speak to anyone. It's taking all my reserves to picture Mason in this space, snooping around a place he has no business in. Cal returns to Luc, and they resume their discussion, voices low between them. My steps are quiet as I explore. Caleb and the other guard note my movements but watch silently as I pass by. There must be at least thirty stations in here and so much coke this place would be a fed's wet dream.

A few offices line the building, and I poke my head into each one. One looks well used but tidy. There's a file cabinet in the corner and a stack of papers on the gray desk. *This must be Luc's.* The papers on the desk don't hold any information I'm interested in, and there's not much else to the office. A vent in the ceiling and a mini fridge in the corner. That's it.

The next office turns out to be a supply closet, but the third door leads to a bare office—just an empty desk and chair in the center. At least this one has a window. It's narrow, probably barely lets in any light, but it's something to break up all the fluorescent bulbs. It's all very clinical in the sense that if you somehow missed the giant loads of cocaine, you wouldn't think anything suspicious was going on.

If this was what Mason had been investigating, what would he have been looking for? Honestly, knowing my younger brother, he has a chip on his shoulder the size of New York, and he'd probably bite off more than he could chew. Not only would he look for product to smuggle back to the Bianchis, but he'd look for a way to stop production—or at least interfere with it.

Oh, god. Is Mason behind the fires?

The question burns like acid. Mason is certainly impulsive enough to escalate to arson, but he'd never want to hurt anyone. In the Culver Street fire, the entire team was killed when the perp blockaded the doors. I can't imagine Mason could be responsible for such a heinous crime.

That doesn't mean he's innocent. It's possible Elias and Leon haven't told you the entire truth.

The world spins, and bile rises in my throat. Just how much have I been kept in the dark?

Cal appears in front of me, a pinch between his brows. "Hey." His gentle voice is soothing, and I throw myself into him. Strong arms band around me, holding me tightly against his chest. His sandalwood cologne fills my senses, grounding me.

I squeeze my eyes shut forcefully. "What if Mason's behind the fires?" My words mumble into Cal's coat, but he freezes in place, body turning rigid under my arms.

Cal's hands press around my arms, and he looks deeply into my eyes. His gaze flicks between my eyes until he finally whispers, "Do you actually believe that?"

My lower lip trembles, and I suck in a wobbly breath. I shake my head.

Cal relaxes, crushing me back to his chest. "Then neither do I."

His belief in me, in Mason, is a breath of fresh air. I've tried to justify that he's an adult who's made his own bed, but it doesn't sit right with me.

"Okay," Cal exhales. "What are you thinking?"

Lucas walks into the nondescript office and shuts the door behind him, offering us privacy from the patrol outside.

A deep breath rattles from my chest, my fingers rubbing my eyes. "Honestly? Knowing Mason, he'd wind up executing a half-assed impulsive plan that would eventually backfire."

Cal and Lucas listen with their arms crossed over their broad chests, hands tucked into their underarms.

"Something impulsive, like setting a fire?"

Lucas makes the same connection, but it only further cements how wrong it sounds.

"I really don't think so. He would never want to hurt someone like that. He's not a murderer."

"Even if he was covering something up?"

Luc's face is contemplative, his question adding a layer of complexity I hadn't yet considered.

"Like what?" Cal asks.

Luc shrugs. "Whoever was actually breaking in. A fire would erase any evidence."

"But they have to know that they're the only ones living in the dark ages. They'd know about the cameras, and it's not 2005. We have the Cloud now. Destroying the hardware is going to be a bitch to replace, but we can still access the footage."

"I think we're making this too complicated."

Both heads turn to me.

"Fires are being set. Why?"

They're quiet for a moment. Then Cal says, "Operations are disrupted, product is destroyed or stolen, crew is reduced. All that combined hits our bottom line. Hard."

"You're missing something."

Cal's eyes light up. "You're right, Bunny. It leaves blind spots we're scrambling to fill, pulling our attention away from our territory. They're snatching up streets left and right as we chase a ghost."

I hum in approval. Sometimes, the right answer is the simplest one. "And who stands to gain the most with each square mile of territory lost?"

Cal and Lucas answer at the same time. "The Bianchis."

The thrill of putting the pieces together wears off, and I'm left with a pit in my stomach. If the Bianchis are behind this...It shouldn't surprise me when criminals are untrustworthy. Growing up in this life, I've always understood there was a balance. If you're not going to sell it, someone else will. At least this way you can have some modicum of quality control. But they'd never strayed from marijuana and protection fees.

"But that would mean...Elias has been behind it the whole time."

My words hang in the air, and I can't help but picture him in his hospital bed. Apparently, Elias was shot in the shoulder the other night, and has yet to wake up from his coma. "Even the bombs?"

Cal's eyes soften. "It certainly looks like it."

"So, did Rose lie to us, or was her information bad?"

Lucas clears his throat. "She doesn't seem like she trades in bad information."

Cal nods, lost in thought as he scrubs a hand over his jaw. "I'm inclined to believe her. But we're not particularly in a position to be too trusting right now."

"We're not in a position to scare away any potential allies, either," I counter. Still, it leads us back to Mason. *Why did he have to get involved?*

CHAPTER THIRTY-TWO

C al takes a step toward me and pulls me to his chest. "I'm sorry, Bunny." His voice is soft, and my eyes fall shut on instinct.

Lucas clears his throat, and I peek up from Cal's hold. "I'm headed back to the house. Everett said we might have some leads on Agapov."

Peter's name sparks a rage unlike I've ever known.

"Did you just growl?" Cal's chest shakes with laughter.

I slap a playful hand over his shoulder. "Shut it."

His lips press together, but the humor still sparks in his gaze.

"We're right behind you," Cal tosses over his shoulder to a smirking Lucas. When the door shuts behind him, Cal slips a finger under my chin. Dark brown eyes search mine, but looking for what? "Does it change how you feel?"

A frown tugs at my mouth. "Does what change how I feel?"

Cal sighs, releasing me and walking over to perch on the edge of the desk. My steps are quiet as I follow him, not giving him the space he's trying to put between us.

"Seeing all this?" He gestures to the warehouse full of cocaine behind the closed office door. "Seeing…me like this?"

His shoulders are rigid under my touch, but I slide my hands over the curve of his neck to cup his jaw and tilt his face toward mine. Without warning, I gently press my lips to his, letting my affection speak for me. The kiss is light, only a few strokes of our tongues before I pull back.

"Cal…" My lips curl into what I hope is a reassuring smile. "It was never a question."

He smiles, relief wiping the worry from the crinkle of his eyes, hands sliding to the backs of my thighs and squeezing gently.

"One day, you'll see all of me. I can only pray you can forgive the darkest sides."

I lean forward, pressing my lips to his once more. I can't verbalize it, not right now, but I think I already have.

Cal's hands slide to my ass, gripping my backside as he pulls me tighter against his body. His cock hardens against my belly, and I groan into the kiss.

"Should I have you here? Right on this desk and leave a mess for Luc to find tomorrow morning?"

I nod, a roguish grin sliding onto my face. Cal's eyes droop with lust as he licks his lips. Hands travel under my skirt, one resting on my hip while the other dips inside my tights. Cal groans when he touches my wet center, and I surge forward to kiss him. Our tongues tangle, and I can't help the whimper when he thrusts two solid fingers inside of me.

Cal smiles into our kiss, setting a punishing rhythm as he works me. "Fuck, you're always so ready for me."

I huff a laugh but don't elaborate that I've been dreaming about this for years. It's easy to fall into his touch when I used to pray that one day I'd feel it again.

Heat burns in my lower belly, filling my senses like the sweetest campfire. Shouts ring out from the warehouse, and my nose scrunches. I inhale sharply, my eyes bursting open. Black smoke pours in from the vent above, and I jump backward.

"Cal!"

Cal swears, rushing to the door and yanking it open. Caleb and the other guard on duty are pulling out fire extinguishers, but it's not stopping the fire from raging. Angry orange flames lick up the walls, heating the room to a sweltering degree. My neck dampens with sweat as I rush toward the door to the outside and tug on the handle. It burns my hand but doesn't budge. *Fuck, someone barricaded us in.*

"Cal, we're stuck in here."

His face glistens with sweat as his panicked eyes dart over the warehouse, over me. Then he digs his phone out of his pocket, dialing someone. Fuck, in all the excitement, I left my phone in the car. The heat rises, smoke quickly filling the vaulted ceiling of the warehouse. Cal hangs up the phone and pulls his white tee off with one hand. My confusion momentarily stuns me, standing frozen as he dashes over.

"Here!" Cal shouts, ripping his shirt in two and tying a strip around the bottom half of my face, covering my nose and mouth. Then he does the same for himself with his other half. "Stay low."

The flames grow brighter, hotter with each second, and a similar panic rises in my chest. My knees scream at me from our crouched position, but I don't dare get any higher. Caleb and the other guard abandon their extinguishers, the fire too great to be contained by their sprays, instead opting to ram the doors down. The walls shudder with each slam against the door, but they don't stop trying. Acid burns in my stomach as I clench Cal's hand.

"There must be another exit. You said there's always another exit." I cough, cheeks burning from exertion. "A back door…something!"

Cal shakes his head. "It's not like we have the fire marshal here to make sure we pass inspections." He swears under his breath.

My hand snakes over to his, lacing our fingers together and squeezing tightly. The heat is thickening, pressing against my lungs as I try to suck in a breath, but all I get is a mouth full of smoke. I cough into the crook of my arm, and Cal's gaze swings over to me.

"Luc's on his way back. He was only a few minutes away when I called him. He's going to get to us."

Anger flushes, and I fight the urge to cough again. "Cal, if they just set this fire, there's a chance they're still here and could stop him from getting to us."

Black smoke fills the air that the flames don't reach, making a hazy film cloud my vision. I can barely see Cal in front of me, and god, what I would give for a window.

My spine snaps straight.

Cal notices, his attention swinging to me immediately.

I hold my hand out expectantly. "Give me your gun."

He opens his mouth to argue, but I cut him off. "Give me your gun. There's a window in that back office that I'm going to climb through. I'll circle the warehouse and open the door. But I need your gun in case they're still here."

Cal's head jerks back, but then somber acceptance washes over his face. He yanks his makeshift mask off his face and rips mine off, slamming his lips to mine. The kiss is brutal, punishing with every unspoken word he pours into it. Then he pulls back, a trembling hand unclipping his gun and handing it to me.

"Listen to me," he rushes, placing his hands on either side of my face, "if there's more than one, or you can't get a good shot—run. Get yourself safe. Do you understand me?"

My mouth opens to argue, but a beam from the ceiling comes crashing down, and we flinch, Cal covering my body with his as the embers catch fire around us. When it settles, we straighten.

"Hurry." He places a chaste kiss on my lips, and I study his face, praying to the gods above that it's not the last time I see it.

I slide my makeshift mask back over my face and check the barrel of the gun, finding it loaded. Without looking back, I cross the warehouse, dodging falling debris and flames as I make my way to the last door on the right. By the time I make it into the room, sweat drips from my temple and under my heavy sweater. With a hasty untuck of my top, I use the hem to twist the knob and open the door. Smoke pours out of the office, but there doesn't appear to be active flames inside.

A *thump* lands behind me, and I jump, twisting around to find another beam having fallen. But that's not all—in my haste to get to the window, I didn't even notice Callahan trailing behind me. Flames cast a wall of fire between us, and I can only stagger backward as Cal takes a running leap through the flames.

A scream rips from my throat as his body sails through the fire. At the last second, he tucks into a roll, extinguishing any flames that caught onto his trousers.

"What the *fuck*, Callahan?"

It distracts me for the briefest moment, but the smoke fills my lungs, and I cough, throwing an elbow to cover my mouth. Cal hustles over, and we cross into the office. The window is about six feet off the ground and a square that's about two feet by one foot. It's a sobering realization that I'm glad Cal followed me. I'm not sure I would've been able to push the desk over in time.

Cal doesn't even ask—he drops into a stance, hands clasped into a stepping point for me to put my weight on. I bounce on my feet for only a moment, and Cal must sense my hesitation.

"Hey," he says, never moving from his ready stance. "You've got this. I've seen you shoot. You'll bust outta here, circle the building, clear whatever is blocking us in, and set us free. Piece of cake."

I nod, the pressure of the situation threatening to suffocate me, but I refuse to let it. Instead, I ground myself, locking my emotions down like I did all that time I spent in Father's closet. I'd listen to his meetings for hours—the only way he'd let me. Since I was born female, I wasn't ever going to be an eligible soldier, but Father wanted me to learn, anyway. So, he shoved me inside his office closet for eight to twelve hours a day, listening in on his meetings to learn the business. While I learned too much for any eight-year-old, it also gave me a sickening claustrophobia.

Cal adjusts himself, smoke thickening the air as I finally place my foot into his hold.

"One, two, three—"

On three, he hoists me upward, and my arms grab onto the window ledge. The plastic lock is stiff under my fingers, but Cal's hold doesn't falter as I work on it. When it finally unlatches, I push open the window and breathe the first breath of clean air in who knows how long. But I can't enjoy it for long. Cal heaves me upward, and I scramble, the ledge of the window scraping along my belly as I crawl through. The smooth shiplap under my palms doesn't offer much in terms of control on my way down, and I land in a heap on the dirt ground.

Standing, I wince. My ankle is sore, but I ignore its protest as I palm Cal's gun and circle the building, staying in the shadow of the walls. Other than the roaring flames, the night is quiet, and I'm afraid I wouldn't hear someone unless they were right in front of me.

I continue, my gun sweeping the area in front of me with each step. Blood pounds in my ears as my vision tunnels, shadows from trees appearing to move in my periphery.

"You're just seeing things. *Focus*."

It feels like it takes too long to clear the corner of the building, and when I reach the front, I burst into a run.

The gravel vibrates under my footfalls, and I skid to a stop in front of the door. There's a thick rope tied around the handles. With a cursory shove, I holster the gun in my waistband and strain to untie the knot, but it's tied so tightly it isn't budging.

"*Fuck*."

The skin on my hands rips with each tug, each pull on the rope. Smoke secretes from the slats between the walls, and hope drains from my chest as a memory of a young Cal flashes in front of me.

My heart is bound to break out of its cage with the way it speeds. Callahan sits in the driver's seat, a hand resting on my thigh, and I can't help the flutter of butterflies that take flight.

"So," he says with a squeeze of my thigh, "you ready for this weekend?"

He's been asking me to go to that damn lake house for weeks now, and I finally gave in. He makes a good point: our families won't know, and we'd be free to be us. Without prying eyes, maybe we could finally take that last step. I know Callahan has slept with one other girl—he told me when we first started secretly dating. But he'd be my first, and I don't think I'd have the guts to do it in his house or mine. Plus, I want it to be special that first time. I chew on my lip, nerves bubbling in my chest.

"Bunny?"

I scrunch my nose. "I thought I told you to stop calling me that."

Callahan laughs, and it's like he's spinning gold. I'm enraptured by the smile that creases his face, the light shining behind his eyes.

"Why would I do that, Bunny, when it so obviously fits you?"

A scoff escapes my chest, but my cheeks flood with heat. Callahan Keane sees through my mask, sees through the biting sarcasm I employ to keep people at a distance.

"You don't think so?" He boops my nose. "Not even when you slip away from me, prancing just on the edge of my traps? Or how incredibly adorable you look when your feathers are all ruffled and your nose scrunches up?"

A newly familiar heat gathers in my belly, and blood rushes to my cheeks. My mouth parts to respond, but the car rolls to a slow. On the shoulder, a car has crashed into a broad sycamore tree. A thick branch has fallen on top of the roof, bisecting the car almost in two. We're off the beaten path quite a bit, and if we hadn't been driving to the lake house tonight, who knows if anyone else would even be here? I roll down the window, the night air crisp. I shiver.

Steam billows from under its hood, and a shaking voice cries from the driver's seat, "Help! We're stuck!" She sounds terrified.

Cal pulls off on the shoulder and throws the car into park. He's quick, flicking open the glove compartment and pulling out a knife, shooting a wink my way. "What can I say? I should be a Scout if the Keane business ever tanks."

He slips from the car right as I open my door, rushing right behind him to help him cut the driver out of her seat. There's two terrified teenage girls in the back seat, so I move to them first. The older one whimpers, clearly trying to stay strong for her mom and little sister. Blood trickles from her temple, staining her auburn hair a deep crimson.

"It's okay. We'll get you out of here."

The memory dissipates, and I dash over to the car and rip open the passenger door. In the glove compartment, a sheathed knife sits. I grab it. Smoke billows into the sky, and time moves slowly, feeling like hours pass as I cut through the coarse rope. When it finally snaps, the rope falls to the ground, and I tug the doors open.

Caleb and the other guard spill outside. They collapse onto each other as they suck in fresh air. My hand moves to shield my eyes from the blaze, but Cal doesn't appear.

"Where's Callahan?"

Caleb continues to cough, and neither offers any answer. My heart lodges in my throat as flames lick the walls of the building. There's still no sign of Cal. The seconds pass in agonizing slowness. Then, Lucas comes running back toward the building, running from the gravel trail that leads to the forest. I should wonder where his car went and why he's on foot, but can't care at the moment.

"Cal"—I point to the burning building—"he's still in there!"

Luc's face blanches. When he doesn't respond, my feet make my decision for me. In the next breath, I'm back in the burning building as smoke clouds my eyes. I squint, but it doesn't help. Black ash and smoke fill my lungs.

"Cal!"

I inhale a billow of ash and cough, heading further inside the warehouse. In the corner, I finally spot him. Cal is slumped over, enveloped in a cloud of smoke. I move without thinking, slinging an arm under his body as I try to lift him. An agonizing groan slips through my teeth as I struggle to lift him upward.

"Fuck," I roar, tugging his arm again and surely hurting his shoulder, but I can't seem to give a fuck about that if it means he'll live. "Work with me, Cal!"

I try again, and suddenly, he goes flying toward me. Lucas appears, sweat dripping over his face as he pulls Cal's body up. He slings Cal's arm over his shoulders and drags him toward the exit. It's all I can do to follow, eyes burning from the smoke, skin blistering from the heat.

Two strides later, we're outside. I collapse onto the ground, sucking in precious, clean air as Cal coughs bedside me. Luc heaves loudly, a firm hand on his chest, and it's then that I notice the blood on his hands, his face.

"Whose blood is that?"

My question sparks interest, and Cal turns his head to investigate.

Lucas shakes out his hands, a curse falling from his lips. "Mine. That damn Agapov," he growls. "I almost had him, and then he slipped into the forest. Looks like he—either by himself or with help—took out the perimeter guards, then tied you in just as I was leaving."

Cal and I look toward each other. This is the closest we've been since that night at the motel. I think we both understand in that moment, too.

We have to go after him.

The building behind us creaks, the structure falling in on itself as flames consume the last of it. The heat of the fire still blisters, still boils against my skin, and I throw a hand up to shield my eyes.

Luc comes loping back from our SUV, a tank of oxygen in his hands. He ignores Cal's protests, slipping the mask over his face and twisting the knob. Cal's hands tremble as he fights to pull it off.

"Her," he demands, pointing to me, "Give it to her first."

My head shakes on its own accord. "No, Cal, you were in there longer. You need it more than me."

"I don't care about me." A deep growl escapes his chest, almost harmonizing with the fire. He tries again, but this time I stop him, a gentle hand holding the mask to his face.

"Cal." Emotion strains with just the single word.

His eyes dart between mine, throat bobbing as he finally concedes. Though only for a moment. He takes three deep inhales then snaps the mask off his face. He stands, towering over me as he slips it over my face.

"You still have my gun?"

I nod, reaching behind me to give it to him.

Cal shakes his head. "Keep it. Shoot anyone who's not us."

He slams his mouth to mine. He tastes of smoke and sandalwood, and I fall into the kiss, but it's over before I'd like it to be.

"Go."

Cal nods, turning to Lucas, who passes him a gun from one of his holsters.

"Protect her with your life," he commands Caleb.

He coughs but stands at attention and nods his affirmation. I wave the guys over to the tank, offering the mask to the one I don't know; he looks like he's about to pass out. Then I turn to watch Cal and Lucas disappear in the trees. The fire crackles behind me, clashing with the crisp night air. A shiver rolls down my spine, and I clamp my teeth over my bottom lip as fear threatens to overtake me.

They'll be fine.

They have to be.

CHAPTER THIRTY-THREE

CALLAHAN

My breaths come in choppy waves, but I press on. Our footfalls are near silent as we track Agapov through the forest. Between the two of us, Luc has the most experience with tracking, so I follow closely behind, head on a swivel as we chase after Peter fucking Agapov.

The temperature drops as we put distance between us and the fire. Soot and ash cover my face and torso. My makeshift mask dangles uselessly around my neck, offering little warmth from the elements. My fury is a furnace, though, its heat warming me to the core.

"You good?"

Am I good? I almost just lost Loren. *Again.*

I don't bother with a response, a growl erupting from my chest answer enough.

"Where did you find him?"

"When you called, I flipped a bitch and shot straight back. A car was hurtling away at top speed, and I just knew." Luc winces, never taking his eyes off the tracks he's following. "I slammed the SUV straight into his shitty blue Tahoe. My head hit the steering wheel, and we stumbled out. I got a shot off before he ran."

Shit. "Blue Tahoe?"

"Yeah, why?"

That son of a bitch. "The car who chased us down after Thorne's bomb was a blue Tahoe."

Luc swears. "So that's one answer we finally have."

I nod, turning back to the task. "Where'd you hit him?"

Luc's jaw flexes. "He twisted at the last second. I think I got him through his shoulder."

I nod.

"I had to make a choice, Cal. Give chase or—"

"Or come back and save us. I understand. You made the right call."

Luc grunts. "Even though you didn't end up needing me. Your wife had it handled."

I smile to myself. She sure fucking did.

The trail of footprints and dribbles of blood takes us north, and we must be a mile away from the warehouse at this point. Then, a pool of blood appears. There's a wide swipe through it, as if someone was dragged through it—or someone dragged himself away. He must be close.

I signal to Luc. He nods, all humor wiped from his expression. With silent steps, we raise our guns and follow the trail of blood.

Around the trunk of a towering sycamore, we find him. Wet breaths wheeze from his lungs. His eyes are closed as he leans against the trunk. His pale skin is colorless, the blood draining from the wound in his shoulder. At first, he doesn't notice us, a groan escaping from his lips.

"Well, well, what do we have here?"

A manic grin splits my face in two. This is the fuck who tried to kill Loren. Who raped her friend. A sick pleasure builds in my chest as blood drips through the web of his fingers. He tries to staunch the bleeding, but he's already weakened. Just to fuck with him, I kick his hand away. Agapov moans, falling over and crashing to the forest floor.

"Oh, you poor soul. You're going to regret coming after my wife."

Luc laughs and crouches. He grabs Agapov's uninjured arm and his right leg and swings the shithead into a fireman's carry. On our trek back to the car, Luc is as clumsy as possible. Agapov groans painfully with each smack against Luc's back.

Ten minutes later, the warehouse—or what remains of it—comes into sight. The flames still burn, the heat wafting over even as we exit the tree line. The gate is still open—there's nothing to keep people out anymore—but Loren and the two guards from earlier are as far as possible while still on the perimeter. A sickly sweet smell floods my nose, and it scrunches on instinct. *Fuck*, the product is burning. My head swims, unsure of how I missed it earlier. *The adrenaline must be wearing off.*

One guard walks the perimeter, gun raised, as he watches for potential threats. Loren sits with her head between her knees, her cream sweater nearly black with ash.

I can't believe she ran headfirst into the flames for me. Thick emotion swells in the base of my throat.

"Get him in the car," I instruct Luc, heading straight for Loren. When I reach her, my hand immediately goes to her back. Her spine is bumpy under my comfort, and I rub circles over the middle of her back. "Bunny." My voice comes out rough, the smoke and ash finally catching up to me.

Loren looks up, her hazel eyes reddened, lashes dark and wet. "Did you get him?"

I nod once, and my wife sniffs.

"Let's go home."

She nods and slips her hands into mine to help her up. I tug her to her feet, not minding in the slightest when she stumbles and falls into me. Her palms are filthy, her nails scraping me as they curl on my chest, but I don't care. She smells of smoke and fire, like ash and soot. I cling to her with every fiber of my being.

From the driver's seat of the SUV, Luc calls, "He's packed! Let's go."

Loren's eyes scrunch, but she doesn't speak, just tugs me by the hand toward the car. But instead of following her, I grab the oxygen tank from Caleb, who sits on the ground, ripping the mask off his face. He doesn't flinch.

"The rest of the guards?"

Caleb's jaw clenches. "Dead. Their throats were slit."

Fuck. Was Agapov working alone, or did he have backup this time?

Looking at the state of Agapov, I'd be hard pressed to think he could do all this on his own. He doesn't seem nearly clever enough to kill six guards without anyone noticing.

"Backup should be here soon. Keep an eye out and report anything out of the ordinary."

They each nod, and I return to Loren. A bit of her sass has returned, sparking behind her hazel eyes as I hand her the mask. She rolls her eyes but accepts it, slipping it over her face without complaint.

"Why do you have an oxygen tank?" Her words are mumbled through the mask, and I fight a smile.

"With the fires and deaths, we started putting them in all the SUVs in case someone on scene needed one. Thank god we did."

The pinch between her brow softens, understanding dawning on her features. She's always been a survivor; tonight only further proves it. Ash and smoke cling to her face, her hair, her clothes. She *survived*. And not only did she survive, she came back to save me. I owe her my life. Not that I didn't already.

If she ever decides she's done with me, I fear she might finally meet the true Callahan Keane. I won't be letting her go a second time.

CHAPTER THIRTY-FOUR

LOREN

Screams erupt from the room. We're back inside one of the torture rooms, with Peter Agapov strapped to the metal chair. This time, I insisted on being inside. Cal must've seen the severity in my face—he didn't object.

The room isn't big, about the size of a standard bedroom that seems to have been converted into a torture space. The floor is mostly clean besides the pooling blood below Peter's body, and the light flickers erratically from the fluorescent bulbs above. Each cry echoes throughout the empty room, and I swallow back nausea. I school my expression as Cal and Matthias play with Peter, slicing cuts all over his skin. His naked body is filthy and caked in blood, and the gunshot wound in his shoulder trickles.

"Will she be here soon?" My voice startles both Cal and Matthias. They look over at me like they'd forgotten I was here.

On the drive back to the Keane residence, Cal sent a message to Rose that we'd apprehended Peter. They decided to bring him back to the Keane's to interrogate, and Rose would come by to land the final blow. I don't know why she wanted to be the one to end him. I can only assume he's wronged her somehow. My stomach clenches as images of Alice's broken and petrified body resurface. Cal lands a suffering blow to Peter's ribs that stuns the lowlife, and sick pleasure curls in my chest.

"She'll be here in a few." This comes from Everett, who steps into the room. He's filthy, too, and a disturbing smile curls the corner of his mouth. His strides eat up the short distance to the center of the room, and he pushes Matthias to the side. As a unit, they work like a well-oiled machine, instinctively yielding to each other's silent commands.

They've done this before.

The thought doesn't churn my stomach like it might have in the past. Instead, I'm grateful for their experience. They seem ready to draw this out, and for Alice's sake, I hope they're able to.

Not just Alice. He hurt you, too.

The unbidden thought takes me by surprise, and a surge of fury courses through my veins. I might have had Cal there to comfort me, but if I had any less training, or had been any less aware of the situation, I would've been his next victim.

My teeth grind together, my fingers curling into fists as I take a calculated step toward Peter. It's like I've fallen into a trance, not realizing what I'm doing until my face is inches from his. The men have fallen back a step, either in confusion over my actions or understanding. I was owed my lick, too.

I extend a hand, and when cool metal touches my palm, I smile. A gash splits Peter's forehead, and his left eye swells shut. For talking such a big game, he's sure trembling like a little bitch. His cracked lips part, and he tries to speak, but nothing comes out. *Pathetic.*

My fingers curl around the knife Cal handed me. The metal warms in my hand, and I adjust my grip, dragging it between Peter and me. His one working eye widens at the glint of the sharpened blade, and he murmurs…something. I can't make it out. But what he doesn't seem to realize is that I'm not looking for answers.

"Where?"

Peter's brows furrow, but Cal understands my question.

"Shoulder. Above the collarbone."

Raw wounds and purple bruises mottle Peter's skin. Cuts from Cal and Everett, the gunshot…Both fresh and dried blood paint his skin. Simple joy bubbles in my chest, and I can't help the curl to my lips. Before Peter can even scream, I sink the blade into his shoulder. It slices through his skin and muscle like butter, hitting bone. Just for fun, I twist the blade. Peter screams in agony, and it's the sweetest music to my ears.

"You're a sadistic little bunny, aren't you?" Cal whispers against the shell of my ear.

I straighten to my full height—at five and a half feet, I'm not tall by any means, but I still tower over the strapped Peter—and a sneer twists my lips, my nose scrunching.

My head tips over to look at Callahan. Lust sparks behind his brown eyes, and his tongue darts out to wet his lip. He lets out a quiet *ooph* when I slip a bloodied hand behind his neck and pull his face to mine, but he falls easily into the kiss. Our tongues tangle, and goosebumps rise on the nape of his neck, his silky hair tickling my fingers.

"Ahem." Everett clears his throat, and we break apart, a dopey smile now plastered onto my face. A pained groan sounds beside us, and I turn back to Peter as Cal's arms slide around my waist from behind. His hold is possessive, and I can feel him staring daggers over the top of my head. Then a gentle kiss presses against my crown, and Cal shuffles me to the side. In a flash, he yanks out the knife still in Peter's shoulder.

Peter swears, but it comes out more mumbled than he's probably aware.

"Who are you working with?" Cal's voice is bitter as death, and a shiver rolls down my spine.

Peter's smile is bloody, stretching across his face as the red liquid coats his teeth. Still, he doesn't answer. Each time I've been in his presence, I've felt something different. First, confusion and apprehension. Then, pure, blinding terror. And now...I feel nothing for the broken man in front of me. When his spirit leaves this mortal earth, all I'll feel is relief he's no longer alive. If that makes me evil, so be it.

Cal drags the bloodied knife over Peter's chest, never pressing hard enough to break the skin. The blade leaves behind a red mark, and Cal presses it under Peter's chin, forcing the man to strain his face upward or risk impaling on the blade.

"You must know how this is going to go." Cal's words are hushed, and Peter's throat bobs. "I can make this more painful"—he presses the blade harder under Peter's chin, and a fresh bead of blood drops—"or you can tell me what you know and I'll make it quick."

I know he's lying; there is no quick or painless for Peter Agapov.

The man strapped to the chair flicks his eyes over the room—Everett standing over Cal's shoulder, me in the corner. A raspy, twitching laugh rumbles out of his chest, which quickly turns into a cough.

"Do you think I don't know you'll make it torturous, no matter what I say?" Spittle mixed with blood drips from the corner of his mouth.

Cal's brows relax, almost as if he's satisfied that Peter didn't tell him. It gives him the chance to continue the torture.

The door opens. A woman strides in, green eyes focused solely on the man in the chair. For a brief moment, they swing to me, widening infinitesimally. She has deep auburn hair pulled into a high pony and a spattering of freckles over her nose. This must be Rose. Despite our late-night call, she looks ready for business, wearing a black turtleneck tucked into combat pants and boots. She looks vaguely familiar, but I dismiss the thought upon recognizing her as the woman in Cal's car the other night. Though she can't be taller than five feet, her aura swells in the room, demanding respect and commanding attention.

And she's not alone, either.

Two men flank her on either side, both silent as they observe their new surroundings. The one on the right is bald with a scruffy beard and a scar slashing through his eyebrow. He looks perpetually angry. The other is leaner, but an icy air flows from his frame, and I doubt he's any less deadly than the other. Their gazes flick over the room, landing on Peter in the center.

"Thanks for the call." Rose's voice is raspy and sensual. She can't be any older than I am, but there's a haunting behind her eyes that tells me she's seen more than her fair share of trauma.

Welcome to the club.

"I'd say 'anytime,' but I hope this doesn't become a regular occurrence."

Rose smiles at Cal's joke, but it doesn't spark my jealousy. It almost feels reverent. Her boots echo with each step she takes toward Peter, the room feeling more and more crowded by the minute.

She circles the chair, and we give her a wide berth. Peter watches her with his one good eye, but he doesn't seem to recognize her. His lack of response sadly doesn't answer why she wanted the killing blow.

When she pauses behind the chair, rigidity sets into her bones. Her sight doesn't leave the back of Peter's head, and her voice rings out steady in the small space.

"May we have the room?"

Cal freezes. "We still need the name of his partner."

Rose's lips twist into a macabre grin. A hand with sharp black nails slides over Peter's neck and squeezes. "I'll be sure to ask."

Cal thinks for a moment, and nods curtly. He slips an arm around my waist and leads me toward the exit. Everett opens the door for us, and we step over the threshold as Peter's incoherent cries begin again. The man with the scar through his brow follows us toward the door and moves to shut it.

"Why did you want the last shot?" Cal asks as we leave.

Something dark shutters in her eyes, a bitter fury eclipsing her youthful features. Her jaw grinds, and when she speaks it's practically a hiss. "He killed my father. You may have known him." Her throat bobs. "Andrew Thorne."

Holy shit. Holy fucking shit. She's Andy's daughter? The implications swirl in the air between us. No one seems to know what to say. And if she's Andy's daughter, that means she's *Mia's* daughter. Rose might be a Thorne, but she's also a fucking Bianchi.

"Oh, and Cal," Rose says brightly, "I hope she forgave you for holding her brother in your torture room all this time."

The door slams shut and an audible lock engages as Peter's cries escalate to a fever pitch. Her words ring in my head, and a fuzzy tunnel blurs my periphery. The color drains from Cal's face. It's all the confirmation I need.

Fury rips through me. My blood boils under my skin, fingers trembling with rage and itching to wrap themselves around Callahan's neck.

This whole time he's had Mason?

"Which room?"

Cal opens his mouth, but I silence him with the slice of my hand. "No. You don't get to speak. Take me to him. *Now.*"

Sweat beads along his hairline, his temple shiny with perspiration as his throat bobs. But his feet move, leading me to the fourth room. Eight beeps pierce the tense silence as Cal puts in the code, then his hand lands on the handle with a deep sigh.

"Bunny," his voice cracks, and the sharp ache I thought had healed splits in half.

I ignore his plea, shoving past him with a rough shoulder as I rip open the door. There he lays, my baby brother knocked out cold on a cot.

CHAPTER THIRTY-FIVE

"Mason!" I rush inside, falling over him as I shake his shoulders, trying to wake him up. Thankfully, he's clothed, unlike the other prisoner, three doors down. My vision blurs as I keep shaking him. A fresh bruise covers the expanse of his jaw. I wince.

Mason groans, eyes fluttering open as he wakes. Guilt flashes through me, and a knot lodges in the back of my throat.

He's been down here this whole time?

I was just down here a few days ago. Were those his cries I'd heard? My shame threatens to swallow me whole. All this time, I've been falling deeper into Callahan's trance, when all along he's had my brother.

"Mason," I whisper, trembling hands cupping his face, wiping the hair from his eyes.

Slowly, my brother comes to consciousness. "Loren?" His voice is scratchy and dry, and another pang of guilt rips through me.

"Bunny, please let me—"

"*No,*" I scream. The room spins as I whirl around, shielding Mason's fragile body with my own. "How could you?"

Cal opens his mouth to answer.

I don't give him the opportunity. "I trusted you. *Again*. I trusted you."

Mason groans behind me, and I spin back to him, sliding an arm under his to heave him out of the cot. "Come on, Mase, we're leaving."

"Leaving?" Cal asks.

I glare at Callahan, and he flinches.

"Yes," I practically growl. "Leaving. *Move*."

Cal doesn't move, but thankfully, Everett tugs him back with a hand on his shoulder. Cal stumbles backward a few steps, watching in silent agony as Mason and I hobble out of the room and toward the stairs.

When we reach the bottom of the stairs, I place a firm grip on Mason's elbow and help him ascend.

"You are my wife, Loren. And it's not safe. You can't just leave."

I look over my shoulder. The sight equally breaks something in me, just as it fuels me. Cal pleads with me with his brown eyes, lashes wet with emotion, but his words are a harsh reminder. He used my love for Mason to manipulate me into marrying him. Now that I have Mason back, and Peter's captured, the threat against our lives is neutralized. Our contract is void.

"Watch me."

Ten minutes later, I'm knocking on a door and praying my friend hasn't written me off just yet. Like before, I took the Corvette. This time, outrage fueled my need for speed, as opposed to panic. The door opens, and Jenna's surprised face meets mine. Her brows furrow as she looks between Mason and me, eyes widening in obvious shock, either at his state—or mine, I haven't had a chance to shower the ash off yet—or the fact that we've shown up at nearly midnight.

I can't tell if we're waking them up, but Jenna wears a pair of high-waisted, striped sleep shorts and a cropped white tank.

"*Sweetcake*," Jude's grumbling voice growls as he stomps into view. Barely sparing us a glance, he slips a hand behind her neck and pulls her face toward him, whispering against her lips, "What have I told you about answering the door at night? I'll get it." Then he kisses her softly, and she melts into his hold.

"*Sweetcake?*" I stifle a chuckle when Jude glares over the top of Jenna's head.

"I checked the cameras first. I knew it was Loren." She pulls out of his grip and lightly swats his concern away. "You brute." Her tone is teasing, and I know my friend—she loves when Jude is overprotective of her.

Jude grumbles, crossing his arms and turning toward us. He wears only a pair of low-slung gray sweats and white socks, muscles on open display.

"So you gonna let us in? Got a kid bleeding out here."

It's an obvious exaggeration, but I haven't spoken to Jude since that day at Strikers. All he did was express concern for me, and I threw it back in his face. I really thought I had it under control. My chin wobbles, and Jude's gaze zeroes in on it.

Without speaking, he turns and stomps toward the kitchen, leaving me to drag Mason in.

"Come on," Jenna whispers, shutting the door softly behind us and taking up the other side of Mason. Together, we help him to their sofa, and when he falls into the plush cushions, he's instantly out. I was too anxious during the drive to ask him any questions, and now I feel too guilty to wake him.

Mason snores softly, and I choke over the knot lodged in my throat. Gentle hands wrap around me, and Jenna pulls me into a hug. Although she's younger than me, her hugs are the closest I've felt to maternal warmth since I was a small child. A whimper escapes my lips, and Jenna just hugs me tighter.

After another minute, she rubs my back. "Let's get you a tea."

"Got anything stronger?" I laugh and wipe the snot from my nose with the back of my sleeve.

"Honey, have you met my husband? Of course I do."

Arm in arm, she guides me to their kitchen. It's dark, only a few lamps on to light the way, but it's a short walk. Their home is cozy and a perfect blend of their mutual tastes. It's decorated in soft grays and creams, open-faced cabinets, and stainless appliances. There's a large window above the sink, and moonlight spills through it. Jude is already sipping on a glass of some clear liquid—gin, most likely—but red wine and whiskey wait on the island. Jenna picks up her glass with a sly smile, sidling next to Jude and snuggling into his hold. There's something so beautiful about them. Jude with his harsh corners and rigid attitude, and Jenna with her soft curves and carefree nature.

Jude's hand squeezes her hip, and she takes a sip of her wine. I pick up my glass, raising it in silent cheers and slamming it back in one go. Jude watches as I move to the cabinet that holds their liquor, pull the bottle of whiskey down, and place it on the island.

I slump onto a bar stool, my face falling into my hands with a groan. "Aren't you going to say I told you so?" My words are muffled against my palms. When I don't hear a response, I peek an eye up.

Jenna wears compassion on her face, but she knows the question wasn't directed at her. Jude's eyes narrow, but there's less heat in them than before.

"Your words, not mine."

I stifle a laugh and purse my lips. Jude takes another sip of his drink to hide his own smile, and that's how I know we're okay. In all the years I've known him, he's never been one to hold a grudge.

"What happened?"

By the time I finish, the anger has returned to Jude's set jaw. He swears under his breath and turns around to stare out the window. Jenna rubs a reassuring hand over his spine, murmuring quietly between them.

"That Keane is no good."

"I know. I think I've always known."

Jude slams the rest of his drink, and I notice the bandage on his knuckles for the first time.

"Why didn't you tell me about the fighting?"

They still, Jenna turning to me with wide eyes.

"It's a gym. Of course there's fighting," Jude counters.

I arch a brow. "The *underground* fighting."

Jenna's mouth parts, then shuts. "Who told you about that?" she asks, but there's no anger behind her words. She's curious, but what I want to know is why I had to find out from the Doc and not from Jude himself.

"Who told me isn't important when it wasn't you." I arch a brow, directing my vitriol to the brooding man with his arms crossed.

There's a tense quiet. Jude shrugs. "I would've told you. Eventually."

"Eventually? Is that the best you've got?"

Jenna raises her hands in defense. "It's dangerous, Loren. A lot of scary guys fighting for no reason other than blood. Most don't even care about the payouts—Callahan certainly never does. They just need an outlet, and Jude's fight nights provide that."

Jude grunts. "What she said."

My eyes roll. Ah yes, a man of many words.

"So that's why you were so upset when I showed up married to the guy?"

"Keane is one of the top fighters. He hasn't lost a fight in five years. He used to come more when he was younger, but now we only see him every couple of weeks."

I wish I could say it was a shock, but it makes sense. Cal has never shied away from his anger, and it doesn't surprise me he found a physical outlet for it.

"When's the last time he fought?"

Jude's brows shoot up. "You don't know?"

"Why would I? We might have been married, but it was in name only. Until a week ago, I slept in a different bedroom." My cheeks heat at my admission, basically having just told him I fucked Callahan.

Whatever. He was—is—my husband, and it's not like they think I'm some blushing virgin.

Jude sighs. "He was here last week."

Last week?

"He was particularly feral, and I had to have him dragged away from the unlucky son of a bitch who went up against him. Pretty sure the poor kid doesn't have any teeth left."

A knot thickens in my throat, and I struggle to swallow. What happened last week that pissed him off?

Flashes of me mauling him, drunk off my ass, rush to the front of my memory, and I cringe. I remember a little about that night, but I remember he never came back to bed.

"I approached him to find out how you were doing, but he just ignored me and left."

That sounds about right.

I sigh. "Could we stay here for a few days? My place was broken into, so we don't really have anywhere else to go."

Jude swears and swiftly exits the room. A door slams in the distance, and I take it he's not coming back.

"Don't mind him. Come on." Jenna wraps a gentle arm around my back and guides me to a room down the hall. It's on the smaller side but has a queen bed in the center with a fluffy duvet and a mountain of pillows. The walls are a soft cream, and the wood floors are light. On the wall opposite the bed, there's a mounted television and a square window on the wall to the left. On the right-hand side is a door, which I assume leads to a bathroom.

A yawn slips free, and I cover it with the back of my hand.

"Thanks, Jenna." I hope she can hear the sincerity in my words, because if I say anything else out loud, I'm liable to break.

She just wraps me in another hug, and I sniffle, cringing at how dirty I must be.

"Anytime."

Then she's out the door, shutting it softly behind her. Mason will be fine on the couch for a few hours, and I'm probably not going to sleep for very long, anyway. The bed beckons, but I wince at the thought of getting in without showering off all the ash and grime first.

Icy water slices over my skin, but I can't bother to wait for it to warm. My limbs move on autopilot as I scrub the smoke from my hair. A lilac scent swirls around, and a weight settles on my chest. I scrape the dirt from under my chipped manicure. Wash my hair again. Scrub my face. Anything I can do to avoid thinking about the past six hours.

When I'm finally clean, I wrap my body in a fluffy towel. It's like a cloud envelopes me, and I almost groan. *Damn, I need to find out where she bought these.*

Fatigue settles over me like a thick blanket, and I stumble back into the bedroom. It doesn't even faze me I don't have any clean clothes. Instead, I slide under the covers and let myself slip into blissful unconsciousness. At least there I can pretend today didn't happen.

CHAPTER THIRTY-SIX

My heart is so full it feels like it could burst. *Callahan stands at the end of the dock, the dying sunset painting him in golden rays of orange and rust, and my breath catches.* He's so handsome. *I snap a picture of him with my camera, desperate to hold on to this memory forever.*

In the distance, crickets chirp and frogs croak. A gentle breeze cools the summer sweat from the nape of my neck, and as the light dies, it snatches the heat with it. Out here on the lake, it feels like our troubles are miles away.

Because they are.

The wood planks creak with each stride, and Cal turns over his shoulder to blind me with one of those million-dollar smiles. A dimple appears in his cheek, and I can't help the fireflies that take flight. He wears only his swim trunks, and his sun-kissed chest is deliciously bare. At his feet lay two popsicles melting from where we forgot them. We were…distracted.

"Come here." *He holds out a muscular arm, and I hurry into his hold. He still smells of lake water from our earlier dip, but his sandalwood cologne shines through. It's a deadly combination, one I'll forever associate with this house, this summer.*

It's our last trip to the lake house this summer. For me, school starts back up on Monday, and with that, we return to reality. Cal graduated last week, after finishing an extra semester of summer school. He's a year older than me, but when I transferred into Pointe Charter, we were in the same grade. With his graduation, it means he's no longer attending PC, and instead, starting full-time in the Keane enterprise. We talked about what we'd do when the time came, and earlier in the summer, we both agreed it would be best we go our separate ways.

I burrow my nose into the curve of his neck, twisting into his body and praying time would just slow down. I think we both knew it was inevitable. Perhaps it always was. But no one told my heart that. I fell hard, and I'm not sure how I'll survive knowing what's around the corner.

"I was thinking..." Cal trails off, pressing a quick kiss to the crown of my head.

I peek up from his chest, and his deep brown eyes sparkle with something dangerous: Hope.

"Yeah?" The word cracks out of me, and I clear my throat.

Cal's gaze flicks over my face. "What do you say we—"

"Yes," I cut him off, longing burning in my chest and tingling in my fingertips.

Cal rolls his eyes, but his hold on me tightens. "You didn't even let me finish, Bunny."

A laugh slips free, and I ignore his nickname for me. It grew on me in the last four months. "I know what you were going to say because I was thinking the same thing."

The words hang unspoken between us: Maybe we don't have to end this. Not just yet, at least. A slow smile curves his lips, and he tucks a strand of damp hair behind my ear.

"What if it's a mistake?"

Fear thickens my throat, but I banish the unwanted emotion. "We'll never know unless we try."

Cal lets out a deep breath, relief washing over his boyish face. "How do you know me so well?"

I raise onto my tiptoes, pressing my lips against his to whisper, "My soul just recognizes yours, I guess."

CHAPTER THIRTY-SEVEN

Bright sunlight streams into the bedroom, and I groan, squeezing my eyes shut tight. The remnants of an old memory, one I've kept tucked inside my heart, float away, leaving behind a familiar ache. A musty smell invades my nose, and it scrunches in recoil. With a peek, I realize not only am I lying on top of my towel—still damp from last night—but that last night did, in fact, happen. Memories flash, but I immediately dismiss them, opting to ignore reality for a little while.

The wood floor is cool under my feet, and I head into the bathroom. I jolt at the sight of my reflection. My hair is a rat's nest, half dry, half damp, and in desperate need of taming. I can't really care about it, though, so I snoop through the medicine cabinet to find a hair tie. Jenna would never leave a guest bathroom empty, so I find everything I need to become semi-human again.

My phone's dead, so I can't text Jenna about my clothing situation, but it turns out I don't need to. Just outside my door is a pair of sweats and an old tee. I might have to go commando, but at least everything's covered.

I dress and pad out of my room in search of coffee. Mason still sleeps on the couch. Should I wake him up? *No, let him sleep. He needs it.*

Warm, roasting coffee wafts into the hallway, and I'm led by my nose to the kitchen. Morning sunlight fills the space, painting the soft colors in bright warmth. Jude types on a laptop at the island, and Jenna pours a cup of coffee. It's quiet, but a different quiet than last night. A weight has lifted off my chest, and I no longer worry that I've lost Jude.

Jenna notices me first, offering me an empty mug. I smile in thanks and pour my coffee, then accept the offered creamer.

"Hey, do you have a phone charger?"

Jenna nods, pointing to a drawer on the far side of the kitchen.

God, even their junk drawer is organized.

I find the right cord and plug my phone into the wall. It was already low on battery at the warehouse and had died by the time we got to Jude and Jenna's.

Jenna pulls out some fruit and eggs, then passes the fruit to me to wash and slice. As I stand at the sink, it occurs to me I'm still wearing my ring. I file the observation away, not ready to think about the implications. We work in companionable silence as we prepare breakfast. I pause every so often to sip from the coffee. Jude clacks away on his computer, and I wonder what business could be so important at seven in the morning.

"Finalizing the next fight night," he says without looking up from his screen.

Did I say that out loud? My face flushes with heat, and I return to my task, even though I'm more curious than ever.

"On a totally unrelated note…when is this next fight night?"

This time he does pause, peering at me from over his screen. Reading glasses perch on the bridge of his nose. I've never seen him wear them before, and I have to stifle the snicker that threatens. I don't want to push him too far.

Jude sighs, returning to his computer with fast clicks of the keyboard. "Tomorrow night. Yes, you can come."

A smile splits my face until my cheeks hurt.

Jude glances up, then does a double take. "Yeesh, calm down. You'd think I just gave you the keys to the kingdom."

I shrug, pinching my lips together. Finally, I'll get to see what the fuss is all about.

"Is that coffee?"

Mason stumbles into the kitchen with an arm stretched behind to scratch his neck. His eyelids are heavy with sleep, and he yawns deeply.

My breath catches, and I drop the berries I was washing into the colander and rush around the island. Mason barely catches me, a *whoosh* escaping him as I land against his chest. My arms wrap around his torso, and I can't help the sob that rips from me.

He's real. He's real, and he's here.

Mason returns the hug after a moment, crushing me between his arms. He might be six years younger than me, but he has at least a half a foot on me and fifty pounds. In the last year or so, he'd really started bulking up.

"You fuck," I say, smooshed against his chest. "What the fuck were you thinking?"

Mason pulls me from his chest, and I get a good look at the bruise spreading across his jaw. Maybe it's the weeks apart, or perhaps I'm seeing him as a grown man for the first time, but the differences between us are

329

more obvious than ever. Where my hair is chestnut brown, his almost has an auburn sheen. Where my hazel eyes are almond-shaped, his are large and brown. I always thought he looked more like our mother, whereas I took after our father, but now I'm not so sure.

Mason studies me as well, and I'm not sure what he sees. I smile under his appraisal, but it feels shaky. Even though it's only been a couple of months, I feel like a different person. I think I grew used to the thorn sticking in my side, growing around it and pretending it was a root instead. For years, I built a foundation around it, pretending it was stable, when really all it took was one brown-eyed monster to send it all crumbling down.

I waver under his scrutiny, but he doesn't seem to look for very long. Instead, a light smile lifts his lips, and he repeats, "Coffee?" Then he skirts around me.

My smile falters. I stare at the space he was just in with confusing disappointment swirling inside my chest. With a shake of my head, I spin on my heel and join the group at the island. In the few minutes of our reunion, Jenna finished breakfast and slides a plate my way.

Berries, sourdough toast with butter, and scrambled eggs. Correction—*cheesy* scrambled eggs.

I smile weakly, thanking Jenna and taking the plate to the round table in the nook off to the side. Mason joins me with a plate, while Jenna and Jude eat at the island. I nibble the toast and eat a few berries before pushing the eggs around on my plate.

Mason scarfs his food down like he hasn't eaten in weeks, and my stomach drops.

What were they feeding him down there? Were they even feeding him?

"Here, you need this more than I do." I scrape the eggs onto his plate, hoping Jenna won't catch my ulterior motive.

Mason just hunches over, shoveling in bite after bite, barely slowing to chew.

"Slow down, you're going to choke."

Mason waves me off, tossing another concerningly giant bite into his mouth. "It's fine." His words are mumbled around his food. It makes me smile.

"We need to talk about what happened."

It's not a question. I need answers, and Mason needs to be honest. Although I'm his sister, there's a reverence there from being an older sibling slash parent. Mason swallows thickly, avoiding my poignant stare. He squirms in his seat, as if he's not a six-foot-two man whose arms are bigger than my face.

"Well? I want to hear it from you."

Mason sighs, his fork clattering onto the ceramic plate. Jenna dutifully ignores his rudeness, but I raise a brow at the carelessness. He reddens, fidgeting with his napkin. "Where should I start?"

"How about from the moment you received orders to enter Keane territory?"

Mason's eyes drop to the napkin. When he speaks, he can't seem to look away from it. "All my life, I've felt like an afterthought. Dad was busy with the business, and Mom was always sneaking off to who knows where. You wanted nothing to do with me, so I entertained myself. Leon barely wanted to be my friend, and it was lonely. I was lonely."

My chest aches with his confession. I never knew he felt like this.

"I feel like I raised myself, but somehow, everyone still compared me to Dad. Nothing I did was ever good enough. I couldn't ever live up to the infamous Francis Catrone." He scoffs. "Elias wouldn't even take me seriously. It wasn't until Leon suggested doing what no one has done before: reclaiming territory from the Keanes."

"Wait—Leon suggested it? He said Elias was the one who thought of it."

Mason's nose scrunches, brows furrowing. "No, it was Leon. He said Elias wanted to test me, since I was a Catrone."

Why would Leon lie about that?

"When I got to the warehouse, some dude caught me. He threw a bag over my head and threw me into a van. When they finally took the bag off, I was in that concrete room. Callahan came downstairs, and at first, I didn't recognize him. But then I realized he looked like that boyfriend you had when we were kids."

He knew about us?

"He took one look at me, and instead of beatings and torture, I got three square meals and a bed. Over the next few weeks, they brought in some entertainment items, and I could use the bathroom whenever I wanted, so it wasn't that horrible. Unless you consider staring at plain white walls torture."

I visibly wince. But he wasn't hurt? Just held inside for several weeks? But then—

"Why is your face bruised?"

Mason scrubs a hand over his jaw and winces. "I was getting irritated with them. They wouldn't tell me why they were holding me. Some dude clocked me a few times to shut me up last night. Said something about not disturbing the boss during his interrogation."

So, Cal hadn't been torturing him this whole time?

My temple throbs, and I rub against the tension. Mason watches with thinly veiled concern, his eyes darting to my left hand. Where I had gotten used to the overly exuberant ring, his eyes widen with obvious shock.

"Loren…when did you get engaged?"

Jenna snorts, and I realize our conversation was not as private as I'd thought. I glare at her, but she fills my baby brother in, regardless.

"She married Keane in exchange for finding you. Ironic, isn't it?" She laughs, and Jude joins in. If I wasn't busy burning under Mason's gaze, I'd be shocked by Jude's rare laughter.

"At least someone finds it amusing," I grumble, unable to meet Mason's gaze. My fingers toy with the frayed hem of my tee.

"I'm sorry," Mason drones, "you married *who* in exchange for *what?*" Anger spikes through each word, and I wince.

But then Mason's chubby baby face flashes in front of me. Visions of present-day Mason blur with baby Mason and certainty inflates me. I won't feel shame for the lengths I'll go for my family. Or rather, for my brother.

Maybe it's pathetic, knowing I love others harder than anyone will ever love me, but it's who I am. A die-hard loyalist. Sue me.

"You married that piece of shit for *me?*" Mason sounds as equally disturbed as he does surprised. Does he not know just how far I'd go for him?

"Mason…" I swallow thickly. "I'd do anything for you."

His face sobers, hearing the truth in my words. Then he stands, falling to his knees in front of me and throwing his arms around me.

His shoulders shake with emotion, and I slip from my chair and onto my knees, holding his face to my shoulder in a tight embrace.

"Don't you ever do anything like that again," I sob into his hair.

Mason just holds me tighter.

CHAPTER THIRTY-EIGHT

fter breakfast, Jude leaves for the gym, and Mason heads off to take a shower. Jenna brought him into the second guest room, then grabbed her laptop and went outside to do some work. Suddenly, I'm left by myself. I trail around the house like a ghost haunting the living and find myself in front of the sizable bay window at the front of their house. Jenna and Jude live in a cul-de-sac—something I've never let Jude forget—and in the bright February morning, the clouds part and birds chirp. The blinding sun mocks my despair, its cheerful rays a stark contrast to the heavy weight of misery I carry.

Their neighbors go about their day, blissfully unaware that evil exists in this world—or even in this neighborhood. On the street in front of the house, a black SUV rolls to a stop. Frustrating—confusing—hope swirls in my chest. A glare flashes, and a car door opens. It slams shut, a loud, jarring sound that makes me flinch.

Dark sunglasses conceal the face that steps out, but it's not

335

Cal. Disappointment floods my chest. I don't care to examine the confusing emotion.

Cohen climbs out of the SUV in his usual all-black uniform, but he doesn't approach. No, he just leans against the hood and crosses his arms over his chest. I'm frozen for a beat, but then I find my strength and charge out of the house, straight toward him.

His face gives nothing away. I land in front of him, hot breaths huffing from my chest. The sun warms my face, or that might be the anger flushing up my cheeks.

"What are you doing here?"

Cohen huffs a laugh. "What do you think, Mrs. Keane?"

I clench my teeth so I don't lose my lid on him. Of course, Cal couldn't just let me go.

Did you really want him to?

"Back to Mrs. Keane, are we?"

The corner of Cohen's lip curls the slightest degree.

I sigh. "How did you even know where I was?"

Cohen arches a brow.

"Why am I even asking? It's Callahan," I say under my breath with a groan. At least this time he chased me—or rather, he sent someone after me. It's something, at least. The realization defrosts the first icy outer layer of my fury toward him. That's what I wanted—*needed*—him to do eleven years ago.

I click my tongue and press my lips into a firm line. With a careless wave at the cookie cutter street, I try to reason with Cohen. "I think we'll be safe here. You can leave now."

Cohen shrugs, eyes scanning the street, ever vigilant. "Unlike you, I don't have a choice."

This time, he doesn't look back, just continues keeping watch over the street. When I reach the front door, indecision tugs at me.

Later in the afternoon, I'm lying on my bed, staring at the ceiling, warring emotions stirring in my chest. On one hand, Cal lied to me. He told me he'd look for my brother—manipulated me into *marrying him*—when really, all along, he knew where he was: down in one of his torture rooms. A shudder wreaks through me.

But no one actually harmed Mason until yesterday. From the sound of it, whoever decked him wasn't aware of his celebrity status. It was a big case of wrong place, wrong time. I arrived minutes after someone had knocked him unconscious. It painted a terrible picture of Cal and his treatment of my brother.

A solemn pressure weighs on me as tears stream into my ears.

A gentle knock announces someone's presence, but I don't bother moving or wiping the tears away.

"Hey," Jenna says softly. She joins me on the bed, staring up at the ceiling with me. "Want to talk about it?"

Where would I even start?

I sigh, the words spilling from me as I share the story of a young girl who fell in love with the wrong boy, only to be haunted by him for years after he betrayed her—or so she thought. Cal's confession might have healed the wound, but it didn't erase the eleven years of heartbreak. Jenna is quiet, the perfect listener as my voice cracks and my tears start anew. She emits only a soft gasp when I finally reach the current events of the fires, bombs, and attempts on our lives.

When I finish, she's quiet. My heartbeat thuds heavily. I focus on the rhythm, counting each beat for almost a minute until she finally speaks.

"Holy fuck." Disbelief drips from her expletive, and the first smile in a while teases my lips. Jenna doesn't swear very often, so when she does, you know it's a big deal. "I mean, I heard some of the stuff from Jude, but never in my wildest dreams did I think what you just described was possible in real life."

A laugh bursts out of me, and I wipe a tear from my eye, this one from humor. "More like an alternate reality."

Jenna joins in easily, and for a moment, I'm just a girl hanging with her friend, having a good time. But when the laughter quiets, and the tendrils of silence creep back in, I squeeze my eyes shut, hoping to preserve the moment longer. It doesn't work.

"How about we forget about men for a while?"

I turn to look at her. She's curled on her side now, hands folded under her head as she watches me. Jenna smiles slowly, and my brows furrow.

"What are you thinking?"

⚭

When Jude comes home, I'm pretty sure his eyes bug out of his skull. Jenna and I are in the living room in the middle of a karaoke duet and singing—screeching—at the top of our lungs. Maybe he swears, maybe he says something akin to "these women are the greatest singers of all time"—we'll never know because the chorus starts back up again. My microphone is a wooden spoon and has been cutting out all night, but Jenna's is a soup ladle and works perfectly—the bitch. We spin around the living room, singing to each other as the song comes to a close. My shoulders shake with laughter. Sweat beads along my hairline as heavy breaths chop from my lungs.

"Okay, this time I want Lady Gaga's part, and you can sing Bruno's."

Jenna's face is flushed, cheeks bright red from either the four margaritas we drank in the last two hours or the fact that we just crushed yet another song. She sobers, a serious air settling over her features. "You got yourself a deal, missy." Jenna jabs out her hand to shake on it, but she stumbles.

In a flash, Jude's steadying her with an arm and swinging her into a bridal carry. "I think that's enough for you two." He carries her toward their room.

I cup my hands around my mouth. *"Boo,"* I jeer.

Jenna struggles to escape, but Jude leans down to whisper in her ear. Whatever he says she must like, because she screeches a laugh, her giggles disappearing down the hallway.

My heart is happy for them, even if a little jealous—and a little bitter that I'm now drunk by myself. I swing by the bay window to find Cohen sitting in the driver's seat of the SUV still. It's dark in the cab, but when he notices me, he clicks on the light. Then he gives me a finger wave. I roll my eyes, hunger gurgling in my belly, and turn to go in search of food. Mason sits at the small table in the nook, eating a bowl of cereal.

"Thank god," he mumbles around a bite. "I thought I was going to start bleeding from my ears."

"Get choked." I flip him off.

Mason laughs and watches as I pull out the box of pizza in the fridge from earlier and grab a few slices. The microwave hums, and I perch against the counter as I wait. My phone vibrates on the counter where it's still plugged in. After breakfast, I realized I needed some time and space from the Keane family, and I've left it in here the whole day. My fingers itch to check the notifications. If I had one more margarita, perhaps I would.

Instead, as Mason finishes his cereal a few feet away, a new anger sparks in my blood. I yank the microwave door open right as it beeps. The pizza is bubbling, and I grab a bottle of water and a napkin and stomp over to sit across from Mason.

Unfortunately, it's too hot to eat, so I have to just wait, stomach grumbling and patience dwindling. Delayed gratification was never really my thing.

"So, what are you gonna do?" Mason's words cut through my thoughts.

I meet his gaze. His bruises are getting darker, but the scruff on his jaw helps hide them. *When did my baby brother get old enough to grow a beard?*

I sigh, blowing a long breath onto the pizza to help cool it down. For once, I don't know what I'm going to do. I hate to say it, but at least when we were kids, it was obvious. Cal cheated and dumped me in the same breath, and I would be damned if I ever begged a man to choose me. I had no choice but to pick myself up off the floor, dust myself off, and move on. But now, here I am in the aftermath of another lie, but this time, no one really got hurt. *Except me.* Mason got clocked a few times, but I'd be lying if I didn't say he deserved it for accepting such a dangerous mission. If that's all that happened to him, he got off easy.

I freeze. Did I just somehow justify a man's lying and manipulation? A shudder rolls through me. *Hell must've frozen over.*

"I don't know," I say finally. At least it's the truth. "What I do know is you're not going back to the Bianchis."

Mason opens his mouth to argue, but I throw up a hand to silence him. "They were ready to throw you away like that." I snap for emphasis. "That family is falling apart at the seams, and I won't let you get caught in the crossfire. I know I'm not your mother, but for the last eight years I've been the one to raise you, and if I have to go mama bear on your ass, I will."

Mason is quiet during my tirade, but a sparkle of relief shines behind his brown eyes. His mouth flaps open twice before he finally speaks. "I did a lot of thinking the past couple of months. They took my cell, and any access I had to the internet, so my only source of entertainment was a DVD player and a stack of books. Three times a day, Tinley dropped off my meals, and sometimes she stayed to chat. She never gave much away, but she made it clear the Bianchis weren't looking for me." Shadows eclipse his face, and his jaw tightens. "I can't go back to a family who saw me as chattel. After everything Dad sacrificed… It's obvious they're on a downward spiral. And I refuse to sink on their ship out of some twisted sense of loyalty."

Pride swells in my chest, and I nod curtly. Looks like my baby brother grew up a bit these past few weeks, after all.

Mason must sense my building emotion and deftly switches the topic. "What happened with Cal?"

A bitter laugh escapes. "He tricked me into marrying him when he had you in his basement the entire time. It's hard to reconcile that every night when he got into bed, he was lying about looking for you."

Mason's face scrunches. "I don't need to hear about you guys in bed together."

My eyes roll. "Oh, shut up. Like I didn't do your laundry when you were a teenager. You know how many stiff socks I threw away?"

His face reddens like a tomato, a vein popping in his forehead.

"Or what about the girls you snuck out at two in the morning? Or when *you* snuck *out?* Did you think I was oblivious?"

Mason stands abruptly, stuttering an excuse as he skirts around me.

I stop him with a hand on his forearm. "Forgetting something?" I raise a brow.

Mason groans but turns back to grab his cereal bowl and take it to the sink. After he loads it into the dishwasher, he makes a speedy escape, and I can't help the chuckle that trips past my lips.

Without our parents, and counting for our six-year age gap, I filled that parental role for him, and even though he's twenty-one now, I find it hard to let that part of me go.

As I sit alone in the kitchen, eating my pizza and trying to sober up, fatigue washes over me. *I'm too old for this.*

The pizza soaks up the tequila, but by the last slice, I'm picking the cheese off. It's the only thing I can eat it on, and even then, I have my limits. I move on autopilot as I tidy up the kitchen, flicking off the lights as I make my way to bed. After a half second of thought, I grab my cell and take it with me.

CHAPTER THIRTY-NINE

I don't even make it past the door to my room before I'm checking the notifications. Text after text, missed call after missed call…but there's only one voicemail. It's from two hours ago, and there aren't any more texts or calls after it. Like he left the voicemail, then turned his phone off. It should make me cringe how many times he tried to reach me, but it doesn't. Instead, it feeds a part of my soul that longed for Cal to chase after me when we were teens.

With greedy—and likely misplaced—hope, I shut the door, sliding down until my ass hits the floor. My finger trembles as I press on the voicemail, holding a shaky breath as Cal's voice floods my ear.

"Shut the fuck up," he starts with a hiss, but when the background noise quiets, I quickly realize that he wasn't talking to me—or, my voicemail, rather. "Ren…Please come home. Let me explain." His voice cracks, and I can tell the dam of emotion he usually keeps such a tight lid on threatens to explode. "Everything I've done has been for you. Give me a chance to prove it to you. I won't let you down." The voicemail ends, and it's just me in the silent guest room of my friend's house. I replay the voicemail.

When the sun peeks over the horizon, my phone's back to almost dead when I finally put it down. Instead of sleeping, I spent the early hours of the morning listening to Cal's voicemail over and over and analyzing his texts. They ranged from frantic worrying to heartfelt apologies, but they all boiled down to the same thing: this Callahan Keane is not who he was at seventeen. Hell, he's not even the same Callahan Keane from Abstrakt last month. And it is time I trust my gut.

By the time I make it into the kitchen, it's well past lunch. The house is empty, and a note on the fridge says Jenna and Jude took Mason to the gym. There's a reminder about the fight tonight, which starts at eleven o'clock.

"Don't worry, I'll be back way before then, and we'll get ready together," I read the last line of Jenna's perfect penmanship. My head throbs, though not from a hangover like you might expect after so much tequila. No, a tension headache seems to catch up with me after so many late nights. It's also still a little sore from slamming my forehead against Peter's the other night. I'm just as shocked as anyone I didn't bruise.

I plug my phone back into the charger. I should probably just take it into my room, but something about that feels too permanent. As the coffee brews, filling the kitchen with a rich roast, my fingers tap impatiently on the counter. Then I rip my phone from the charger and dial a number I should've already called. She has yet to answer my calls, so I haven't been sure if she wanted to talk or not. Guilt still sours my stomach, knowing she was another piece of collateral damage just by being my friend.

It rings three times, and disappointment swells. Just like all the times I've called before, I know she won't answer. I want to be there for her, but it's obvious she's hiding from the world. I debate leaving a voicemail when silence greets me instead of her usual peppy voicemail recording.

"Hello?" My voice is shaky, and static crackles. "Alice?"

"Yeah?" Alice's voice is raspy, like she also just woke up.

Emotion clogs my throat, and I swallow thickly. "Hi, babe. I just wanted to call and see how you're doing." I wince. Of course, she's not doing well. Fuck, I'm an awful friend.

There's a long pause. My mouth flops open as I try to think of something to say to cover up my blunder. The coffee machine hisses, the cup finished brewing, but I ignore it.

Finally, Alice laughs. It's unsettling, a twisted and bitter laugh that makes me flinch. "How am I doing?" Her tone is drenched in sardonic fury. "How the fuck do you think I'm doing?" I've never heard her swear before, and I'm stunned speechless. "I was held at gunpoint, raped, and beaten for days on end. I actually started praying for death. And now, when all I want is to sleep, you keep calling. So, leave me alone, Loren. You've done enough."

The phone clicks, and I'm frozen for several long seconds. I'm left dazed, fingers trembling as they press the phone to my ear. That's not my friend. My friend has never raised her voice a day in her life. Not that she doesn't have every reason in the world to do so.

That's because she's no longer the friend I once knew.

The realization is heady, striking me deep in the gut. I flinch, hand flying to my belly in some semblance of comfort. It doesn't help. Despite her words, I can't be angry with her. She would've never been in my house if I hadn't asked her for help. It's the worst possible case of wrong time, wrong place. She deserves to light the world on fire, should she choose, and I'm happy to take whatever punishment she deems necessary. All I can do is hope she'll realize I'm not going anywhere. No matter the vitriol she throws, I won't give up on her. She's so young, just a year older than Mason, and an orphan herself. I'll be damned if she goes through this alone.

After pouring a concerning amount of creamer into my coffee, I head out to the backyard and soak in the sunshine. It's been a rainy few days, and god knows I could use the warmth.

An unknown number texts me, and from the preview, the sender says they're Rose. How did she get my number? The text is simple, with only two words.

It's done. - Rose

Peter must be dead then. *Good.* I only feel relief that he's gone from this word.

I shoot her a quick text back.

Fight night at Strikers tonight. I think we should talk.

Then I close the thread out, not wanting to think about her or the sequence of events she threw into motion with the bombs she dropped last night just yet.

Mia Bianchi's daughter. Andy Thorne's daughter. God, how did it get so complicated? That makes her one of their two daughters, the ones he was grooming to take over his tech empire. Thorne Enterprises provides IT and cybersecurity services to some of the largest corporations on the east coast. Their systems are impenetrable. And Rose is the heir to the entire company. That must be how she got my number.

Something tugs in the back of my mind, half-formed connections swirling around, but I don't have the brainpower to work them to completion. Instead, I move on with my day, keeping my hands busy and my mind empty. I spend a few hours cleaning the house—my way of thanking Jenna and Jude for letting us stay. When it's dinnertime, I rifle through their fridge and set out to make the easiest dish I know: pan-seared chicken with fluffy rice and sautéed veggies. Just as the rice finishes, Jenna, Jude, and Mason walk into the kitchen.

"I'm gonna grab a shower real fast." Mason darts to the other guest room, leaving Jenna and Jude to amble in by themselves.

"Thanks for cooking." It sounds like it pains Jude to thank me, but I don't take it personally. The only person who he ever sounds happy to talk to is his wife.

Jenna playfully swats him and moves to wash her hands and set the table. When we're all seated, a comfortable silence settles over the meal. Mason crashes in a moment later, grabbing his plate with apologies muttered under his breath, wet hair dripping onto his gray tee.

"So, are you ready for tonight?" Jenna asks as she takes a bite of chicken. "Mm, this is good." Her words are mumbled around her chewing.

"Physically?" I gesture to the same pair of sweats and shirt she gave me yesterday. "No. Mentally? Fuck yes." I've always read about fight nights in other romance books, and it's always sounded so dangerous and mysterious. I'm practically foaming at the mouth. "I need to figure out something to wear, though." The clothes I was wearing when I showed up like a crispy rat got thrown away first thing that morning—there was no saving them.

Jenna smiles brightly. "I got you covered."

⚯

Music blares, and I fight the instinct to cover my ears. I've never seen Strikers like this before. I never even knew it had a basement.

"You've been holding out on me."

A rare blush stains the ridge of Jude's crooked nose, and he grumbles some sort of dismissive answer. Jenna slides her arm through mine, and we head down the stairs together. She had a vision alright. Wearing a faded band tee of Jude's, I belted the waist and slipped into a pair of black fishnets. I borrowed a pair of black combat boots from Jenna and a leather jacket from Jude. Basically, I was wearing both their closets. Jenna offered a fresh pair of underwear, but that's where I drew the line. Besides, the T-shirt-turned-dress falls to the middle of my thighs, so as long as I don't bend over, I'll be fine.

Jenna wears a black corset top tucked into black cargo pants, giving off a cyberpunk vibe that I love on her. It's so different from her usual look. After we smoked out our eyes and curled our hair, she said that she and Jude sometimes like to play. My cheeks had flushed with heat, and I had to look away, unsure if I was flustered or just jealous. Then she made a comment about my ring, saying I had no room to talk, but I just brushed her off and swiped a red lipstick on.

Right before we left, I changed my mind about my hair, and threw the curled strands into a high pony, pulling a few pieces out to frame my face. Despite the chill to the air, I knew it would be blistering in Strikers' packed basement. I felt sexy as fuck, and I was determined to have fun.

"There's a bar on that side," Jenna yells over the thrum of music, pointing to a compact bar with a line forming already. "But if you just want your whiskey, we can steal some of the good stuff from Jude's office."

"Yes, let's do that." I didn't want to waste my night standing in line when I just planned on getting a whiskey, anyway. "Don't do anything stupid," I direct to Mason, who's already looking around the room like he's got stars in his eyes. He doesn't answer, so I nudge his shoulder, snapping his attention to me.

"Yeah, yeah." He folds into the crowd that's forming, and I have to take a deep breath.

He'll be fine.

"He'll be fine," Jenna says, reading my mind and leading me to Jude's office. She covers her hand over the keypad, keeping the code safe from wandering eyes, and then we slip inside. The music immediately deafens, and I crack my jaw open, trying to pop my ears.

"Goddamn, it's loud out there."

Jenna cringes. "Yeah, I should've warned you. Sorry about that."

I wave her off, taking in Jude's office. It's nearly identical to the one upstairs. And by that, I mean it's boring as fuck. There's a brown desk with a black office chair and a lamp in the corner. The only difference with this office is there's a bar cart off to the side and a couch next to it. There's a window that shows the ring just outside, but the shutters are mostly closed, offering relative privacy.

Jenna pours me a drink while I peek through the shutters.

"Damn, it's packed out there."

Jenna hands me the glass, and it's icy in my palm. The amber liquid is rich, a delicate heat burning my throat with each sip. She has a glass of red wine and perches on the edge of the desk.

"Yeah, we rarely have two fights so close together, but tonight was a special occasion."

"Oh yeah? For what?"

Jenna doesn't answer. I look at her over my shoulder, and she just mimes locking her lips and throwing away the key.

Okay. Whatever that means.

I slam the rest of the whiskey back, and the heat washes through my limbs. Without a second thought, I slip out of the leather jacket and drape it over the back of the couch. "Ready?"

Jenna takes a healthy swig of her drink and nods. "By the way, if you ever need to get in here, the code is 0317."

0317? "That's random."

A flush stains her cheeks, and her eyes drop from mine. "It's the day we met."

"Oh, my god, that's so cute." Shock stuns me. "I didn't know Jude could be that sentimental."

Jenna laughs, a tinkling, infectious bubble that has me joining in easily.

"Come on, let's go." She links her arm through mine again, and we exit the office.

The door locks behind us, and we're immediately pressed into the suffocating heat of a hundred bodies. It's a mix between women wearing next to nothing and men who look like they'd eat me for breakfast.

She tugs me along until we reach a dance floor. I guess while they wait for the fights to start, people work off their bad days here. A wide berth surrounds us wherever we go, and at first, I think nothing of it. When we get to the dance floor, we move to the beat and lose ourselves in the house music. A sheen of sweat covers my exposed skin, and I feel freer than I have in a long time. Mason was safe, Alice was safe—scarred, but safe.

A grateful smile curls my lips, and my face tilts toward the ceiling. The bass thrums over my skin, pounding against my eardrums, but I'm acclimating. It's then that I realize there's a noticeable bubble surrounding us, as if no one dares get in our personal space. Seriously, I can extend both arms out straight and wouldn't touch a single person besides Jenna. In a packed basement like this, it's an oddity.

"Do we smell?" I joke, although I'm grateful that strangers aren't pressing against me. But seriously, this is weird.

Jenna winces. "Jude's broken a few noses and fingers for touching 'what was his.'" She uses air quotes around that last part.

When I finally get it, I double over in laughter. "Holy shit, only Jude would do that." A stitch forms in my side.

"Not just Jude." Jenna points her chin over my shoulder.

What?

I spin on my heel, and there he is.

Callahan Keane. My husband.

He watches with a burning lust that rakes over my skin, goosebumps breaking out the longer he stares. He doesn't move, just stands with his arms crossed over his chest and a gleam in his eyes that tells me he's been standing there for longer than I realize.

A forceful push from Jenna breaks me from my stupor. I stumble forward. In a flash, Cal catches me, just like he always has.

His hands slide down my arms to my waist, tugging me against his chest. When we're breaths apart, I finally speak. "I need to hear you say it to my face."

Cal deflates under my palms. His brown eyes twinkle with emotion, but this time, we don't run.

"I'm sorry, Ren. I'm so fucking sorry."

CHAPTER FORTY

"I didn't trust that you could fall for me again without some scheme. I should've had more faith in you. In us."

His words hang in the air between us, and I suck in a choppy breath. He lied to me for months, extorted me into marriage, and kept my brother in his basement. But in the next breath, my anger fizzles out of me. Sure, he lied, but it brought us back together. And our marriage might've started as a mutually beneficial arrangement, in the last week, I realized that while it might have been unconventional, in my bones, I know we belong together. Plus, Mason was never in any real danger. Still, he needs to own it.

"And?" I arch a brow.

Cal smirks, eyes darting between mine. Then he sobers, his throat bobbing as he swallows. "I should've never lied. I was a coward."

"*And?*" I repeat.

He sighs, relief flooding his features as he realizes I've already forgiven him. Somewhere in the discovery that Mason has been safe this whole time, I came to understand that Cal was terrified of losing me. His every action proved it. Each time he placed a new brick in our relationship, he was proving to me he loved me. And I think after I recognized his fear, it made me take a long, hard look in the mirror. How much vitriol had I spewed at him in the beginning, throwing the harshest of accusations and lies back to him? I was no better. But if we can get through this and come out the other side, then we can get through anything. Together.

Cal's palm is warm against my cheek, and I lean into his touch. "I'd follow you anywhere, Ren. Anywhere you lead, I'll be your shadow. Every step I take is toward you. Through any fire, through any agony, I'm yours."

It's all I needed to hear. A smile curls my lips, and I press my lips to his. He captures my face between his wide hands, claiming my heart once and for all. I slide my arms around his neck, but my tee rises, and I immediately pull away and tug it down.

Cal's eyes flash with something fierce, something…predatory.

"Bunny, are you not wearing panties?" His tongue darts out to wet his lower lip.

I shake my head slowly.

"Oh, you naughty little thing."

"Attention, Strikers." A voice booms through the speakers, cutting over the music. "Gather 'round; the first fight is about to begin."

A wicked smirk upturns the corner of Cal's mouth, the dimple coming out in full force. Heat gathers in my core as he consumes me with his undivided attention. As my arousal pools between my legs, I realize what a bad idea it was to turn down panties. My face floods with heat just as Cal lands another scorching kiss. Then his hand slips into mine, and he tugs me toward the ring. As we cross the room, I look around for Rose. She never texted me back, and I don't see her anywhere. I guess we'll have to talk some other time.

"Wait, I need to get Jenna." I look over my shoulder, but she's being escorted by a beefy man who isn't Jude. I recognize him as another trainer from Strikers.

Cal hides me behind his vast frame as he parts through the crowd, ignoring the grumbling men who dare to complain. When they see who it is, their faces pale, and they fall over themselves to apologize. Cal ignores them, continuing to push through until we're near the front, but there's still a few rows of people in front of us. Then he pulls me in front of him, my back to his chest as his hands wrap around my waist.

The crowd roars as the bell *dings*, the fight ensuing. It's bloodier than what you see on television, and where I once might have cringed, I now watch with sick fascination as a tooth goes flying. I cup my hands around my mouth and scream, lost in the theatrics of it all, when Cal's hand drifts lower, trailing against my thigh. The fighters circle each other, hands raised in a ready position as one throws a left hook. His opponent dodges, tossing back an uppercut that should've been the end. Lost in the thrum of the crowd, I'm zapped back into my body when Cal's fingers trail along the hem of my tee.

My eyes widen, glancing around, but no one's paying attention to us. His hand crawls up the back of my thigh, finding the center of my heat. The pumping music and roaring cheers swallow my moans, my head tilting back on Cal's shoulder as he teases my entrance.

His other hand reaches down, and against the screams of the crowds, he tears apart my fishnets. I gasp, legs trembling when I feel the tension of the fishnets snap. The crowd cheers as one fighter knocks the other out, deafening my ears. Then his fingers are back, unimpeded by the foolish tights. He swirls them around my entrance and drags his lips over my exposed neck.

"Fuck, Bunny. Have you always been an exhibitionist, or is that just for me?"

His fingers curl inside me, and stars explode. The heat of the hundred bodies around us cheering and screaming only spurs me further as Cal works me over.

Right as I'm about to fall over that cliff, he pulls back, circling my clit with drenched fingers. The angle is different since I'm in front of him, but the knowledge that he's touching me, getting me off in front of all these people, is a heady explosive. Fuck, if he just whispered in my ear and told me to come, I would.

"Ladies and gentlemen, who's ready for the next fight?" The announcer throws his arms out and circles the ring.

Somehow, the crowd gets even louder, and a smile splits my face in two. I join in, screaming until my throat burns.

"Let's hear it for The Surge and Snake Eyes!"

Two fighters touch knuckles, and the fight begins anew. My heart is pounding, excitement swelling until my eyes practically cross. Cal's fingers resume their teasing, dipping in and out of my entrance as he swirls my arousal around. It drips down my leg, and the naughty picture we make almost makes me explode. My eyes dart around, the bodies pressing around us doing nothing but heightening my pleasure.

"Is my pretty wife ready to come?"

355

I groan, turning my face into his shoulder and biting his black shirt. Cal's fingers twist inside of me, hitting my spot with every stroke. My core pulses, and I whimper.

"Be a good little wife and come on your husband's hand."

I detonate, falling apart with a cry that's swallowed by Cal's shoulder. His rhythm doesn't change, just continues twisting inside of me as I tremble and shake. My legs give out, but his other arm wraps around my waist, holding me up.

Finally, after several moments, he slows, thrusting gently inside of me. Cal presses a gentle kiss to my crown, and I melt, spinning in his hold and wrapping my arms around his neck, no longer caring. No one's paying attention to us. Cal's soft lips yield to mine. Our tongues tangle, and I slide my fingers in his hair, holding the strands tightly as I kiss him.

Cal pulls away with one last kiss and beams. Before I can say anything, a bell dings, and Cal's eyes flick behind me to the ring.

He beams, a twinkle of something I can't decipher behind his hooded brown eyes.

"That's my cue."

What?

"It's time you see every part of me." With that, he slips from my hold and pushes through the crowd of people.

They part for him instinctively, and I marvel at the sheer power he exudes. The crowd swallows me, bodies pressing in on every side as Cal approaches the ring. His smirk never drops, and my tongue practically wags at the bulging muscles when he pulls himself into the ring. In a move that shouldn't have surprised me, he bends one arm backward to drag his shirt off by the back of his neck, his toned body on display for the crowd. Women scream, but his gaze never leaves mine. It's like we're in our own bubble, no one else existing but us as he flicks the first button of his pants open. When he languidly drags the zipper down, it's like he's giving me my own private strip tease, and I fight the urge to touch myself. I just came, but goddamn, the need is curling inside me again.

Cal pushes his pants down, toeing out of his shoes and socks and leaving his clothes in a pile. The referee collects his clothes without a word and tosses them off to the side. When Cal finally drags his gaze from mine to his opponent's, I admire his body. Years of fighting and working in the family business has toned him into a muscular god. My core throbs, but it's not until I see the reddened skin around a fresh tattoo over his chest that my mouth parts.

Even from here, I can see the swirling font that spells *Ren* over his heart, sitting untouched in the center of vicious flames that lick up to his collarbone.

Cal's eyes gleam with something nefarious, and before he taps knuckles with his opponent, he shoves his index and middle fingers into his mouth. He never breaks his eye contact with me as he sucks my cum and arousal off his digits. It's intoxicating the way he pulls my strings taut without even touching me. I don't even notice the bell rang until his opponent swings straight for his face. I gasp, hands flying to my mouth in shock. There's no way Cal sees it coming, but he dodges at the last second, a smirk playing on his face as he turns from me to face his opponent.

This fight is different, a tension I hadn't known before flooding my bones. I know Cal is a beast of a fighter, but it's been so long since I've seen it for myself. The opponent, Red Mist, throws combo after combo, trying to land any blow he can on Cal, and I'm practically gnawing on my fingers as Cal evades.

After a minute of no contact, Cal bounces on the balls of his feet and laughs. Then he drills into Red, fist over fist raining down on him. It's brutal, but I can't look away. Cal has a manic gleam to his eyes as he pummels Red into the floor of the ring. It's a massacre, obvious that Cal was just toying with him at the beginning. The tight coil in my chest loosens. Then something blunt stabs into my side.

"If you want your brother to live, I'd suggest you come with me."

I stiffen, the threat whispered into my ear, freezing me in my place. But while the threat itself is sickening, it's the voice that turns my stomach. The gun in my side presses against me harder, and I have no choice but to comply.

CHAPTER FORTY-ONE

"Leon?"

Leon practically rips my arm from its socket as he drags me through the crowd, his other arm keeping the gun pressed steadily against my side. He's wearing a dark sweatshirt with the hood up, but I know it's him. He tugs me up the stairs, and I nearly trip at the pace he sets, but I can't care. Where is Mason?

"Leon, where are we going?"

"Shut up," he growls, jabbing the gun harder into my side. Entering the main gym, he pulls me to the back, where an emergency exit is propped open. The chilly evening air rushes against my heated skin.

I shiver, goosebumps breaking over my skin. "Leon, what are you doing?"

"I said *shut up!*"

Before I can block the attack, the back of his hand strikes my cheek. My head twists with the force of his blow, and I cradle my face. Heat scorches my cheek, and I'm positive it's already red and welting.

"What the fuck?" My words wobble out of me in disbelief. The events of the past few months swirl in my brain, and I slot the puzzle pieces together. Hell, even last night, Mason said Leon was the one who put him up to the mission. But why?

Leon's eyes are frantic as he drags me down the alley, auburn hair oily and shadows darkening under his eyes. His once full cheeks are hollow, and his pulse visibly thrums in his neck. He levels the gun at me.

The realization tumbles out of me. "You're Peter's partner?"

Leon laughs, and it's so unlike the boy I used to know. He's younger than Mason by a few months, but something has aged him terribly. Acid burns in my throat at the cruelty sparking in his eyes. This man sent my baby brother to a certain death and killed Nathaniel, Andy, and so many more. He got Alice abducted and raped. A red haze settles over me, and I plant my feet against the concrete.

"How did you know where I was?"

Leon bares his teeth in what I think is supposed to be a smile. "Oh, Loren. You should've been more careful with how much detail you put in your planner. It was all too easy to know when and where you'd be. Plus, I had some help. Tonight, however, I knew you couldn't resist the infamous fight night once you learned of it."

My stomach twists. "I guess I should've given Peter some more credit."

Leon laughs incredulously. "Fuckin' Pete? He had his uses, but he was an idiot. A hotheaded idiot, but a fucking idiot." Something dark flashes behind his shadowed eyes. "I told him we had to stop with those fucking fires." He's becoming distracted, his anger tangible. "But no, he wanted to keep setting them. And I had to clean up his shit. I even left a note threatening Mason to make that fucking Keane strike first and ask questions later." Leon grumbles, as if his threats against my brother were nothing more than a pesky letter from an unwanted suitor.

Fuck. Was Leon the one slitting their throats and killing the guards?

The thought sickens me, having known him since he was born, but I return to his earlier confession. *He had more than one partner?* Who is the second? As much as it plagues me, I shake it off; it doesn't matter right now.

"Where is my brother?" My voice is steady, but fear still strikes through me.

Leon smiles, but it doesn't reach his eyes. He extends an arm, and my eyes follow, mouth parting in horror. Mason lays on his side, trussed up in a hog tie. A startled gasps chokes me, and I rush toward him.

Leon blocks me. His face is gaunt but deadly, and I take a shaky step backward. The night chills my exposed skin, and I can't help the shiver that grips me. Leon wets his bottom lip, and a memory surges to the front of my mind.

"Cal, I can't." I giggle into the phone. Butterflies spark in my belly as Cal's laugh filters through the phone.

His dark chuckle does something to me, and I almost give in.

"Come on, Loren. Who am I gonna tell?"

He makes a good point, but it kind of defeats the point of telling him who my crush is when he's my crush. A forbidden coil tightens around my chest, and I decide to deflect.

"How do you even know if I have a crush?"

"Because like it or not, I know you, Loren Catrone."

The way he says my name has me floating on a cloud. Still, I'm not brave enough to say it out loud. Just daring to think it while living in the Bianchi estate is practically treason.

"So, who do you think my crush is, then?"

Cal pretends to think, humming into the phone. "Well, I think we might have something in common."

"Oh, yeah?"

My eyes glance to my door, and I notice it's open more than I'd thought. Leon stares at me from the crack, an unreadable expression contorting his round face. He didn't hear me, right? No, there's no way he knows who I'm talking to.

I cross to the door and stick my tongue out. Leon skitters away.

I shut the door. "And what do we have in common?"

The memory dissipates like smoke. Leon definitely heard, and who knows how long he spied on me? Was Leon…jealous? Did he have feelings for me? Was this all some sort of sick and twisted revenge plot because I didn't return them? He's way too young for me to have even looked at twice, especially when I was sixteen. Leon would've barely been ten.

The questions swirl inside me, and my stomach clenches. Leon circles me, his footsteps crunching over the gravel. I flinch. Mason is unconscious, but how? There's a red welt on his temple.

Leon pauses behind me, his gun trailing over my back. "It should've been me."

"Leon, you know I care about you, but I've never seen you more than a friend. A brother, even." Somehow, my words are steady as they tumble out, and Leon comes to a halt directly in front of me. The familiar scent of gin washes over me with each breath. It smells like my mother.

Shit, he's drunk.

Strain cords his neck, his face flushed. He scoffs. "I gave up on you when you chose to run back in that burning warehouse for Keane.

Before then, I'd even packed your apartment to move you back into the house. That's how much I loved you." His left eye twitches. "When your little friend showed up, all she could do was lie and say that you'd never love me. I showed her just how wrong she was."

His manic smile is gruesome, and he taps the barrel of the gun against my chest. "Pete tried to scare you away with those bombs." Something humorous sparkles behind his dilated pupils. "And even when he got the wrong car at the publishing house, he even chased after you all the way to the highway, shooting at you. All to show you just how dangerous Keane and his life was. Don't you see? I could've protected you from that. That would've never had to happen if you were with me. You would've been safe with *me*. But you didn't care. No, you had to run into a burning building for him," he growls, spittle flying as he hisses in fury.

For a split second, his attention slips from me, some invisible memory playing out before his eyes, and I make my move.

I dart toward him, hands ready to wrest the gun away, but he snaps back to attention, swinging the barrel at my head. The metal is icy against my forehead, and a cool calm settles over me, dampening my fear in a way I've never experienced before. I suck in a deep breath.

"You won't shoot me." My tone is incredulous, and Leon's eyes widen infinitesimally. "Leon, I've known you since you were in diapers. You can't shoot me."

Leon sputters incredulously. Then he hardens, jaw clenching once again. "Loren, this had nothing to do with you until you chose to throw yourself into the middle of it."

"You had to have known I was going to come after my brother. You think I'd just let him disappear?"

The gun wavers, but I press it tighter against my forehead, calling his bluff. Or rather, what I'm fucking praying is a bluff. Leon scoffs, ripping the gun away, only to press it against my chest.

"Your brother?" He laughs, an unsettling noise that echoes against the empty alleyway. "Try *our* brother. I sent him to Keane, hoping he'd get snatched up. It would've been the perfect excuse to start a war."

His words jumble around my brain, but I'm stuck on the fact that he said *our* brother. My brows furrow, trying to understand the implications, but it's too much. That would mean...

"Your whore of a mother had an affair with my father, then passed off the pregnancy like it was Francis's. She did everything she could to escape, even if that meant finding the bottom of every bottle in the house. I only found out a few months back when I found a letter from your mother in his desk, begging my father to not tell Francis. Pete was already working on getting into the States, and now I had to get rid of two brothers instead of just one." He swears, as if killing two brothers— one of them mine—was nothing more than a minor inconvenience.

The dots connect with rapid fire. The gin, the guilt, Leon's deceitful ploys. Suddenly it makes sense. Why my mother couldn't be bothered with raising us once Mason was born. Why their marriage drifted apart.

"Mason was born seven months before me, which makes him..." Leon trails off as he waits for me to put the pieces together.

Holy shit. Mason is technically the second son, then. With Elias in a coma and no guarantee he'll wake up, Mason stands to inherit the entire Bianchi enterprise. My jaw falls to the floor as the information implodes in my brain.

"What the fuck?"

Leon laughs cruelly. "Now do you get it? He has to die. This time, I won't miss."

Cal's retelling of that night at the port flashes in my memory.

"Leon really didn't know when to shut the fuck up," he growls. His fingers trail circles over my body, goosebumps chasing after his touch.

I lean my head on his chest and nuzzle into his warmth. Cal was alive, relatively unharmed, and Alice was back safe. Not so sound, but safe, at least.

"Then what happened?"

My head bounces on Cal's chest when he scoffs. "Someone on the Bianchi side started shooting. It all happened so fast, and we dove for cover. By the time we got a few shots fired off, Elias was bleeding out on the ground, and the rest of their men fell back. I didn't like the guy, but he was better than his father. We dragged him to the car, and Matthias dumped him on the hospital's front steps as Cohen brought Alice inside."

His own brother didn't even try to save him?

Cal's fingers trail lower, gathering the heat between my legs and swirling against my clit. Any thoughts of another man drift away as he works me higher and higher, whispering the filthiest praise against the shell of my ear.

"You tried to kill your own brother?" The implication is dangerous. That would mean Leon is much more dangerous than I'd thought. He's not misguided—he's homicidal. Suddenly, my previous bravado washes away.

Leon freezes, turning to face me with a sickening barbarism flashing in his bloodshot eyes. I try to swallow over the knot thickening my throat. Leon takes a solitary step forward, and I retreat backward a step. Like a macabre dance, he steers me like cattle until my back presses against the concrete exterior of Strikers.

"As soon as I'm done here, I'll make sure his coma is permanent."

I tremble against the icy concrete, frozen with dread, as he presses the gun against my temple once again. This time, fear seizes my breath.

"You could've been my bride, Loren. Too bad you bet on the wrong man."

CHAPTER FORTY-TWO

L eon's looming threat swells as his smile broadens. Is this really how I'm going to die? At the hands of some entitled child?

Adrenaline floods my limbs, and the tingling sensation ceases entirely. In a blink, I'm back in control of my body.

With a roar that could shatter mountains, I launch off the wall, taking Leon by surprise. The gun scatters to the ground, a shot firing into the night. We tumble to the ground, and I unleash my fists on his face, his ribs, anywhere I can inflict damage. Blood sprays over my face with each blow, and I lose myself against the warm liquid.

Leon's nose caves with the next blow, blood spurting down his mouth. He coughs, choking on the blood flooding his mouth, but I don't stop.

This is the man who sent my brother to his death, who partnered with Peter fucking Agapov to traffick women, who planned to kill *me*. Worst of all, he raped and abducted Alice. I try to reach for any ounce of sympathy but return empty. I lose myself in the blows. When my knuckles split, I punch harder. When my wrist cracks, I roar in Leon's face. He doesn't move below me. Still, I don't stop.

Hands grab my shoulders, yanking me off his battered body. I screech, the blood-curdling cry echoing in the alley, and turn my fists on the man who dares to pull me away.

Familiar brown eyes narrow as they dart over my face, flicking with some mix of approval and concern. A growl reverberates from my chest and splits my lips.

"Bunny, it's me."

Features come into focus. A chiseled jaw covered in five o'clock shadow. Brows furrowed with protective concern. Hands squeezing the tops of my shoulders as he gently shakes me in front of him.

"Loren." He says my name like a deity worthy of worship, and my head tilts to the side. He watches with storms raging behind his brown eyes, and when I blink, I snap back to my body.

Turning on my heel, I take in the massacre I managed with just my fists. Feeling tingles back in my hands, and my job might seem finished by anyone else, but not to me. Like a ghost, I float toward his body, feeling a kaleidoscope of emotions. Pity, rage, disbelief…everything except guilt swirls inside my chest.

Leon's face is concave, a mess of blood, tissue, and teeth that makes him look like a victim of an animal attack.

Not an animal. Me.

Next to him, just out of his reach, lays his gun. If he were three inches closer, he would've been able to use it against me like he'd threatened. Instead, I pick it up, the weight of it lighter than I expected—or maybe that's shock setting in.

I raise the gun, aiming for the cracked open skull of the boy I grew up with. My finger trembles on the trigger, but before I can squeeze, a steady hand stills the pistol. I don't look away from Leon, and Cal comes to stand in front of me.

"Bunny, he's gone." Cal's voice is barely a whisper, but it feels louder in the alleyway. "You did it."

A single tear slips out of the corner of my eye and falls on my cheek. "That's what I thought about Peter, too."

Cal straightens, eyes boring into the side of my face, but I can't look away from Leon. He nods once and steps out of the way.

This time, when the barrel of the gun lines up with Leon's cracked skull, I don't tremble; I don't hesitate. I plant my feet firmly on the ground, ready for the kickback. When I pull the trigger, it's the easiest shot I've ever fired. The bullet slices through Leon's forehead, ricocheting blood over my legs. My lip curls into a sneer, and I hold the gun off to the side for Cal to take.

When it's out of my hands, I take the first full breath in what feels like hours. Light spills into the alley as Jude pushes outside. He halts, eyes tracking silently over the scene, from Leon's mangled face to my bloody hands, to Mason's groaning form.

Mason.

In a flash, I'm by his side, trying to untie the rope but coming up short. Sobs finally wreak my body, and I collapse on the ground. Calloused hands cup my face, but I squeeze my eyes shut. Tingles prick my fingertips and sound deafens as I try to stay afloat in the panic attack. Whispered words flutter through my hair, and the tickling sensation grounds me.

Cal cycles through nonsensical words of comfort while rubbing my back. The heat of his palm steadies me, and I finally open my eyes. Cal is crouched in front of me, one knee on the ground as he swipes my falling tears with his rough thumbs.

"It's okay, Bunny. I'm here. You did so well, Loren."

Off to the side, Jude slices through Mason's ropes and helps my brother sit up against the building. He lifts a trembling hand to his temple and curses.

Cal tucks the wispy pieces of hair that I'd left down behind my ears, pulling my attention back to him. He looks at me with such awe and concern it slots something foundational back into place. With a cry, I launch myself into his arms. Cal catches me with a sway, crushing me to his chest.

I bury my face into his neck. His sweat and sandalwood cologne floods my senses, and I squeeze him tighter. He's back in his clothes, and the heat of his body warms mine. Then his hands slide to my ass, and suddenly I'm lifted into the air. The world shuts out as I let him carry me wherever he's taking me. I don't care where we go, or that my ass is exposed, as long as we get the fuck out of here.

A car door opens, and Cal slides into the back seat with me still cradled to his chest like a koala. He doesn't take me off him, just settles into the seat and adjusts my legs so they're off to the side instead. The car rumbles to life beneath us, and warmth from the heater and Cal's body lulls me into a deep slumber.

Just before I lose consciousness, Cal's lips dust against the crown of my head.

"You did such a good job, baby. I'm so proud of you."

I try to respond, but it comes out as a whimper, and I fall asleep.

CHAPTER FORTY-THREE

My hands tremble as I clutch my books to my chest. Mom waved me off when I said I was too nervous to eat breakfast, and I wish she would've asked me why I was so nervous to start at Pointe Charter. Switching schools in the spring semester of my junior year was like sneaking into a theater halfway through the movie. Switching to the school the Keane family attends? It's like she wants us to be eaten alive.

Books slip from my clammy palms, and I readjust them. Mom gave such a stupid answer why they were switching Mase and me. As if I believed the bullshit that she wanted us to have our own identities separate from the Bianchis. At least at Roswell Academy, people knew not to mess with us.

But no, that wasn't enough for her. She wanted me to lose all my friends and social standing all in one fell swoop.

Bitterness swirls in my chest as a bell rings. I pull the crinkled schedule from my pocket and find my third period. Math.

Ugh, I hate math.

English and history are my favorite subjects. I was actually looking forward *to the book report capstone for my English class this semester. Everyone always dismisses* Romeo *and* Juliet *as overdone, but no one seems to find the beauty in the star-crossed lovers. The worn copy sits in my book bag that's slung over my shoulder, and I resolve to lose myself in the cracked spine during lunch.*

With only three wrong turns, I finally make it to Algebra II a few minutes late. My face heats when the teacher stops talking mid-sentence to welcome me. Mr. Koplin is fit and looks to be in his thirties. He holds out an arm, and I hand him my schedule as instructed by the front office. He initials next to his class, and without looking up, he introduces me to the class.

"Everyone, this is Loren Catrone. A transfer from Roswell Academy."

There are a few gasps, but thankfully, no one says anything. It seems it's obvious to the class about the caliber of students that attend RA: children of the Bianchi enterprise. I'm not sure if Mr. Koplin is new, but the reaction causes him to stop skimming the rest of my schedule and look around the room.

"Let's show her a warm Seagulls welcome."

The class grows quiet, and he sighs in resignation, handing my schedule and directing me to sit in the only open seat in the back.

"Alright, let's continue, shall we?" He returns to his whiteboard, and the squeaky dry erase marker echoes my steps to the back of the classroom.

When I slide into the chair, I drop my book bag on the floor. The books that didn't fit crowd my desk. There's a boy staring at me, not even trying to hide it. For ten minutes, he doesn't look away, and I finally have enough.

"Can I help you?" I whisper-hiss as I turn to face him.

The boy has the most beautiful deep brown eyes and boyish charm already dripping from him. When I speak, the brightest smile takes over his face, and the cutest dimple pokes in his left cheek.

"I think we're going to be good friends, Loren." His voice is smooth, and

butterflies erupt in my lower belly. The longer he keeps my attention, the more I feel captivated by the boy with brown eyes.

He smirks and reaches a hand over. "Callahan."

I gingerly take his hand and shake it once. "Loren Catrone. Callahan...?"

Callahan doesn't release my hand, just keeps shaking it as he stares into my soul.

"Just Callahan."

CHAPTER FORTY-FOUR

"**R**eady?" Jenna enters the room, shutting the door behind her softly.

Butterflies erupt in my belly, but I've never been more sure of a decision. I nod, a bright smile burning my cheeks.

In the vanity, a new woman faces me. With a few pieces left to frame her face, she piled her chestnut hair atop her head. A glow radiates from her skin, her hazel eyes twinkling with unshed emotion.

It took me about an hour to shape my hair and paint my face, but the results were so worth it. I went with simple glam, dark lashes, and mauve lipstick. Given the day, my cheeks are naturally flushed, but I added a soft pink blush on top and a shimmery highlighter on the highest points of my cheekbones. Altogether, I look refreshed, which is saying something after the events of the last few months.

When Cal and I got back to the Keane residence after fight night, he made Doc check out my hands. Turns out I had a hairline fracture in my wrist and had to keep it wrapped for a few weeks. The broken skin on my knuckles left thin white scars, but even as I feel the rigid tissue now, all it does is fill me with a sense of pride. For years, I learned to defend myself in the ring, but I'd never had to actually fight to survive. But twice now, I've fought. And twice now, I've won.

Over the next few months, we helped right the Bianchi house and Mason's ascension of power. With Elias still in a coma, Mason was the next in line to be the head of the family. A tentative truce has been wagered between the Bianchis and Keanes, and Cal's been helping to teach Mason the ropes. It's gone surprisingly well so far, but if I know my brother—and my husband—there's an expiration on Cal's goodwill. Eventually, Mason is going to want to launch himself full speed ahead without the training wheels, and I'm nervous for that day. It doesn't help that another warehouse was set on fire two weeks ago. It happened while Mason was over for dinner, and I knew my brother wouldn't do something like that.

It begs the question: Who else is out there that wants to take the Keane business down?

Jenna picks up the white tulle and slides the comb into the base of my bun on the crown of my head. Her eyes twinkle with emotion and she sniffles, wiping a tear from the corner of her eye.

I stand, my dress falling into place. The material is soft under my palms, and I release a shaky breath. It's the most beautiful gown you could imagine, and it's what I should've worn the first time around.

I scold myself. *No, the first time around didn't count. This is the real wedding.*

Its sweetheart neckline leaves my shoulders and collarbone exposed, and the boning of the bodice gives the illusion of a corset. The floral lace covering my breasts and waist transforms into vertical layers of ruffled tulle, almost resembling feathers as it falls to the floor. My feet are bare, and the only jewelry I added were a pair of drooping diamond earrings and Cal's necklace. I know now that he put a tracking device in it, but that doesn't bother me. It actually makes me feel quite safe. My left ring finger feels empty without my ring, but Cal made me give it back to him just so he could symbolically place it back on my finger.

I had rolled my eyes, but it's sweet. Given recent events, it's comforting.

Jenna hands me my bouquet of blush pink peonies, and I take one last look in the vanity. I'm filled with an overwhelming sense of need to get down that aisle so I can kiss my husband. For real, this time.

Jenna slips her arm through mine, and we exit the bedroom. The lake house we spent half the summer at is just as I remembered it, with log walls and rustic furniture. When we discussed where we'd renew our vows, we decided to take the trip north to the cabin. This time around, only our closest friends and family attend. A pang pulls in my chest. I wish Alice was here, but she took off a few weeks ago, and no one's heard from her since. Cal says they'll keep an eye out for her, but she likely fled Roswell, and if she needs space to heal, it's probably best to give her that. With any luck, she'll be back to the old Alice soon.

She's not the only one missing, either. Tinley is gone, too. No one—not even Mason—has heard from her since the fight night where everything changed. If not for the resignation letter on Cal's desk, I'd think she disappeared into thin air. I try not to worry about everyone all the time, but it's difficult after so many hard losses.

The dirt is warm under my feet, the sun shining through the sycamore trees. A gentle breeze plays with my veil, and our loved ones turn as I round the corner. Mason stands off to the side, a teary smile matching my own. I throw my arms around him, careful not to mess with my hair too much.

376

He kisses my hair and whispers, "Happy for you, sis."

Tears burn my eyes, but I don't let them fall. Mason props his arm out, and I slide mine through his. This time, he'll be here to walk me down the aisle. Warmth spreads from my chest, my heart thudding as Jenna takes her first step down the aisle. We planned to keep the ceremony short, so everyone stands as she throws peony petals onto the ground.

At the end of the aisle, where the forest blends into sandy shore, Cal stands in a warm brown tuxedo and crisp white shirt. His eyes are glued to me, and I heed the command of their pull. Without thinking, I march toward him, catching Mason by surprise. He scrambles to catch up, and together, we walk the twenty feet to my heart.

When we reach the end, Mason squeezes my hand and places a gentle kiss on my cheek. Then he takes a spot in the front row. Matthias stands behind Cal; since I only have Jenna, Cal had to pick just one of his brothers.

This time, Matthias doesn't seem so upset to see me marrying his brother.

The group here today is quaint, with only about ten people. Everett is at the front of the crowd, and Darla links her arm through his. Their faces shine with pride. Mason and Cohen are on my side of the aisle, watching with warmth in their eyes. Jude stands stoically in front of Jenna, his gaze never leaving his wife. Tears burn my eyes, and my attention is pulled back to Callahan. Before we start, I hand my bouquet to Jenna and slide my hands into Cal's.

"Hi," I whisper.

"Hi, Ren." His voice is rich, and I squeeze his fingers. He squeezes mine back.

"You ready to get married? Again?"

Cal throws his head back, and laughter rumbles from his chest. It's a perfect late spring day, with a gentle breeze swirling and birds chirping lyrically. It's made only more perfect by this ceremony.

"Ren, I've been ready to marry you since I was seventeen."

My heart swells, and a tear slips over my cheek.

"You look so beautiful, sweetheart."

Blood rushes to my cheeks, and I feel them heat. "Thank you. So do you."

We're interrupted by Lucas clearing his throat. "You ready, love birds?"

I look to Cal and smile widely. Brown eyes twinkle with love, and I fall even deeper for this man.

Lucas speaks, but I can't pull my attention from Callahan. The fresh shave of his jaw, the twinkle in his eyes, the dimple in his left cheek that's ever present today. When it's time for our vows, Cal's throat bobs.

"Ren, I knew from the moment I laid eyes on you, my life was going to change. You stole every breath from my lungs, occupied every thought in my mind, and you weren't even trying…" He tails off, humor sparkling in his eyes. "Before you, I was sentenced to a life of misery. Locked in the cage that was my name—my *duty*—I dreaded waking up. Then suddenly, there was hope. You, Loren, are my hope." He swallows thickly, and I squeeze his hands. "When I broke us—*broke you*—a piece of me died." He laughs bitterly. "Fuck, all of me died. I wandered with no purpose, no direction but my father's. I spent every day of four years wondering what I'd say to you, if I'd ever have the chance to see to you again."

Cal exhales a long breath, and he blinks away his tears. My lashes are wet, and I make a note to thank Jenna for the waterproof mascara.

"Ren," Cal continues, but the tone sounds like he's reciting something from memory. "Is your life as bleak as mine? Fuck, I hope not. I'd pray to any god that would listen if it meant you weren't living this misery."

My breath catches, and I realize he must be reciting the letter he wrote me. The one that was stolen when Leon broke into my house.

"Each day, I wonder what this world would look like if I'd chosen differently. If I had chosen you. God, what a different life we'd be living in. I can't help but think we'd be happy. We could run away together. What do you think? You and me, somewhere far away from all the blood, all the history. Would you run with me? If I found you, would you take my hand and put your faith in me one more time? I know it looked bad, but you have to believe me. I would never betray you. Not then, not ever. My heart is forever held in your palms. Should you choose to tend to it like a bird with a broken wing or crush it between your gentle fingers, your choice is my fate. Oh, what a merciful death that would be. Ren, if I ever get the courage to mail this letter to you, please write me. Tell me I haven't lost you forever. I think the only fate worse than death would be knowing I have."

I swallow thickly, but Cal continues.

"If you can find it in your heart to forgive me, I'll be waiting in our spot each year on your birthday. Rain or shine, I'll wait for you until my dying breath. Please, oh please, put me out of my misery." Cal clears the emotion from his throat, starting anew. "Loren, I don't know how else to say I love you, but I plan to show you every day for the rest of our lives. I promise to protect you, to worship you, and to never take you for granted again. I'll spend the rest of my life on my knees if it means you'll spend even a second loving me back."

Cal's barely finished speaking when I throw my arms around his neck and press my mouth to his. His steady arms catch me, wrapping around my waist and clutching me tightly as we kiss. A cheer erupts from our loved ones, but we pay it no mind, until Lucas clears his throat.

"I didn't even say you could kiss the bride yet," he grumbles.

I playfully swat an arm toward Lucas, but Cal commands my attention once more, thumbs swiping over my cheeks. I cradle his face with my hand, and he twists to place a gentle kiss to my palm, whispering, "Your turn, darling."

My stomach clenches, but this time, in need. I need to drag my husband by his tie into a closet and do things to him that would make a nun blush.

Until then, I straighten, returning my hands to his to hold.

"Callahan...Sometimes I wonder how my life would've played out if I had ignored the boy with intelligent eyes and a curious sort of kindness. Perhaps the way it happened was the way it was supposed to. Perhaps it was always inevitable. I'd like to think that we were always inevitable, and the journey we went on during our years apart was necessary somehow. What I've learned is that there's a boundless well inside of me, and it's overflowing with my love for you. I can't breathe without feeling the depth of my love for you, and I never want to again. I may have forgotten once, but I promise that from this moment forward, every breath I take will be for you, for us. I've always loved you, Callahan. Even after my last breath on this earth, I will love you."

Cal smiles, and my heart thuds against my ribs. Somehow, we manage to wait for Lucas to speak the five words, and we collide like a force of nature. His hands wrap around my face, cradling me as he worships me.

"For the second time, let's hear it for Mr. and Mrs. Callahan Keane!"

Cheers erupt around us, and we break from our kiss, leaning our foreheads against each other's. My heart swells, and I can't help the laugh when he sweeps me into his arms, carrying me back down the aisle.

"Where are you going? We've got a party to start!" Cohen shouts as Cal leads us to the cabin.

"Start without us," he throws over his shoulder. Then, just to me, he whispers, "I've got a marriage to consummate."

A giggle so unlike me escapes my lips, and Cal growls, speeding up as he kicks open the door to the cabin.

EPILOGUE

In the dreamscape, his senses are overwhelmed with her scent. Sweet almonds and the ripest of summer cherries flood his senses, and he burrows into her. His arms wrap around her waist, and for a moment, he thinks he's imagined the laughter that spills from her lips like golden sunshine. But no, he hasn't imagined it.

He peeks open one eye, and relief floods his chest. Chestnut hair is fanned over the pillow next to him, and his wife mumbles something in her sleep, a slight curl to her mouth. His cock aches at the sight of her, just as it has every day since he met her. Even though it's been ten years since they married, she still elicits the most primal of responses from his body. His hand slips over the curve of her waist, pausing momentarily over the swell on her belly. She's due next month, and he thanks the universe again for giving him a second chance.

A screech follows a fearsome bellow, and a tiny body slams into his chest. A whoosh of air escapes him, and he catches the wriggling girl with matching chestnut hair and brown eyes, a perfect blend of the two of them.

"Daddy, Mommy, wake up! Santa came!"

His wife grumbles beside him, peeking up from under her arm. "Time to wake up, monkey?"

Their daughter nods emphatically, and his wife meets his gaze.

He nods, too. "Time to wake up, Bunny."

❧

Dear Reader,

Thank you for reading Through Any Fire. I hope you enjoyed it! Stay up to date on advanced reading opportunities by signing up for my newsletter at: katherinecarterauthor.com

Watch for Alice's story, coming Fall 2025. You can pre-order With Any Luck now!

Please don't forget to leave an honest rating/review! It would mean the world to me. Thank you!

CALLAHAN
BONUS CHAPTER

The days blur together as I wade through the shit that is my new role. The Keane family is now under my stewardship, and it's never ending, wrangling the respect from the older generation that still sees me as a five-year-old kid chasing his dad around. When he died eight months ago, it should've been the greatest day of my life. For the first time in years, I woke up with the weight of his expectations suddenly lifted from my chest. The first thing I did was open my phone, my thumb hovering over Loren's contact. It probably changed from when we were kids, but I never could delete it.

Then I remembered just how my father died. *A heart attack in the middle of the night,* the coroner said. He might have left this world the most anticlimactic way possible, but it served as a reminder of just how dangerous my world can be. Loren was out. She was safe. And I had to leave her in the past.

God knows I broke her soul in two, but she'll never know mine was shattered into pieces so small I couldn't possibly ever mend it back together.

I've filled the empty cavity with temporary fixes, but nothing has ever come close to stitching me back together.

It's with that same empty soul that I find myself at Abstrakt tonight. Last week, someone burned down one of my warehouses, destroying the product and killing three of my men. Kyra said she'd listen for chatter, and the city better pray she has something for me. I was about to go on a warpath.

There's an electric current thrumming through Abstrakt, and I scan the lounge with little curiosity. It's a new club that opened a few months ago, advertising its exclusive lounge and nightly shows. The upper echelon of Roswell are here on any given night, and if I'm to find anything, it would be here.

My tumbler of whiskey is cold in my palm, and I take a sip. The heat is delicious, and I take another drink. Across the room, Kyra delivers drinks to a group of men. She flirts with a coy smile, walking her fingers up one's shoulders. She's the best at finding the dirt on those around us. We're due to meet in a half hour to discuss her findings. I continue my surveillance. It's a quieter night, but some invisible force sizzles under my skin.

That's when *she* walks in.

My world stops turning, my heart stops beating. She looks around the room, nerves etched in the pinch of her brow. She's wearing a black silk dress that barely covers the delicious curve of her ass, and my cock swells behind my fly. Loren sucks in a sharp breath, eyes darting around the room as if she's looking for someone. *Is she looking for me?* My fingers itch to touch her, to pull her toward me and never let go.

What is she doing here?

My feet move without instruction, heading toward her, but she's circled by Caleb Ferguson. He approaches her from behind, and they exchange a few words. Then his hand lands on the small of her back, and he guides her toward the bar. Steam practically shoots from my nostrils as rage flushes my skin. He's going to lose that fucking hand.

They bring their drinks back to the couch in front of the fireplace, bantering back and forth. My tongue thickens, sound draining from my awareness as my entire center pulls toward her.

God, she doesn't even know the power she holds over me. Even to this day, all she'd have to do is ask, and I would burn every bridge to ash for her.

Caleb leans toward her, and I decide I've had enough of him tonight. I'll ship him straight to security detail after this shit he's pulling. He won't understand why, but I'm staking my claim. Loren Catrone is *mine*.

I approach the couch just in time to catch his last words. "Every woman drinks red. But you don't?" He tucks a strand of hair behind Loren's ear.

I see fucking crimson.

"She drinks whiskey." My voice rumbles out, and I hold out my glass to Loren, who looks up at me with shock. Her delicious lips part in surprise, and I can't help but remember how they taste.

How *all* of her tastes.

My cock hardens almost painfully, but I ignore it.

God, she's even more beautiful than she was at sixteen. She's taking her time looking me over, and I do the same. Hazel eyes flecked with green and gold sparkle with lust, and her pulse thrums against the base of her neck. Her hair falls in loose waves around her shoulders, but I can still see them tense with apprehension. She's older, as expected, but even more radiant than I could've ever imagined, and I'm surprised I'm not bleeding out on the floor with how fiercely she pierces me with her gaze.

Caleb says something, but I ignore him.

"Bunny." Her nickname falls from my lips without a second thought, and I watch with immense satisfaction as she flinches. Anger sparks behind her hazel eyes, and they narrow with residual heat.

"I'm not your bunny. And I don't drink whiskey anymore." She takes a long swig of her red wine, and I have to stifle the groan that threatens to slip as I watch her delicate neck swallow.

I arch a brow, her fire intoxicating and addicting, and finish the last of my drink. Meanwhile, Caleb is still here. It's been eleven fucking years since I've seen the only woman who can make me believe in a higher power, and Caleb needs to get the fuck out of here. I shove the empty tumbler into his hand.

"Get another." My gaze slices to Caleb, and he flinches. "And this time, keep your hands to yourself."

He frowns, but leaves anyway. With our recent losses, I can't afford to lose anyone else, but that's the only reason he's leaving here alive tonight. That, and his father would kill me. Or try to, at least. I'd hate to wipe an entire bloodline out, but for Loren, I'd do it. Happily.

I take Caleb's seat on the couch, and Loren sits silent as a ghost as she stares at the fire.

"You know, the silent treatment is sexy. Means I'm under your skin."

She whips around to face me, narrowing her eyes. "You wish."

I'd walk barefoot over broken glass for this woman. I shoot her a wink. "Of course I do. I'm not afraid to admit it."

She sets her jaw, and her fingers curl into fists. Her anger is a heady aphrodisiac, and it's taking everything in me to not reach across and slam my mouth to hers. Are her lips still soft, like I remember? Does she still whimper right as she's about to come?

My fingers move without a second thought, and I tuck a strand of hair behind her ear. She sucks in a breath, and I freeze in response. My index finger burns where it touched her.

"Why are you here, Bunny?"

The Loren I remember jolts back to life with her anger. She hated when I started calling her that. I always thought her false pretense was even hotter, so I never let up. Then it stuck, and she eventually learned to accept it.

"I'm here…" She trails off for a beat before she seems to find her resolve. "Because I need your help."

Sweeter words have never been spoken. "What do you—"

"Here." Caleb holds a fresh glass of whiskey, and I grind my jaw, never looking away from Loren. God, I can't believe she's here in front of me. If not for my cock that threatens to break through my pants, I'd think I was stuck in one of my nightmares.

"Thank you, Caleb." Loren accepts the drink, trading her wine for the whiskey. I stifle the smirk that threatens to tease. *I knew it.*

She shoves the glass into my hand, and for the first time in eleven years, our fingers brush. Electricity sparks my blood to a boil, and heat flushes through my body. Fuck. It's like I'm breathing the first breath of clean air after years of smoke and fire. I don't know how I'll ever go back.

I don't have to.

The thought startles me, but I don't dismiss it yet. If she needs me, perhaps I can use that to my advantage.

"What's happened? Why are you coming to me?"

Loren grinds her jaw together, and anger flashes through her hazel eyes. But then she visibly deflates. "Mason is missing. He…" She trails off, gaze dropping to her lap. "He wanted to be made, so they gave him a task."

Shit. Of course she'd go looking for her brother. He's been stirring up a shit storm the past few weeks, but he hasn't broken. He refuses to answer my questions, but as soon as I found out it was Mason Catrone in one of my secure rooms, I issued an order to my team not to harm him. Mason's given three square meals a day, and I recently had a DVD player and television sent down there. He's basically at a luxury resort. Just one without windows or fresh air.

But I still don't know why he was snooping around the Culver Street warehouse.

I press a finger below her chin to tilt her face toward mine. "What kind of task?"

She licks her lips, and my gaze falls to her lush mouth. With my thumb so close, I want to tug it open and shove my cock inside it.

"They wanted…"

Invisible memories play behind her eyes, and I can't help but feel grateful that I was the one who caught Mason. She might not like it, but fuck if I can ever let her go again. She's going to be pissed, in fact. But I don't care. I'll suffer the blisters of her fires happily if it means she's back in my life. This time, I'll bind her to me with every tie I can.

Plans swirl in my mind. Loren once mentioned how beautiful Wisteria Pointe was near the coast, so I'll get that reserved when I get home. I'll start the paperwork to change her name tomorrow.

"Wanted what, Bunny?"

You. I want you, Bunny. And I'm going to have you.

Fuck, she's going to be pissed when she finds out I've had Mason this whole time, but he's safest where he's at. For now, that is. I just have to have faith that she'll understand.

Loren Catrone is a force of nature. But soon she'll be Loren Keane, with even more power behind her name. My cock hardens to the point of pain.

I'm never letting her go again.

No matter what it takes, I'll make her mine. I will make her love me again, even if it's the last thing I do.

NOTE FROM THE AUTHOR

Last year, when I wrote The Fool's Errand, my debut romantasy, I truly thought writing a book was a one and done thing for me. While I'd always dreamed of writing stories, I never knew what I wanted to write. After I finished TFE, I was lost. I'd fallen in love with writing, but my well was dry. Once again, I didn't know what I wanted to write about. Then I had this idea of teens from rival families falling in love, and fate getting in the way. It spider-webbed into different stories for the characters introduced in Through Any Fire. I'm so excited to continue writing their stories. And if you're wondering where Alice ran off to, well, you'll just have to stay tuned. I hope if you liked TAF you'll follow along this journey.

At this point, I'd like to ask if you would please rate and/or review Through Any Fire on Amazon and Goodreads. Whether you loved or hated it (or thought it was just okay), I would be so incredibly grateful. Reviews, both positive and negative, are the lifeline of indie authors and I hope you can take just a few moments to share your thoughts. Thank you for taking a chance on my novel! It means the world to me.

Artist Credits
Dear Reader: @luardraws
Page 21: @marssketch
Page 390: @vinc_ry
Commercially licensed. No AI.

ACKNOWLEDGMENTS

Wow, where to begin? Last year was a whirlwind, writing and publishing The Fool's Errand within four months of the initial concept. It was exhilarating, and I loved every minute of it. However, afterward, I felt zapped. It was a difficult transition, moving from the reader space to the author space, but I did it, and I couldn't have done it alone.

To KC, one of my dearest friends: thank you for being the ultimate hype woman. You listened to every single rant, breakdown, and questioning of TAF's existence. You filled my stores with renewed dedication each and every day. From the bottom of my heart, thank you.

To my author group chat: thank you for being the glue that held me together, and for always being honest and supportive. It takes a village, and I'm glad I'm in yours.

To the artists I've worked with to bring Loren and Cal to life: I am ever grateful for your talent and dedication. It's a unique experience to envision fictitious characters and have them brought to life so exactly how you picture them in your head. Thank you for bringing my babies to life.

To everyone at my favorite local wine bar, Divided Vine in Gilbert, Arizona: thank you! To find a spot that's so welcoming and intimate is special, and I'm so thankful I found yours. I spent countless hours here writing, editing, and doing tedious admin work. Thank you for always providing a cozy space to do so.

To my See-You-Next-Tuesday friends: thank you for being my tether to the real world. Thank you for asking how my writing is going and celebrating my wins with me.

And finally, to my loyal readers: thank you for your ever-constant support of my books. It brings such joy to me knowing so many of you see the potential in me and continue to share your love for my books and engaging with my content any chance you get. Thank you. It does not go unnoticed.

TRIGGER & CONTENT WARNINGS

Trigger Warnings: abduction, alcohol/alcoholism, assault, blood/gore (graphic), bombs/explosions, death of a parent (discussed, not on page), drugs/drug use, fights, fires, gun violence, home invasion (off page), infidelity (in the past, no present day cheating), intimidation, murder, attempted rape (on page, of the main character but not by the MMC), rape (not of the FMC, off page), sexual assault, sex trafficking, suicide (brief mention, not of main characters), threats, torture (graphic), other potentially disturbing and explicit scenes.

Content Warnings: explicit sex, mature language.

ABOUT THE AUTHOR

Katherine Carter lives in Arizona, USA with her 3 cats and approximately 142 book boyfriends she's collected over the years. As an avid reader, Katherine loves to escape between the pages, losing herself in the adventures and fantasy and romance. She'd always dreamed of writing, but had always thought it too out of reach.

And then she realized, the only one stopping her was herself. Her debut novel, The Fool's Errand, is the culmination of her childhood dream to become an author and the years she spent thinking up mismatched characters and adventures. This passion project was born out of a spark that quickly blazed into a full-blown inferno that took over her every waking thought. She can't thank you enough for giving her a chance.

Follow along her socials for the most up to date information on current projects and opportunities to read her next work early!

TikTok @KatherineCarterAuthor
Instagram @KatherineCarterAuthor
www.KatherineCarterAuthor.com
KatherineCarterAuthor@gmail.com

ALSO BY KATHERINE CARTER

Check out Katherine's debut romantasy, The Fool's Errand!

e33777fe-6a63-4c9b-8472-23e6feb2de61R01